YOU ARE NICK THIRKIELD
AND YOU ARE ABOUT TO
REOPEN THE CASE OF YOUR
BROTHER'S ASSASSINATION

Fourteen years ago, your late brother, then
President of the United States, was shot down
while riding in a motorcade. Now you have
proof that the investigation of the assassination
was a fraud, and the men behind the killing
are still very much in power.

With your family's vast financial resources behind you, you reopen the case—and plunge into the nightmare labyrinth of sex, violence, be-
trayal, and corruption that will lead you to the
strange and shocking solution to the mystery,
and to a conspiracy that threatens America itself . . .

WINTER KILLS

"A triumph . . . a savage depiction of a world
in which fiction and reality are mingled to
manipulate, exploit and kill . . . It puts Condon
in the first rank of American novelists."
—*The Sunday New York Times Book Review*

"Powerful . . . riveting!"
—*Publishers Weekly*

"Guaranteed to curdle your blood!"
—*Atlanta Journal-Constitution*

W9-BFC-909

Other Dell Books by Richard Condon:

THE MANCHURIAN CANDIDATE

THE VERTICAL SMILE

ARIGATO

AN INFINITY OF MIRRORS

MILE HIGH

RICHARD CONDON
WINTER KILLS

A DELL BOOK

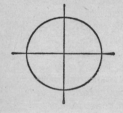

For
JOYCE ENGELSON,
The Smartest Girl in Town

Published by
DELL PUBLISHING CO., INC.
1 Dag Hammarskjold Plaza
New York, New York 10017
Copyright © 1974 by Richard Condon
Dell ® TM 681510, Dell Publishing Co., Inc.
Reprinted by arrangement with
The Dial Press
Printed in the United States of America
First Dell printing—July 1975

Minutes trudge,
Hours run,
Years fly,
Decades stun.
Spring seduces,
Summer thrills,
Autumn sates,
Winter kills.

—The Keeners' Manual

Nick Thirkield once told Keifetz that being in the same family with his father and his brother Tim was like living in the back leg of an all-glass piano. It was uncomfortable, it was noisy, and everyone could watch whatever he did; not that he could do much. Nick looked grim when he said it, but he could look grim when he said Merry Christmas, because he had strong, family-based reasons against showing his teeth when he smiled.

Nick got out of the glass leg of the family piano when he went into the oil business in Asia. Sixteen years later (on the day Keifetz called) he was doing another "favor" for Pa by sweating out the job of drilling superintendent on the shakedown cruise of Pa's drilling ship *Teekay 60*. "There is two hundred million bucks sunk in that ship, kiddo," Pa said on the phone from Palm Springs. "Don't get any scratches on it."

Nick had been twenty-eight days checking out the equipment on the ship at the Mitsui yards at Tamano in Japan. For a week he was afraid he just wasn't going to catch on. He was really stuck and he knew it. And Pa had the kind of brass to give him a set of cuff links for neglecting his own business to take on the hideously responsible job of checking out the first satellite-controlled, deep-water oil-drilling ship ever built and never floated in all history before.

The Marine captain took charge only when the ship was in transit. Once Nick told him where to park it, Nick was handed the command. Wherever they were became just another drilling site. His head almost came to a point. When Keifetz called, Nick was finishing deep-water tests in the South China Sea, about a hundred and two miles north of Borneo. They had been testing the ship in open ocean for seventy-four days, with Nick averaging fifteen hours every day, because everything had to come out right for Pa, because that was the way Pa felt about things. There were times when he wished he had gone into vaudeville or had just let Yvette Malone rub coconut oil onto his back on some Caribbean island. The *Teekay* was to oil rigs what the Apollo moon wagons were to piston-engine airplanes. The *Teekay*'s working position in heavy seas, which could be a mile and a half deep over the precise point where they would drill for oil, was fixed by signals from Pa's own navigation satellite in orbit around the earth.

When the ship's position for drilling had been fixed, all four hundred and forty feet of it slammed about by one-hundred-and-ten-foot-high waves, it had to hold that place for a month or more, without anchors, under automatic control of computers, while an oil well was drilled in the seabed six thousand feet below to a depth of twenty thousand feet. For every thrust of wind or shove of wave, eleven thruster propellers and six hydropones were lowered through the hull in retractable turrets spread along the length of the ship's bottom, fixed at right angles to the hull, providing the required counterthrust, moving the ship sideways or swinging it on its axis.

When the ship was holding, Pa's satellite rechecked the ship's position over the oil stored under tremendous pressure six miles beneath it—more than four hundred miles beneath the satellite. When Nick was ready to drill, part of the ship's bottom slid away, and a thirty-five-foot, ninety-ton blowout-preventer stack went down through the hull, through the moonpool at the middle of the ship.

The whole ship revolved around the framework of

this ninety-ton stack, so that the drill could always remain stationary whichever way the sea was running. The drill string was run down the middle of the stack to make the strike. In time an oil field would be pumping out of the seabed at a mile and a half under the ocean. Every wellhead would be piped. All the oil from every well would be run to four-hundred-and-fifty-foot-tall vertical floating spars that could hold three hundred thousand gallons of oil each and feed it into Pa's tankers while they were anchored to the spars hundreds of miles out at sea. People back home would still be able to drive to the movies in the old eight-thousand-dollar family jalopy, and sometimes get killed driving home by having to breathe the air so many cars had polluted, because *Teekay* was going to make a continuing supply of gasoline possible—at about triple the cost per gallon, if Pa had anything to say about it.

When Keifetz called from Brunei, two of the thrusters weren't responding, so the ship wasn't steady enough over the well. That was no good, and Nick was chewing out two computer mechanics.

Nick had two oil rigs working off Brunei. He leased the rigs from Pa. One of Pa's companies had ninety-three semisubmersible rigs out on long-term lease. Pa ran a fleet of seventy-one tankers called the Hatch Farm fleet. Now he had *Teekay 60,* but he insisted he wasn't in the oil business. "I got myself some exposure in there, certainly," Pa said to Nick. "Oil is money. But there's gunna be a switchover one of these days and I'm not getting stuck with a lotta iron."

The *Teekay* was one hundred and three miles north of Brunei when the Keifetz call came in.

"Listen, Nicholas," Keifetz said, "my crane-hoist operator on the Number Two rig just fell off the ladder."

"What the hell can I do about that?" Nick asked. "I have problems out here, fahcrissake."

"He's dying in the DeJongg Hospital."

"What am I—the chaplain?"

"He wanted to talk to me, so I went in. It's wild.

Listen, Nicholas, he says he was the second rifleman when they killed your brother. He wants to tell you about it."

"Tell him to go to a health farm with a telephone and to call Horse Pickering," Nick said. "I'm going to get a call from Pa any minute now, and the electronic abacus he installed on this ship is acting like a half-wit."

"The chopper from the *Teekay* is here now picking up pipe valves," Keifetz said. "I'll get it right back there to bring you in."

"What the hell is the matter with you? I'm sorry about your crane operator, but he doesn't have half the troubles I have. *His* father is probably *dead.*"

Keifetz said, "Nicholas, you don't think I'd get you into a flap over nothing, do you? I mean, talking loose about your brother has made about sixteen people dead."

"I'm running very important tests out here!" Nick yelled into the telephone.

"Baby, you can be back there in about three hours. How long can this guy talk? He's dying."

"Fuck him," Nick said.

"Listen, Nicholas, the people have a right to know. They're the ones who took the big screwing when it happened. I'm sending the chopper back. I think you should come in here. Make up your own mind." Keifetz hung up.

Nick knew he would have to do what the vast television audience expected of him. If your brother was President of the United States and he was assassinated, the viewers like to think you will avenge him. Or at least take an interest.

Nick Thirkield was a man of moderation in food, drink, and friends. He worked, as much as possible, at hard manual labor that kept him out in the sun. His brown, violet and white eyes lay like Easter eggs in a

basket of squint lines. His body was as dark as a cinnamon stick. He was a blocky, strong-looking man, neither tall nor short. He had blond hair, and he wished
he had the nerve to dye it any dark color. People could
spot him too easily—people like Pa—unless he wore a
hat. All his physical characteristics separated him still
further from Pa and Tim. They were both very tall,
red-haired men who walked as though they were trying
to hold a bowling ball between their thighs. Pa was
covered with freckles, a disgusting thing, and he had
the diction of a street urchin. Nick's cinnamon tan
made his teeth look neon white. They were exception-
ally good teeth, but few people (his dentist, Yvette
Malone and certain members of the Glee Club at Cor-
nell) knew about that, because he refused to show
them when he smiled. When he did smile he conveyed
rue. He was ruing Pa's marble teeth, which looked as
if they could have been ripped out of a merry-go-round
horse. Pa flashed the teeth on and off as if they were
traffic lights, increasing the pace when he was cheating
someone, which was most of the time.

Tim had been all teeth and hair. Take away everything on Tim's face except those finger-length incisors
and that half kilo of hair and everybody from Pennsylvania Avenue to the high Himalayas would still recog-
nize him. A buffet dinner for fourteen could be served
on Tim's dinner-plate front teeth, but Tim's inner life
rarely had any relationship to his toothy smile. He was
a politician-grinner. Nick told him, "I don't know how
you and Pa can grin so much. You're both supposed to
have a lot on your minds. I mean, they keep saying
you're the most powerful man on earth. How can you
grin all the time—maybe even when you're asleep—
knowing that?" Tim answered frankly for once. He
said, "Toothy smiles are an announcement. They pro-
claim: 'Observe my genuine equine boyishness, the
charm you jes' have to trust.' "

"My mother met Hermann Goering once. She said

he was the most charming man she had ever met," Nick said. "Most people who trusted that charm got their arms broken."

"That's what people's arms are for," Tim kidded. But was he kidding?

Tim had to be cynical, hard and shifty because he was a real politician. He had had a minimal education and he had never worked for a living; he had worked at getting elected. Nobody was better at that than Tim—unless it was Pa for Tim.

Nick worked for his own oil company, Jemnito International, of which Pa owned 18 percent of the profits. Pa had fought for 50 percent of the profits, but Nick had dug in, and they had fought it out face-to-face and by telephone for one entire winter, Nick cutting him down and down and down. Nick had finally had to sign away an equal percentage of what Pa said he would inherit in Pa's will (which was nothing but blackmail, Nick told him), but Nick didn't want a dime of Pa's money anyway (it would be like being a receiver of stolen goods, he said).

"You are a real cold-ass kid," Pa told him admiringly.

"And you are a real crooked, greedy negotiator," Nick said.

"What the hell is this? That's how it's done. You wanna win, you play to win. Start handing out breaks to the other guy and it only means you wanna lose. You don't give away millions, like you just did, to make thousands, for what you think—for about five minutes—is some fucking principle. You must be some kind of a nut or a Jesus-freak."

"Just figure it that I'm against free rides," Nick said. "For me and anybody else."

"You gotta take care of your*self,* Nick. Nobody else will. Look at me. I don't know how I made it this far all in one piece. Shit, you'd think I have the best security in the world, but I'm telling you if I started to look around me at the people closest to me, I wouldn't sleep nights. Take Nolan, an army General, my roommate at Notre Dame. I made that son-of-a-bitch, just because he happened to get assigned to room with me in a jerk-water Midwestern college. But let anybody come to him from Texas with a hard-luck story and he'd cut off my balls to help him out. All right. Take Cerutti. Cerutti is not only the best research-and-development mind in the world outside of two Japs and a Swede who can't speak English, he is a full professor I bought right out of Yale, the big time. All right. He's sick. He can't stand people around him. So I made it possible that he didn't have to earn a living like every other rope-puller in the world. Sure, he's a very smart, imaginative man with the best analytic mind except three guys I couldn't communicate with. I pay that reclusive little prick two hundred and fifty thousand dollars a year to handle all investigations for me and make them come out right, and I bought him a whole fucking island to himself so he wouldn't have to look at people. So what happens? He thinks I'm just a little Mick on the make. He thinks he's *superior* to me. And I'm telling you this. If he *did* deign to talk to people, this ego-maniac egghead, the first thing he would do would be to pull me down just to make himself look superior."

"Pa, for Christ's sake," Nick said. "You're seventy years old or something and you look great. Also, you're getting a more than fair salesman's commission for a couple of telephone calls, and next year that'll bring you in about four hundred thousand dollars and help your own son to get started in business besides."

"Nick—you're going to be out on oil rigs working with your hands with no shirt on, and you're going to be taking home sixty-four percent *more* than I get for actually bringing in the business."

"Right. Because it's my company. I'll make the com-pany—nobody else—while I stagger around with it, paying out eighteen percent to a salesman. And that's why I don't have to wait around until they read the will on *your* money."

"You're a hard kid, Nick. It nearly breaks my heart."

They looked at each other right at that second and they both began to laugh. They fell about laughing together, and it was the first and last time they ever did.

Nick had a buffer against Pa and the oil business, a man named Keifetz. Keifetz wasn't as old as Pa by easily fifteen years, but he had been more of a father than Pa had ever wanted to be. Keifetz was on his side, not on Pa's or anybody else's. He was a powerful, hairy man with a comic-strip moustache like Stalin's mother's and a right hand that could maybe punch holes in the average office safe. Keifetz could hold liquor, pacify women and explain politics. That was the shaman side of him for Nick: he could explain politics to Nick the way Lionel Barrymore had been able to explain the common cold to Dr. Kildare. Nick used to think that there was the Democratic Party and the Republican Party. It had taken Keifetz a long time to explain why this wasn't so, but after that, after Nick had been able to comprehend that there was only *one* political party, formed by the two pretend parties wearing their labels like party hats and joining their hands in a circle around their prey, all the rest of it came much easier. Pa said Keifetz was a fucking radical. Nick felt much safer with Keifetz than he ever had with Pa.

Keifetz got 3 percent of the Jemnito profits on a ramp basis that would get him up to 7 percent if the profits kept increasing. He didn't get the percentage because he was Nick's very reliable friend. Keifetz was the best tool-pusher and all-around oil man they had in the business in South America, the Near East, Asia or anywhere else.

Nick owned all the shares in the company. He had invested two-thirds of the money his mother had left him. Pa had invested information and clout only.

Jemnito was headquartered, in an intricate tax troika arrangement that seemed to exhaust tax collectors, in the Republic of San Marino, in the Faroe Islands, and in Bhutan, but was operated out of London as an Irish-Nigerian company. It was currently producing oil off Bangladesh and in the South China Sea off Brunei. It was about to begin negotiations for the concession to prospect on the Great Barrier Reef off Queensland, Australia. All oil leases exploited by Jemnito were obtained by Pa from his many friends, who were government ministers, reigning generals, sultans, presidents and others well disposed and dispersed.

Nick liked the oil business for solid reasons. It kept him remote from his father, who had believed in thrusting the world on Tim while ignoring Nick. So Nick ignored Pa. Pa had bought immortality for Tim—a sainthood for a family that had everything. Pa got what he wanted. The other reason Nick liked the oil business was that it produced the dramatic kind of wealth his father respected. Pa found it difficult to measure men who had only three, four or even five million dollars. People who had less than that did not exist for Pa any more than plankton existed for a whale.

But no matter how hard Nick tried, Pa looked right through him. Nick told himself Pa couldn't see him because he wasn't President of the United States. It was all pretty silly stuff and it hurt. Nick answered all of it by keeping ten or fifteen thousand miles between them.

Nick's mother (who had conducted the Albany Symphony Orchestra, with Dame Maria Van Slyke as soloist, in a performance of "Rastus's Dream," Mrs. Thirkield's own composition, at a charity concert held at Palazzo Bonetti, her home and shrine near Utica, New York, where her second husband, Gabriel Thirkield, manufactured superior harmonicas) had insisted that Nick learn to play the piano really well. Nick had studied piano formally from the time he was five until he was twenty-two. When he was moved across the continent to his father's house after his mother's sudden death, Tim had told him (Nick being nine at the time and Tim almost twenty-four) that Pa considered piano playing to be "faggy," this delivered in Tim's bland, wary way from behind his remote gray eyes. The put-on was part of Tim's famous emotional detachment, which also, Nick came to see, kept him out of conflict with Pa. It was a projection of calm weakness experienced tensely. Nick finally discovered that his brother was always fearful that Pa, or the world (in that order), would catch him out in a mistake. Despite the heroic detachment, it tended to make him excessively dependent on other people.

Tim's big piano warning had the wrong effect on Nick, who concentrated with redoubled vigor on his piano studies, until Pa actually remarked how much he was beginning to enjoy listening to Nick play. As soon as he said it, Nick stopped playing on the full piano when Pa was near. He played on a silent practice keyboard. As he got older and went away to school, on the occasions when he did visit Pa he would set up the silent keyboard in his father's sight and play on it lustily. For many years he actually believed he was depriving Pa of pleasure. Later he understood that Pa probably thought that reading books was "faggy." There were books in all Pa's houses but they were placed far from where they could corrupt Pa. Pa owned paintings and sculpture, but all he appreciated about any beauty was how much it had cost him and how much he could stick the next buyer for it. Pa hardly ever drank his own wine, because that would be cutting into capital. "You don't have to read books, kid, if you can read a balance sheet," he told Nick (when he was fourteen) in a rare bit of father-and-son tenderness. Pa wasn't a Philistine, Tim explained, he was more of a barbarian. To put it one way: Pa was not one of Nick's friends, but Nick loved him.

Nick had three friends. Keith Lee, his oldest and most seldom seen friend, was the son of Pa's Chinese butler. Next came Keifetz, who had been working with

Nick since Nick had rushed to the Orient in 1958, when Pa had gotten him and his mining engineer's degree an offshore job with Gulf. Last in calendar order (but first in the heart of her countryman) was Yvette Malone. Nick was in love with Yvette Malone, but just the same she was his friend. Three strong friends were a lot for a rich man to have, Tim had told him. But Tim had been like Pa, he hadn't wanted friends, just people on whom he could be dependent and who were certified to appreciate his wit and wisdom. It all worked out backward. Why not, Nick thought. By 1974 the big difference between Tim and Nick, Nick felt, was essentially that he had three friends, and Tim, although dead for fourteen years, had approximately three hundred million.

Nick flew off the pad on the high stern of the *Teekay* on a rainy night. He was the only passenger in the ship's twenty-six-seat Sikorsky S-61N that Mitsubishi had built under license for Pa (Pa having gone into Japan with his money and his specialists as a spiritual part of the treaty MacArthur had produced). It was fully amphibious, with twin stabilizing floats, and was cleared for all-weather operation. It had a 275-mile range.

The chopper had a crew of three, and ordinarily Nick would have visited with them all the way in to Brunei, but he had been telling Pa for the past seventeen days that the *Teekay* was as perfectly checked out as it could ever be, and still he couldn't get away to get back to his own business, because Pa now wanted him to start all the goddam tests over again for the third time. Sometimes he wasn't exactly clear on whether he was lurking around Asia with dirty fingernails in order to stay away from Pa or whether Pa was delighted to pile time on him to keep him in Asia safely out of the way. But safely out of the way of what? Or did he go through all these elaborate rituals just to bug Nick. They both knew at least three men as qualified or more qualified to run the shakedown on the *Teekay,* but Pa had insisted that he do it, then do it over and over. Someday he'd have to have a long talk with Pa and try to find out who was staying out of whose way. It was a pain in the ass to belong to any family, he thought, but to be in the same family with Pa was like having an anal fistula and having to run the hundred-meter dash in the Olympics. He moped in a seat at the back of the chopper trying to figure out what he could do to get off the goddam *Teekay.* Maybe Keifetz would have an angle. He supposed he should get laid or something now that he would be ashore, because he would be crazy if he didn't, even if he was too goddam exhausted to get his pants off.

When they put down at the Shell airport in Brunei, Keifetz was there sweating Tiger beer. It was ten thirty at night, pouring down some hard January rain.

"Seasonal weather," Keifetz apologized. Nick realized that he had never bothered to find out Keifetz' first name. Maybe Keifetz didn't have one. He liked it the way it was, just Keifetz. Who ever called a tiger Eddie Tiger?

"Is he still alive?" Nick asked stiffly, because he had to carry out being sore at the way Keifetz had hustled him off the drill ship.

"He'll hang in until he talks to you." Keifetz wrestled Nick's suitcase away from him, waving amiably at the customs officer and speaking to him in rapid Bahasa.

The Jemnito company car was a 1965 Dodge half truck. Nick sulked and Keifetz pretended he had traffic problems until they got out on the highway, then Keifetz said, "This crane operator has been with us four years, which is pretty fantastic. I signed him on first in East Pakistan. When we moved he showed up on the next job. I asked him how come. He said it was a privilege to work for Tim Kegan's brother, you dig?"

"Oh, shit."

"After he came to, he knew he was a goner, so he asked me if I could get you here and he told me why."

"Who is he?" Nick asked with irritation.

"His name is Turk Fletcher. When he signed on he even had a reference. It was a to-whom-it-may-concern letter from General Nolan—that friend of your family."

"General *Nolan*? *James* Nolan, Tim's old commanding officer?"

"That's him. You know him?"

"I never met him. He's been Pa's caretaker up at Rockrimmon, in Connecticut, almost ever since the war was over. This man's name is Turk Fletcher?"

"Yeah."

"I know most of our guys. I never heard of him."

"So he was in the cab fifty-one fucking feet over your head whenever you came aboard. Whatta you want?"

"Okay, tell me."

"He said he was Number Two rifle when they killed your brother."

"Oh, come on! You're a fanatic on this. There was no second rifle."

"Only according to the Pickering Report."

"Do you believe this guy?" Nick was incredulous.

"Let's say I believe there was a second rifle."

"Suppose there was a second rifle. What am I supposed to do about it?"

Keifetz shrugged. "Let me put it this way: the Pickering Commission didn't want to know anything about a second rifle so why should you—right?"

"Now, listen, Keifetz—"

"Every doctor on that job said there was a second rifle."

"Newspaper talk!" Nick had read more than very nearly anyone about his brother's murder, but he had known what he wanted to believe, and he had stayed in Asia most of the time after that, or in London or Paris, except for when he had the breakdown because he was taking the whole thing too big. All he knew as he stared at Keifetz was that fourteen years after everything had happened he just didn't want to hear that there had been a second rifle, because that would just stir everything up again. It could get Pa all agitated and active. He would pull Nick into some crazy vengeance scheme, and that would put an end to Nick's life without father. Talk or proof about a second rifle couldn't serve anything except to keep him away from running his own company for another three months. Tim was dead. He'd been dead for fourteen years. No big deal of another presidential commission investigation would bring Tim back to life.

"Look," Keifetz said, "how many times I gotta say it? Go ahead, Nicholas. Turn your back. What the hell do you care?"

"Are you asking me or telling me?"

"I already told you plenty of times." Keifetz had raised his voice. "Abe Weiler won a Nobel Prize for medicine, and I went to school with Abe Weiler. He is the doctor who pronounced your brother dead. I wrote to him. He answered back exactly the way he told the newspapers in the official medical report—that your brother had been hit front and rear by two different rifles. You allow the shot in the back of the head because the Pickering Commission told you to—right? Okay. The other bullet knocked on the front door."

"That's a cute expression."

"Boy, that's what this dying man, this Turk Fletcher, needs, some of your famous sarcasm."

"Willie Arnold was a Communist," Nick said irrelevantly. Not irrelevantly for him, because Pa had trained him all his life to use sentences like that, but irrelevant to the question.

"Would you believe the Hearst papers on Communists?" Keifetz asked.

"Of course."

"Okay, so I'm a Victor-ola. The Hearst papers, in 1960, the year your brother was killed, said that in assassinating the President, Willie Arnold had, quote, served the Communist cause its worst setback in forty-six years since its baneful inception, unquote. Okay, tell me something. Would you believe the late J. Edgar Hoover on Communists? In 1960 J. Edgar Hoover said—"

"Never mind, fahcrissake! I was crazy to bring it up. What do I talk politics with you all the time for? Why don't I back you into a good argument about piano techniques?"

"I'm sorry, Nicholas."

"You are so goddam self-righteous about the Joseph Alsop columns you were able to memorize."

"Still, right is right."

Nick stared at him with his Captain Bligh look. "Keifetz, this is a family affair. If the man in this hospital was part of a conspiracy that murdered my brother, I am going to find out about the rest of the people in the conspiracy."

"I hoped you'd say that. I am proud of you. I honestly am."

What have I said, Nick wondered. Is this a John Wayne movie? How could I commit myself like that? Keifetz was a dangerous mental case where Tim was concerned and Keifetz would never let him forget what he had just said. It meant, for Christ's sake, he had been manipulated again, and he would never be able to prove that he had been manipulated. Someday he was going to decide he had had enough and fire this son-of-a-bitch.

There was a parking space in front of the hospital. They waited in the air-conditioned lobby. "Enjoy the cool while you can," Keifetz said. "The air-conditioning breaks down here every hour on the hour."

"What are we waiting for?"

"Fletcher is going to be able to go .through this only once," Keifetz said, "so I borrowed a lawyer from Shell to take a deposition."

The lawyer brought a stenographer with him. The lawyer's name was Chandler Tate. The stenographer was a Javanese girl named Sis Ryan. Keifetz led them to Fletcher's room. There was a screen around the bed and two chairs on either side of it. Keifetz leaned over and spoke directly into Fletcher's ear. "President Kegan's brother is here, Turk," he said. Fletcher opened his eyes, but he didn't look at anybody.

"We are going to swear you in, Turk," Keifetz said. Sis Ryan moved a Bible under Fletcher's hand on the bed. Tate read the formula to Fletcher from a typewritten slip. Fletcher repeated that what he was about to say was the whole truth, nothing but the truth, so help him God.

The iodoform smell was sweet and heavy. The flat fluorescent light poured age down on all of them except Sis Ryan. Fletcher's face was as lined as a phonograph record. His voice was a hoarse whisper.

"State your full name, please," Tate said.

"Arthur Turkus Fletcher."

"Your address, please."

"Dallas. Texas."

"How old are you?"

"Fifty-eight years."

"We will hear your testimony now."

"I shot President Kegan."

"How?" Nick asked the question involuntarily.

"I was second rifle in Hunt Plaza on February 22, 1960. I hit with both shots." His voice had no color because he was saving everything. "First rifle missed with his second shot. I fired from the sixth floor of the Engelson Building, from behind the President's car."

Nick corrected Fletcher. "You mean you shot from the TV Center warehouse," he said.

"There never was any shot from there," Fletcher whispered, sweating like a mollusk. The people around the bed glistened. Keifetz' thousand-mile blue shirt had dark loops under each arm. "That room up there was just a decoy. They left the phony rifle there. A mail-order Carcano, fercrissake. I couldn't hit you from here with no Carcano."

"Where was the Number One rifle?" Keifetz asked.

"I shot on a line with him," Fletcher said. "At a high angle where you gotta watch your azimuth and you gotta figure your lead time with a big car that's bound to pick up speed after them first two shots. Number One shot from behind the fence with the bushes in front—up on the grassy knoll to the right of the car and a little above. I shot three seconds—about thirty yards—behind him."

Tim loomed up in Nick's mind wearing a dark jacket with a yellow silk lining that had horses printed on it. He could smell the smoke from Tim's Cuban cigar. He could see Tim's eyes mocking him. Tim's eyes could either use you or you were useless. If you were useless, the eyes were indifferent, but if there was something else seen there that could possibly hoist Tim, the eyes sparkled with attention and flattering concern.

Fletcher gasped with surprise at the intensity of a serial pain that had just scampered through him. Then he continued to speak slowly, leaning against the ramp of the pain. "First shot to the back of his head. Second shot beside the spine. Near side. I went into history. The way the fortune teller told my momma I would, two hours before I was born."

Keifetz looked at Nick. Nick seemed to be trying to memorize the square inches of Fletcher's face. This man killed Tim, Nick was telling himself incredulously. He could reach out and touch Tim's murderer, but he couldn't see anything evil in his face.

Pa had made Tim the President. This man had un-made him. Between the two stood an odd stranger, a shimmering figure of memory in TV newsreels. A zero called The Wit and Wisdom of President Kegan. Teeth. Ellamae Irving and her orogenic brassiere. All that red hair. The man who had stared down the Russian Chairman. Women. All sizes of women. A rusty-haired man in white pajamas. A head on a celluloid button. Vietnam.

This exhausted, dying, staring body on the hospital bed, whose face had less expression than a baseball glove, had exploded all of it, had made the wlonk presidential cartoon disappear. It was ridiculous.

Fletcher stared upward as though the ceiling were a crowded movie screen that was offering a spectacular starring himself back in the days when he had never bothered to think about dying.

Toward the end of November 1959, Turk Fletcher came out of the barbershop of the Baker Hotel in Dallas. Just about twenty-three years before, he had gotten the first manicure of his life right there. He had admired the manicurist, Harleen, so much that even after she left to marry the biggest grapefruit producer in East Texas he had continued to patronize the Baker barbershop. He kept track of his haircuts, as he kept a careful record of nearly everything, in case the Internal Revenue ever questioned his expenditures. He had been pleased to note that he had had two hundred and eleven out of two hundred and seventy-six haircuts in the barbershop at the Baker.

On the way out, inhaling the wonderful odors of tonics and cures, the steaming towels and the good clean soap, his back to the barber, who was staring with horror at the ten-cent tip Fletcher had just given him, he was bumped into by a short, stocky fellow who just didn't give a goddam where he was going. If the little fucker couldn't see him, he couldn't see a hole in a forty-foot ladder. The man's hands apologized for him before his voice could say it. They grabbed Turk sincerely and set him right. Then he came right out and said, "Say, ain't you Turk Fletcher?" Fletcher nodded like a billy goat (excepting he sure didn't smell like one right at that minute). "I seen you shoot in Crystal City and at the big chili cookout up to Nito Bennett's ranch."

"Win a little?" Fletcher asked smarmily.

"Some. I know maybe a dozen people who think you're the finest rifle shot alive."

"Purely fine of you to say it."

"Would you do me the honor of acceptin' to drink with me?" This fellow was something else, Fletcher thought. "It would purely be a pleasure," the stocky man said, "and more than that."

He had a bright pink face as if barbers had been pinching at it day and night. He had a curvy, white, bartender's haircut. The part in his hair was a pink, flat, straight ribbon. He was wearing a sure-thing mail-order suit, so he had to be country bred. He had kind of a crude-oil look to him, a good, old-time look. "Call me Casper or call me Junior," he said. "The name is Casper Junior. And I hope, with all respect, that you'll let me tell all my people that you asked me to call you Turk."

"Call me Turk," Fletcher said in his slow, hoarse voice.

They went up to Casper's suite of rooms on the fourth floor. Fletcher thought suites of rooms were a great way for a man to chouse his money and make it all nervous. Nobody could live in more than one room at a time. People were outside most of the time anyways. He'd never lived in anything bigger than one room in his life. But, oh hell, it wasn't anything to get chuffy about.

"In town for long, Turk?"

Casper was the kind of a fellow who polished a bottle with a towel before he poured your drink. He had to have been a bartender before he found the money to throw away on hotel suites. Turk had never seen a bottle of bourbon so undusty. Casper poured them both drinks in a pair of bathroom glasses, then it turned out the little fucker had a goddam icebox right in his parlor. He pulled a bowl of ice out of it, put two lumps into each glass—as if one cube wasn't cold all by itself—then put the bowl back. Casper must have learned about life from a correspondence course, Turk figured.

"I live here in East Dallas now," Turk said.

"What about your Rifle Association work?"

"Well, that was no life. I was as homeless as a poker chip and the West Texas food wasn't gettin' to me. I got a mean little stomach, and the best thing is like cheese, so I come back into Dallas where I could get it any time of day."

"But what about rifle shootin'?"

"I still shoot for the side money. The boys still like to bet if I can hit it or I can't."

"The rifle is sure your meat," Casper said. "We was talkin' once out in Bryson, Texas—the town named for the great actor?—or no, maybe it was Littlesam—hell, no, I think it was in Bryson—about what the fortune teller said to your mother?"

"I guess ever'body knows that story." Turk meant it. He was sure everybody in Texas knew that story.

"Well, you'll sure as hell go into history as the best marksman in the world in your time or any old time."

"No," Fletcher said reluctantly. He had thought a lot about it. "Tom Frye could beat me with a Remington Nylon sixty-six, twenty-two calibre. And I know Zeiser can take me with benchrest rifle rules, because he has goddam well done it."

Casper filled Fletcher's glass with more of the same fine drinking whiskey.

"Then maybe the prediction means you're gonna shoot the most famous man in the world," Casper said with a broad grin. "That sure would put you into the history books."

"I guess it would." He sipped at the whiskey and stared at the wall. "Hell, come right down to it, Wigger and Anderson can both take me with a small-bore rifle."

"That's a different story," Casper said. "Them boys is full-time record-book shooters."

* * *

Over the next month or so Casper Junior saw a lot of Fletcher. They would run into each other accidentally at first. Fletcher saw nothing unusual about that or about Casper's hero worship. They began to dine together once a week, always at the best places, such as Old Warsaw, or Arthur's, or Town and Country, and with Casper always grabbing the tickets. Turk felt Casper was the kind of a man who liked to spend money. Turk had given his life to Texas, but that hadn't made him rich, although he knew he was meant to be rich. It took a rich man to keep grabbing dinner tickets like these, and if Casper wasn't rich it would be poor manners to let on that Fletcher thought that Casper was just pretending to be rich.

Suddenly, for no reason in this world, Fletcher lost his job on the crane.

The foreman just came up to him on the third payday and told him he was through. Fletcher wanted to know how come, but the foreman just walked away. Nobody could understand it. "Why, it wasn't a week ago that this same little pissmire was tellin' me an' ever'body else that I am the best crane operator in the entire Southwest. I mean, I've known that man and he has known me and my work for near to eight years," he told Casper.

It put him off his feed. It turned his stomach all sour. He had saved, sure. But if you had to spend what you had saved, that was wrong. He was just not a spending man. He was a man who had respect for money. He worried himself sleepless about keeping the nurses and doctors sweet at his momma's nursing home. It was true that Momma was paid up for life at the nursing home and that they all loved her there, because you just couldn't help loving her and because she had left the nursing home everything she had in her will, but just the same Momma said he plain had to send her cash money twice a month. He knew the nurses and doctors took it away from her before she ever got it but that everybody treated her nicer after they stole it from her. She was a real old lady. She slept most of the time, but once, when he had forgotten to send through some cash right on time, they had started pinching her and they made her get up and walk in the windy halls late at night instead of letting her sleep.

Fletcher hadn't been without some money coming in since he was twelve years old. He was scared. He didn't tell himself what a good batting average he had as a steady earner. He never reminded himself that he had one hundred and two thousand, four hundred and six dollars in four banks around the state. He just said to himself that he was forty-four years old and his momma needed him, but that he didn't have any son to take care of him when he was old like Momma.

His stomach got so bad he could eat only chili. They had to stop eating in all the expensive places because he couldn't stand to see all that money being paid out just for cooked food. By the week after he was fired they were having dinner together three times a week at the Spanish Village in Cedar Springs or out to Joe Garcia's in Fort Worth. Casper had got so he just didn't want to talk about anything except how Turk was heading straight for the history books.

"You know what I found out?"

"What?"

"Fletcher means 'maker of arrows.' "

"I didn't know that," Turk said. "I'm good with a rifle, but I never handled a bow and arrows in my life."

"No. That ain't it. It's a meaningful symbol. You are a maker of arrows who is going to pass into history because of the way you can shoot. A rifle, that is."

"I always knowed I was meant to do big things," Fletcher said. "My momma taught me that from the time I was about fryin' size. That was my heartbreak. I mean, I can shoot a rifle, but I was never stretched. I mean, I got all the shitty details in the army. My momma used to tell me I might be Viceroy of India, so, what the heck, anything I ever did never seemed like anything to me. I never seemed to be able to climb into the real money. They was like fifty bandidos around Dallas and Houston and ten other Texas towns all bulgin' into the big money while I was just a workin' stiff, and I ain't even that now. I been turned down for three jobs in a row, and that never happened before. They ain't any crane work left for five hundred miles around. All I have to keep me goin' is what is keeping Momma alive—we both know I'm gonna pass into history. But when?"

"Turk? I know a man who'll make you rich and *push* you into history if you'll point your rifle and shoot Tim Kegan when he rides by."

"I guess we both know a coupla hundred of them," Fletcher said glumly. "Right here in Dallas."

One Sunday afternoon on the way back from a big country rifle shoot at Fort Peters, where Fletcher made himself five hundred and twelve dollars betting on himself and Casper made maybe ten times that much, they were rolling along home in Casper's big sand-colored Cadillac with the thin red stripe all around it when Casper said, "Seen the papers, Turk? Kegan is beggin' the Russians to be nice to us again."

"I never read newspapers," Fletcher said. "They say one thing today, then they say something all different a week from now."

"Don't you care what happens to your country?"

"Pew, Junior. Everybody in Dallas cares about that. Let them take care of it. I don't have a head for politics."

"Well, you can write this down in your little book," Casper said. "Kegan is just asking for it."

"Ever'body in Dallas knows that too."

"All right. Then you know where the people of Texas stand. And the whole oil-depreciation allowance."

"Junior, first I got to get me a job, then you'n me can talk about politics. Okay?"

"Would you take twenty-five hundred dollars and all expenses to spend a little time on a ranch?"

"Doin' what?"

"Showin' a man how to shoot a Garand rifle the right way so's he can run it good enough to pot Tim Kegan ridin' past in a car?"

"No shit?"

"Twenty-five hundred dollars cash. And here's where the class comes in. My boss doesn't blink an eye at money. He'd like to buy hisse'f the mental comfort of knowin' they was two men shootin' at Kegan instead of just the one, and he'd feel best of all if one of them was a shooter like you."

"I sure as hell don't seem to be able to get any other kinda work."

"Sixteen thousand, five hunnert net for doin' what you do better'n anybody alive. For maybe sixty seconds of work. Sixty seconds to pot the most famous man in the world and push yourself right into history."

Fletcher turned his head slowly and stared at Casper with all of his catcher's-mitt expression. Casper kept his eyes on the road. Fletcher enjoyed talking about good-sized chunks of money. He had obliged a fellow once before and had shot down a tortilla politician in the State of Vera Cruz because he'd been paying for his momma's keep in Winship Falls, New York, for twenty-seven years. Money didn't berry out on bushes.

"Shoot a man like Kegan and you never get to spend the money," Turk said tentatively.

"Oh, yes, you do. My boss is just as big a man as Kegan. They ain't nobody he don't know and he's talked around about it to alla them. I mean, everything is settled. You goin' to get top cooperation from the very top people."

"Who is your boss, Casp?"

"My boss is a man who knows the cool-headed way

you handled a job of work in the State of Vera Cruz,
Mexico. And he admires you for it."

"A fact?"

"Sure is. Now—what do you say?"

"I got to think about it," Fletcher said. "I am not
quick, but I am thorough."

Fletcher made a chart in his room in East Dallas after mulling things through with two bottles of Pearl. He
wanted all the facts right in front of him in good-sized
letters so he could think the proposition through. A
man who took a running jump into anything deserved
to sink up to his hat. He stared at the chart, sipping
beer.

ALL DALLAS FRETS.
HE IS A TRAITOR.
SAVE AMERICA?
MOMMA—HISTORY IS MEMORY.
SIXTEEN FIVE—IS IT ENOUGH?
THINGS TO WATCH FOR.
WHO LEAKED VERA CRUZ?

No reason to trust Casper any more than anybody
else. Hell, the man who had hired him for Vera Cruz
was dead for over four years, and they had already
hung somebody for killing the fellow he had shot. But,
by God, Mexico didn't have the budget of the government of the United States. Boil up the federal people
and they could really go after you. There were a lot of
newspapers back east that were sure to make a big
thing out of somebody shooting down a President.
Man, they'd sure have to grab somebody—though it
would all cool off as soon as they settled on who was to
blame. He wondered if it had been that little fucker
Casper who got him fired off the crane. Goddam pissmire. Sure, Casper made everything look easy, but the
money wasn't right. The money was an insult to the
President. The head honcho had to have so much

money he could never count it. Shooting a President was a big job. They needed the best man there was.

Two nights after Turk got back from some ranch in the west country somewhere, when he and Casper had settled down over a couple of bowls of red and some good cold Pearl beer, Casper said, "Did y'all think of what I was sayin' to you on the ride back from Fort Peters?"

"Yes, I did."

"How do you see it?"

"The basics is what bothers me."

"That was a mighty generous price, Turk."

"I do not agree."

"How much do you have in mind?"

"Fifty."

"You just have to know that cain't be."

"I know what cain't be all right. It's your figure of sixteen five net."

"We are willin' to come up a little, Turk, but you gotta know our overhead. The other rifle, his assistant, paying police, sweetening Feds, flyin' us up and back, hotel bills, tips, meals, laundry, rifles and rounds, car rentals—I mean, you are just part of the over-all."

"I bet you are paying the other rifle plenty more."

"I'm not so sure about that. We are Texas people and so are you, and we wouldn't stand for that. But even if it was a few dollars more, you'd have to say he's a city feller and his overhead is higher."

"I'll go for thirty-five."

"Turk, I think you should know that everybody in this gets a life-insurance policy made out to whoever he says. That is the kind of a man we are working for."

"I appreciate that."

"On the line."

"That is real courtesy."

"Ten-day term insurance for one hundred thousand dollars face value, and we pay the premiums."

"Junior, you seem to know so much, you must know

I got fifteen for the work in the State of Vera Cruz, and that was back-country stuff. This is right out there in front, and you know it."

"We are going to be spending upwards of four hundred thousand dollars just to put you at the end of a board so's you can jump into history. That's worth a lot, Turk."

Fletcher shoveled in the chili and chewed thoughtfully. He didn't speak for almost ten minutes. When he finished bowl number one Casper called out to the waitress for two more.

"Twenty-five thousand," Fletcher said at last.

"Twenty-two thousand, five hundred gross," Casper snapped. "That is, including the twenty-five hundred for the shootin' lessons."

"I guess that'll be all right," Fletcher said, "providin' you pay it over on the mornin' of the day."

"Absolutely."

"Abso-abso-*abso*-lutely," Fletcher said. "There is one thing I am stickin' to, Casper. If I don't get my money on the morning of the day, I plain ain't goin' to work."

On the morning of the day, February 22, 1960, in a furnished room off Walnut Street, Turk Fletcher put on the Philadelphia policeman suit they had given him to wear. He packed the disassembled rifle, a civilian suit, a green-and-brown-striped bow tie, a heavy wrench and *Western Stories* in the boughten bag he had brought along from home. He locked the bag, then he snapped a padlock on the hasp he had welded to it. A man had to do his own independent thinking to stay in one piece with a crowd like this, he thought. He hadn't liked the sound or the look of the Number One rifle from the time he had first set eyes on him at that fake-ass ranch in Arizona. The little basser was just a cheap gangster and some kind of a fairy fellow too.

At seven thirty Casper knocked at the door and Fletcher let him in.

"You are sure something to see in that suit," Casper said. "There has always been something gentling about a policeman to me."

He gave Fletcher an envelope and they sat down at a round table to count it out. It was all there. They shook hands. "I know you are going to do a fine job," Casper said.

"I am going to do my best," Fletcher replied, then Casper left.

At ten minutes after eight, young Willie Arnold, the Number One rifle's "assistant" (shee-yut), a blubber-lip who looked as if he couldn't drive nails in a snow-bank, came to pick up the boughten bag and take it to Room 603 in the Engelson Building, where he would lock it in. They didn't speak. Willie wasn't *his* "assistant." Willie just stayed out in the hall. He handed Fletcher the key to 603. Fletcher handed him the boughten bag. Willie went right back down the stairs. He sure looked boogered.

Fletcher went back inside and folded the money into a money belt and put the belt on. He thought how, if anyone had ever told him when he was twenty-one years old that the day would come when he would be paid twenty-two thousand, five hundred dollars for a morning's work, he just would have thought that person was crazy. He had very much in mind that they had agreed to pay him so handily because when the police came asmokin' for him—as they all sure as hell had it all set up—they would find all that money on his poor dead body, and that would be sure evidence that he had been the man who had shot the President. He giggled softly to himself, purely enjoying the surprises that were coming to some people.

He was down on the street in front of the building when the police patrol car with only one man in it pulled up at nine twenty. The driver looked pale. He hung onto the wheel to keep from shaking. He was a thick-looking basser.

It was a four-minute drive to the Engelson Building.

The car stopped at the delivery entrance. Fletcher got out.

The driver's name was Bailey Bissett. He said to Fletcher, "I don't know what you'll be doing up there, but I'll be waiting right here with the engine running when you come down."

"Well, fine," Fletcher said.

"When will that be?" Bailey Bissett's voice squeaked he was so spooked. "When will that be?"

"About twelve thirty-six, I figure. Be brave, son." Turk went into the building.

He walked up the six flights of service stairs and let himself into 603 with the duplicate key. He locked himself in. The boughten bag was on the floor. There was no furniture in the room except one chair. He went to one of the two windows that faced Hunt Plaza. The plaza was empty of people. The traffic was moving through under the railway bridge at the bottleneck. It was nine thirty-nine. The presidential motorcade was due to move through at about twelve twenty-five.

He assembled the rifle with admiration. It was the sweetest goshdarned rifle he had ever fired. It was a U.S. Rifle Calibre .30 M1D sniper fitted with a Lyman M84 scope that had a cross-wire reticle and a rubber eyepiece on a special 26-inch barrel. It weighed nine pounds, less the magazine. It provided semiautomatic fire on a closed bolt. Fletcher had had a metal outline stock made for the rifle at Fort Worth. It was fitted with a foam-rubber cheek pad. The special stock was only slightly wider than the barrel itself, making the weapon into one long magic wand. He whistled "Little Joe, the Wrangler" as he chose bullets from a box with delicate care. He propped the rifle up against the wall, then changed into civilian clothes. He stowed the police uniform in the suitcase, took out *Western Stories* and settled down in the chair to wait, looking at his watch about every eight minutes.

At half past eleven he put the magazine back into

the suitcase and did fifteen minutes of setting-up exercises so his circulation would be normal when he went to work. He looked down at Hunt Plaza. About a hundred and fifty people had collected to see the President whisk through. More were coming in.

He watched Number One rifle drive the panel truck marked AIR-CONDITIONING along the Euclid Avenue channel, drive off under the railway bridge, then turn off to the left into Rackin Boulevard. Fletcher knew he would circle around into Market Street, then turn again into Klarnet to get to the parking lot behind the fence at the top of the grassy knoll. The truck had plenty of time to get into position. No other cars could get in behind the fence because Willie Arnold had roped off the space between two NO PARKING stanchions early that morning. When the Number One rifle backed the panel truck in, he would crawl to the back of the truck, take the rifle case from Willie, use the back gate of the truck as a benchrest for the rifle barrel and shoot through the fence and the protecting bushes. He'd make his two shots, close the back gates of the truck, slide into the driver's seat and glide away.

On schedule, Captain Heller's lead car of the Political Squad in front, drawing the procession into Hunt Plaza on the President's tour through the city to the Liberty Bell, outriding motorcycles in front of and on either side of the President's car, the Vice-President and many members of the presidential staff in the cars following, with the President's physician riding eleven cars behind, the motorcade swung into Hunt Plaza and moved toward the invisible line between the two rifles that bisected the square.

Fletcher's hands were sweating lightly, but no more than when he had competed against Zeiser and had put four consecutive shots into a one-inch hole at a hundred yards. The President rode along in the open car beside the mayor of Philadelphia. He was grinning broadly. Fletcher tracked with him. The procession turned sharply to the left and headed due west toward the underpass of the railway bridge. Number One would fire in four seconds. Fletcher counted deliberately under his breath, tracking through the scope smoothly just above and to the left of the President's head.

The President jolted backward. Fletcher saw the mayor's body jerk sharply to the left and knew the Number One rifle had missed with his second shot. Fletcher squeezed the trigger. The occipitoparietal section of the President's skull went out while the mechanical components of the rifle moved swiftly to deliver the second shot. The camming surfaces on the inside of the hump on the operating rod of the rifle engaged the camming surfaces on the operating lug and rotated the bolt counterclockwise. The residual pressure in the gas chamber and the momentum of the operating rod and bolt extracted and ejected the cartridge and cocked the hammer. The operating rod carried the bolt forward and fed the cartridge into the chamber as Fletcher tracked the car above and to the left of his target, dropped the rifle muzzle slightly and squeezed the trigger a second time. The bullet passed the gas port, crossed the plaza and slammed into the President's back.

Fletcher turned and stepped away from the window with the same involuntarily formal movements he had used so many times to step out of position on a firing range during the years when he had been an inspirational demonstrator for the National Rifle Association in the Southwest. He propped the rifle against the wall. He took the heavy wrench out of the suitcase. He used it to turn the joint on the wide vertical heating pipe that ran from ceiling to floor in the southwest corner of the room. The pipe came apart as he had designed it. He lowered the rifle into the pipe. He secured it in suspension from a wooden rack that he had built into the false pipe at the joint. The rifle hung straight downward. He reassembled the pipe, tightened the joint, put the wrench back into the suitcase with the police uniform and *Western Stories,* closed the bag and left the room. He locked the door behind him. He turned upward to the stairs to the roof, crossed four building roofs before he went down to street level again, to emerge in the heavy pedestrian traffic of Market Street. It was a glorious day, not a cloud in the sky and with a bright sun overhead. It looked like they were going to have a wonderful winter.

Twenty-seven minutes after he had made the two shots he was riding out of Philadelphia on a Greyhound bus to Cleveland. He worked his way back eastward from Cleveland by plane to Albany. He was sitting in Momma's room at Winship Hall and watching television while she slept when he saw Joe Diamond shoot down Willie Arnold in the basement of the Philadelphia Police and Courts Building while Arnold, handcuffed to a Philadelphia detective and surrounded by more than seventy Philadelphia police, was being led to a waiting police car.

Turk grinned broadly as he watched. They sure were a slick bunch of guys.

Fletcher was grinning as he stared at the hospital ceiling.

"Who hired you?"

Fletcher said, "Man name of Casper Junior remembered me as a shooter around the state when I was doing demonstrations for the National Rifle Association. I never seen him before. I just know there was one man paying all the bills."

"Don't you have any idea who that could be?" Nick asked desperately.

"I got an idea, sure. But that don't mean nothing. I got an idea it was the man everybody in Dallas was so proud of for doing it—Z. K. Dawson, the oil man. I mean, he coulda organized it. He sure knew ever'body."

"But you don't know it was Dawson?" Keifetz asked.

"But—look, here—just a minute," Nick said. "What about Willie Arnold? The Pickering Commission proved that Willie Arnold shot my brother. What about Arnold in this thing?"

"Willie was kind of a coffee-runner for Diamond," Fletcher said with exhaustion. His voice sounded like a surgeon's xyster scraping a living bone. "Willie ran errands, and they had him to be the spare fall guy. I was Number One to take the fall, but I used my head, so they made Willie take it, then Diamond killed him before he could talk to ever'body and crap on ever'thing." His voice had fallen to a whisper.

"Turk," Nick said, "do you think the rifle is still hanging in that steam pipe in Room 603?" He leaned over close to Fletcher's ear to say that.

"Sure. Why not?" Fletcher spoke thickly. "Nobody but me knew about it. It's right there, covered all over with my prints for when the time came when I had to prove I killed the President. An' I taped my own name to the rifle too, because nobody was able to tell me whether fingerprints could just fade away."

Nick leaned close to Fletcher's ear again. "You are garbage," he said intensely. "You are a back-shooting murderer. Nobody but me is going to get that rifle, and when I get it I'm going to rip your name off it, and I am going to polish it with a cloth so that nobody will be able to tell it was you who fired it. You aren't going into history, Turk. You are going straight to hell."

"Needless to say," Keifetz said to Tate and Sis Ryan, "that part doesn't go into the deposition."

Fletcher flopped his head over to face Nick, breathing shallowly and rapidly. "Don't—do—that," he pleaded. He kept staring at Nick. Keifetz stared into Fletcher's popped, beseeching eyes and said, "Jesus, he's dead."

"Well, it wasn't unexpected, was it?" Tate said.

"I'll get the cops to lift his fingerprints and get us some mug shots," Keifetz said. "They belong with the deposition."

"We'll have that ready some time tomorrow afternoon," Tate said. He and Sis Ryan shook hands with both men and left.

"Keifetz?" Nick said.

"Yeah?"

"When you called me on the *Teekay,* what did you mean about sixteen people being dead?"

"What the hell has happened to you? We been over this ten times already. Sixteen people are known to be dead because they had some kind of information about the assassination."

"How many of them died within a couple of months of when Tim was killed?"

"Twelve, maybe. Maybe fourteen. Why?"

"I am trying to figure out something."

"They were people who should have been called before the Pickering Commission. Except they were never called, because one was shot through the head, one hanged herself in a Philadelphia jail. A Philadelphia reporter was thrown out of a window. A woman who had taken some home movies that day was dropped over the side of a cruise ship. A reporter was shot to death in a California police station. Sixteen were killed. Nobody will ever know how many were threatened to make them run and shut up, but there's nearly a dozen on the record."

"But the people who were killed just knew something. Like some shred that when put together with other shreds would tell who the killers were?"

"That's right."

"Well, Fletcher not only knew something, he was one of the people paid to shoot Tim, he says."

"Right."

"Then how come he survived for fourteen years? If they were out killing people who had little shreds, how come Fletcher got away?"

"Well—"

"How long has he worked for us?"

"I thought about four years, but it could have been six."

"And he said he just wanted to work for us for the kick of working for Tim Kegan's brother?"

"That's what he said."

"Well, I think he wanted to work for us because we're about the last place his former employers would think of looking for him."

"I think you're right. Yeah. That's it. But let's stay with the big point. Whoever paid to kill your brother paid other people to smother all the evidence, no matter where it popped up or how fast it popped up."

"But that would take police cooperation."

"More than that. Beyond that. Whoever arranged it sure got the cooperation of the FBI and the Pickering Commission. If the same guy had been in charge when they murdered Julius Caesar, Shakespeare would have been short one play, I can tell you. Never have so many been clammed up by so few."

"It's crazy. It's like the whole government was dropping acid."

"It's been crazy for fourteen years. You just started to notice it."

"I don't see how everybody could let it happen."

"Well, *you* let it happen. And the American people got three marvelous days of television out of it. Outside of that they didn't seem to be shook up. You try telling any one of them that there was a second rifle—just a second rifle, don't confuse them—and see what happens."

Nick was dazed. He stood up and sat down and walked to the window, then went over to look down at Fletcher's body.

"It's more droll than you know," Keifetz said. "One of the White House Secret Service detail who was on the job in Philly that day announced that he wanted to testify before the Pickering Commission about the failure of the Secret Service to take proper precautions to protect the President. They indicted him. Yeah. On the wild charge of trying to sell government files. And the Pickering Commission announced they just didn't have time for stuff like that. Get it? This guy was working on the President's detail that day, fahcrissake."

"Where is he? We've got to find him and talk to him."

"He was number sixteen. He's dead."

When the police and the photographer came in, Keifetz fell into Bahasa, and they went to work taking prints and mug shots of Fletcher. Keifetz freed the room for the resident and two nurses about twenty minutes later. It was a quarter to two in the morning when he drove Nick to the VIP guesthouse. Every insect in the surrounding jungle was alive and sounding. "Room eight," Keifetz said at the main door. "Right down the hall."

"Thanks."

"What's the next move?"

"I have to think about it."

"Don't think too much. It always slows you down."

"That is insubordinate."

"That's what you have me around for."

"Just shut up, will you do that?"

Nick, in white pajamas, lay across the bed in the guesthouse. He tried to think about Yvette Malone, but she wouldn't come into his head. Tim had been dead for fourteen years. The whole world was satisfied (except maybe a few Frenchmen) that the man who had killed him, Willie Arnold, had paid the penalty. Siegfried had floated off down the river on a leaf at last. The past was out of sight. The thing now was to know what was wisdom. Was all this why history contained so little truth? Was the history of all time piled up in a refuse heap at the back of humanity's barn, too ugly to be shown, while the faked artifacts that were passed around for national entertainments took charge in the front parlors? Could the seven hack lawyers of the Pickering Commission, with a new President for a client, decide that two hundred million people could not withstand the shock of history?

He got up from the bed wearily. He carried his attaché case to the table in the room, opened it, took out a book of piano scores and a folding practice keyboard. He laid the keyboard across the table and pulled up a chair. He leaned on his feet, but the weight of his body rested on the chair so that his trunk could move freely. His arms assumed a slightly stretched position at a higher level than the keyboard to facilitate the velocity of octave and chord playing. However, he was careful not to assume a high forearm position, because that could make the functioning of the muscles so unreliable that virtually none of the finger strokes would be entirely exact. Fortunately he had short forearms, which were most advantageous for the velocity of octave technique and let him execute swing strokes easily and surely.

He began with the slow practicing of fast scales in order to limber up, decomposing every movement into its components. To keep his finger action clean he executed the swinging movements of his fingers in a way exactly corresponding to the way they would be executed in fast tempo. He decomposed the action of his thumb and divided its movements into the preparation and the stroke, instead of executing a single, unbroken swing stroke.

Nick was equally thorough in everything he did, once he had decided it was important. He had the gift/curse of total commitment totally arrived at because he was a literal, systematic man. As he thought of the invisible face that had ordered Tim to be made dead, he started to break down all of the movements that might have been initiated within such a man's mind.

As with: what to do if he found Fletcher's rifle? As with: the succession of broken comma chords in the transition in the first movement of the Waldstein Sonata. His upper arm performed energetic vertical movements added to the rotation of the forearm, the passive movement of the wrist and the slight bending of the elbow joint. Everything worked together interdependently, capable of being stopped only if the censor in the mind ordered all of it to stop.

The Pickering Commission had operated like arms, elbows and fingers upon a silent keyboard. They had played all the notes—the score was surely there to be read, but they would not allow it to be heard. The commission had announced Stephen Foster when they were actually playing Wagner. Surely, critics who had followed the true score should have pointed that out.

As he played, two immediate decisions became apparent. He had to find the murderer-hirer; and somehow his father would have to be persuaded to help him. Then he felt sleepy. He put the keyboard and the score book back into the attaché case, lay down on the bed, forgot he was wearing white pajamas, and went to sleep.

A car picked him up at eight o'clock in the morning. It drove him to Keifetz' office in Brunei, but Keifetz wasn't there. Nick put in calls to his father in Palm Springs, to David Carswell, his manager in London, and to Jake Lanham on the *Teekay*. Daisy, Keifetz' gorgeous Filipina secretary, lined up plane tickets to Philadelphia from Singapore via London. While he waited for the calls to come in he tried to figure out the time-zone ratios to keep from thinking of the holy hell Pa was going to raise when he heard that Nick had left the *Teekay*. Well, maybe not. Maybe even Pa would rate nailing Tim's murderer over, at the most, six hours more on a drilling ship. The Lanham call came in first. Nick told Jake he was to take over as drilling superintendent until Pa's people came aboard, and he emphasized that Jake was to get a written release from them certifying that the *Teekay* was in perfect condition. The London call came in about ten minutes after Jake's. Carswell had a hard time fighting his way out of a sleeping-pill haze. It was eleven o'clock the night before in London. Nick had to repeat his name several times to get through to Carswell's recognition level.

"You know who I am now?" Nick abominated Carswell because he was a fink of Pa's.

"Perfectly all right," Carswell said. "Missed the name at first. Playing the wireless too loud, I suspect."

"That is a transparent lie, David."

"What? Will you repeat that, please?"

"Write this down," Nick snarled.

"Try to speak more clearly, Nick."

"I arrive at Heathrow at ten o'clock Tuesday morning on BOAC 713 from Singapore," Nick shouted. "Go to my flat and pack a bag with winter clothes for me. Meet me in the VIP lounge and bring me a heavy overcoat, a muffler, a hat and long woolen underwear. What I am wearing now could kill me in Philadelphia in January."

"What about the *Teekay?*"

"I'll tell you about it Tuesday morning. And don't take that tone of voice."

"Your father will not be at all pleased, nonetheless."

"Did you make a list, you twit? Did you write it all down? You sound all doped, and I need those clothes."

"Not to worry."

"Next—pay attention, goddammit—call Miles Gander at the Petroleum Club in Philadelphia and ask him to hold breakfast for me Wednesday morning."

"He's about to go bankrupt, you know."

"Just call him. Save your comment." Nick detested Carswell doubly each time he was forced to talk to him, because Carswell's whole air made him act like such an ass.

When Carswell disconnected he was wide awake enough to put in a direct-dial call to Thomas Kegan in Palm Springs.

Nick's call to Pa was still delayed, but the charter was waiting to fly him to Singapore. He told Daisy to talk to Pa and to tell him that Nick had finished the tests on the *Teekay* and was on his way to Palm Springs. When he got outside, Keifetz was waiting to drive him to the Shell airport.

"What did you decide to do?" Keifetz asked as they drove away.

"Find the rifle."

"Better take a couple of witnesses. But lay off newspaper guys."

"I'll have Miles Gander as a witness."

"Poor Miles," Keifetz said. "He's going bankrupt."

"That's certainly the world's worst-kept secret. I'm going to ask Miles to find me a Philadelphia police official as the other witness."

"The Philadelphia police didn't smell very good in 1960."

"It can't be helped. The rifle is a murder weapon, and it's their turf. Anyway, we'll outnumber him."

"Then what?"

"If I find the rifle?"

"What else?"

"Then I'll take Fletcher's deposition and prints and photographs—which you will airmail out to Palm Springs by tomorrow afternoon—together with the rifle, and my father and I will go to the President and ask that the investigation be reopened."

Keifetz was coming in the office door after seeing Nick off when Pa's call came through. He told Daisy he'd take it.

"What's up, kiddo?" Pa said.

"Nicholas is on his way to the States."

"What about the *Teekay?*"

"He finished the tests."

"Maybe he thought he finished, but he doesn't finish until I say he's finished."

"Anyway, Mr. Kegan, he's on his way."

"Why is he having breakfast with Miles Gander?"

"I don't know, Mr. Kegan."

"Listen—you know, and I know you know."

"Mr. Kegan, how do I know? Maybe he meant to tell me, but he was out of here like a shot this morning."

"But you saw him?"

"Yes, sir."

"Okay. Why is he having breakfast with Miles Gander?"

"A man who worked here died last night. Before he

died he confessed that he had been the second rifle when they killed President Kegan."

"Why didn't you tell me that?"

"Nicholas wants to tell you himself."

"What's Nick going to the States for?"

"The guy who was dying told Nicholas where he hid the rifle. Nicholas is going to Philadelphia to get the rifle, with Miles Gander and a police official as witnesses."

"No press!"

"No, Nicholas won't call in the press. He also got a deposition and fingerprints of the man who died—Arthur Fletcher. Those are going out to him by registered mail to your address—probably tomorrow night."

Pa hung up on him.

Nick loved Singapore, but he wouldn't see it on this trip. Something eccentric happened to him every time he got to Singapore. The last time, there had been an epidemic of over four hundred Chinese believing that their penises were retracting into their bodies. Rickshaws had rushed past him from all directions carrying appalled men whose friends, sitting beside them, held on firmly to the imperiled part to prevent it from disappearing up into the lower abdomen.

On this visit all there was to do was to climb down out of the Bonanza and climb up the first-class ramp of the BOAC flight. He had thirty-four hours of sitting ahead of him to Philadelphia, with a three-hour-and-forty-minute layover in London. There were six other passengers in the first-class section, all men. The man in the window seat ahead of him was an unconscious hummer who was improvising Grieg over and over again. It was crazing. Nick moved to the last row in the section, but it was a long time before he could no longer hear the humming.

He decided not to eat or drink until he got to Philadelphia, hoping that that would help him to survive better. He was flying in the wrong direction for minimum jet lag, because as the plane went westward it got earlier and earlier, but his body clock couldn't understand that. Eating and drinking only made it worse. His head had to be clear when he got to Philadelphia. Goddam Keifetz and Fletcher, he thought uselessly. Responding to them like an altar boy, he had reverted to the most obvious comic-book cliché—his brother's avenger. He decided that he must be afraid of Keifetz' contempt, with all that hissing steam about marching on the White House. How old does a man have to be before he stops finding things out about himself, he thought. He knew more about himself than he had ever wanted to know by the time he was twenty-one. Well, there were clouds and there were silver linings. When he got to London he'd be able to call Yvette Malone. That almost made the whole devious business worth it. No poking and probing (in a psychological investigator's sense) there. He knew all he had to know about Yvette Malone. She was beautiful. She had a disposition as soft as the down on angels' wings. She was from Texas, but that was an accident of birth, and even so it wasn't all bad because, in its unmysterious way, Texas had made her very rich. As far as Nick was concerned, that was all anybody needed to know about anybody. Find out who her mother's aunt was, and the first thing you know, you discover you are sleeping with the sister of a first cousin of yours. Besides, marginal information about anybody merely reduced to the least the ecstasy of concentration upon the center of the warm sun. Yvette felt the same way. He was just another oil man, and she collected oil men. She liked the way he looked and tasted, she figured he was not from Texas, because he talked like a Yankee. That's all she wanted to know. It was gratifying to wallow in the generous gifts of pleasure of a woman like Yvette and know that she was giving because she wished to, not because it made her a peripheral part of history to screw the half brother of the late, great Timothy Kegan, once President of the United States.

Yvette Malone lived an idyllic life anywhere it was the comfortable, fashionable place to be. She had a big, fat house on the Avenue de la Bourdonnais (on the right side of that privileged street), and she was willing to fly anywhere except Texas. She insisted on screwing on an "exchange of presents" basis. She always gave

Nick gaudy underwear. He had seventeen sets of silk underwear in five pastel colors. After the first time, when she had explained her policy, he had given her a Hiroshige print. After that she had guided him toward stockings. She said stockings were more impersonal. He didn't think he really understood her, but he liked barter-banging very much.

Nick was unmarried; had never been married. He was forty-one years old. More and more he had been thinking he should marry Yvette Malone. He couldn't think of even one small reason against it. They could breed some people to whom he could leave all that underwear. Marriage was a tricky business. When Tim had married Mary Elizabeth McGlade he had certainly never expected he would be a widower at twenty-two, while he was still at Yale. And he had remained a widower, because Pa had underlined that since the tragedy had happened anyway, and terrible as it was, no one could change it, it should be viewed as a political asset: The Man Who Had Remained True to a Precious Memory. Tim had agreed, partly because he felt that way (at the time), but even more because it meant big action with the hundreds of women who had wanted to console him.

Tim had appreciated women because they brought out the actor in him. When he got bored with himself he changed women and got himself a new personality. Except for Pa's implacable resistance, Tim would have been an actor. Tim had been a wholesomely vulgar man who had believed in a good mirror when he saw one.

Tim's women always ended up sad, Pa's mad. Nick preferred his own women glad. Not that it always worked out that way, thank God.

He hadn't seen Yvette Malone for more than four months. He took her picture out of his wallet and propped it up in front of him. What a beautiful thing she was, he thought. She had kind of burnished brown hair—red hair, really—and eyes as green as avocados. She was so smart she could speak Italian, French and German with a Texas accent. He was suddenly direfully needful to be in some kind of contact with her, so he asked the steward for some notepaper and began to write her a letter. "Dear Yvette," he wrote, "I am wearing the lime-colored silk underwear and thinking of you. But when do we get out of the underwear phase? Not that I want ties. But pajamas would be nice. You must be yearning for a letter like this. You have ninety-six pairs of stockings I know of. Why don't we switch? I'll give you underwear and you give me navy-blue lisle socks, size eleven.

"Disaster has struck. When I explain it I realize everything is going to sound like a bad movie, but are there any more good movies—were there ever any? This family secret has to come out sometime (between us, that is), and the whole framework of the events leading to the reason why I am on my way to Philadelphia and Palm Springs without the slightest chance that I can stop over in Paris long enough to make love gives me as good a chance to let the skeleton out for an airing as I guess I'll ever have. To put the whole thing bluntly: Timothy Kegan, a President of the United States, was my half brother, and now a man has just died in Asia who said he was just one of the people hired by somebody to kill my brother, so now I have to rush into the labyrinths of this melodrama, extract the answer to the enigma (which is probably that a man named Z. K. Dawson was the man who hired the killers), confront my unpredictable father with all that is happening, and, generally as well as particularly, have my life light up TILT for the next month or so. It is brutally stupid because it is so wastefully silly. There is not one chance in a million that, after fourteen long years of covering tracks ruthlessly, the man (Dawson, if it is Dawson) or men who paid for Tim's death can ever be found. But I have to do it as the Avenging Brother, because entertainment has taken over culture and we all live in a movie, or worse, in a mid-morning TV soap outcry.

"I cannot imagine that you will continue to stay on in the coldest city in the world (in January). You are probably on the beach at Grenada right now. I can't wait to get to London to call you to find out."

He put Yvonne's letter aside, because writing about Pa and what he would be walking into with Pa had brought out his never-absent dread of seeing Pa again. He would be in the worst sort of a position: the fink who brought bad news to Thomas Xavier Kegan about his most sacrosanct property—the dead son who had made him the revered father of the late President.

He didn't remember knowing either Pa or Tim until he was nine years old. For the seven years before that he had been a Thirkield, not a Kegan, because his mother had divorced Pa and had made him pay her a huge sum of money without a murmur. Whatever Pa had done to deserve the loss of such a lady (and all that money) must have been at least slightly disreputable.

Nick had known Tim for eighteen years. Then he subtracted the three years when he had been nine then twelve and Tim had been off to war. Then he subtracted one of the two years at the end of their time together, because he had fled Pa and America to go into the oil business in the Middle East when he was twenty-five. Tim was dead two years later. The salvaged single year had been made up of fragments of disconnected pieces of time—short bursts at the White House, at Palm Springs, at Camp David, at the Walpole, or on the yacht—and always it had been tacitly agreed that Pa wouldn't be there. All told, he had known Tim for only fourteen years out of the forty-two of Tim's life. Fourteen had been plenty. Tim was Pa and Pa was Tim. What had made Tim such a glorious achiever (Pa, always Pa) had made Nick faceless. Tim was gloriously dead at forty-two. Nick was merely indefinably alive. Even Yvette Malone had never remembered him long enough to write him a letter spontaneously. True, she always answered his letters—which was a different thing altogether. Nick brooded that he might live to be twice Tim's age and exist as a sort of vegetable unless he could master Tim's knack for living so warily. But he'd be damned if he would, because it was a knack Pa also had. Pa's idea of being lusty and alive was to fart at a state dinner, then nearly laugh himself into a hernia. He supposed that both he and Tim had been born with souls resembling Pa's soul. Then, by a great stroke of luck, Nick's mother had taken him away from Pa and he had been saved. After his mother had been killed in the car with Gabriel Thirkield, Pa had ordered Nick to come home, although Pa wasn't there, because there was a war on and serious money to be made. Nick had been nine. To his great relief (and even greater joy after Tim got to the White House) Nick kept the name Thirkield, because Mama's will said if Pa tried to change it back, Nick wouldn't get one cent of her money (which had all been left to him). Pa deeply respected that kind of logic. Tim was off in the war. The head of the house at Palm Springs was Pa's Chinese butler. It had been a big change from the leafy, green, temperate coolness of Harmonia, New York, to Pa's fortress house in the desert. It was all like another planet.

The object Nick missed most was his mother's dear old Rolls, which her father had bought for her in 1927. Mama had worked on it herself, fiddling with the engine, changing tires and oil, washing it like the family pet it was. Every other day Mama and he would drive the cook, who sat on the back seat, to the meat market in the village. The butcher would bring the meat out of the shop to the car on tray after tray so that Mama and the cook could look it over and choose. Then Mama would drive the Rolls back to Harmonia Hall, and the butcher's boy would pedal out to deliver the meat, arriving an hour after them.

He remembered the epergne at the center of Mama's table on which she would place the bowl filled with homemade caviar on the one day a month when she would invite the locals in to be enthralled by her music. Mama made caviar out of tapioca, fish broth, squid ink and lemon juice, which allowed each guest to have as much caviar as he or she wished. "It would be a cruel thing to give these good, provincial people a real caviar habit," Mama had explained.

Tim had been twenty-four when he went into the war, in London, on the staff of Major General James Nolan, head of the socially blessèd Ultra action group, which plotted and wove behind locked doors that were themselves within a series of locked doors. No one but General Nolan knew what anyone in Ultra was doing. Long after the war it was finally revealed that Tim had been Nolan's cryptanalyst. Nolan was a Texan and a West Pointer and a former roommate of Pa's at Notre Dame. General Nolan awarded Tim a Presidential Citation for, he said in the accompanying recommendation, breaking a Spanish code that transmitted Spain's African intelligence about weather conditions around the Ouagadougou region of French West Africa. Four months before the war ended, well after the invasion, Tim was transferred to General Patton's (colorful) Third Army as aide-de-camp to Major General Anthony "Tuffy" Godwin. Here Tim had won, on General Godwin's personal citation, the army's Silver Star for leading a Tank Medium M4-A3-E8 into an action across the Rhine near Martonsburg in the Hilda Hess sector "at immeasurable personal risk in a feat of incomparable daring." After the war Tuffy Godwin had joined Thomas Kegan's bustling, belching rabbit warren of subornment in Washington as Procurement Officer in charge of Pentagon entertaining. Pa was very proud of Tim's military decorations.

Tim had gone to Yale law school before the army, because lawyers screwed up the country best. After the war Pa okayed two years for him at the Yale drama school, because the theater was good training for politics, but he made Tim finish off with a master's degree in political science at Harvard nonetheless. Cross an American lawyer with a political scientist and you get a mad scientist, Tim told Nick.

Pa had had General Nolan made a papal count, and the General agreed to manage Rockrimmon, a Kegan estate in Connecticut, for all his years after the war. Rockrimmon was the one family property Nick had never been invited to visit. General Nolan was the one old family friend he had never met. Tim said General Nolan provided Pa with "disreputable diversions" there. Tim had used Rockrimmon now and then as a hideout when he attended out-of-town tryouts of musicals in New Haven ("Not since Woodrow Wilson has an American President shown his degree of passion for the American popular theater") so he could take the young ladies of the casts to Rockrimmon and screw them.

By 1950 Tim had been elected to the House of Representatives. By 1955 he was in the Senate. At the end of his first week in the Senate, Pa opened Tim's active campaign for the presidential nomination. Before Pa masterminded a presidential campaign, a successful candidate had pretended to wait for his party's nomination to come to him. Pa said that was a lot of shit. He said Tim would have to go into a few primaries to make everything look good, but that was what the party system was for: to let the bosses handle the rest. He said it was a waste of time and money to run in all the primary convention states except where a candidate had to to keep up appearances. Sometimes winning a few primaries could punch up the whole script and fool all of the people all of the time, was how he felt. Pa believed in using his money and his power where it could count most—in nonprimary convention states where the political professionals really controlled their people. For three years Pa had been spending big money to find out, state by state, what it was that made each

key delegate jump. When he needed their votes for the
first big ballot at the nominating convention, his supply
of jumping beans proved to be inexhaustible.

The marvel of the Presidency, Tim told Nick over
and over, was the dramatic acceleration of the action.
By his records, until the time he had entered the House
he had scored four hundred and seventy girls. By the
time he entered the Senate, only five years later, he had
scored nine hundred and three girls, which was pretty
fantastic acceleration itself, Tim said, considering it
had taken him a lifetime to make it to four seventy.
However, from the day he had announced for the Presidency until the day he was inaugurated the score had
soared to nearly sixteen hundred (three the morning of
Inauguration Day)—which showed what the power of
entering the highest political office could do. "Boy,
when you enter, you really enter," Nick had said admiringly.

Because of his interest in the theater and related arts
Tim tended to screw actresses more than others, but
his favorites had also included a Belgian princess, an
Eastern chief of government, thirty-four heiresses, one
hundred and fifty-three models, nine professional tennis players, many lady lawyers, doctors, astrologers
and chiropractors, two hundred and ninety-one newspaper and television women, some ordinary taxpayers,
a population of the wives of senators, ambassadors,
congressmen and the more powerful businessmen, labor leaders and industrialists in the United States,
Western Europe and the coastline cities of South
America—and one lady astronaut.

When Nick was in his early twenties and Tim was in
the White House manufacturing acutely dangerous
missile crises during his first eleven months in office,
Nick had counted and concluded that all the great
leaders had done that sort of quantity copulating—
Julius Caesar and Atatürk were examples. Nick was
forty-one now, and he marveled at how little effect this
consideration had had on him, thus separating him

from leadership, perhaps because he had not over-screwed. He calculated that he had slept with about twelve or sixteen women in his life—and he didn't have any idea whether this was average or underaverage. He didn't envy Tim, because of the prodigious complications arising from Tim's copulations along the way, although Tim had said that most of the betrayed husbands felt honored. It was the goddam press, Tim said, that cost him the most ass. They had forced spectacular strains on Tim in making him try to find places to screw. Eluding the press had been a superhuman feat. Therefore, most of the time there was an air of catch-as-catch-can, of improvisation, about Tim's sexual feats. Many times he would have despaired that he would ever meet the circumstances in which he could screw a lady when, suddenly, walking with her alone in a White House corridor and spotting an empty cloakroom, he would push her in there, enter her among the overcoats and furs, standing, then put them both together again and continue along the corridor to the reception, the lady almost unable to believe that such a thing had happened to her. The White House Secret Service detail learned to cooperate with maneuvers like that, although the Chief was ever nervous that one of those women could be a plant, and he would have borne the blame if the President had got himself stabbed or shot in some employees' rest room.

Just the same, all the horrible difficulties notwithstanding, sometimes late at night while he tried to sleep under mosquito netting beside a field of pumping rigs four hundred miles from places only about eleven people had ever been to, knowing that the native women with their smells were not for him, Nick would become wistful. But when he got back to the cities he refused to make any big effort to get women into bed, because it made him feel Pa inside him, and he could not live with that. Early on, he had concentrated on the piano instead. It wasn't a substitute, but it was a comfort.

He got off the plane to stretch his legs at New Delhi. He stayed in his seat at Beirut. When the plane was airborne to Frankfurt he decided to risk having a half bottle of champagne. After the wine he fell asleep, and slept until the plane reached Germany. In Frankfurt he marched the letter to Yvette straight to the airport post office and sent it as registered mail. He used registered mail only for love letters. As the plane headed out toward London he felt the old bafflement again—a permanent confusion of doors slamming in his face, lights going off, distant voices singing that there was absolutely nothing to worry about, all of it repeated over and over again until, manipulated and bored, he had turned away, along with most of the rest of the people, telling himself, as they had told themselves, that the Pickering Commission was the receptacle of the consciences of seven wise men, seven just men who had pored themselves almost blind over every scintilla of the evidence, which had at last filled twenty-six volumes. These great men had finally decreed, separately and together, that there had been no conspiracy, that there had been only one lone, mad killer. Repeat: no conspiracy. Repeat: no conspiracy. With the help of the reassuring press—that greatest single continuing conspiracy of modern civilization—life had gone on, the nonconspiracy untroubled. Nothing could change except the truth.

The plane began its descent into London.

David Carswell was easy to spot in the VIP lounge at Heathrow. He was the opposite of a jolly fat man. He was a mean fat man who explained away his fat by claiming he had diabetes. He was eating buttered sugar buns, slurping coffee and pouting like the spout of a pitcher when Nick came up to him. In greeting, after two years of separation, he said, producing an even more intense reaction than usual from his employer, "I am frightfully worried about this *Teekay* desertion."

"You don't look it," Nick said.

"Your father isn't going to like it at all. Not one bit."

"We are not going to talk about it."

"It took you five months to set it up, and now you just walk away from it." His accent was plum-perfect Oxbridge with just a soupçon of Hammersmith.

"Aarrgghhh!" Nick said.

"I think that is a desperately unfriendly attitude to take, Nick. It is hurtful and really uncalled-for."

"Did you bring my clothes?"

"Marian could not find the winter underwear in your flat."

"Did you buy me some winter underwear?"

"The shops were not open. It was far too early."

"You brought everything else?"

"Yes."

"Thank you."

"Whether you think so or not, Nick, I am entitled to

an explanation about the *Teekay*."

"If you had brought the winter underwear you would be entitled to an explanation."

"You are being monstrous."

"Do you have any silver?"

"Yes."

"Call Marian. Send her to my flat. Tell her to look in the bottom drawer of the highboy in the second bedroom. Tell her to bring the underwear here."

"Who will run the office?"

"I don't care if it burns. Get me that underwear."

Carswell got up. He waddled away three steps, then turned. "I can have them bring a telephone to me here."

"Oh, no, you won't. Go to a booth and shut the door."

Nick glared at his back. The twit. He ordered tea. He was impatient to get Carswell out of there for good so that he could talk to Yvette at his leisure. It took Carswell twenty minutes to get back.

"Marian will be here in about an hour," he said.

"Did you talk to Miles Gander?"

"He will be *charmed* to have breakfast with you tomorrow morning."

"Good." He decided to fire Carswell as soon as he could find a replacement. "That's all. You may go, David."

"It *is* Monday morning. I *do* have an extraordinary amount of work to do."

"Well, go and do it."

They shook hands limply. David waddled away. Nick asked for a telephone. He dialed Yvette's number in Paris and instantly she was on the line.

"Yvette? Nick."

"*Nick?* Oh, boy! Are you in town?"

"London airport."

"Oh."

"I am dazzled to know that I am this close to you. The Channel and a little hunk of France is all. Nothing like half the world between us."

"How come you're at the *London* airport?"

"I put it all in a letter to you and mailed it in Frankfurt."

"I may not see it—I mean for a couple of months. I'm going to the States in about two days."

"Where to?"

"New York first."

"How long will you be there?"

"Through January. Then Jamaica or something."

"Can we have dinner Thursday night? I have to go to Palm Springs but I can make it to your place by eight on Thursday."

"Oboyoboyoboy."

"It's been almost four months."

"I know."

"Just talking to you is too much. I don't know how I can be this close and not see you."

"Don't even say it, Nick."

"Okay. So long."

"I love you, Nick."

He hung up in a pink daze. He drifted to the newsstand and bought paperbacks and magazines. Marian arrived with the underwear in a plastic shopping bag. She was a short, thin girl in a miniskirt. If she couldn't afford to wear a long skirt in London in January, Carswell must be underpaying her.

"I had a crazy cabbie," Marian said. "He must be fleeing the police. Aren't taxis supposed to have speed governors?"

"How much do we pay you, Marian?"

"Twenty-three pounds a week. Why? I didn't miss finding the underwear the first time round. David forgot to tell me."

"Give me your notebook."

In fullest holograph he wrote a note to Carswell saying that henceforth Marian was to be paid thirty pounds a week. That should annoy the repulsive twit, he thought. Marian stared at the note. "But—why, Mr.

Thirkield? I'm really not very good at anything in an office. Honestly, I could have missed your underwear the first time this morning even if David had told me."

"You weren't good at anything in an office because you were underpaid," Nick said. "Now that you will be paid properly you will improve enormously."

"But I don't want to spend my life improving at this. If I could find a husband I'd be away from you like a shot."

"Perfectly all right."

"You may not understand it, but you are trying to obligate me, Mr. Thirkield. It's as though thirty pounds a week were my price. This could change my life. This could make me so obligated that I would stop looking for a husband and turn into an office creep like a girl David Carswell."

"What do you want me to do, Marian? I'll do whatever you say."

"That's all right, Mr. Thirkield."

"I'll take it back. Here, we'll tear it up."

"No," she said glumly. "That's all right. It's my problem now, innit?" She turned away from him and walked toward the exit of the lounge.

The pink haze had lifted again.

Nick's plane touched down at Philadelphia at four thirty-five that afternoon. He checked into the Petroleum Club.

"You are looking worse than I have ever seen you look, sir," the reception clerk said genially.

Nick was very much pleased. "I've been on an airplane from Borneo."

"Travel is terrible punishment, sir."

"Please tell the operator to post Do Not Disturb signs all over the switchboard. That includes my father—I mean, most of all my father."

"Yes, sir."

"And please send a man up to wake me at eight thirty tomorrow morning."

He slept for fifteen and a half hours, until the bell captain shook him awake. At nine fifteen he shambled into the baroque Victorian dining room with its magnificent portrait of Edward VII as a young man, by James Richard Blake the immortalist. The room was a womb of the past in deep green and heavy gold. Miles Gander was waiting for him, a thin and melancholy man with a high bald head and heavy black-rimmed glasses. They told each other that each was looking very well indeed. Nick was ravenous. He hadn't eaten for two days. They ordered at once.

"Somebody said you ran into a string of dry wells, Miles."

"Quite an advertisement for an oil geologist, wasn't it?"

"Need any money?"

Miles shook his head in a melancholy way and went on nibbling at a piece of toast. He was smallish, with a birdlike face and a squamulous nose, as though he were an evolutionary map of reptile-into-bird-into-man.

"I cannot stand David Carswell any longer, Miles."

"He is impossible. But he knows everything."

"We are too small an operation to fit in a fellow like that."

"But whom would you get?"

"I thought I'd ask you."

"A desk job? No," he said sadly. "I'm a geologist, Nick—but I thank you." Every shading of Gander's manner was melancholy, indicating that bankruptcy can be depressing but also that he had deeper malaise than the loss of money. "If you can't bear Carswell, try Ed Blenheim in Tulsa."

The food arrived. Nick attacked an enormous pile of scrapple, about which Edward VII had said (in that room), "Philadelphia is filled with people named Scrapple, and they all have biddle for breakfast."

After a while Miles said, "What did you want to see me about, Nick?" He coughed lightly. "It couldn't be about the job, because you wouldn't have had David call me if it were."

"I need your integrity," Nick said.

Miles winced.

"A man who was working for Keifetz fell off a crane in Brunei. He knew he was dying. He confessed that he had been one of the two men who had shot my brother."

"My God!"

"He told us where he hid the rifle. Here in Philadelphia. So I wanted to ask you for two favors. Can you arrange for me to meet a high-ranking police official? Second, will you come along with us as witness that the rifle has been found—if it is found?"

Miles wet his lips. He took a sip of water. He had a

mouthful of black coffee. He dabbed at his mouth with a napkin, drying it. "Yes," he said. "I can do those things."

"Thank you."

"When do you want me to do this?"

"Now, if you can."

"I'll go out to the hall and telephone." He got up abruptly and left the table. Nick thought he had become a different man since the bankruptcy. He had to need money. He decided to press it on him. He ordered more scrapple, with poached eggs and fried apples, and more hot toast and coffee. When he was in Asia, he had dreamed of scrapple—a divine marriage of American Indian cornmeal with the genius of German sausage.

"Well, we were lucky," Miles said when he came back. "An inspector of police named Heller is on his way over."

Nick said, "I don't believe you when you say you don't need money. Let's get this straight, Miles. I am your friend, and there are things you have to make yourself accept from friends. I am worried about you. I want you to tell me how much money you will need, and that will be that."

Miles's eyes suddenly brimmed with tears, but they held. He looked away, and after a time the tears were gone. "The fact is, Nick," he said, "I would have grabbed that offer last night. But everything was settled last night. I have the money. I don't need to be a bankrupt."

Deputy Inspector Frank Heller came into the dining room in full uniform, fruit salad across his left chest and a gold badge that gleamed like a searchlight under the commendations. He was a beefy, red-faced, heavy man with hard eyes. He shook hands as though it were a karate maneuver. He sat at the table, refused breakfast, because he never ate breakfast, he said, grudgingly accepted some coffee, then asked if there was any raisin bread, then asked if he could have some red currant jelly to go along with the raisin bread.

"Why not have some lamb with the red currant jelly, Frank?" Miles asked.

"The scrapple is great," Nick said.

"Scrapple? Well. I'd like to try some scrapple." He nodded to the waitress. "What's up?" he asked Miles.

"This is all very delicate and confidential, Frank, as you will see," Miles said.

The inspector grunted. It was like a random hit on a bass drum. He looked quickly from one face to the other. His eyes had large pouches of blackness under them, as if he had rubbed them with sooty mittens. "Everything is," he said.

"Mr. Thirkield is the half brother of the late President Kegan," Miles said. "We work together in the oil industry."

Heller nodded with automatic, sympathetic appreciation, then he caught himself and went on the defensive.

"We did everything humanly possible to protect your brother here, Mr. Thirkield. But you can't protect anyone from a nut. I hope you realize that."

"I don't know anything about it," Nick said. "Two days ago in the Far East a man confessed to having killed my brother."

"Impossible."

"And he told us where he had hidden the rifle. In Philadelphia."

"Out of the question."

"His name was Arthur Turkus Fletcher."

Heller grunted again. It had a threatening sound. Boar hunters have heard the sound. The food arrived, so they stopped talking until the waitress left. Heller attacked the scrapple as if it were trying to devour him first. He finished everything on the plate before he spoke again. "You read the Pickering Report?" he asked Nick.

"The short version."

"There was no second rifle."

"Inspector," Nick said with all the innocent arrogance of his relationship to the late President, the late President's father's billion dollars, and the thirty-seven thousand, nine hundred crunch people his father knew in the crevices and on the pinnacles, "when you finish your coffee we will go out of here and see if we can find that rifle. The rifle will have Fletcher's fingerprints on it, and taped to it we should find his full name. As you will discover, the prints will match the fingerprints of the man who confessed, taken two days ago by the police in Brunei, on Borneo. They will also be shown to be the prints of a man who worked for eight years as a professional marksman for the National Rifle Association with the rating of Master. When we have all those things in hand I will give you a certified copy of the deposition Fletcher made in Brunei before he died. Then you will be asked and Mr. Gander will be asked to make a deposition as to what you will have witnessed this morning. My father and I will then take a complete copy of this record, with the weapon, to the President to request a reopening of the investigation under a congressional commission. That is all."

There was a delay of ten minutes while the desk located the club's engineer so that he could lend the expedition a large wrench. They drove to the Engelson Building in a black police car that had a uniformed police driver.

They found the manager of the Engelson Building in his office. The inspector explained that they wanted to make an examination of Room 603. The manager looked the room up in a notebook, then dialed on his telephone. "Mr. Kullers? This is David Coney, the building manager. I wonder if we could trouble you for a few minutes for a look around your office." He put his hand over the receiver. "He wants to know what for," he said to Inspector Heller.

"The steam pipe," Nick said.

"The steam pipe, Mr. Kullers," Coney said into the

phone. "Thank you." He hung up. "There are no steam pipes in this building," he said. "This doesn't involve Mr. Kullers, does it?"

"How long has he leased 603?" Heller asked.

"About four years."

"Probably not, then," Heller said. The four men went to the elevator.

Lettered on the door of 603 were the words JOHN KULLERS and VENDING MACHINES. Coney knocked. A voice told them to come in. A rumpled, red-haired man wearing heavy black horn-rimmed glasses exactly like Miles Gander's was alone in the room checking figures at a desk, his back to the two windows.

"Cops? Why cops?" he said.

"Are you Kullers?" Heller said in a hard voice.

"Who else?"

"Go down the hall and smoke a cigarette or wash your hands or something. You can come back in ten minutes."

"What for?"

"Listen—it would only take a little time to get a search warrant, but I can get one."

"A search warrant to find a steam pipe? There it is." He gestured. "And while you're getting the search warrant see if you can find the two milk machines somebody palmed on me at Bryn Mawr last Friday. What is there to search? I am a one-man operation."

"Do I have to get a warrant?"

"You can search, but I am staying."

Heller shrugged. He took the big wrench to the vertical heating pipe.

"That never worked," Kullers said.

"It isn't even supposed to be there," Coney added.

There was a sleeve joint halfway up the pipe. Heller tightened the wrench around it, applied force and turned. The sleeve fell to the floor around the pipe with a clatter. The inspector and Nick separated the pipe and looked downward.

"I'll be a son-of-a-bitch," Heller said. He lifted a

star-shaped wooden rack out of the pipe. Attached to the rack was the barrel of the .30 M1D. Heller lifted it out very carefully by the tip of the barrel and the rack.

Nick felt light-headed. His hands began to shake hanging beside him. He had never looked at a rifle and seen it to mean certain death before, designed for death, accomplished only in death.

"What the hell is that?" Mr. Kullers said. "I'll tell you one thing. That ain't mine."

Heller sent Mr. Coney down the hall for some towels. Miles Gander stumbled to a chair and sat down heavily. He looked ill.

"What was that doing in there?" Mr. Kullers asked shrilly. "Don't think you can pin that goddam thing on me."

Coney came back with a large, soft roll of paper towels. Heller carefully wrapped the rifle on all sides then secured the package with Scotch tape from Mr. Kullers' desk. "This goes to the lab," Heller said grimly. He left the package on the floor, and moving very deliberately to increase his menace, he walked behind Mr. Kullers' desk and lifted him to his feet by his shirt and tie. "You make one sound about what you saw here this morning and you will be the sorriest little man in this state," he said. He dropped Kullers. He turned to the building manager. "That goes for you too. You understand?"

The manager nodded: very bright eyes.

"Well, fuck you for a start," Mr. Kullers said, whacking Inspector Heller across the back of the head with a large, heavy, green Scotch-tape dispenser and dropping him to his knees. "I am an American citizen, you Cossack, and you can take a flying fuck back to Poland."

Heller picked himself up and charged. Nick slammed himself between the two men. He was less bulky than the inspector but he was twenty years younger, and he was able to back him against the wall and hold him there, talking right into his face.

"There is simply no call for this, Inspector," he said. "No call at all. Mr. Kullers is absolutely right."

"You are goddam right I am right," Mr. Kullers yelled. "No more Mr. Nice Guy. I am going to bring you up for invading without a warrant, you fucking bellhop."

Heller nodded to Nick that he was in control of himself. Nick released him. Heller went straight to the rifle, picked it up and left the room.

"Will somebody tell me what this is all about?" Mr. Kullers said, disheveled and red-faced.

Nick walked to the window and stood beside him. He looked down over Hunt Plaza. "That gun was fired from this window," he said, "to kill President Kegan."

Kullers gaped. Coney lifted his right hand to the side of his face. "Well, why didn't he say that?" Kullers asked. "All he had to do was say that. Who would go around blabbing a thing like that? You could get killed just knowing a thing like that."

All the way down in the elevator David Coney kept saying, "I don't like it. This is bad. This is trouble. I don't like it."

On Market Street Nick and Miles Gander walked slowly in the general direction of the Petroleum Club in Rittenhouse Square.

"Who hired Fletcher?" Miles asked.

"He didn't know. There was a go-between. He said he thought it would be someone like Z. K. Dawson."

"It sounds like Dawson," Miles said. "I've worked for him. I've heard him sound off against your brother because of the depletion allowance. But threats to the allowance made a lot of Texans feel murderous. Still, Eldridge Mosely was Dawson's man."

"Mosely had nothing to do with this foul business."

"I didn't say he had. But Z.K. made Eldridge the governor of Pennsylvania. Z.K.'s money was all over the presidential nominating convention. If Z.K. had been as smart as your father, he could have made

Eldridge President. But when your brother was dead it was suddenly Z.K.'s turn—wasn't it?"

The post was delivered at the Avenue de la Bourdonnais at nine fifteen ayem. A houseman in a starched white coat signed for the registered letter from Frankfurt. He gave it to a parlor maid, who took it up the white flying staircase to Madame's personal maid, who walked it across two rooms to Madame, who was making elaborate lists having to do with the organization of her packing for both New York and Jamaica.

Madame let out a yelp of pleasure when she looked at the envelope, stopped her work and sat down to read the letter. She asked the maid to bring her a cup of tea. She read the letter smiling, with total absorption.

She stopped smiling. A look of shock that almost immediately turned into a look of loss set itself into a mask of tragedy. She covered her face with her hands and began to weep.

WEDNESDAY NIGHT, JANUARY 30, 1974
—PALM SPRINGS

Nick was on the ground at the Los Angeles airport at four ten in the afternoon. He chartered a helicopter to fly him to the pad at Pa's rambling white stucco house south of Palm Springs which had once been called "the western White House." Flying in over the Springs, he was able to identify nine of the great houses wherein Tim had screwed his hostesses. When they flew over Lola Camonte's pleasure complex he grinned with vicarious pleasure as he thought of the dozens of long, friendly talks Tim and the great Mexican star had had, one lying atop the other. Nick wished he could have seen her in the last great scene, which Tim would always allude to but refused to be explicit about. Just thinking about that last scene made Tim howl with glee.

The chopper went in over Pa's own eighteen-hole golf course, which was as green as Ireland in the middle of the desert and set down there not only because Pa liked uncrowded golf but as a buffer between Pa and his security men and anyone else in the rest of the world who might like to take a shot at Pa.

Li Hsi was standing beside the pad with a security man, waving wildly and looking exactly as ageless as when Nick had first seen him: standing at the front door when the huge car had driven nine-year-old Nick to the house. Si was an extremely scrutable Chinese who could whoop and weep and waffle at the drop of a hat. Si wrapped his arms around Nick and giggled madly as he welcomed him home. Si was probably the only Chinese out of some 800,000,000 who had always called President Kegan by his first name.

"How long you gung be here?" he asked happily.

"Until about like three o'clock tomorrow afternoon."

"Ah. Long time."

"I should be in Australia right now. But I have to talk to Pa."

"Pa not here."

"Not here? When will he be back?"

"Tonight. Mebbe ten o'clock, twelve o'clock. You eat with Keith?"

"I sure will."

"I fix. Eight o'clock. What you like to eat?"

"Anything."

"Anything so long is chili and noodles, hey, Nick? I fix."

On the way to Nick's apartment, which was in its own cottage about sixty yards from the main building, Nick asked Si if his father's library had the full twenty-six-volume Pickering Commission Report.

"We have. But only make you sad, Nick. No good."

"You told me all learning is good."

"I bring. I send Keith as soon as he come."

Keith was Si's son. He was a psychiatrist with the Riverside County medical staff. He was a fine doctor, a better chess player, a good painter, a great cellist, a loving husband and a gaga father. He had married a third-generation Californian whose great-grandparents had been working Eskimos who, Keith said, had overshot Nome with a dogsled. Their three children were as Oriental as pandas. The whole family spoke Californian that twanged like a banjo.

The twenty-six volumes of the Pickering Report arrived by golf cart as Nick finished unpacking his bags. He settled down at a large desk with the volume that covered the time slot of the assassination which Turk Fletcher had described. It was as though he were reading a ponderous fairy tale written by lawyers. Except for its description of Hunt Plaza and the route by which the motorcade had crossed it, the official account was like the testimony of a witness in Rashomon—totally different from what Fletcher said had happened, yet immovably sure of itself. Three hours later a security man knocked at the door to say that dinner was ready.

Nick and Keith had a grand reunion while Si beamed on them. They had been through more together than most boyhood chums. Keith had admitted Nick to the Riverside Hospital as his psychiatric patient a year after Tim's killing. Nick was in the hospital for five months, and the treatment was continued at Pa's house for four months after that. Having put Nick together again, Keith handled him like eggs wherever Tim or Pa were concerned. Nick's emotional collapse had happened because he had been able to sleep less and less as he waited for Pa to come to tell him that it would be necessary for Nick to take Tim's place to get Pa's work done.

But they didn't talk about that anymore. Keith watched him closely, wondering if Nick thought like that anymore, but Si joined them at table, so there was no clinical talk. Si had made them Chinese noodles cooked in won ton, then covered with a thick rug of chili, which they ate with two bottles of cold white wine from the North Coast counties. Si chortled, wept and burped through the meal, pausing now and then to take a phone call in the pantry. Nick was having the best time he had had since being in bed with Yvette Malone, and he was achieving a form of double-think: while he enjoyed the presence of his two oldest friends he levitated Yvette over the kitchen table mentally so that he could be with her simultaneously. At that moment Si asked his perpetual question: "When are you getting married, Nick?" At last he had something definite to report. "It just happens that I almost asked a girl to marry me the day before yesterday," Nick said.

"Oh, boy," Keith said. "Wait till Grace hears this. She'll give a big party whether you can come or not."

"What did the lady say?" Si asked. "When is the wedding day?"

"She didn't say anything. She went right on talking as if she hadn't heard me." Nick really enjoyed this fantasy.

"You must have surprised her," Keith said. "You have to lead up to things like that."

"Maybe I did surprise her. Maybe I was too sudden."

They heard the sound of a chopper coming in from Palm Springs. "The boss!" Si said joyfully, leaping to his feet and standing behind Nick's chair to pull it out as he got up.

"I'll slink out the front door," Keith said. Si guided Nick along the shortcut to the helicopter pad.

The area was densely lighted by flood lamps on high poles. Two security men had taken their positions on either side of the pad to watch all approaches. Two more would be with Pa in the chopper. The helicopter was a ten-seat U.S. Army utility tactical transport whose lengthened cabin had been luxuriously refitted. It had been made by Bell and fitted with a Lycoming T53 L-13 engine that could cruise at a service ceiling of twenty-two thousand feet over a range of three hundred and fifteen miles. Pa used it to get to his jets at the Palm Springs airport and sometimes to go into L.A.

Some people scramble out of helicopters, but it is a thing that takes practice. A security man pushed a ramp elevator up to the door of Pa's machine. He stepped out on its platform into the glaring theatrical lights and was lowered gently to the ground like a ballerina in the arms of the first dancer, at half the speed of a gently falling leaf. Pa was wearing a scarlet linen waistcoat under a white bawneen jacket. He had a sheared mink overcoat across his left forearm and a large billycock bowler on his head. His face was so deeply creased with lines that it looked as though it had been plowed by a combine. He was smoking a thick black cigar. He smiled horrendously when he saw Nick, displaying what looked like row upon row of huge white false teeth that seemed to have been made of mother-of-pearl.

"I knew you'd be here, you little son-of-a-bitch," he bawled. "What's this I hear about you screwing Carswell's secretary in London?" The two men came together and embraced with a great show of fake feeling.

"Carswell is through," Nick shouted over the sound of the engines.

"Don't be a chump," Pa said. "Where are you going to find another guy who knows his stuff like Carswell?"

"I'll run Jemnito, Pa. You're just a salesman working on commission."

"Some salesman. Who got you the Alhart field in Tanzania? Who set you with Somoza in Nicaragua? Who's gonna fit you into the North Slope after someone else figures out how to get the oil out? Me, your commission salesman." He threw a long bony arm around Nick's shoulders and began to march him off to the house, asking Si, who trotted beside him, if he could find him three roast beef sandwiches and a bottle of beer.

"Hey, you guys," somebody yelled behind them, "wait for me!"

Nick turned and had the satisfaction of knowing that his father could not have known he was going to be there, because a small blonde, with muscular legs and a mouth as depraved as a Venetian principessa's, wearing a fantasy pink-and-blue mink coat in wide checkerboard squares, was descending on the miniature elevator. Pa gestured to her angrily as if she had been a stowaway. "Get the hell out of here," he yelled. "Get back in that chopper. Eddie will take you back to Chicago and I'll call you next week."

"I will like hell," she shouted. "My ass is sore now from riding in your goddam airplanes."

"Eddie!" Pa yelled at the top of his voice.

"Yes, sir?" a short gray-haired man yelled back from beside the lift.

"Put her in the De Mille cottage and give her a bottle of booze. And see that she doesn't bother anybody. I'm going to have a visit with my son." He took Nick's arm and dragged him quickly into the main house. Si bolted the door after them just in time, because the young woman's small form hurled itself against it and she hammered on it with her fists.

"Jesus." Pa grinned. "If we only had some way to tell they had a temper when they first looked good to us, right?" He kept walking. Nick followed him through a complex of corridors to the "small" sitting room that adjoined his father's sleeping quarters. The room was decorated with photographs, busts, medals and paintings. Tim with Malraux and De Gaulle. Tim with Khrushchev. Tim with Adenauer. Tim with the Supreme Court. Tim with the cast of *Hello, Dolly* at Rockrimmon. Tim with the cast of the Bolshoi Ballet at Rockrimmon. Tim accepting honorary degrees. Tim with Harold Macmillan. Tim between Floyd Patterson and Archie Moore. A life-size portrait of Tim in oils by James Richard Blake, famed for his portrait of Edward VII. Tim with the senior class of Wellesley at Rockrimmon. Tim with Dr. Martin Luther King, Jr. A bust of Tim by Edward Delaney. An illuminated display case of Tim's decorations: the Vatican State Order of the Golden Spur conferred "motu proprio"; the Order of Charles III (Spain); the Order of the Elephant (Denmark); the Order of Merit of the Principality of Liechtenstein; the Yugoslavian Grand Star; the Grand Cross of the Legion of Honor (France); Polonia Restituta (Poland); the Grand Cross with Collar (Italy); the Baden-Powell Medal for the Perpetuation of World Scouting (Britain)—all earned through connections of Pa's before Tim had attained the Presidency. Far at the back of the piano, somewhat blocked from view by a large cabinet photograph of Tim wearing a ten-gallon hat shaking hands with Oveta

Culp Hobby, there was a small framed snapshot of Tim with Nick, grinning at each other over a net on Pa's tennis court, Nick not showing a single tooth.

The north side of the living room displayed a rank of eleven transaction tickers that were even then reporting on stock, mineral and commodity markets. Pa picked up the tape of the nearest one reflexively and looked at it. "Drink?" he asked mechanically.

"Maybe some cold white wine."

"What were you looking at the Pickering Report for?"

"When did Si get a chance to fill you in on that?"

"I called from the plane before we got to LA."

"Well—that's what I came out to see you about."

"The Pickering Report?"

Si came in with the sandwiches and the beer. He took Pa's hat and coat. Pa asked him to bring Nick a bottle of white wine.

"Tim," Nick answered.

"What about Tim?"

"Pa, this is going to jolt you, but I have to tell you."

"Okay, tell me."

"I was there three days ago in Brunei when a man named Turk Fletcher confessed on his deathbed that he had been one of the two riflemen who had shot Tim. No—wait!" Nick stood up, cutting off his father's protest with a raised hand. "This man told us where he had hidden the rifle in Philadelphia. I went there with the police and we found it. It is covered with the man's fingerprints. It has his name taped to it."

To Nick, Pa's face was terrible to look at. The thousands of things that seemed to be trying to crowd through his memory into a recognizable place in his consciousness had jammed right behind his eyes. For Pa the moment was one of total release from the tensions of fourteen years, the bursting out of a long black tunnel. To Nick, Pa's eyes seemed to scream. His face seemed to be falling apart. Tics began under his left eye and at the right corner of his mouth. For Pa the great moment had finally arrived. It had happened as he had dreamed it would happen, and the effect of it on him was transmogrifying. Nick saw that his father had turned dead white. He was all white—white seventy-four-year-old skin, with watery blue eyes and ketchup-red and white hair held in place by large outjutting white ears.

Staring at Nick, Pa began to weep, contorting his face into shocking grimaces, dragging clanking sobs out of his chest, causing his head to shake with the regularity of a metronome from side to side, denying what he had done but seeming to deny what Nick had said. He stood motionless, his face glistening wet, an appalling noise machine. Nick wanted to vomit.

Si returned with the wine in a cooler. He set it down calmly. He went to Pa and led him slowly out of the room, permitting him to continue to weep without stop. He took Pa into the bathroom and closed the door between them and Nick.

While Si was helping Pa pull himself together again in the bathroom, Nick poured himself a glass of the cold wine, his hands shaking badly. He gulped the wine, then went to the piano and began to play Mozart mindlessly.

After about fifteen minutes Pa came back into the room alone. Si had left the bathroom through another door. Pa took up a half of a thick sandwich, poured a glass of beer and sat down to listen to the music. Nick played through to the end while Pa ate the three roast beef sandwiches.

Pa finished the last half of the sandwich almost at the same time that Nick touched the last chord. "If this guy Fletcher was the second rifle when they killed Tim, how come he was working for you? Who hired him?"

"Keifetz hired him."

"But why with you? All the way out in Asia?"

"Keifetz says sixteen people have been killed because they had little scraps of information about Tim's murder. Fletcher had the biggest scrap of all, the main piece to the jigsaw, and we think he probably figured that whoever was looking for him—that is, looking for him to kill him—probably wouldn't think of looking for him in my company."

"But how come Keifetz hired him?"

"He was a good crane operator. Besides, he had a letter of recommendation from your friend General Nolan."

"*No*lan? James Nolan?"

"Tim's old commanding officer. The man who runs Rockrimmon for you. Whoever he is, I never met him."

"I'll be goddamned. You mean, he sent this killer to Keifetz?"

"No. Not really. Fletcher was carrying around an old to-whom-it-may-concern letter from General Nolan."

"Who was the Philadelphia cop who went with you and Miles to find the rifle?" Pa asked.

"Inspector Heller."

"Oh, yeah. Who else was there?"

"The manager of the building and the occupant of 603, a man named John Kullers."

"We'll have to get a deposition from every one of them. I'll handle that."

"The police are doing that. Heller took the rifle to the police lab, and by now they're checking the fingerprints—and whatever else they do—with the FBI."

"That's real evidence."

"We had a Shell lawyer take a deposition from Fletcher, the second rifleman, in Brunei. Keifetz got the Brunei police to lift Fletcher's prints and take his photograph. Those are all in the mail now and on their way here."

"To this house?"

"Yes."

"Then we have a case. We have a case," Pa said. "We are going to take this to the President."

"I hoped you'd say that, Pa."

"You did a wonderful job, Nick."

Nick blinked with gratitude. He felt a hard, dazing blow of almost paralyzing satisfaction. Pa had never said anything even distantly like that to him before. It was a glorious feeling. It was a feeling of glory. He clung to Pa's words the way a groggy fighter clings to an opponent until his head clears. "I think it should be a congressional investigation," Nick was able to say, "not a presidential commission."

"We won't have much to say about that."

"Yes we will. If the President refuses, we'll take it to the press and TV. Anyway, no President would want to be solely responsible for the shameful necessity of a second time around in the investigation of the murder of an American President. He wouldn't dare to risk anything as sinister as the Pickering Commission again."

"Nobody would want it. But they would risk it," Pa said.

"What do you mean?"

"I think we have to watch everything ourselves. With my people. We have to have a place in the investigation. You could be his liaison with the congressional committee. That would be good politics."

Pa looked glassy. Si must have sedated him, Nick thought. Pa began to wander about the room, picking up pictures of Tim and rambling in his speech. "I am thinking about how we took the first primaries. Believe me, politics in a state like that involves a lot of money, and I mean under-the-bridge, over-the-table, and tucked-in-a-box-of-cigars money. All of it for a little state whose primary vote isn't even binding on the delegates it elects. Shit, I put out ninety-seven hundred primary-day workers alone. And we had the most gorgeous TV commercial you ever saw of Tim leading those three tanks across that Hilda Hess sector in Germany to liberate that beleaguered infantry column. Jesus, he looked great. And there was one showing

Tim very solemn, very respectful, holding his book under his arm while he was awarded the Anne Knauer-
hase Prize right here in my library. We made a real
noise in that shitty little state, kid. We got fifty-three
real movie stars to turn out and roam up and down the
state yelling Tim's name. Sickleton's people began to
sneak in some money to the opposition in the primary,
and I called up the son-of-a-bitch who was their head
honcho and I said that if they didn't pull out every
goddam Sickleton dime, Old Baldy wouldn't even be
considered as Secretary of State."

Pa stopped and stared at a large photograph of Tim
wearing the full headdress of a sachem of the Cherokee
nation. When he turned to face Nick his eyes had filled
with tears, but the sedation Si had given him held him
down. "And all that time and later—and before—and
during," he said, "everything I did, every buck I spent,
every threat I made, I was just leading Tim along the
road to meet that bullet." He sat down helplessly.

"Pa, there's a couple of more things," Nick said
evenly.

"Like what?"

"Willie Arnold was not one of the riflemen. Somebody sold that to the commission."

"Do we have to start this all over again?"

"There were two riflemen. Fletcher was one. He
talked a lot about the other one. That's the whole point
of the new investigation. The commission didn't care
who killed Tim—they only wanted to prove that there
was no conspiracy. Well, there was a conspiracy. Our
new investigation has to establish who hired those two
riflemen and Willie Arnold."

Pa didn't seem to be listening. He was dazed, but
Nick told himself he had to be getting the point. Pa
himself had said what they had to do.

"Pa?"

"What?"

"Every doctor who attended Tim after he was hit—
and the doctor who performed the autopsy—said Tim

had been shot from front and back. But the Pickering Commission twisted that. They shifted the whole emphasis to rationalize *why* Willie Arnold had shot Tim, not *whether* he had done it. Then they buried the autopsy report for the next seventy-five years.

"Pa, listen to me. If we're not sure of all the facts, it's because they were changed so often and so fast by the Pickering Commission, whose job it was to make sure of the real facts and bury them before the investigation was over."

"All right, Nick," Pa said steadily. He seemed to have himself together. "We'll quit talking and do something." He sat down at the switchboard and took up the phone. "Get me Fred Frey, the police commissioner of Philadelphia." He hung up. "Play something on the piano, Nick," he said. "I have to think a little."

Nick went to the piano and began soothes by MacDowell. Pa stared at the Blake portrait of Tim. In about four minutes the telephone light went on and Pa picked up.

"Hello, Fritz? Fine. How are you? Fritz, you'll understand why I have to take kind of a guarded tone here—do you have a lab report on that rifle yet?" His face clouded with irritation. "What rifle? This is Tom Kegan. Don't kid around. Listen, you have a cop named Heller—Inspector Frank Heller—right? Okay. Well, yesterday morning at—what time, Nick?"

"Quarter to eleven."

"At a quarter to eleven your man Heller in the presence of my son, Miles Gander—you know, the geologist—and two other witnesses, both residents of Philadelphia, found one of the rifles that was used"— Pa faltered, his voice broke—"was used in Hunt Plaza in 1960." Nick moved away from the piano in tension while Pa listened on the telephone. "Why would I try to make a clown out of you?" Pa said to Frey. He became incredulous. "Nobody told you anything about it?" He looked across at Nick blankly. "Well, you better call Heller in, Fred. You better untangle your options. I'll be waiting right here in Palm Springs for your call." He disconnected.

"You heard it," he said to Nick.

"Heller must be waiting for a confirming report from the FBI before he takes it to the commissioner."

"He's a crook," Pa said. "I mean, I feel that." He got up and began to wander around the room again. "Nick, I hate to let them have another shot at burying all this. Everything I stand for resists the idea of taking what is absolutely my own vengeance to the government and asking strangers to avenge my son."

Nick was bland. "That's the way it has to be, Pa."

"Is it? Are we supposed to turn everything over to a pack of lobbygows again? A strung-together scarecrow of mediocrities who are only interested in making sure the United States doesn't look like a banana republic, a bunch of failed lawyers who were able to eat well only because they were eating at the public trough?"

"How long have you felt this way?"

"From the time I talked to Mosely twenty-seven hours after Tim was murdered."

"But you went along, Pa."

"I had to go along; there was carefully nurtured doubt! There were men convincing me that it would be scalding America with shame and disaster—and maybe even revolution—if I stood up and pointed a finger at some figure in American life and charged that he had paid to have Tim shot down in the streets. Yes. I went along. Because they gave me Willie Arnold's body as representing Willie Arnold's guilt, and I bought it because there was nothing else to do."

A telephone light went on. Pa picked up. "Yes, Fritz? What's the scam? What? That's crazy. You'd better haul Heller up on your carpet, my friend. Whaaaat? Dead? Heller is *dead?* How? When? What happened?" He listened, staring at Nick with consternation. "Listen, Fred, I'm going to put my son on the line and he's going to give you the names and addresses of the three witnesses who saw Heller find that rifle and take it with him out of the Engelson Building. Hold on." Pa put his hand over the mouthpiece. "Heller is dead of a heart attack. It happened some time this morning. The rifle has disappeared." He gave Nick the telephone.

"Commissioner? I am Nicholas Thirkield, Mr. Kegan's son. Yes, sir. Miles Gander. At the Petroleum Club. The building manager, David Coney. The third man ran a business in vending machines which occupied Room 603. His name is John Kullers. That's K-u-l-l-e-r-s. Yes, sir, I will report to you and make a sworn statement." He hung up.

"I'd like to make a deposition here, Pa, and send it in. I have to go to New York tonight."

"This cop Heller was on the case in Philadelphia when Tim was shot," Pa said. "He was a captain then. He seemed to run everything."

"Could Heller have been working for the man we are looking for?"

Pa nodded blankly.

"When Heller got the rifle, could he have tried to blackmail whoever the man is?"

"Yes. He probably tried to sell the man the rifle."

"And the man killed him?"

Pa nodded.

"Then it isn't a total loss. If all that is true, we know the man is still alive—that he survived these past fourteen years with the rest of us."

Pa grinned. His plaque teeth revealed themselves row on row. They shone in the light like files of ivory. His eyes crinkled and his creased face showed two little Santa apples under each eye, all rosy and shiny. Nick knew he must be thinking of death for someone else, that he was summoning ruin and pain for whoever had caused this thought to make him smile so wondrously. "Yes," Pa said, "the son-of-a-bitch is still alive."

Thomas Xavier Kegan was a professional Irishman and a professional American—each kept separate from the other. The operative word "professional" is, as a noun: (a) one who professes to be skilled in and to follow assiduously the calling or occupation by which he habitually earns a living; (b) one who trains himself in the skills required for theoretic and scientific exploitation of an occupation, as distinct from its merely mechanical parts, which raises the occupation to the dignity of a learned profession.

Annually, for thirty-one years, Pa had been Honorary Grand Master of a St. Patrick's Day parade, which he attended in one American city or another. He kept a card file of eleven thousand, four hundred Pat-and-Mike jokes which he told, with a "brogue" that was a mixture of Polish, Japanese and Italian accents, at Holy Name Society breakfasts, at banquets given by the Friendly Sons of St. Patrick and the Knights of Columbus, at alumni dinners at Notre Dame and Holy Cross universities; and he had been known to tell Irish dialect stories to Eamon de Valera in The Park.

He was a member of nineteen Irish fraternal societies in Boston, New York, Liverpool, Capetown and Manchester. He had been granted the Freedom of Bodmor Truth in Rathfarnham, sponsored by Lord Butterfield himself, aged ninety-nine years. He had been awarded the Daithi Hanly Medal for Gaelgoiri twice, with its accompanying certificate made out to his Gaelic name, Tomaltac X. MacAogain. He owned offshore Irish oil leases. He wore green neckties and buttonhole shamrocks for the week preceding and the week following the anniversary of the death of Cromwell. He had disciplined himself to be able to tolerate Irish instrumental folk music, a talent that is almost impossible for the nonnative to acquire. Four times he had been offered the ambassadorship to Ireland by four importuning American Presidents (including his son), but each time he had, agonizingly, to refuse. He owned an Irish copper mine, an assembly plant for joining together the parts of a certain popular automobile, and an Irish road-building company of some prominence among politicians in Dublin. He had barmbrack flown to him twice a week, to Palm Springs, from O'Keefe's own bakery in Schull on Roaringwater Bay in West Cork—and boxes of carrageen.

These partisan manifestations were droll. If he had known the truth, he might have needed to be restrained with wet winding sheets and might (almost) have returned his many papal honors and his Irish marching society medals. Ethically and ethnically Tim's Presidency would have had to be declared unconstitutional. Significant electoral votes, as ethnic as soda bread, such as those of the Commonwealth of Massachusetts, would need to have been bestowed retroactively upon his opponent.

Thomas Xavier Kegan had no Irish ancestry. His father's name had not been Kegan nor had that of any of his progenitors. Further, his ancestral family had all been Lutherans. The family name was Kiegelberg.

In 1849, at age twenty-six, Thomas Kegan's grandfather, Jakob Kiegelberg, a peasant from Scheraldgrün, a small Alpine village in the Bernese Oberland of Switzerland, had emigrated to join the California gold rush. The Kiegelbergs had always been cursed with arrogance, feeling themselves as people apart from and above the world because of their uniqueness in the mountain-and-snow-locked valley. Of the 606 people living there, 310 were named Marton, 126 were called

Ketcham, 170 were known as Lear, and for 234 years, until Jakob Kiegelberg left the valley, only one family was called Kiegelberg.

When Jakob had made his fortune in the northern gold fields (the Ornstein Nugget) he moved to southern California, where he married Gertrude Garfunkel. In 1868 their son, Heini, absconded with his father's principal savings, which caused his father's death. Heini fled to San Francisco, where (using the name Hank Kegan despite his heavy Scheraldgrün accent, conferred by his father) he built a large saloon in the Barbary Coast district of the city and named it Kegan's. As Hank Kegan, Heini married an Italian girl from the Lugano area of Switzerland (Maerose Carnaghi).

On New Year's Day 1900, Heini and Maerose Kiegelberg-Kegan had a son born. His name was Thomas, then pronounced Toe-mahss. The infant's parents and all records of his true family name at baptism, Kiegelberg, were destroyed in the great San Francisco earthquake, which began on April 18, 1906. The authorities entered the boy's name as Thomas Kegan, taking the name from the child's father's saloon. Little Tom was raised by the Little Sisters of the Poor in a sound San Mateo boarding school for the children of the rich. The Little Sisters gave him the name Xavier at his confirmation. His father's considerable estate appreciated at the Crocker Bank.

Ever endowed with the mystical gift of piercing the heart of any matter instantly if the heart of the matter concerned money, Thomas Kegan sought and was granted a court order that forced the Little Sisters of the Poor (how he hated that designation!) to release him into the guardianship of the prestigious Wall Street law firm of Swaine, O'Connell, Cravath & O'Connell. He wanted his money put to work. At fourteen he qualified to enter the University of Notre Dame, and was graduated from that institution with honors for sports, religion and Irish studies. At eighteen he enrolled at the Wharton School of Business at the University of

Pennsylvania, where he won two graduate degrees in accountancy and advanced finance in three years.

In 1923, at twenty-three, he was ready for the expanding bull market and for Prohibition. He was also readier than most when the slide began in 1929 to transmogrify himself into a ruthless bear. By 1934, at thirty-four, he had increased his father's pleasant eight-hundred-thousand-dollar legacy to a far pleasanter five million, six hundred and forty thousand dollars in cash and shrewdly bought (meaning entirely with bank loans) Chinese boxes of real-estate parcels in eleven American cities worth thirty-one million, one hundred and fifty-six thousand dollars (a 1934 evaluation). He realized a net profit of two hundred and seventy-three million dollars from even shrewder investments in liquor stocks and liquor production, using them to circumvent the Prohibition law. He sold his liquor interests to eastern Mafia families whom he had helped to establish and who had worked for him in the mid-thirties, and reinvested the funds in founding personal loan-financing companies in twenty-eight states to provide welcome short-term small loans for his fellow Americans at 39 percent annual interest, and in three competing pharmaceutical manufacturing companies, which were to grow and expand (in the sixties) to produce 9,400 kilograms (2.5 billion pills) of amphetamines and 5,382 kilograms of methamphetamines, which was 61 percent of the total (U.S.) market, as well as 23 percent of the tranquilizer and sleeping-pill market, with marketing problems greatly diminished through the help of the same grateful Mafia families. He balanced his cash investment in these home products and home banking with heavy buying into weapons-producing firms so that he could later feel he was backing up the Vietnam war effort when that effort cried out for help. He had done most of his major investing well before the wondrous 1960 decade.

Fourteen years after Tim's mother's death, Pa married his new, beautiful and in every way splendid wife,

who became the mother of Nicholas one year after
that. She divorced Pa two and a half years after that
when, to her chagrin, Pa had infected her with a con-
tagious catarrhal inflammation of the genital mucous
membrane due to *Neisseria gonorrhoeae*. For this af-
front Pa paid Nicholas' mother ten million dollars and
the custody of Nicholas.

In her modulated farewell Mrs. Kegan called Pa a
guttersnipe, and for whatever reason far, far back in
his extraordinary snobbism, which concealed his lack
of belief in his own worth, Pa accepted this description
as true. Therefore, after Mrs. Kegan became Mrs.
Thirkield (and was later killed) he was forced to feel
deep ambivalence toward her son.

Nicholas knew well that his mother had been nega-
tively moved by his father. She had not withheld her
opinions of Pa during their son's plastic years. By the
time Nicholas was nine and his mother was dead,
Nicholas had been formed by her opinions and was
unable to feel other than infinitely superior to his father
and to his half brother.

This was not Pa's fault. More likely it was the fault
of the necessity that had made Heini Kiegelberg-Kegan
steal from *his* father, thus affecting his conscience and
making him seek punishment by accepting snarls and
humiliations from other older men whose advice
helped make him rich. This cringing attitude in his father may have signaled the basic family inferiority to
little Thomas, a six-year-old boy, so that even after a
succession of brilliant accomplishments, when a beautiful woman of the world for whom he had the most respect was impelled by her shame to call him a guttersnipe, he had accepted that as truth, and in so doing
had confirmed the belief in this of his wife and son.

As the years took Nick and his father wider and
wider apart, this confirmation gave authority to her
teachings to her son. His half brother, Nicholas observed, was merely a satellite of his father and was
therefore of the same common substance. Nicholas had

been given reason for his undeniable arrogance by the towering nature of the superiority he felt for (a) the President of the United States and (b) a self-made multibillionaire—together the two most imposing American institutions.

Tim never knew this, because Tim had skin thicker by far than the blood that is thicker than water. Tim loved his silly little brother, who he thought was silly because he worked so hard to alienate the source whence all good things flowed—Pa. Nick was "little" to Tim because Tim was six feet three inches tall and Nick was about five feet nine. Like all tall men, Tim figured everyone else's hostile acts in terms of the number of inches of height the offender lacked.

Only Pa thought he knew what the deep displacement between himself and Nick was all about. His son obviously thought he, Thomas Kegan, was a guttersnipe. Nick saw it somewhat differently but in effect just as clearly: his father held him in contempt because he would not let his father run him as he had run Tim, because although his father was of a caste to give orders to Tim, it would be altogether unseemly for him to attempt to give orders to Nick— circular frustration, circularly arrived at.

When Nick awoke in Palm Springs the next morning it was half past ten. He was still exhausted from so many airplanes. He remembered the Philadelphia police commissioner and scrambled out of bed, was showered and dressed in twelve minutes, then called the kitchen to ask them to send him a pot of tea to his father's office.

Pa looked like a heap of ashes tied up in golfing clothes. As Nick came in he shook his head sadly. "I talked to Philadelphia. Miles Gander has disappeared."

"Miles is always traveling. That's the kind of business he's in."

Pa nodded blankly. "Yeah. But the Engelson Building manager and John Kullers of 603 are dead."

"Dead?"

"Suicides, Frey said. But he doesn't believe it."

"No," Nick said.

"I told Frey I'd pay for an all-points on Miles. And I put my own people out to find him."

"And Heller didn't die of any heart attack."

"Three out of five people who saw that rifle are dead. In twenty-six hours."

"And the rifle is gone," Nick said. "And no depositions could be taken. Did the package come in from Keifetz this morning?"

"Not yet. But you gotta give it another day. This isn't 1955. They walk the mail in now."

"I can't explain it—but John Kullers knew he was going to be killed when he saw us find that rifle."

"We must find Miles." Pa stared at him with great concern. "And suppose Miles is dead? We'll still have Fletcher's deposition. But that isn't enough without the rifle. We can't go to the President with just that deposition. But what would we be going to the President for? To persuade him to reopen an investigation. Until we find the rifle or find Miles we could start our own investigation."

Nick looked away from his father. He was in the oil business. He wasn't a policeman. He didn't think that the fact that three other people had died because they had seen the rifle meant that he might be killed himself. He just thought of the time it would take and the time he would have to spend with Pa that he could be spending with Yvette Malone. Then he thought of Kullers and Mr. Coney. They certainly hadn't asked to be declared into this thing. They were dead because they happened to be standing in the wrong place, and, to a large extent, they were dead because of him.

"People would talk to you because you're Tim's brother. They'd talk to you because of me in other cases. You and me and Tim are a powerful combination, Nick, and I'd give you as many trained men as you need."

The light on the switchboard turned on. Pa picked up the phone. He listened, then handed the phone to Nick. "It's for you. A call from Brunei."

Nick took the phone. "Hello? Yes, Daisy." He listened. His face changed into a twist of grief. "No!" His legs seemed to give way. He leaned on the desk. "This is terrible. This is the worst. Daisy—Daisy, please—try to pull yourself together. Daisy, I know, I know—he was a fine man. But there was something he was trying to do and I have to know. What happened to the deposition and the fingerprints?" He listened. At last he hung up.

"Keifetz is dead," he told Pa. "The lawyer who took the deposition is dead. The stenographer is dead."

"Is the deposition in the mail?" Pa asked harshly.

"No. It was with Keifetz. We are supposed to believe he fell off a rig and drowned."

"Then that's the end of that."

"No," Nick said grimly. "The deposition is only lost, Pa. Like the rifle. Somebody has them, and we have to get them back."

Keifetz was dead. Keifetz had been more of a father to him than Pa had ever been. Kullers was a total stranger, but he had been a valiant man, and his death somehow meant more to Nick than Tim's murder had. Life was all a thing of trying to make contact. He had made it with Keifetz and Kullers. It had eluded him with Pa and Tim, and no interminable talk about families could change that. He felt a need to avenge Keifetz. The same man had bought the deaths of all those people. He had bought a blood lust for Nick at last.

To get the meeting over with so he could begin a manhunt, Nick asked Pa to have his agency people check out the National Rifle Association, to confirm that Fletcher had worked for them and to see if they had any fingerprints and photographs.

"What else?"

"We ought to try as close a total comb-out of Texas as we can, to try to run down a trace of this Casper," Nick said. "But most of all, can you set a meeting for me with Z. K. Dawson?"

"Sure. When?"

"Anytime beginning tomorrow. I'll be in New York. Either at the Walpole or at Butterfield 9-1845. Meantime please tell me what you know about Dawson. He's just a name to me."

"Z. K. Dawson is the richest man in Texas. He owned Eldridge Mosely. Eldridge was oil business in Pennsylvania, and Dawson was big oil business in Texas, Oklahoma and Colorado. In Saudi Arabia and Venezuela. In Algeria and the Gulf. He wanted Eldridge to be President, but he had to settle for Vice-

President—and you know what John Garner said that
was worth. But Dawson didn't see it that way. I say he
had Tim killed to put Eldridge in the White House.
He's the greediest man we ever had in this country."

"You agree that he was probably one of the men
who paid to have Tim killed?"

"He had the most reasons. He was against everything Tim did and everything Tim stood for. And he
owned Eldridge Mosely. . . . Who lives at Butterfield
9-1845?"

"A girl. I'll have to have Jake Lanham take over for
Keifetz at Brunei. That means you have to put your
people aboard the *Teekay* right away so he can get
off."

"I'll handle it," Pa said.

Nick caught a twelve ten plane to New York. He sat in a daze sipping cranberry juice and mourning Keifetz. He should have paid him more. Why was he so stingy with everything? He remembered Keifetz' uncle, an old dermatologist named Harry Lesion. Keifetz used to send the old man a hundred-dollar bill whenever he thought of it. He'd have Daisy dig out the old man's address, Nick decided, and send him the raise Keifetz should have had. He got to the family flat at the Walpole on upper Madison at a quarter to six. He took a bath, left a call for seven thirty, and went to bed so he would be as fit as possible for an evening with Yvette Malone.

Yvette Malone was a lightly bruised woman of about thirty who had been trampled by a man named Malone in holy matrimony and who had been fleeing ever since to almost anywhere it was emotionally comfortable, because a love of emotional comfort was all she had been able to salvage out of a marriage that had happened ten years before, when she had been even more defenseless. She had married one of those men who are retroactively determined to fly a Spitfire in the Battle of Britain or to become the leading climber of the Sherpa people for the first conquest of Everest or to pitch four consecutive no-hit games in the 1928 series against the Yankees—almost anything superlative if it were fictional or unattainable. He punished his wife for being denied these ambitions. After two years of doing the dishes for this prince of obscurity Yvette got out of town and moved to Paris. She divorced Malone.

As contracted, Nick called from the lobby of the building at exactly eight o'clock and rose like a randy eagle to her flat on the twenty-eighth floor. They didn't speak much for the first hour—mostly there were grunts, moans, wails and shrieks. He threw himself at her, ran his hands up along her legs under her dress and grabbed everything that was waiting there. He scooped her up and ran down the short hall with her into a bedroom with a large bed. He threw her on it, then threw himself on top of her and began to flop about trying to kiss her and get out of his clothing while refusing to give up his hold on her crotch. She got his clothes off at about the same time he got hers off. It was fierce. It was poignant. It was noisy. And it was very, very carnal. As they were reaching a third climax he proposed to her. But he did it just before she moved into exultant chords of orgasm, bellowing "Yes, yes, yes!" to the extraordinary pleasure of the moment. He forgot she always responded just like that and thought she had agreed to marry him with enormous enthusiasm.

Forty minutes later, while they were getting ready to sit down to dinner in the kitchen, as he opened a bottle of French wine she had smuggled in with her, he told her how happy she had made him by accepting his proposal so happily.

"I don't know what you mean," she said.

"I asked you to marry me, and you yelled 'yes' three times."

"Nick, I couldn't have."

"Why not?"

"Because I can't marry you."

"Why not?"

"Just because I can't, that's all."

He put the bottle down with the corkscrew impaled in the cork. "I think I deserve more of an explanation than that. Have you met somebody else whom you'd rather marry?" he said stiffly.

"Oh, for heaven's sake, Nick. There isn't anybody else, and I've cooked a very good dinner, and we can certainly talk about anything else in the world except about getting married."

"Just answer one question. Do you refuse to marry me?"

"Yes."

"Ever?"

"Yes."

"Then I can't even stay here, much less eat your dinner."

"Well, I'm certainly glad you didn't propose the minute you got out of the elevator. At least we got something out of this evening."

"Listen, Yvette—you've said about thirty times that you love me. You certainly act as if you love me. You certainly couldn't be more sure that I loved you. Are you just generally against marriage because you had that one bad experience, or what is it?"

"I can't marry you, Nick. That's all there is to say about it, and that's all I'm going to say about it."

As he started to protest, the telephone rang. Yvette answered it. "It's for you," she said.

Baffled, he took up the telephone. It was Pa. "Nick? Pa. You're all set with Dawson. The house is on the Muskogee road, outside Tulsa. He'll see you tomorrow afternoon at four o'clock."

"Thanks, Pa."

"Before you leave the Tulsa airport set the car's odometer to zero, then drive out on the Muskogee road for one seven, point four miles. It'll be a white house on the right-hand side."

"Does he know what I want to talk about?"

"He knows you're in the oil business. He probably thinks it's about a deal. He's an odd bird. He keeps fresh money in laundry sacks and runs all his meetings lying down in a dentist's chair."

Nick hung up. "That was my father," he told Yvette.

"I've heard of him," she answered curtly.

"Listen. What the hell is the matter with you? I haven't seen you for almost five months, and it's like all that time you've been studying up on how to chop me down."

"Everything's changed."

"What? How?"

"I have to have time to think."

"What has changed? What could possibly have changed? I talked to you from London a couple of days ago and nothing had changed."

"I am not going to talk about it until I get it worked out."

"You are so going to talk about it! I want to know what has changed?"

"If you force me to talk about it, I swear to you, Nick, that that could be the end of it for us. I don't think I want it to be the end." She began to weep. "I know I don't. But it's hard. It's very, very hard."

He walked to her and tried to put his arms around her. She moved away from him, eluding him. She said, "Please just sit down and eat this marvelous daube."

"What the hell, Yvette," Nick shouted. "How can I eat? How can we sit here staring at each other and pushing food into our faces to keep from talking about whatever it is you won't talk about?" He stalked out of the kitchen along the hall to the front door, grabbed his overcoat and hat and left, slamming the door. Yvette sobbed into her hands at the kitchen table, thinking about the lies Nick's father had spread all over the world about her father.

The weather was sunny and mild when Nick got to Tulsa. While he waited for his baggage to come up he called Ed Blenheim, who was out. Nick said he could call Blenheim again at about seven o'clock. The secretary gave him Blenheim's home number. Nick picked up the rental car, set the odometer, and went out to find the Muskogee road.

The white house was where it was supposed to be. It was a very modest house for a man with eight hundred million dollars and wells still pumping as if they had no bottoms. It stood about a hundred feet off the road and looked as if they kept chickens out back. He rolled the car up the driveway. He checked the voice-activated recording equipment he had stowed in the glove compartment. The meeting would be picked up through the microphone in Nick's signet ring, then transmitted from the house to this recorder in the car. Pa thought of everything. Pa didn't own a big, rich Japanese electronics complex for nothing.

As Nick got out of the car the front door of the house opened. A short fat-faced old man with a big belly and curvy white hair came out and asked Nick what he wanted.

"I'm Nick Thirkield."

"Who?"

"Tom Kegan's son."

"All right. Come on in." The old man didn't wait for him. He went back into the house and left the door open. Nick went in through the high-ceilinged hall. He entered the only open door. The old man was stretched out almost flat on a dentist's chair with his eyes closed. His stomach dominated the room. The old man was like a big fat bullfrog with the wearies. "Close the door and set down," the old man said. Nick sat in an over-stuffed Grand Rapids chair. The wallpaper was hideous. Cord was showing through different parts of the carpet.

"What's on your mind? My boys tell me you got a small company but that you're doin' all right in the South China Sea. Do you need money for that Australian operation you got comin' up?"

"Do I? Have you heard anything?"

"No. I ain't heard a thing. I'd tell you if I had. But nobody's goin' to drill on that barrier reef in your lifetime. The pollution nuts took care of that. What can I do for you?"

Speaking very deliberately, Nick told the old man about Fletcher, and how he had found the rifle. He didn't mention Keifetz or the other five who had died. When he finished, the old man lay on the chair as if he were asleep, his domed stomach rising and falling as he breathed.

"That's a funny goddam thing to come all this way to tell me about," he said at last.

"You are an extensive operator in the Southwest," Nick said. "I wondered if you might remember a Dallas man named Casper or Casper Junior."

"I don't think that's exactly what you wanted to ask me. I think you're trying to figure out a way to tell me you think I was the prime mover who got your brother shot."

Nick didn't answer.

"A lot of people think that. Why, I do not know. You tell me. If you got any ideas on that subject, you tell me. I'm a big producer in the war industries, and your brother was a politician who was hell-bent for war, and he could have doubled my fortune."

"Only in the beginning, Mr. Dawson. Only for the first eleven months."

"He tried to get World War Three going over Berlin. He doubled, then he tripled the draft. He called up a hundred and fifty thousand reservists. He demanded that the Congress provide fallout shelters instantly while he ordered the development of a household-attack warning system. Your brother was reckless and irresponsible to an extreme degree, but I wouldn't have had him shot for that, because it was good for my business. Why, the Pentagon's own study of the war in Vietnam concluded that your brother transformed what they called the 'limited risk gamble' of the Eisenhower administration into a 'broad commitment' of American forces at war. Your brother was a crisis-eating President. That is the only way that kind knows how to convey the illusion that he is accomplishing something—which he wasn't."

"You keep talking about his first eleven months. Everything changed after that."

Dawson chuckled. It sounded like oil bubbling in the earth at the bottom of a well. "How about that goddam space program? Well, Jesus Christ, an awful lot of money was made out of that, but the more nonhuman the project, the more it appealed to your brother. But everything he did helped me, just the way it helped his daddy. Your brother was good for business. He was a helluva lot more conservative a President than Eisenhower. All his policies were set to profit big businessmen. He was his daddy's own true son, and I don't have to tell you that they don't come any more reactionary than that. Why would I shoot a man who kept thwarting the dreams of the niggers?"

"Only at the beginning. Only the beginning."

"That's all there was, sonny. Only a beginning. He went to Berlin to say 'I am a Berliner,' but he never went into the state of Mississippi and said 'I am a nig-

ger.' He was a token President with token policies, and
he fooled 'em all most of the time. All that talk about
how he was gunna put through a law to abolish the oil
depreciation allowance was purely horseshit. And the
biggest bunch of horseshit was the bunch that got everybody convinced that your brother was antibusiness
in every area—in taxes, wages, finances and federal
spending. Take a look at his Medicare proposal, how
he dragged his feet on civil rights legislation, the way
he encouraged government contracting, and his whole
yammer about poverty at a time when just about
ever'thing the poor needed was in surplus supply. And
you have some crackpot idea that I had him shot?
Sonny, your brother reduced taxes by ten *billion* dollars in the short time he was in office. Your brother
worked like a nigger to make the rich richer. He was a
faker from the word go, but if we started going around
to shoot the fakers, there wouldn't be enough bullets,
sonny. So let's let it go. I am seventy-nine years old,
which means I've outlived a lot of bubbleheads like
your brother. I never did give a holler about what people said, and I care less now. But I know who killed
your brother."

"Who?"

"All that talk back at the time about me gettin' your
brother killed plain upset my daughter. And she's a
good old girl. So I hired me some sleuths and reminded
a lot of people in Washington that they owed me a few.
We worked at it and we found out who did do the killing, then I showed the whole report to my little girl,
and after she seen it I threw the whole thing into the
furnace."

"Who killed him?"

"Now, your brother was a frivolous man. He didn't
do much more for his country than help the rich and
improve the social life in Washington. He did
ever'thing off the top of his head, and he was an arro-
gant, cold-ass son-of-a-bitch. But you're his brother,

and that's something like being a daughter when it comes to this kind of feelin'. So I'll get you started towards where you want to go."

"Who killed him?" Nick said loudly.

"The Philadelphia police killed him," the old man said. "A man named Cap'n Frank Heller was in charge of the operation. Best thing for you to do is to talk to Cap'n Heller."

"He's dead, Mr. Dawson."

The old man blinked. "Then try his sidekick, Lieutenant Ray Doty. They were the Philadelphia Special Squad, which was the Political Squad fourteen years ago." The old man's almost-round right hand, whose stubby fingers made it seem like a bear's paw, dropped to the side of the chair and pushed a lever. The chair came full upright. He swung it around to face Nick. Stiffly he got out of the dentist's chair. Nick stood up. He was herded toward the door.

"Goin' to Dallas, sonny?"

"No, sir. I have to see a man in Tulsa about some oil business."

"Who's that?"

"Ed Blenheim."

"Good man. What'd you want to see him about?"

"I have a job for him in London."

"Where'll you put up in Tulsa?"

"I don't know yet. First time in Tulsa."

"Try the Gusher Motel at the airport. It's a good clean place to stay even if I do own it myself. I'll phone ahead and tell them to fix you up."

"Very kind of you."

The old man stood on the porch and watched Nick back the car down the driveway and out onto the Muskogee road.

FRIDAY, FEBRUARY 1, 1974—MUSKOGEE ROAD

Halfway to Tulsa, ahead of Nick's moving car about two hundred yards down the road in the approaching dusk, a car had been run off the road. A woman was standing on the highway near the wrecked car. She was trying to flag Nick's down, waving a red-and-blue scarf. He braked and stopped near her. She was a shockingly pale woman in her middle thirties with exquisitely sculpted features. She had a bleeding gash at the right side of her forehead.

Nick asked, "Can I help you?" thinking he had wandered into a James Bond movie, remembering old-time warnings about weird holdups he had read of in the old *American Weekly* at Harmonia, New York; obliquely worrying that this might be some kind of Women's Liberation attack in which other equally smashing-looking women would rush out from behind trees and bushes and would all gang-bang him.

She had a voice with the texture of pecan pie. "If y'all would be kind enough to ride me down the road a piece so I can find a telephone back there at Jane Garnet's Corners—"

"Jump in," he said.

"A cah deliberately drove me off the road! Ah swear they were hopheads."

"We'd better find you a doctor."

"The proper thing is for us to introduce ourselves."

"How do you do?"

"I am Chantal Lamers."

"Happy to meet you. I am Nicholas Thirkield."

"Thoykeeld?"

"Yes."

"A handsome and unusual name." She slammed the door. "I'm just dazed. I swear those men tried to drive straight into me."

It was getting dark. Nick switched the low beams on. After not more than five minutes of driving they came to a collection of buildings grouped around a gas station. Nick leaned out of the car and asked where they could find a doctor. The gas pumper pointed to the house next door. The woman got out of Nick's car and ran inside, holding a handkerchief to her forehead.

"She get hit by two weirdos wearin' a 1967 Thunderbird?" the gas pumper asked. "Man, they were flyin'. Lemme tell you, they had eyes just like four sleepy rocks."

"Where's the police?"

"Jessacrossa highway."

Nick crossed the road and made a report to a young trooper who called ahead to Muskogee to have a 1967 Thunderbird stopped. Then he needed a better description of the car and the victim's name and license and insurance. Nick told him the victim was in the doctor's office and he'd send her over. When the woman came out she had a plaster on her head, but she didn't look as pale. "He gave me a big drink of grain alcohol," she said happily. Nick took her to the young trooper and she completed all the forms. Her car was rented, and the trooper told her to refer the car-rental people to him.

When they got back to Nick's car Nick said he was on his way to the Gusher Motel at the airport and that he'd be glad to drive her into Tulsa. She said the airport was exactly where she wanted to go. As they drove in she told him she had been visiting her parents in Muskogee, where her father ran the oldest pharmacy in town. She lived in New York, where she worked for the *National Magazine.* She was ticketed on a flight that would leave at six fifty-five. Nick said he was in Tulsa on oil business.

They got to the airport at six ten. He invited her for a drink, but she said no, because she'd face a lot of red tape at the car-rental office and she had to check in at the flight counter. She thanked him earnestly, staring nearsightedly into his eyes, holding his forearms tightly. She was as tall as he was. She had deep black hair worn in a Dutch-boy cut. She had a strong, sensual, classic face. He decided she was an interesting-looking woman. Her mouth came together into one large, loose cushion.

"If you ever come through New York I'd love to have that drink with you," she said. She wrote down her telephone number at the magazine office, explaining that they had a system that bypassed the switchboard and went straight to her desk. She kept thanking him for his kindness. He stared at her legs as she walked away from him. Not since Yvette Malone had he seen legs like that.

He arranged to have the rental car picked up at the Gusher Motel, bought a *Tulsa Tribune* in the motel lobby and was checked into room 1364. He asked the bellman how they could have a number 1364 in a one-story motel. The bellman said the numbers started at 1351 because this one was part of a chain of motels which at the time the Gusher was built had 1350 rooms. Nick got no special greeting at the desk, so it was hard to say whether Mr. Dawson had bothered to tell them he was coming.

There were still twenty minutes to wait before the time when he said he would call Ed Blenheim, so he settled down to read the local newspaper. Tulsa was an oil capital, so the paper was big with oil news. On the front page he read: GEOLOGIST SUICIDE IN EAST. Miles Gander had been found dead of monoxide poisoning in a closed car near Trenton, New Jersey. He dropped the paper. Miles Gander was dead from having agreed to have breakfast with a friend. He telephoned Pa.

"Pa? Miles is dead."

"I know. My people found him. Nobody thinks it was a suicide. Did you see Dawson?"

"Yes."

"What did he say?"

"He said the Philadelphia police organized Tim's murder. The man in charge of it was Captain Heller."

"Our Captain Heller?"

"Who else? Dawson said the man to talk to now is a police lieutenant named Ray Doty. Can you set me with him?"

"I'll take care of it."

"I sure have a rotten feeling about Dawson. He even smells like death."

"Call me in the morning for details on Doty."

Nick called room service and ordered some tea. When it arrived a small ginger cat wandered in with the waiter. Nick watched the cat scoot under the bed, but it was time to call Ed Blenheim.

Blenheim couldn't take the job because, to his absolute amazement, he had just, five minutes before, had a big surprise offer—which he had accepted—from Z. K. Dawson personally. "He just called me up. Z.K. himself," Blenheim said in an awed voice. "It's raining big jobs today."

When Nick hung up, he felt a different kind of worse about Dawson. He poured himself a cup of tea, and because he never used milk or sugar, filled the saucer with the milk and put it on the floor next to the bed. The cat came out of hiding to lap at the milk. Sipping tea, Nick called his airline to make a reservation on an early-morning flight to Philadelphia. The reservation was confirmed for 8:50 A.M.

At the periphery of his vision, Nick saw the small saucer of milk on the floor next to the leg of the bed. As he sipped the tea he looked down to watch the kitten lap it up.

The kitten was dead. She was on her back with her

eyes open, stretched taut, bent backward, looking like a bow, in agony. But she was very dead.

Nick emptied a bottle of aspirin tablets. Carefully he poured the meager amount of milk out of the saucer into the bottle and capped it tightly. He called the bell captain to find him a roll of aluminum foil and some Scotch tape. The man said everything was closed. Nick surprised himself by saying he would pay ten dollars for it. It arrived in ten minutes. While he waited he changed his departure reservation to a flight leaving at nine fifty-five that night to Los Angeles. He called Si to tell him he would be coming in. Si told him a car would be waiting at the Palm Springs airport. It would be too late to use the chopper, he said, because the noise would wake up the boss.

Nick wrapped the dead cat in thicknesses of aluminum foil and made the package secure with tape. He packed the cat into his attaché case. He went to the motel restaurant, ordered a large steak, even allowed the waiter to talk him into the doughnuts called "French fried onions," and marveled that he felt both hungry and refreshed after someone had tried to murder him. The curtain was torn aside. He was frightened because he was intelligent, but he was also gratified that he would not have to pretend to carry on this feud of vengeance for Tim across fourteen years. He had to find the killer to stay alive, the best reason. Whoever it was he was pursuing—and it simply had to be Dawson—knew he was coming and feared him enough to try to kill him. That made whatever Nick would have to do all the clearer. He was accumulating evidence.

He got to the Palm Springs fortress at eleven thirty-five. Pa was waiting for him in the "small" sitting room.

"What happened?" he asked irritably. "You're due in Philadelphia for lunch tomorrow with Doty."

"Dawson tried to kill me, Pa."

"When?" Pa was confused. His aged, leather face offered new diagonal seams. "You called me after you left him, you said."

"He sent me to stay at the Gusher Motel—which he said he owns—then someone put poison in the milk intended for my tea, which I gave to a cat who wandered into the room—and that cat was dead in seconds."

"Poison!" Pa spat out the word with contempt and disgust.

"I poured it into a bottle and I wrapped the cat in aluminum foil. Let's see what a lab says. Let's find out if whatever killed the cat is the kind of stuff that would make Inspector Heller's death look like a heart attack."

"You're really right on top of this thing, Nick." Pa looked at him as though he were seeing someone new. Pa also had a look on his face that said if they had poisoned Tim instead of shooting him he wouldn't have had much respect for Tim.

"Well, anyway," Nick said, "if the lab report checks out, we'll have to ask for an autopsy on Heller. Maybe we haven't got much solid evidence now that Fletcher's deposition and the rifle have disappeared. But we have one helluva newspaper story that could shake any government into reopening an investigation."

The idea panicked Pa. He almost exploded with passion. "Absolutely not," he said so loudly that Nick knew he was suddenly frightened. "I'm not going to barter Tim's place in history with yellow journalism. We've had enough government-by-printing-press in this country." He stared at Nick, breathing heavily. "You've got to go out and dig up evidence. Real evidence. You have to do it. No one else can do it, and I'll have the agency cover you with security men around the clock."

"No."

"Why not?"

"Because that might just stop somebody from trying to kill me when I'd have the chance to grab him and hang onto him."

"Then you have to take a gun."

"No, Pa. I don't even know how to use a gun."

"Then will you take a blackjack? You don't need lessons for that."

"Okay, I'll take a blackjack."

"And brass knuckles. So they stay down when you hit them."

"Okay, Pa."

"It's my fright as much as it is yours."

"There is plenty to share, Pa."

"But we have to do it. We can't take this. I am proud of you, Nick."

"Don't get sloppy, Pa."

"I can't believe that I once thought you were just another piano player."

"Pa—what was the agency able to find out about Lieutenant Doty?"

SATURDAY, FEBRUARY 2, 1974—PHILADELPHIA

Lieutenant Ray Doty was retired from the Philadelphia police department. He raised Cornish hens in Amalauk, New Jersey. He was eight years older than Frank Heller. They had been partners on the force since 1939. They were both rough men. When the new mayor decided he needed a kind of task force to keep organized crime (and other special problems) in line in Philadelphia, he formed the Political Squad. Heller and Doty were it. Heller was the brains, although he put in a lot of rugged muscle too. Doty was the hammer.

Doty was sixty-eight years old when he agreed to meet Nicholas Thirkield in the restaurant of the Barclay Hotel. He was as slight a man as Heller had been thick and tubby. He was tall, skinny-looking, very strong and had bright red skin. He came complete with a cockade of stiff white hair worn in the style identified affectionately by Captain Heller as *der Bürstenhaarschnitt*. His eyes, much like Captain Heller's, had all the warmth of two set mousetraps. He smiled a lot, showing his teeth.

Nick and Doty made a memorable lunch of snapper soup, imperial crab and pineapple chiffon pie. They also made small talk.

"Tomorrow is Frank's funeral," Doty said. "I can't believe it. We were partners for thirty-five years."

"I met Captain Heller briefly," Nick said. "Seemed like a very nice fellow."

"Was he on duty?"

"Yes."

"Then he wasn't exactly nice. He had a whole different spirit, you might say, when he was on duty. We always had the roughest jobs."

"I bet."

"I been running a chicken farm for eight years, and, believe me, I ain't relaxed yet. Not that I like it. You know—once a cop, always a cop."

The agency had paid Lieutenant Doty two thousand dollars to talk to Nick, and in the sense that it would probably be his last big contract, he really wanted to give a money's worth. But in the right way. The safe way. After lunch he took Nick into the manager's office and frisked him for transmitting/recording devices, then they bundled up in heavy overcoats and went out to sit on a bench in the sun in Rittenhouse Square. There was no one nearer to them than sixty feet. There were no leaves on trees to conceal parabolic mikes.

"Did the Philadelphia police set up my brother to be killed?" Nick asked.

"Set him up, yes. Cover, yes. But we had nothing to do with the killing."

"Who paid you?"

"I don't know. They paid Frank, and Frank paid me. Frank said the less I knew about that the better—and he was right, of course."

"You never knew anybody from their side?"

"I knew, yeah. One time—well, like a couple of times—we used my chicken ranch for meetings, because nobody could find it to bug it. It was always the same guy. A plump little guy with a bartender's haircut. Short. Talked like a cowboy."

"But I mean—how did they come to you? I mean, a stranger can't walk into the police department and ask them to cushion the murder of the President."

"Well, look—first it wasn't the police department. It was the Political Squad. That was Frank and me and six men working three patrol cars when he needed them. We were in charge of all arrangements after the mayor talked to the advance man, and we had maybe two hundred and seventy cops assigned to us for the detail after that on a big job like a President."

"How did their man get to you?"

"He didn't get to us. He got to Joe Diamond. Joe knew everybody in the department and who did what and who took contracts, so the actual work was like all organized through Joe, then Joe called us in to like routine everything and handle the cushion."

"How? Tell me how it was done," Nick said.

"Before anybody could get anything done they had to talk it over with Frank. You gotta understand that."

Captain Heller's wife's name was Myrtle. She was a merry-faced woman whose rosy cheeks came from making so many of Mom's Zimsterne and Schwabenbrötle for her master and her seven children—Hans, Franz, Fritz and Wolfie, and Käthe, Kläre, and Katerina, who were called, naturally, Ku, Klux and Klan in school. In the Philadelphia police department the Heller house was known as Little Germany. The house was in Philadelphia's Germantown section.

Years before, Captain Heller had trained his non-German wife to set a Swabian table. After years of work with her, he considered that her Flädle were superior to his mother's, her Schwarzwalder Kartoffelsuppe not yet as good as his mother's. However, no one, not anyone, could equal her Maultaschen. And she scraped his Spätzle from the board by hand as per the high ruling of the Stuttgart Municipal Restaurant Council. She knew as much about making Spätzle as his grandmother!

At home Captain Heller spoke German to his children, English to his wife. The family drove in three Volkswagens (and on one Honda), one of which Myrtle was intent on borrowing for the evening on behalf of her son Wolfie when she put her head in at the door of Captain Heller's study, with its ancient, black, enormous furniture, carved and columned, which had been brought from Swabia by Captain Heller's grandfather eighty-seven years before and which left very little circulating space in the small room. There were only four pictures on the walls of the study: a mezzotint portrait of Richard Wagner by the München Master G. Bocca; a signed photograph of Feldmarschall August von Mackensen at the Heldengedenktag ceremonies with Adolf Hitler; a portrait of the German Crown Prince, and one of General Von Blomberg. There was a fading typewritten record of the statement made that day (dated March 17, 1935) by General Von Blomberg pasted at the bottom of the photograph: "It was the Army, removed from the political conflict, which laid the foundations on which a God-sent architect could build. Then this man came, the man who, with his strength of will and spiritual power, prepared for our dissensions the end they deserved and made all good where a whole generation had failed." The third wall decoration was a small painting of Ernestine Schumann-Heink by Shannon-Philips in the costume for Ortrud in *Lohengrin*. Beneath it on the wall was an identical portrait of Mme. Schumann-Heink, in seven colors, executed in needlepoint. This was the work of Captain Heller. It had taken him thirty-seven months to complete, working twenty-two stitches to the inch.

"There's a man at the door," Myrtle said. "His name is William Casper. And can Wolfie have the car tonight?"

"Ach," Heller rumbled. "I should have told you he was coming. Do we have schnecken for the coffee?" He did not mind English to his wife in his own house, because he loved her and had forgiven her for having been born of Scottish people in Pittsburgh.

"As commanded," Myrtle said, "we have the standard minimum of nine schnecken."

"And fresh coffee?"

"You and your guest will be issued two cups of fresh coffee each, as per regulations of this house. You can sign for them in the morning."

Heller frowned. He did not understand why she always joked about the coffee and the schnecken. "Send William Casper in," he ordered.

Myrtle held out her hand. "The keys to the white Volkswagen, please."

"The *white?* Why the white? It is the second newest. And I don't like the way Wolfie steers. He has not smoothness. He is abrupt with the wheel."

"Wolfie has changed his driving style altogether," Myrtle said. The captain found the car keys in the drawer and handed them over. "Tell them nobody leaves for their dates until I am finished with this man."

"They know, Frank. Believe me, they know." She patted his cheek and left the room. Very shortly afterward William Casper knocked at the door and came in.

"Cappen Heller?"

"Come in, sir. Close the door." Heller got up from behind the desk, walked to Casper and said, "Put your hands against the wall and lean into them."

"What the hell for?"

"We have voice prints now. We will make sure you are not wearing a recorder or a transmitter. Then we talk with total security."

Casper leaned, and Captain Heller frisked him. Then he held a chair for Casper and returned to his own chair behind the desk and started the recorder with his knee. "Coffee is coming. Do you take schnapps with the coffee?"

"What is schnapps?"

"Whiskey."

"Oh, *snaps*. Sure, I take a snaps now and then."

"We will not talk business until the coffee comes."

"Sure is cold up here." He saw the instantly offended expression on Heller's face and quickly amended that. "Not *in* here. *Up* here. In Philly."

Myrtle came in with the loaded-down tray. Captain Heller pulled up a bottle of bourbon from behind him and laced the coffee with it. Myrtle left. As she opened the door, from down the hall and from up the stairs came the voice of Buddy Holly screaming a song of ruined young love, but decently far enough away so that the raw rock sounded pleasant. The coffee smells blended with the whiskey smells and the bouquets of bay rum and witch hazel that rose from Mr. Casper.

"Now we will talk," Heller announced.

"You seen Diamond?"

"He told me."

"But you didn't say you was on."

"I talk my own money. Nothing is settled until the money is settled. And I am aaalzzo speaking for the share of my partner, Lieutenant Doty." Within otherwise wholly native American speech, which had been formed in Dover, New Jersey, Captain Heller always pronounced the word as "aaalzzo," one of his few lapses (in speech habits).

"We want to buy your experience, Cappen."

"And my protection."

"Thass right."

"One thing must be clear. Everything must be done only from my plan. From the plan I will lay out."

"Well, sure."

Heller grunted. He could grunt like a Westphalian blue-ribbon boar weighing in at maybe three hundred and twelve kilos. He sipped coffee. "How much?" he asked.

"Remember, when I give you a figure, it is cash."

"Did you think a thing like this could go on the American Express?"

"My boss will go all the way to twelve thousand, five hundred."

"Then forget it."

"That is a big piece of money for a morning's work."

"A morning's work? How long do you think they take to hang you, my friend? How long it takes for the rope to break your neck, that is only how long is the work that goes into this."

"Well—I don't know—I might be able to get an okay for twenty thousand."

"I will now tell you what you will pay. Fifty thousand. Try the schnecken." He pushed the plate toward Casper. "My wife makes them herself. You will faint, it is so delicious."

"I ain't much of a sweet tooth," Casper said, breaking a schnecke into three pieces and tasting one of them. "God *damn,*" he said with delight. "Man, that is *good!*" Having gone through enough of the motions of driving a hard bargain, Casper was no longer interested in pretending to haggle. The price had been set. "Okay, Cappen, fifty thousand."

"Half now."

Mr. Casper took a large brown manila envelope out of his side pocket. He took a sheaf of banknotes out of it and counted out twenty-five thousand dollars slowly in one-thousand-dollar bills. His lips moved silently. He pushed the money across the table to the captain, who recounted it rapidly, opened the top drawer of his desk, dropped the money in and locked the drawer.

"When does he come to Philadelphia?" he asked.

"Washin'ton's birthday. Two-two Feb. Gives us about eleven weeks. Say—how does she make these buns?"

"The pure, sweetened yeast dough is sprinkled with cinnamon, chopped walnuts, raisins, citron, and a sugar sheet, then rolled into snail shapes and baked in brown sugar and honey." He was very pleased that Casper had asked the question. "You mean his own people are setting him up?"

"Well, we gotta get him here, don't we?"

"I will see Joe tonight."

"Then that's all, then." Casper stood up.

"Please pay the second half of the money, into my hand, in this house, on the morning of the day the work is going to be done. Or nothing happens."

"Fair enough."

Heller escorted Casper to the front door and helped him on with his coat. They shook hands. Casper left.

Heller turned into the house as a patrol car rounded a corner to drive sedately and at a discreet distance behind Mr. Casper's car.

"Wolfie!" Captain Heller bellowed. A young man of nineteen appeared instantly from a room off the hall. "Ja, Poppa?"

"Where are you going tonight?"

"I am taking the girls to the Bingo," he said in German.

"Of course. You want the car to help your sisters. Where will you go with it when you leave them off?"

"I have a date. With Harriet Wilmerding."

"A good family. But, aaalzzo the Volkswagen is from a good family."

"Yes, Poppa."

"Take care!" his father barked.

Captain Heller marched past his son into the parlor, where his sons and daughters were waiting in two rows. He glared at them over the great pouches of blackness under his eyes, because the girls had their hats on. "All right!" he said in German in a parade-ground voice. "It is Saturday night. You have done good work all week, and now you play." They all smiled. "But there is bad weather out there tonight, so you must take care. Tonight the girls will return at eleven fifteen." The girls groaned. "Fritz and Wolfie will come home at twelve thirty. Hans and Franz at one o'clock. Remember! I will be waiting."

He stood at the door, kissed each one as they went past and gave each one a secret sum of money. After they had gone he settled down with Myrtle in the crowded study and concentrated on his needlepoint. At twenty minutes to eleven he said that Doty would arrive to pick him up in six minutes.

"Will you be late?"

"I will be home at twelve twenty."

"If you are having a good time," she said, smiling, "make it twelve twenty-two. Just give a shout as you cross the threshold so I can set the clocks by you."

He drew a chair close to her and kissed her ear. "Why are you always making fun of me?" he whispered.

"Because it gives you tremendous pleasure."

"You know too much," he said with a heavy German accent. He kissed her ear again.

Captain Heller came out of his house the moment Lieutenant Doty sounded his horn. They sat in the car while Heller counted out eight one-thousand-dollar bills and gave them to Doty. They were wearing civilian clothes.

"You owe me five hundred dollars change," Heller said. "He paid twenty-five up front. I get fifteen. You get seventy-five hundred. Then four hundred apiece for the patrol-car boys—it cheats them out of about sixteen bucks apiece but maybe you'll need it for your chickens."

"That's sure as hell great with me," Doty said.

"You are sure that's okay? You think that is eminently fair?"

"One hundred percent, Frank."

"Good. Aaalzzo there is another twenty-five due when the show gets to town."

"Same split?"

"Correct."

"Sensational."

"Now we go to Diamond's saloon."

Doty moved the black police car downtown.

Joe Diamond's saloon was called the Casino Latino. It had a big barroom in front. Behind that was a smaller room that Diamond called the nightclub. It was very dark in there. A piano played all the time. Out at the center of the bulked tobacco smoke four girls took turns stripping every now and then. When they had finished they went back to sit with the customers. Joe kept a king-sized mattress on the floor in a pantry behind the kitchen for any cop who wanted to get laid.

But only cops. He wasn't running any joint. Most of the cops preferred to stay in the big lighted barroom. It was both a club and a bourse for the Philadelphia police. It was the favorite club, because policemen known to Joe (which was 86.3 percent of the entire force) got a check for only every second round of drinks.

All grades spent their off-hours at Joe's. It was only two blocks from police headquarters, but also precinct men from every section of the city showed up there throughout the day and night to set contracts. For example, if a citizen wanted a neighbor beat up, he would go to the Casino Latino, talk his problem over with Joe, and Joe would cast the right cop for the job. If an out-of-town dealer wanted to set up an operating base at a new school and housing development in the suburbs, he would buy his heroin from Joe, as a wholesaler, but Joe would set the okays to operate from the police in the new district, who would be represented at the Casino Latino. The waiters handled crap like traffic tickets and summonses.

Joe Diamond, who had made it all possible for citizen and law-enforcement officer alike, had two great love affairs with life: money and policemen. He was sexually hung up on both. He just—well, he liked the way they smelled. He liked to grip them tightly. He liked to pack money and policemen in a crowded room and rub against them as he moved around. He patted young cops on the face when they were very clever. There were three young cops who were so low on the pole that he goosed them every now and then, but he made it up instantly by buying them drinks. He knew the cops who would kill for the right money. He knew the cops who would steal for him if the setup was right. He knew the plain gorillas. He had respect for one policeman. He was frightened of one policeman. When he lay in bed in the dark wondering if he wanted to go to sleep, his reveries were conscious dreams about Captain Heller.

Captain Heller (and by association, Lieutenant

Doty) was to Joe Diamond the most policeman that existed anywhere to a man who knew himself to be a connoisseur of policemen. Captain Heller was the Political Squad, accountable to nobody but the commissioner (who was a politician). Only Joe Diamond and a few dozen dead guys knew Heller was there. The work of the Political Squad was so tricky that Frank Heller had to be the best operating cop in the United States just to be chosen to handle work like that.

But if Heller was Joe's hero, Joe was like a mother and wife to the rest of the guys just the same. He was good for a touch of up to a hundred dollars for only five percent a week, but he wouldn't lend more than that, because it made bad friendships in the end if he had to turn the guys in for nonpayment. He got the cops a better than fair share of all the narcotics business in the city. Whoever was in vice or stolen goods or retail extortion had a call from Joe the week he started in business, and honorable and convenient arrangements were made to pay off both the precinct and downtown.

Joe ran a string of about a dozen, sometimes up to twenty, call girls. He cheated them whenever he could, because he hated women who could go into a business like that. He insisted that they put out to cops for nothing, and he beat them up if they refused. He also insisted on absolutely clean underwear. If a girl went out on a date with dirty underwear and he asked the customer about how was her underwear and it wasn't right, he would kick that girl unconscious, because every one of those girls knew how he felt about that. Class showed, he explained to them vociferously, in little things like that.

Joe Diamond was a dumpy man with an oatmeal face and four gold front teeth. Other than that he was easily as good-looking as a basket full of assholes. He was a sharp dresser. He took care of his hair. He shaved twice a day. He smoked thirty-five-cent cigars. He knew abortionists and clap doctors, and if a cop didn't have the money, he made the cop let him pay for it. He had operated the Casino Latino for eight years, and it had been an important place from the start. Joe was an overachiever about making people understand that he was afraid of absolutely nothing and nobody. He re-established that two or three times every night in a loud voice. He was his own bouncer. Everybody knew he carried a piece in an ankle holster, which was why he walked with a gimp. He was not only the best-connected man in Philadelphia but he was very big about saying who he knew in New York and Cleveland, in Vegas and Miami. You asked Joe for something and he delivered. If he couldn't—well, he didn't. That was Joe—a very butch fag. He had his faults, certainly. He deducted for social security and withholding from his people, but he didn't pay it in. If he was a sadist, it was because that was what anybody was quick to call anybody who beat up on women in public. But what the hell. He was a helluva guy, if he said so himself. He believed in palmsmanship, and if he didn't drink with you, it wasn't because he didn't like you, it was because he had a lot of blood sugar and had to be careful.

Heller and Doty sat in a far corner of the big barroom, and everybody gave them plenty of room. Captain Heller was well known not to be a fraternizer and showed up in the Casino only for business reasons. They drank rye and ginger ale—just enough to keep the lips moist. Joe was making his rounds of the tables, copping a feel wherever he could. He hadn't seen them come in and they didn't send for him, but when he saw them he ran to their table.

"Welcome to my place, Captain," Joe said. "Hello, Lieutenant. Are they taking good care of you?"

"We'll be in the square in twenty minutes," Doty told him.

Joe told a couple of jokes. Nobody laughed. He fought to buy them another round of drinks until Doty told him to get the hell out of there. Heller and Doty left the saloon and drove to the south side of Ritten-house Square. Ten minutes later Joe got into the back seat beside Captain Heller. He told himself he would give his life if he could have Doty's job for one year.

"Casper is all settled," Heller said.

"Oh, great," Joe said.

"But there is still plenty of work. First and fore-most—who takes the fall?"

"I have a guy in mind, if that is gonna be any help to you. It is strictly none of my business, I am just the middleman here, but this is a kid you won't believe for this job. This kid spent two years in Poland—after he got outta the Marines—and in Poland, in the capital of Poland, he went to the American Embassy and said he wanted to be a Polish citizen."

"He's a Commie?" Doty asked incredulously.

"What else? Also a Marine. Also very stupid."

"Why do you think he would want to work on this?"

"He is a Cuba nut. He hands out leaflets on Market Street every weekend. He thinks Kegan is oppressing Cuba."

"What's his name?" Heller asked.

"His name is Willie Arnold."

"Check him out," Heller said to Doty.

"You know what this kid does?" Diamond asked rhetorically. "This kid pushes shit in his spare time, and he sends the money he makes to Cuba."

"If he checks out," Heller said, "we'll pick him up. Then he'll go to you to fix it, and we'll have a little lock on him."

"Okay."

"Now, who do you have for an alternate?"

"We need an alternate," Doty said.

"The natural is the shooter they are bringing up from Texas," Diamond said. "In fact, there isn't any-body else."

"They're bringing a man all the way up from Texas?" Heller said. "When will he be here?"

"He's not a racket guy. Just some farmer. Casper said he would bring him here like a week ahead of the date."

"Call Ray when you know," Heller said. "That's all. Good night, Joe."

Diamond got out of the car thanking his friends. They left him in mid-sentence and drove away. Heller looked at his watch. "This is great. I can be home and sitting in the parlor before the girls get home. Step on it, Ray."

Three nights later Captain Heller sent word to Diamond that he wanted to see Casper at his house. When he had frisked Casper, when the coffee and schnecken came in and Myrtle had left, Captain Heller said he had developed his plan. Casper held up his hand. "I don't know nothing about plans and I don't want to know. We got to keep this thing compartmentalized. My job was to contact Joe Diamond, then, later on, to bring the shooter to him. My other job was to make the money deals. The way I see it, the best thing is if you tell the whole plan to Joe Diamond, so he can deliver the shooter to where he's supposed to be. The fewer people who know about the plan the better."

"I agree with you one hundred percent," Heller said.

The night before Casper brought Turk Fletcher to Philadelphia, Heller, Doty and Diamond had a meeting at Doty's chicken ranch. They sat around the kitchen table with their hats on. Doty mixed chicken feed while they were talking.

"This is the last meeting, Joe. All right. This is the drill. He will be on his way through the city to the Liberty Bell. I take him up Market Street, then we snake around through Hunt Plaza as if we were going under the railway bridge. There are a lot of good things about this route. The Texas shooter will have good elevation from the Engelson Building. Here are two sets of keys to Room 603, where he will work. He should be planted there by about half past nine in the morning. Ray will work out the details with you and how we'll want to deliver him. Aaalzzo, Hunt Plaza is good, because Willie Arnold works in the TV Center warehouse. Ray will give you a cheap rifle, which you will have Arnold plant in the TV Center room on the top floor overlooking the plaza. And some cartridges for him to throw on the floor. Ray gives you the details. After the hit and after we have established him in the building, tell him to go home and wait there in case we need him. If we need him we'll send a patrol car for him. Tell him nobody gets paid until the job is all over. Ray gives you the details." He stared heavily at Diamond.

"And you know what you do—right, Joe?"

"Yeah. I know," Joe mumbled.

"There were a lot of things to consider here," Heller said by way of apology.

"And that's it," Lieutenant Doty said on the bench with Nick in Rittenhouse Square. "Frank was just a born leader."

"How did they find Diamond?"

"Who?"

"Casper and his people."

"It figures they were passed along by the Mob. Diamond was with them in Cleveland and Chicago and Detroit—a long time."

"Lieutenant—I was with Heller the day we found the rifle. Where's the rifle?"

"He never said nothing to me, Mr. Thirkield."

"But you know how his mind worked. He didn't take the rifle to the lab. Where would he go with it?"

"I think he would put it away somewhere, then he would contact Casper to sell him the rifle."

"He knew where to find Casper?"

"He didn't say so. But I bet he had Casper tailed back to his own house in Texas. Waste not, want not was Frank's motto. He was always saying, 'If you're always ready, you're always glad.' "

"Who did Casper work for?"

"Frank never said."

"Did he have any ideas?"

"He had a theory."

"What theory?"

"He said Joe Diamond was the first man in. He thought it was probably a Syndicate hit."

"He believed that? He believed the Mafia would

want to kill the President?"

"What the hell—that's their business, isn't it?"

"But—why?"

"How do I know? But we once heard a very big Syndicate man say Kegan took a two-million-dollar campaign contribution from the boys and then never did anything for it."

"That just isn't possible."

"Look—Kegan could have been hit by anybody. There were a lot of grudges flying. We think the Mob did it. But whoever did it still has one terrific amount of clout fourteen years after it happened. It was good to see you, Mr. Thirkield. Good luck." Doty got up from the bench and walked rapidly away. Nick went back to the Petroleum Club to call his father.

Pa got on the phone. He said, "I've been waiting for your call. I sent the dead cat and that poisoned milk to Standard Laboratories in Glendale. I just got the report back."

"What kind of poison kills that fast?"

"We're up against some real pros. If you hadn't brought that cat, they could never have figured out what killed it."

"Why?"

"Why? The milk shows no poison. How about that? But the cat had a terrific immunological reaction. It died from—wait, I gotta read this off—anaphylactic shock. So they went back to the milk and isolated foreign matter, which turned out to be about four drops of red pigment of a guinea pig's blood. It would have turned you bright blue."

"Maybe they got that into Heller."

"Maybe."

"But he died in his own house."

"First we have to find out if that's how Heller died. I talked to Fritz Frey. He is going to try to clear an autopsy on Heller."

"The funeral is tomorrow morning."

"Did you see Doty?"

"I just left him. Heller set Tim up for the murder. Pa, I think I might have a hunch where Heller put that rifle. I may even have a hunch who killed him."

"Who?"

"He probably tried to sell them the rifle, and they agreed to talk about it, and they went to his house. He has a real coffee ritual for visitors. Maybe they put the stuff in his coffee."

"And maybe the rifle is right there?"

"Right. Will you call Frey again and say I have this hunch and ask him to send me a reliable man to go with me to get it if it's still there?"

"I'll call him right now," Pa said. "Stay where you are."

In twenty minutes the front desk called to say the police commissioner was waiting downstairs.

The commissioner was sitting in a large limousine. Nick got in. The driver took the car out into the stream of traffic. Nick said, "I didn't mean to get you out, Commissioner. This is only a hunch."

"Where is the hunch?"

"It may sound simple-minded, but Heller was such an intense family man, I am guessing that the only place he would think the rifle would be safe would be in his own house."

Frey looked at Nick blankly for a moment, then he said, "That's right." He told the driver where to take them and told him to use the siren.

When the car pulled up in front of Little Germany, Frey asked Nick to wait in the car. "This is going to be a delicate and personal visit with Myrtle Heller as well as being a police call."

Myrtle greeted him warmly. She took him to the kitchen, which was the largest room in the house. She poured him a cup of coffee, put a schnecke on a plate and set it in front of him. "Take care of yourself,

Fritz," she said. "You smoke too many cigars."

"I never light 'em."

"But the juices. Who would have thought it would be his heart? Two weeks ago he had a department checkup and the doctor said he had the heart of a twenty-five-year-old."

"Myrtle, look . . ."

"What's the matter?"

"It might not have been his heart."

"But the doctor said it was his heart."

"We have some new evidence. I mean there's a chance that—well, I have to say it to you—Frank could have been poisoned."

"Poisoned? In his own house?"

"Did anyone come to see him that night?"

"A woman was here. Just a routine call, Frank said. I showed her in. I brought them some coffee."

"Do you remember her name?"

"I remember everything about that night. I always will. She said her name was Mrs. Casper."

"Think you could identify her in a lineup?"

"I'm sure I could. She was a pretty woman about thirty-five, but she had silver hair."

"Did Frank keep any records of his meetings here?"

She smiled proudly. "No one kept such meticulous records as Frank. He taped every phone call. And he taped every meeting, then he filed it all away—why, you can't imagine. Come in here with me." Myrtle led the way to Captain Heller's study. She went to a long filing box on his desk. "This is just the card file for meeting tapes," she said. "You should see the boxes with the card files to locate the telephone-call tapes." She opened the box. "Go ahead. Look up Casper. It'll be there."

Frey riffled through the cards. There was one Casper card with three entries. It said:

CASPER, WILLIAM—Dallas (?) Texas. Five feet

seven, 190 lbs. White wavy hair which curves
over the forehead. Contempt for money. Recorded:
November 28, 1959. No. 1364
December 1, 1959. No. 1371
February 18, 1960. No. 1409 in Code P

Myrtle was looking over Frey's shoulder. "I don't
know what 'Code P' means," she said. Frey thought
silently that it probably stood for "payoff." There was
no card for Mrs. Casper.

"It could be he didn't have time to make out a card
for Mrs. Casper," Frey said.

"That would mean the tape is still in the machine,"
Myrtle said. She went to the window seat behind Heller's desk and opened a large walnut cigar box. There
was a four-track cassette recorder fitted inside it. Frey
leaned on the EJECT button. A cassette popped out.
Written on the cassette was "MRS. WILLIAM CASPER."

"I'll have to take this along with me, Myrtle."

"What is happening?"

"I came here myself this morning because we have
all been such good friends and I know you trust me."

"I do trust you, Fritz."

"We want your permission to conduct an autopsy."

She looked at him helplessly.

"It won't delay the funeral," Frey said. "We can
have it done this afternoon, and he can be back at the
funeral parlor tonight."

"Is it police business?"

He nodded. "If he was poisoned."

"Do I sign something?"

Frey took the papers from his pocket and a large
black fountain pen. She signed without reading the paper. "Don't let my kids know about this, Fritz."

"Not if I can help it."

"That's right."

They walked toward the front door. "We're talking

about moving to Arizona," Myrtle said. "The kids want it."

"Year-round sunshine."

"Frank is all over this place, except he isn't here."

"He was a man."

"He was a great man," Myrtle said.

"Oh—there's just one other thing. I wonder if I could pick up the rifle Frank brought home last Wednesday? They need it down at the lab."

She looked at him oddly. "Don't you remember, Fritz? You sent for it Thursday morning."

"The rifle?"

"It was a patrol-car cop. A skinny little guy named Marek, with a weak handshake."

They stared at each other.

"Fritz—did I do wrong to let him take the rifle?"

With Nick, Frey played back the cassette tape at police headquarters.

HELLER: Come in. Shut the door. Hands against the wall, please. Lean on the hands. . . . Sit down here please. . . . Coffee?

WOMAN: No coffee.

HELLER: What can I do for you?

WOMAN: You called Mr. Casper. You said you had the rifle. I came here to buy the rifle.

HELLER: Good.

WOMAN: I would have thought we had been more than generous.

HELLER: You were fine. But this is a separate transaction.

WOMAN: How much?

HELLER: What is it worth to you?

WOMAN: It doesn't matter. No matter what I say you'll say it's not enough.

HELLER: Try me.

WOMAN: Five thousand dollars.

HELLER: Not enough.

WOMAN: All right then. Five thousand and one dollars.

HELLER: You have committed a federal offense here. The death penalty for a federal offense depends on the mode of execution of the state in which the offense was committed. In Pennsylvania we use electrocution.

WOMAN: How much do you want?

HELLER: I will bring the rifle tonight to Hunt Plaza at eleven. [*There is the sound of a knock on the door.*] Come in. [*Door opens. Sound of cups rattling on a tray.*] Ah—coffee and schnecken. Thank you, Myrtle.

MYRTLE: You're welcome, dear. [*Sound of door closing.*]

HELLER: So—Hunt Plaza at eleven. We will meet under the railway bridge. You will hand me twenty-five thousand dollars cash. I will hand you the rifle.

WOMAN: That's a lot of money for a rifle.

HELLER: It's a lot of money for anything.

WOMAN: I think I will have some coffee. No—please! Let me pour it. . . . Let me freshen yours. . . . My God! It's a quarter to twelve, and I have to get to the bank if I'm going to buy that rifle.

HELLER: As you wish, dear lady.

[*Recording is terminated.*]

Nick asked for a copy of the tape, then the Commissioner asked if Heller and the woman had been talking about what he thought they were talking about.

"They were haggling over the price for the rifle used to murder my brother, Commissioner Frey."

"That's what I thought," Frey said sadly. "Frank finally overpriced himself."

"May we have copies of the two tapes filed for Mr. William Casper?"

"You can have copies and voice prints on all of them, Mr. Thirkield. And a copy of the autopsy report."

"Maybe you'd better include the autopsy reports on the Engelson Building manager and John Kullers."

He took the train to New York. When he got there it was a wet, cold winter evening. He was baffled by the emergence of a Mrs. Casper who had left the antilife substance in Heller's coffee. Just by showing up out of nowhere she had widened the inquiry. He had to pass all of this along to Pa for Professor Cerutti, Pa's house mastermind.

There were many more people than taxis at Penn Station. He did not have the courage to roam the streets looking for a cab. He waited for ten minutes before he understood that he was going to have to fight for a cab to get one. He fought off three men (who had body-blocked two women), made it into a cab, slammed the door and locked it instantly. There was no thought in anyone's mind that he should have offered to share the cab, because everyone there knew that everyone else there was probably a homicidal maniac who carried a concealed ice pick that would flash out and pin the cab-sharer's heart to the back of the seat. The driver, locked inside a steel compartment behind the wheel, didn't want to know who rode, who killed whom or who didn't. Everything but the street traffic hurried across the funeral parlor of the western world in taut silence and with frightened faces. Even with the doors locked and a good grip on the black-jack bestowed by his father, Nick sweated out the passage to the protected inner zone of the city, where no junkies were permitted to wander around unless they had an assured source of supply.

He felt locked in the ultimate stasis on concentric levels of self and civilization. He responded against the savagery and the threat of the city automatically: he moved out within his mind to defy his father. To throw off the threat of collective insanity from the most dangerous place in the world he hacked at the central suffocation of his life—his father.

He wasn't aware of how his mind was reacting, but Nick was so committed to impressing Pa with his intelligence and efficiency, his daring and skill, that he compromised in his mind with what his father had not wanted him to do, telling himself he had to do it to get results, that there was no other way: he decided to bring the press into the investigation. He was certain that he could make a written agreement with them at the outset that would control them. He reasoned that he would be able to control them until Pa could be brought to see why the cooperation of the press was necessary and give his permission to let them publish.

Nick decided he could negotiate press assistance on a copyright basis. It would be his story. He would lease the story to them with explicit conditions.

He had to do it, he told himself. Lieutenant Doty had said the Syndicate had found Joe Diamond for whoever had paid to have Tim killed. Nick had only the vaguest idea of what the Syndicate was; he supposed it was another way of saying "Mafia" and labeling organized crime. If the Syndicate had agreed to provide a man to do the killing, then it followed that they knew who had asked them to find the killer. As impenetrable as the situation had seemed a few hours before, he now saw that all he had to do was to find a way to reach the Syndicate, whatever that might be. The press knew such people. Until the woman from the *National Magazine* had had her car accident, Nick hadn't known any part of the press, but he knew someone now.

Mr. Zendt, the managing director of Pa's hotel, took Nick personally to the family apartment, a three-story penthouse in the tower of the hotel. It was an extraordinary apartment at the very center of the mire of twenty-five million people and all of their lights. And Pa believed in comfort most after matters of money and power had been settled. The colors of the apartment soothed: muted ivory against pale orange, green and soft blue. There was a living room that was three stories tall; a dining room, library, a large foyer and kitchen on the main floor; four bedrooms, four baths and two studies on the upper floors. The first-floor study, with blue walls and white woodwork, had another installation of Pa's replicas of the White House telephone system, by which, he bragged, he could reach anyone in the world who was lolling about near their phone within six minutes. Pa had stolen all the records and systems of the White House switchboard, including every public, private and hideout telephone number of some six thousand people in the world. Pa bragged that he could reach the Metropolitan of the Russian Church during Mass through a phone in the tabernacle.

Nick knew that as soon as he arrived at the desk in the lobby of the hotel Pa would be flashed on the special equipment so that he could know Nick was in residence in New York. "Information is the key to everything," Pa taught. The thought made Nick sweat. Suppose Pa had the whole place bugged? Why was he supposing? Of course Pa would have it bugged. That meant (a) no meetings with the press at the apartment and (b) he would be crazy to invite Yvette Malone up into one these bedrooms, because she was so operatically vocal in the sack. Therefore, when Mr. Zendt asked whether Nick would like to have a cook while he was in residence, Nick declined; no entertaining. God, what a waste, he thought.

A man came to unpack him and to take out his clothes to be pressed. Two chambermaids turned down the beds in Tim's beige and brown room, which had one green velvet chair and one green leather chair into which Pa had had screwed commemorative tabs establishing that Tim had sat in his own two chairs.

Nick put in a call to Jake Lanham in Brunei. While he waited for it, he walked aimlessly around the room, staring out at the rare beauty of the city when seen at night from a height of seven hundred feet. The view made him thirsty. Remarkable things could happen in buildings in which Pa stayed, because he had the foresight to own everything. He called down for a bottle of Montrachet '59, a dry white wine of which the Vicomte Henri d'Emmet had said it caused one "to be drunk on one's knees, with the head bared," but of which the Vicomtesse d'Emmet (to some the greater authority) had recorded, "Very great, but the very best makes the veins swell like whipcord."

By the time he had spoken to Jake Lanham he had drunk a third of the bottle and felt himself to be one-third wider and one-half longer. Jake was willing to stay on, managing Brunei, with a 20 percent raise (less than Nick had paid Keifetz). Then Lanham said that Keifetz had died thirty-five hundred dollars light in petty cash. Gulping, Nick said that was "all right." He was thinking of asking Lanham if he'd like to take Carswell's job in London, but after hearing news like that, he decided he didn't dislike Carswell quite so much.

After another glass of wine he couldn't stand being separated from Yvette Malone any longer, so he called her. Maddeningly, she was not at her apartment. He told her answering service to tell her to call him. If she didn't want to get married, what the hell, they wouldn't get married. He sipped at the wine, then hoping it wasn't too late for magazine office hours—but it was the only way he knew to reach her—he suddenly called Chantal Lamers at her desk number at the *National Magazine*.

Chantal Lamers was happy—he was even willing to estimate that she was *very* happy to hear from him. She would be stimulated and delighted to have dinner with him. They agreed on the Canopy for eight thirty, just about two hours ahead. The moment he disconnected, the switchboard flashed again. It was Pa.

"What are you doing in New York?" Pa asked.

"I wanted to see a friend."

"What friend?"

"You don't know her."

"Oh. A *friend*. Well, the agency confirms that Turk Fletcher worked for the National Rifle Association, and they will get us photographs of him. No line on Casper in Dallas. Did you know your pal Keifetz clipped us for thirty-five hundred bucks?"

"How did you know that?" Nick gasped.

"I keep in touch, kid."

"Well, Keifetz didn't clip anybody. I authorized the withdrawal."

"Like hell you did." Pa hung up. Nick felt himself swelling up with rage, although it was probably the Vicomtesse d'Emmet's prognosis for people who drank too much Montrachet. He called down for a car and driver to pick him up at eight fifteen. He thought of ordering a car to pick up Chantal Lamers, but he decided he didn't know her well enough.

He felt a little drunk. He decided to take hot and cold showers. He thought about sending out for some tanked oxygen or maybe some propranolol, because he had to be sharp for Lamers if he were going to maintain control of the press. He started for the stairway to go to the upstairs bedroom when the doorbell rang. He shook his head, took a deep breath and went to the door. He opened it on a large, bulky man wearing a Chesterfield overcoat, a blue woolen scarf and a bowler hat who was pointing a pistol at his stomach. The man jabbed the barrel of the pistol into him and backed him across the entrance hall, kicking the door shut behind him. "Don't talk," the beef-cheeked man said. "There is nothing to talk about. You are going out that window." He had a pronounced British accent.

Nick leaped to the wall at his right. He pressed the alarm button that the Secret Service had installed for

Tim within the columns of the decorative paneling. Rapid bells and heavy gongs began sounding simultaneously. A full-throated siren began to moan. The bulky man took his eyes off Nick in astonished panic, as though he could not shoot him because his orders had been to thrust him out the window. Nick threw a bronze bookend from a recessed shelf. It struck the man at the side of his bowler hat and sent him staggering backward into the wall. Nick lunged for the man's gun wrist, holding it with both hands, forcing it downward. The man dropped the gun and hit Nick heavily in the face with a long, left-side swing, then dropped him to his knees, screaming, by applying deep pressure with his powerful left hand to a nerve terminal in Nick's elbow. Nick let go the man's wrist. The man kicked him in the right temple, spun around, opened the front door through all the noises of the alarms, and sprinted down the hall. Nick lay there unconscious for fifty seconds or so until a swarm of house security officers, followed by Mr. Zendt, came pounding down the hall into the flat. The whole assault had taken less than two minutes.

They walked Nick around the room while he said to Mr. Zendt, "My father wouldn't want anyone to know about this, Mr. Zendt."

"Not a word, sir."

"Do we even have to tell the police about it?"

"He left a gun, Mr. Thirkield," the chief security officer said. "We have to report the whole thing."

"But the police are cooperative," Mr. Zendt said. "And you'd goddam well better make sure of that, Flicker."

"Mr. Thirkield is gunna have to talk to them," Flicker said.

"I have a meeting at eight thirty," Nick said. "If they can get here in time for me to make the meeting, I'll be happy to talk to them."

"Otherwise tomorrow?" Flicker asked wistfully.

"Sure. Why not?"

The telephone rang. "That would be my father," Nick said. "He has heard about the attack no doubt." He walked unsteadily away from them, then turned to ask if Mr. Zendt would have another bottle of wine sent up. If it affected the meeting with the *National Magazine,* too bad. He needed it.

He closed the door of the study and picked up the phone. "Yes, Pa?" he said automatically. It was Pa. It wasn't Yvette.

"Did they nail the son-of-a-bitch? He must be somewhere in the goddam building." Nick figured that the British hit man must have called Pa himself to make sure he was filled in.

"Not yet. He wore a derby hat and sounded like he came from London."

"London?"

"Carswell probably sent him."

"No jokes, kid. This is very bad. I don't give a goddam what you say, we are putting a security team on you."

"All right, Pa."

"How did you fight off a professional with a gun? I can't tell you what a terrific feeling it gives me that you actually saved yourself by fighting off an armed man."

"Thanks, Pa."

"I don't want the cops giving this to the papers. Leave it to me."

"Pa, something very big happened in Philadelphia this afternoon. I drove out with Commissioner Frey to Heller's house to look for the gun. We didn't find it, but we got voice prints William Casper and a woman who calls herself Mrs. Casper made in Heller's office. He was one of those nuts who records everything. But the thing is, all of a sudden there is a woman in this case. A woman in her middle thirties with silver hair, Mrs. Heller says, and Commissioner Frey is sending copies of the tapes to you so that Cerutti can analyze them."

"You are absolutely terrific, Nick."

Nick felt the glow beginning at his toes and starting upward. "It just happened to happen, Pa," he said.

"Well, I am telling you that you are solving this case." Pa hung up. When Nick returned to the big room only Mr. Zendt was waiting.

"Was it your father?" he asked nervously.

"Yes. He just wondered if we had caught the gunman, that's all."

"We'll have him within the hour, Mr. Thirkield."

"The *hour?*"

"We have only two floors of rooms and suites for transients. The rest are all leased apartments. In order to get up here the man would have had to check in to one of the transient accommodations or he would have had to ask at the desk for someone who had an apartment and who would clear him with the desk before he could get upstairs. The security officers are making the check on the transient rooms first. They think he returned to one of them to wait until a chance came to get out of the building. In the meantime, Mr. Thirkield, we have these photographs taken of people who checked into the hotel in the past forty-eight hours or who inquired at the desk to call on a tenant in the building."

"You photograph people who check in?"

"We photograph anybody who enters the lobby. If he goes to the desk we also record him to synchronize with the photos. Your father insists on this."

Nick pulled the seventh picture from the top of the stack. "That's the man," he said. Mr. Zendt turned the photo over. "He checked in at six forty-five yesterday evening. We had a reservation from a travel agency in Malta."

"Malta?"

"We'll get him. It is as hard to get out of this building as it is to get in."

The wine arrived. The city detectives came in right

behind it. Nick reidentified the photograph of the man, said he had British speech and probably a bruised head, while Mr. Zendt talked to the front desk and came up with information that the man had registered as Martin Keys and that he had a British passport. The police took the gun and left to work with the hotel security on a comb-out of the apartments in the building. A house physician appeared. He pressed a sedative on Nick, but Nick had a glass of Montrachet instead.

Chantal Lamers seemed to have lost the skinny, pale look he remembered her having. How could he ever have thought she was skinny, he asked himself. She wasn't merely "interesting looking" anymore either. She was an absolute gas to stare at. He began to have actively lewd thoughts as he watched her cross the restaurant to join him. *Join* him? More than lewd, he estimated—lewder. She was shucking off her coat as she hurried toward his table. As she leaned far forward to free her second arm, still walking, he had to grip his chair compulsively to keep himself from diving head first into her beckoning décolletage. He shook the china on the table as he arose, dismayed by an instant erection. He had lived alone too long, he decided. He dropped a napkin in front of himself in a gesture of diffidence, not to say personal daintiness—as a matador might work with a cape—but not in time. Miss Lamers was a fly-watcher. Most women were fly-watchers, but Miss Lamers was a fly-starer. She had seen it, hefted it mentally, and the experience allowed her to feel all the happier about everything.

You are involved in multiple grisly murders, he told himself. It is your responsibility to convince this woman that the essence of American history is within the grasp of her journalism, so that she will lead the way to the topmost reaches of the management of her magazine and possibly bring to justice a man who has killed more people than Landru, and yet he was peeking down the front of her dress and manufacturing erections.

She wore a tiny nile-green patch where the unsightly bandage had been. She wore matching eye makeup, and that startled him, because he knew that women who wear eye makeup and ankle bracelets were usually just as unaccountably lewd as he was. He had thought of her as being far more serious than that. He wanted to notice whether her dress gave her any of the thirty-one hundred extras that the work of Madame Grès conferred on Yvette Malone, but he could not bear to take his eyes away from that neckline.

He was appalled to realize that the urgency of being with Yvette Malone was disappearing from his mind with the speed of the evanescence of the Cheshire cat. What disturbed his deepest sense of self, his image of what he was and had always been to himself, however, was that seventy minutes after a man with a gun had been determined to throw him out of a skyscraper window, he could pursue such lascivious thoughts, pursue them as a groupie pursues an employed rock singer. Then he knew he should not have thought of the man with the gun. It was spoiling everything. Instantly he lost the erection. He felt like a living Indian rope trick.

"Are you all right, Mr. Thirkield?"

"Oh, yes. Thank you. I did feel a little odd for a moment. Perhaps I stood up too quickly."

"Your face seems a little swollen too," she said.

"I ran into a door."

"How marvelous that you were able to come to New York so soon." Her Muskogee accent was fruity and gorgeous. She talked like a field hand in *Gone with the Wind,* which he had seen in Bhutan.

"Something to drink?" he murmured.

"A Gibson, please."

"Two Gibsons," Nick told the table captain, even though he deplored gin. People who drank gin simply walked differently. The captain departed on the run, because Mr. Thirkield's father owned the restaurant.

They dined on fillets of brill poached and glazed in Mornay sauce; coq au vin cooked in La Gaffelière '61. They finished a vanilla soufflé with pieces of biscuit soaked in kirsch and anisette. The food was so good they talked less than they thought they would. The wine was so good that they talked more than Miss Lamers thought she should. Nick had a marvelous time: the bodice, that slack red cushion of a mouth, the food and her anecdotes—about actors, jockeys and politicians (including several racy ones about the late President Kegan)—all built his euphoria. "You must know two thousand people more than I'll ever know," Nick said.

"I never *met* those people," Miss Lamers murmured. "It's just that I usually take my lunch to the office and eat it in our file room, which has all kinds of stuff we can't print about people like that."

"I'd sure like to read the file on Tim Kegan," Nick said.

"Are you a Kegan admirer?"

"He was my half brother."

Miss Lamers dropped a spoon. "Oh, dear God," she said, "and there I was ruffling my mouth with those awful stories about him." She blushed like a peony. "I am just terribly embarrassed."

"Oh, please! No. He would have loved those stories—that is, those particular stories. Anyway, Tim is why we're having dinner—in a way. I mean, when you hear what it is, you'll know the story is important. It is so important that before I start I'll have to ask you to keep total silence on it—that is, until my father and I say you can print it."

"Your father?"

"Yes. Is that okay?"

"I—well, I guess so."

"The story concerns the fact that I talked with the man who fired the second rifle at my brother's assas-

sination. In a way, considering the findings of the Pickering Commission, you could call it the third rifle.
That's enough to start with, isn't it?"

"My God, yes."

"I'd like to talk to your editor. If we can reach a
written understanding that the story is mine, that it be-
longs only to me under the protection of common-law
copyright, I will tell him everything I have found out
about my brother's murder."

"This is simply fantastic, Mr. Thirkield." Her large
eyes got larger. He noticed that they were violet. He
had read that actresses were supposed to have violet
eyes, but this was too much.

"There is also a woman's angle. I mean, there is a
woman involved with the assassination team."

She suddenly got pale with excitement. "I'll call my
editor right now," she said. She walked out of the dining room rapidly.

The hire car drove them to the *National Magazine*
building. She held his hand tensely in the car all the
way across town. She smelled very good. They walked
hurriedly across the plaza to the building's night entrance. Miss Lamers signed them in. They rode up to
the main editorial floor. It was ten fifty-two, the recep-
tion-area clock said.

The office of the managing editor, Harry Greenwood, was totally bare and functional, with a desk, two
chairs, a picture of the founder on the wall and sealed
windows. Greenwood was a tall, almost languid man,
younger than Nick, with an elaborate Harvard Yard
accent. His working uniform was less than severe, because, he explained, he had been at home across town
when Miss Lamers had telephoned. He had just gotten
there before them. The stitching around his lapels
seemed tattooed on. Nick feared to look down in case
he might find two-toned shoes. Before he shook hands
with Nick, Greenwood paused to rinse his hands with

Guerlain's cologne from a large cut-glass bottle.

"Please sit down," he said. It was an unctuous voice. "Miss Lamers told me what you have in mind, Mr. Thirkield, and I am greatly excited. I took the liberty of sending down for some photographs of you, just to be sure we were talking to the right man—so that is quite satisfactory. How does this letter agreement look to you? Are you warm enough? Would you like a drink?" He slid the magazine's letterhead across the bare desk. Nick studied it. He passed it back and nodded. Greenwood signed both copies. Miss Lamers signed as witness. Nick folded his copy and slid it into his inside pocket. "We have evidence to prove," he said, "that the Pickering Report is all wet."

"Prove?" Greenwood said.

"We think we have enough evidence to go to the President and ask that the investigation be reopened." It occurred to Nick vaguely that he was overreacting to his distaste for Greenwood by being maybe a little too sweeping in his statements.

"Is there any way we can help you?"

"That's why I'm here, actually. We've come to an area where we need help."

"What's the area?"

"Organized crime. For starters, I'd like to see everything you have on Joe Diamond."

"Well, sure. We're loaded on Diamond. If we aren't, we should be."

"I have to know where he came from—which geographical area of national crime. We think someone who knew him from the old days came to him in Philadelphia with what they call the 'contract' to have my brother killed. We think that if we can find out who dug up Diamond for the organizer of the assassination, we'll be able to buy from them—in one way or another—the names of the people who came to them."

"Very logical," Greenwood said.

"My God, yes," Miss Lamers chimed.

"Get the Diamond files, please, Miss Lamers," Greenwood directed. She left the room with the speed of a bird.

"I was a great admirer of your brother," Greenwood said nasally.

"Everyone was," Nick said.

"What was he really like?" Greenwood asked after a few minutes of silence.

"He had wit and wisdom," Nick said. Miss Lamers returned with a stack of three thick file folders which she handed to Greenwood.

"Newspaper clips," Greenwood said and flopped the folder on the desk. "Post-arrest stuff." He dropped the second file. "Personal. This is the one. Read through it. Take your time. We'll go out and see if we can find some coffee." He handed the file to Nick. Greenwood and Miss Lamers left the room.

Nick went through it slowly. Joe Diamond had started as a hanger-on with the Cleveland Syndicate. The Syndicate, which had begun in the pre-World War I period, had originally been partly the Mayfield Road mob (Sicilian) and partly the Purple Gang of Detroit (Jewish). These two Cleveland elements combined with an Irish group in 1913 when a brawling circulation war began between two Cleveland newspapers, the *News* and the *Plain Dealer*. The Mayfield Road mob worked for the *News*. It kept them in training for the big upcoming opportunities of Prohibition. The gang congregated in the Woodlands section of Cleveland, where 213 murders were committed between 1918 and 1930, and where 98 houses of prostitution flourished. Yussel Schell, a/k/a Joe Diamond, was a Woodlands boy born in 1910, just too late to cash in on the big Prohibition action but ready to learn his trade in the Depression years when he worked for the Syndicate as a bouncer in gambling joints and doing collection work on the Ohio-Kentucky border. According to the file, at about the time World War II ended he went back to

work for Samuel "Gameboy" Baker, whom he'd
worked for in the Syndicate, this time as assistant muscle (and the boss's gunsel, which doesn't mean what it
sounds like) at the Lookout House near Covington,
Kentucky, and, in the winter season, at the Island Club
in Miami Beach.

Gameboy Baker, until Frank Heller came along, was
Diamond's lifetime idol. He tried to model everything
he did on Gameboy's example in every way. Gameboy
taught him that cops were terrific people—strong, action men, and if you were always on the right side of
the cops they could do plenty for you. He also took
pains to explain that you should never admit to making
more than 35 percent of what you were actually making if you were working with cops, because they always
tried to take as much as they could get. Joe took Gameboy literally. He came. To love cops. Gameboy said
that about Joe and always got a laugh. It is hard to say
what made Joe Diamond so crazy about Gameboy
Baker. Gameboy was a schmuck.

The four Cleveland fellows who owned the Syndicate, with an outstanding assist from two Sicilians,
were Jews operating in Cleveland, Canada, Kentucky-
Ohio, Florida and Arizona. Nobody else in the business operated with a spread like that. They were
pumping out real money in Arizona when everybody
was looking at Vegas—not that they have stopped. Joe
Diamond left the Syndicate in Tucson to join Lansky's
operation in Cuba, which kept him in Cuba straight
through the war, because he made some solid political
contacts there who put him into the narcotics industry.
Sometime in the early fifties Diamond came up with a
bundle and opened a restaurant and a bar in Philadelphia, influenced by the glamour of Gameboy Baker's
development of the famous Odeon Grill in Vincent
Street in Cleveland, which was, and still is, *the* place to
eat.

When Greenwood and Miss Lamers came back Nick

said, "Well, it's a line, I guess. He started in Cleveland, so I should start there too."

"Let me talk to our people in the morning," Greenwood said. "We have the best people in the country on organized crime."

"Can I call you about eleven?" Miss Lamers asked Nick demurely.

"We can pinpoint this thing," Greenwood said. "This is an area I know we can deliver on." Greenwood and Nick shook hands good night. Miss Lamers and Nick left the building together, he mumbling that he would take her home. She protested that she could easily get a taxi. "While I have a car and a driver?" he said. "Don't be silly."

She gave the driver an address on East Thirty-first Street. "Please call me Chantal," she said.

"Why?"

"It's my name!"

"Oh. I see. How pretty. Means pertaining to song, doesn't it?"

"Just as Nicholas pertains to Santa Claus, doesn't it? My mother was French, and that's what she called me."

"My mother was from Utica, New York."

As the car rolled down Park Avenue she said, "I've never been on a story as big as this. This story has become the most romantic thing that could happen to me."

"You must have been about fourteen when they killed Tim."

"Ho-ho."

"Well, I hope you get a raise and a chair of journalism at Harvard out of it. You've been very helpful to my father and me."

"It's very easy to be helpful to you." She stared at him wide-eyed. He had a very clear feeling that things were going to happen if she played her cards right.

"I'm very glad to hear that," he said huskily, then he

cleared his throat involuntarily and the sexy effect was gone. "I hope we'll be working very closely together."

"You're so tan," she murmured. "God, it's gorgeous."

"It's really occupational."

"I see you on the bridge of a ship scanning the horizon through narrowed eyes, seeking something, perhaps someone who you and you alone know is waiting for you over the edge of the world." She blinked. "I certainly hope we will be working closely together."

"There will be a lot of traveling on this story."

"And a lot of danger?"

"Perhaps. But not for you."

"I can't get over how—out of all the people in the world—we came together for this. Where were you a week ago today?"

"Brisbane. Australia."

"Brisbane! The Coral Sea. Stone fish. Captain Cook sweeping north through that treacherous channel."

"I'm really not up on the area."

"You crossed the world from the Coral Sea to find me in Oklahoma. *If* —and I accent and emphasize that 'if'—those two men had not forced me off the road—"

"I hope they got those guys."

"But we were meant to be. Weren't we meant to be, Nick?"

"I'd say definitely."

She sighed like a cello. Nick had to take his hat off and place it over his erection this time. It was all beginning to make him nervous. He had just proposed marriage to an entirely different woman, and he had been all torn up when she turned him down. What had happened to that emotion? He was being inconsistent. He was responding disloyally. It was the sort of thing that Tim might have done.

"Uh—what kind of a fellow is Greenwood?"

"Who?"

"Your editor."

"Oh, fine. Harry is fine."

"I suppose it's a pretty close relationship—writer and editor."

"On some things, yes."

The car stopped at Chantal's apartment house. They sat there for a few seconds in a mock absent, undecided sort of way. Nick discovered he was holding her hand.

"Won't you come up for a drink?" Chantal said.

"Thank you. I'd like a drink very much."

They got out of the car with elaborate movements. They walked together to the entrance of the towering apartment building, then Nick stopped and turned. "I'll have to tell the driver how long he'll have to wait," he said. Chantal caught his sleeve calmly and unnoticeably. "Why don't you just send him home?" she murmured, eyes appropriately cast down. Nick cleared his throat again and ran lightly back to the car. "I'll call the garage if I need a car," he told the driver. " 'Night, now."

Chantal's apartment was attractive, unexpectedly not like her at all, done in chrome-and-glass Italian modern—low, blocky, impossible furniture, with a lot of mauve and light green everywhere, and a blanketing smell of pot hanging over all. Before Chantal disappeared she put a large goblet of Yugoslavian red wine into his hand. He decided to concentrate on his own disapproval of Tim and the way he had leaped from woman to woman to woman. He had spent six weeks at the hospital under the care of Keith Lee complaining bitterly about all the ass Tim had managed to get, and when he had exhausted himself on the subject, naming the names of women who were absolute pillars of the national establishment, Keith had "explained" Tim's commitment to exchanging old bodies for new. Nick reasoned that the worst thing that could happen to him, especially after a year of such intensive psychotherapy, would be if he allowed himself to conduct his life as Tim had done. Not that he could deny himself sex totally. That would be carrying a silly compulsion ridiculously far.

He had never really discovered if he was like Tim. He was here, in this woman's drug-fumed apartment. He hardly knew her, but just the same, in about fifteen minutes he was going to be lying absolutely naked on a bed beside her. If he loved Yvette, could he have put himself in such a spot? Did he and Tim have so much in common as half brothers that he really had no control over his disloyalty to the woman he loved? At least Tim hadn't been disloyal. After his brief marriage he had never committed himself to any woman. Keith Lee had said, "As in the song, Tim was a motherless child. The operative word for Tim's endless excursions into endless vaginas—that long tunnel in which there is no light—is 'seeking.' He was endlessly searching for Mama. Of course he couldn't find her, but he peered closely into almost every woman he met. Because it is a tremendous distinction, a tremendous thing to have over other women, to screw the President of the United States, Tim got to do even more searching than other men with his problem. No matter how much they appeared to look like his dear mama's photograph, his search was still never satisfied. When a search is never satisfied, it must continue, because the point of the search is that it fail. Of course if he found a mama, sex with her would be forbidden anyway, and that is the point of the whole search and what makes it endless."

Nick was about to attempt to put the parallel to himself and get to the true bottom of where, really and exactly, he stood with Yvette and she with him, when Chantal came back into the room wearing the goddamndest getup he had ever seen, making self-analysis impossible. She was wearing a sensible sweater and skirt. She had gone inside and had changed into a sensible sweater and skirt and a pair of sheep's-wool-lined bedroom slippers. It was a sensible sweater, because the way her chest bobbled around in there he knew it was all alone. The way the slippers called attention to her improbably perfect bare legs made it better than even money that she had nothing on under the skirt. She was extending a box half filled with funny cigarettes. "Want to light up?" she asked and sat down on the sofa beside him. Music was playing from somewhere in a distant room, but not too distant.

"Beautiful music," he said, exhaling a pound and a half of smoke.

"It's an open-end machine."

"Very sexy."

"It can play for seven hours."

He pulled her. He pushed his fingers along the soft skin of her sides under her sweater to her breasts. She had nipples like thumbs, and her breath had begun to fall out of her like a marathon runner's. He distinctly heard her say, "I think I'm falling in love with you." He kissed her, a kiss for its own time, unending. By manipulating a simple zipper he discovered that it was quite true that she had nothing on under her skirt. He decided that Tim had been utterly right.

They outlasted the open-end machine by thirty-two minutes.

When he awoke he was as naked as a nixon. He felt wonderful. It was eight thirty-eight on a digital clock on a widely sunny morning. He yodeled eight bars from "Der Bürgenstock Ewig." It brought Chantal running into the room. She had nothing on either. It looked great.

"What's the matter?" she said with alarm.

"Come here."

"I can't."

"Why not?"

"I'm making breakfast."

"But the spatter. You must be delicious. Come here."

"I have to get to work."

"You are the most marvelously depraved woman I have ever known, and you are never going to leave this place again. Neither am I."

"Oh—honey—"

She approached near enough to be pulled down. "I'll show you how to liberate a woman," he said. "I have never felt more like liberating a woman in my life."

The garage sent a car. Nick dropped Chantal off at the *National Magazine* building. She told him she would call him at the Walpole as soon as Harry Greenwood established a line to the Syndicate people in Cleveland. Nick had gotten more euphoric with each block they rode uptown. "I don't think I've ever awakened on any day of my life as happy as I felt this morning," was one of the things he said.

"It was the pot." Chantal could have had postcoital depression. She was wearing the same clothes she had worn the night before.

"I have to tell you something."

"No, please, Nick. Please don't tell me anything. I mean not anything that would naturally follow a sentence like that at a time like this."

"Why not?"

"Because it will inevitably be about your past, and just for this morning I'd like it a lot better if I could tell myself that both of us had been reborn."

"Why—that's beautiful, Chantal."

She patted his hand.

"But you sound sad," he said.

"Do I? Well, the time to exult is when there is an absence of pain. I exulted all night, Nick darling. Now—well, it's back to the same old chains."

"Not necessarily."

She smiled at him.

As he rode uptown alone he was happy that he hadn't said any more. First things first. He had to establish where Yvette stood before he went forward with a new claim. Anyway, what the hell. Chantal had been marvelous—but Yvette was Yvette. Even if she wouldn't marry him. She had it, whatever it was that held his total attention, night and day. Chantal cared.

He could feel that. He could feel that as if he were a living Ouija board. Maybe a little part of it was caring about his money. Maybe a bigger part of it was caring about Tim and what he had overachieved. But that could be the entire trouble with Yvette. She had too much money. It was a mistake to allow women to get money. It changed everything. Who would make the millions and millions of beds? Who would listen to the tens of millions of children? Chantal Lamers needed him, cared for him, and after a few more nights like last night—if he could stay in the satyric condition he was in—she could learn to adore him. Where had she learned all she knew! Poppaea Sabina, a titleholder, was a Salvation Army lassie compared with Chantal in the field of sexual erudition. But, still, there was something absolutely wild-making when a woman refused to marry a man.

As he walked across the lobby of the Walpole he had to admit that when Pa bought anything he really maintained it well. This was the classiest hotel in New York, and the food in one of Pa's restaurants last night had been up to the best of first-class food he had ever had anywhere—beyond Si's chili and noodles. Tack another fifty years on Pa's life and the whole country would be looking great, because Pa would own it all.

There were two messages at the front desk. It was nine forty in the morning. Both messages were from Yvette. Well! So she wanted to make it all up, did she? She had probably thought everything over and now wanted to marry him. If so, what stand should he take? He felt the grab of guilt. He stared at his own face in the elevator mirror all the way up to the tower. He telephoned her before he took off his coat and hat, but she wasn't there. Where could she be? Why wasn't she home at such an hour of the morning? Could she have been out doing what he had been doing while he was in the same city with her? He loved her. She understood things about him that no one else understood. She had never laughed at his long woolen underwear (the most sensible winter garment a man could wear) the way Chantal had laughed at it this morning. Certainly a girl as honest as Yvette wouldn't play games by calling him, then letting the phone ring and pretending not to be there when he called back?

He went into the kitchen to get a glass of milk and

found Pa, in a beautifully tailored green-and-white-checked jacket, sitting at a table by the window eating the second half of a grapefruit.

"What the hell were you doing at the *National Magazine?*" Pa asked.

"How did you know I was at the *National Magazine?*"

"A hoodlum tried to put a gun on you and throw you out the window last night. Do you think I'm going to let you walk around alone from now on?"

Nick blushed with enormous gratification. As he had observed himself, Pa maintained his properties. "Thanks, Pa."

"Who did you see?"

"The editor."

"Harry Greenwood?"

"Yes."

"How come you know him?"

"I met a woman in Oklahoma who works there. I called her and she introduced me to Greenwood."

"Where?"

"At his office."

"What was the woman's name?"

"Chantal Lamers."

"I never heard of her. Did you screw her last night?"

Nick glared at him.

"I forgot. You're the Boy Scout in the family. Tim always shared information on his broads."

"I thought we had reached a general understanding that I'm not Tim."

"I want to know what you told the magazine."

"Pa, listen—"

"You did it. You told them." Pa resumed eating. He stared downward at the traffic pattern. He looked murderous. Nick took the letter agreement out of his pocket and put it down on the table beside his father. Pa read it without touching it. Then he said, "You aren't as dumb as I thought. This is something, anyway. Leave it with me." He wheeled around in the chair. "Okay. What is it all about?"

"It's open and shut," Nick said. "We have to find out where Diamond came from so we can find the people who agreed to find a murderer for the men who decided to kill Tim. The only way a civilian can get to the top of organized crime is through the press. So I went to the *National Magazine.*"

"I see."

"If you know a better way, let's do it."

"It depends on who you talk to, Nick," Pa said. "Do you really think a bunch of entertainers at a magazine are going to know who to talk to?"

"Pa, they have people who do nothing else but work with organized crime!"

"You could have asked me."

"To find one top gangster out of thousands?"

"You didn't ask me. But let it lay. What did the magazine people do for you?"

"They expect to have the name of a contact before noon today."

"Okay. It's a lot of shit, but as soon as they tell you, I expect you to tell me."

"Did you come all the way to New York for that?"

"I go into the hospital in an hour."

"Hospital?" Nick was bewildered. Pa had seldom looked this well.

"The quarterly checkup. Three days every three months. That's how I made it to seventy-four. Maybe you'd better stay right here until I get out."

"I can take care of myself."

"The name of the killer who went after you last night is Martin Keys. He got out of the hotel with the late-afternoon shift of cooks. Now listen to this. After he got out of the building, all in the clear, he came back to his room just to prove he had never been involved. He walked in the front door, sauntered across the lobby and asked for his key. Then he went to his room. Zendt sent for the cops. Now—ready? Our camera record shows that *this* Mr. Martin Keys is not the Mr. Keys who had registered. However, Nick, he was carrying the first Mr. Keys's passport, but with his own—a different—picture in it. The first Mr. Keys, as you know, was dark and bulky. The second Mr. Keys is shortish, with ginger hair and a ginger moustache. But the little bastard didn't know about the concealed cameras, so the cops are working him over right now. I called Ben Kiely, the chief inspector for the East Side, and I told him to beat the living shit out of him."

"How do people get into businesses like that?" Nick asked earnestly.

"Laziness," Pa said. "Lissen, Nick, you better know, I have an invisible team all over you around the clock wherever you go, you understand?"

"Do you own the agency, Pa?"

"In my kind of businesses you've got to own a national detective agency. I pay it in, take that as a tax deduction, then get it back as profits. And I get top security at wholesale or better."

"What hospital will you be in?"

"The Anglican Memorial."

"Do you own the hospital, Pa?"

"Use your head, kid. There is no business today that can compete with owning a hospital." He ticked the points off on his long fingers. "No credit for the customers, and they pay in advance or out on their ass. Next, supply and demand is constant. Third, a unique product—pain—right? A hospital is a hotel for pain, but what hotel gets those prices? Christ, the laundry alone throws off enough to pay the orderlies and the lab. And you should see the net figures on what one of those labs makes. I own twenty-seven hospitals in nineteen cities, kid, and I'd like to have fifty more." Pa patted Nick on the shoulder as he went past. He turned at the door.

"My advice to you, Nick, is own whatever you use—forget railroads and, naturally, the postal service, because you wouldn't use them. Break everything down into food, shelter, clothing, diversion and dying—then own everything. I was luckier than you, because I bought everything in the Depression when you could get useful industries for a nickel on the dollar. I live absolutely free now. I own farms, cattle, freezing firms, airlines, ferry services, the best restaurants, French vineyards, California vineyards, Scotch distilleries, hotels, resorts, apartment houses, housing developments, shopping centers, three great tailors, sixty-two whorehouses where they're legal, two cable-TV companies, a set of satellites and a national undertaking system—and other useful things, like pharmaceutical houses, wholesale loan-sharking and twenty-seven hospitals. And what have you got? A lousy twenty-million-dollar oil company, which, like all other oil companies any day now, is going to run out of oil or be taxed out of business or be expropriated by the locals." He left the kitchen, with Nick staring blankly after him. Nick heard the front door slam.

He found a box of matches in a kitchen drawer. The telephone rang. He ran to Tim's study for maximum comfort. It was Yvette.

"Where were you?" he wailed.

"At Gristede's. Why?"

"Oh."

"The last time I called you," Yvette said sweetly, "it was one thirty in the morning, but still I expect you noticed how I did not greet you with a 'Where were you?' "

"I've gotten very, very involved in this thing."

"I bet."

"I don't want even to talk about it. I'm scared witless that you could get mixed up in it—the way other people have."

"Okay, honey."

"It's wonderful just to talk to you."

"I used to think I was in love with you, but now—"

"What?" He was terror-stricken. He had about as large a reserve of cool as a Pittsburgh steel smelter at full production.

"—that I've known you for three whole years I know I'm in love with you."

He groaned.

"Why the groan?"

"It was a groan of ecstasy. I love you, Yvette. I have loved you for three years, but more every day, more wherever I was and you weren't there, more every month and every year. I am simply crazy about you, Yvette." Bye-bye, Chantal, he thought. Quoth the Thirkield, never more.

"I am very happy. Right now."

"Then we can get married?"

"Shall we have dinner tonight?"

"I'm waiting for a call about Tim. They are trying to set up an appointment. I may have to fly to Cleveland."

"Can you call me by six? I'll be back here at three. I'm having lunch out, then I'll come right back here."

"Absolutely."

Chantal Lamers called from the reception desk downstairs at eleven fifty. She was taken up to Nick at the tower. She was knocked out to be there. "Is this where he lived?"

"Yes. This is it," Nick said.

"Oh, it's beautiful! I can just feel him everywhere in the atmosphere of this wonderful place."

"My father put little bronze tabs on the chairs in there—if you'd like to see those."

"I would. Oh, I would!"

He took her to the chairs. She read the identical inscription on each: PRESIDENT TIMOTHY KEGAN SAT HERE 1955-1960. "My God," Chantal said. "I cannot tell you what a wonderful feeling this gives me."

"He used that john," Nick said, gesturing vaguely.

Chantal ran into the loo and shut the door. He went out to the living room again to wait for her. When she joined him, after what he thought was an inconsiderable length of time, she asked if there was some souvenir she might take with her.

"How about an ashtray?" he asked.

"Oh, my God, that would be heaven, darling. But would it be really his? Would he have tapped one of his famous cigars on it?"

"I'll get you the one from his bedside," Nick said. "He not only tapped his famous cigar on that but frequently kept his vitamin C pills on it."

"Oh, Nick, dearest."

After she had stowed a hotel ashtray in her purse she told him that ever since the killing of Willie Arnold, Evander Milship, the magazine's organized-crime person, had had as his hobby the background and career of Joe Diamond. "He was able to actually pinpoint the man in Cleveland to whom the someone you are searching for had gone to find a man in Philadelphia who would undertake the job. The man is now a *very,* very highly placed member of the Syndicate. Evander says he was the protégé of a founder-member named Moey Dalitz or Davis. This man's name is Irving Mentor. He was the immediate superior of Diamond's lover, a man named Gameboy Baker. Irving Mentor is the man, Evander said this morning, who had smoothed everything out with the Sicilians so that Diamond could come back from Cuba after the war."

"That's great," Nick said. "But can your man set a meeting for me with Mentor?"

"He's already set a meeting. Harry Greenwood has had Evander working on this all night."

"Where?"

"Mentor will be sitting alone in the back of an El Dorado Cadillac in Vincent Street, in Cleveland, directly across from the Odeon Grill. Now, you'll have to remember certain things. You must get into the car

from the traffic side. Get into the back, beside Mentor.
You then say your name and tell him you are from
Monroe. Eleven tonight."

"Monroe, Alabama, or Monroe, Mississippi?"

"No. Monroe is some man's name. Just Monroe."

"Okay. It's like some kid's game."

"It's for identification. Anyway, it's what he told
Evander you have to do. Mentor knows what you
want, but he won't cooperate for less than fifteen thousand dollars. But we'll pay it."

"No, no. I'll pay it."

"No—really. We insist."

"No. It gives the magazine too much of a lock on
the story," Nick said. "It's too early to put yourselves
in a proprietary position, because it isn't your story
yet."

"But we are vouching for the quality of Mentor's information. You would be paying out fifteen thousand
only on our say-so."

"I knew I'd have to pay somebody something.
What's the difference? This way I'll be paying with
confidence."

Chantal sighed. "All right, then. I hope this doesn't
get Harry Greenwood angry."

"If it does, you tell me."

"Thanks. The next thing is—I've been assigned to
the story and to you. We'll be traveling together."

"No."

Chantal was shocked and hurt. "No?"

"Listen, Chantal. A lot of people have died because
they got too close to this story. Anyway, Mentor
wouldn't talk if you got into the car, because you'd be
what they call in his business a corroborating witness.
You stay here for this one, and you can interview me
with a tape machine when I get back."

"Suppose you don't get back? What happens to the
story then?" Her voice was coldly professional. "You
are closer to all the facts than anyone alive. If anybody
is killed, your name should be at the top of the list."

"When you come right down to it," Nick said, "I'm the only one they won't kill—not yet anyhow."

"Why not?"

"Because I have passed everything I know—and all the evidence I have piled up—along to my father. If I got killed that would be the capper. The President would be absolutely forced to reopen the case, my father would set up such a hue and cry."

"Then, in good faith, I think we should spend the afternoon right here, and you should spill everything you know about the case, down to the smallest detail, into a tape recorder so the magazine will have the story when, as, and *if* anything happens to you."

"That wasn't the deal I made," Nick said. "First, the magazine helps me to run down the people who located Diamond for the killers. When that is all sorted out, then we sit down and work out the whole story."

She put her arms around his neck and kissed his throat softly. "Don't do any part of it," she said. "Don't go to Cleveland, and to hell with the story. Your brother is dead and nothing can bring him back. I couldn't stand it if anything happened to you. God, you could be tortured if they think they have to find out all you know." Dropping her arms, she clung to his crotch with fear and devotion. He laid her on the floor as if she were a department-store dummy. Then he laid her—on the floor.

Pa's gargantuan hospital, whose lab threw off such great figures, towered considerably higher along the East River, north of the Queensborough Bridge, than the white cliffs of Dover. Pa had settled down in a three-room suite, the equivalent of the owner's cabin on an ocean liner but more luxurious. He had a duplicate of his White House switchboard, with its eighteen direct lines, installed beside his bed. There was no smell of iodoform in Pa's suite. There was a gentling scent of Jolie Madame which Pa sprayed on his two nurses three times a day. For decoration, the Metropolitan had sent four important pieces—two paintings and two sculptures. There was a magnificent vaseful of two dozen long-stemmed roses from the directors of the hospital. But most decorative of all were the two nurses, Eve and Rose, beautiful young women with brave, starched white caps and great big knockers. One of them was reading to Pa from *Barron's Weekly,* the other was feeding him grapes, when Nick arrived. Pa seemed so content that Nick could hear the regret in his voice when he asked Eve and Rose to leave him with his son.

"How'd you like to climb one of those, kid?" he asked when they left.

Nick shrugged.

"How did the magazine meeting go?"

"I have a meeting in Cleveland at eleven tonight with a man named Irving Mentor who is at the top of the Syndicate."

"Never heard of him."

"Why should you?"

"Nick, when I say 'even you,' I am reaching away out to the edge of the world, right? But even you may have heard of Frank Mayo. Did you ever hear of him, Nick?"

"Certainly. Frank Mayo, the grand vizier of the underworld."

"Do you know of a bigger hood?"

"I don't know any others."

"Frank Mayo will be here in about ten minutes. We'll ask him about Irving Mentor."

"Gee, Pa, how come?"

"Because I've been in the whiskey business and a few other businesses since the twenties. Frank was my partner in a lot of things. Punks who were street-corner hustlers when I was a big man with these guys are now big bosses. That's the 'Gee, Pa, how come.'"

"Who don't you know?" Nick asked with a sudden flash of hatred.

"Well, I don't know you, kid, but it doesn't throw me, because you don't either."

"If the *National Magazine* says Mentor is a big man, then he has to be a big man in crime," Nick said.

"Would you ask Frank Mayo to recommend a newsstand? It's the same thing. Business is business. Frank knows. Those punks wouldn't know a Syndicate executive from Mary Miles Minter."

Eve popped her head into the room. "Mr. Mayo is here, Mr. Kegan," she said gaily.

"Send him in," Pa said.

Salvatore Verdigerri, a/k/a Frank Mayo, a/k/a Frank Brown, was a flawlessly dressed man in elegant charcoal-gray flannel, with a carefully knotted black knitted Mafia tie and immaculate fingernails *without* polish. He sounded perpetually hoarse, as if he spent the mornings bawling out police captains at the top of his voice. He had quiet assurance and the gift of geniality. He could have been about five years younger than Pa, Nick thought. Of the two men Nick would have found it far easier to believe that Pa was the criminal, Frank Mayo the tycoon.

Pa became manically hospitable. He directed Mayo to a wicker chair. He introduced Nick. He asked how Mr. Mayo had liked the two nurses, Eve and Rose. Then he said, "Frank, wait'll you hear this. I got an actual salame de felino and a culatello di Zibello from Parma, direct from Parma, and fifteen pounds of grana from Montecchio—absolutely gorronteed straveccione—just like the old days."

"How? How did you get it?" Mayo asked with amazement.

"Interest is the key to life," Pa said. "I sent a man over in my own plane with a blank check and he came back with it. But that ain't all, Frank. I got a whole case of Brunello de Montalccino 1945. Right here."

"Holy Jesus."

Eve and Rose came trooping in with tea carts loaded with slices of salame and culatello, oblong hunks of parmigiano cheese, glasses and three opened bottles of red wine.

"Holy Jesus," Mr. Mayo said again. "Don't tell anybody I'm so crazy about this kind of food, because I'm supposed to be a Sicilian." His voice was really so coarsely hoarse that he might have had a touch of syphilis of the larynx. He took a bite of the cheese very daintily, staring at Pa while he chewed it. "That has got to be eight, ten years old," he said. "I don't know where you can get eight-year-old parmigiano even in Parma, fahcrissakes."

"I'm going to send you a wheel of it," Pa said. The nurses poured the wine and the men sipped it reverently. "Eat!" Mr. Mayo said to Nick. "Jesus, just try that culatello."

Nick dug in.

"That's some glassa wine—right, Mr. Thirkield?" Mr. Mayo said to Nick.

"I'll accept a case," Nick said, and that broke Mr.

Mayo up. When he recovered he said, "What's on your mind, Mr. Kegan?"

"Frank, I am going to tell you something that I will not tell to anybody else—and you know what a tight trap I have."

"Go ahead, Mr. Kegan."

"Nick and I are on the trail of the bastards who killed my boy, Tim."

"Son-of-a-*bitch!*"

"Okay. Frank, did you ever hear of a pezzo da novanta in the Syndicate named Irving Mentor?"

"Mentor?"

"M-e-n-t-o-r. Irving."

"No. Never. A pezzo da novanta? Never. And I am two hunnert percent sure." He glared at Nick to defy him.

"Frank, this is very close to me."

"Look, Mr. Kegan—there could be like a coffee-runner who works for some paperhanger who has a son who is like maybe a barber who cuts hair for Syndicate fellas, but, believe me, there is no pezzo da novanta name of Irving Mentor—believe me, I am telling you."

"This is the straight story, Frank. Somebody in Cleveland gave the contract to Joe Diamond to hit my son Tim—your President."

Nick blinked.

Mayo and Pa stared at each other. Mr. Mayo poured another glass of wine. Looking at the glass, he sighed very lightly before he spoke again. "You always hear about these things too late. I knew about it right after. But it wasn't a business thing. They did it on their own."

"Frank—I'm with *you*," Pa said. "But now my son needs to talk to the man who gave Joe Diamond the contract, because he will know who paid the bills."

"Mr. Mayo," Nick said, "if you are talking to Cleveland, maybe you could ask who this Irving Mentor is."

"Who told you about him?"

"The *National Magazine*."

"Aa! They think Big Jim Colisimo is still operating."

"Nick is supposed to meet this Irving Mentor at eleven tonight," Pa said.

"Well, that's a long trip for nothing, Mr. Thirkield," Mayo said. "Why don't you let us cover it for you?"

"We have a lot of questions we want to ask him," Pa said smoothly. "But thanks, Frank, just the same."

Mayo stood up, brushing his fingers lightly. "I'll call you tumorra," he said hoarsely. He shook hands with both of them.

"I'll send the rest of the case of wine with the wheel," Pa said.

"You're gunna make me a hero in my house," Mayo said. "I'll call you as soon as I know something. Okay?"

When Mayo was gone Nick sipped the unctuous red wine and nibbled on the heavenly cheese.

"We know Mentor is nothing," Pa said, "but that doesn't make it a wild-goose chase. That's why you have to go."

"I have to go just to have it on the *National Magazine*," Nick said. He felt sad because a chance at the big time had just eluded Chantal. She had enough stardust in her eyes to bread a veal cutlet.

"You better get moving," Pa said.

When Nick called Yvette from the airport it was six twenty and he got her answering service. He left a message that he had been called to Cleveland and that he would call her from there. He got to downtown Cleveland at ten twenty. He called her again from a telephone booth at the Statler, but he got the answering service again, which reported that Mrs. Malone hadn't yet called in that night. Nick told them he was calling from Cleveland, that he would try again in the morning.

He walked slowly through the winter night. He stood in front of the Hollanden Hotel watching the street. At three minutes to eleven an El Dorado Cadillac parked directly across the street from the Odeon Grill. The driver got out from behind the wheel and sat in the back seat of the car. He was an endomorph—a circular mass of flesh wrapped in a camel's-hair overcoat complete with a belt. Nick sensed instinctively that he wore vicuña underwear.

It had begun to rain. The area had reached its peak-for-the-night traffic about a half hour before. Nick crossed the street slowly. He grasped the traffic-side door handle of the Cadillac, opened the door, looked in at a Buddha face impaled upon a flashy cigar, and said, feeling as if he were playing pirates, "I'm Nick Thirkield. Monroe sent me."

"Get in," Irving Mentor said.

Mentor smelled like a lived-in steak house. "You

brought the money?" he asked. Nick handed him a flat package.

"Better count it," Nick said.

"Bet your ass." Mentor counted it. "Okay," he said. "The contract to Joe Diamond came from Gameboy Baker."

"And?"

"And what?"

"Tell me about it."

"Joe Diamond was from my old neighborhood. He was a thief when he started out, and he stayed a thief. He got his hand caught in the till in Tucson, and he had to run, because Gameboy couldn't help him. Moe and Sam put out an offer on him. When he heard about it he was in Florida. He got so nervous he killed two Sicilians who didn't even have nothing to do wit' him, so he knew he was now like in double trouble. You know what I mean?"

"Vaguely," Nick said.

"So he got a job in Cuba. By the time the Rappaport boys knew who he was, Joe was in bed wit' every fagele Cuban politician. So when he told the biggest politician what the Rappaport boys were willing to do to him as a favor to Sam and Moey and the Sicilians, this politician called Max—he's the oldest Rappaport brother—to his office, which it is like surrounded wit' soldiers and wire, and he tells Max he wants to make sure Max protects his friend Joe Diamond. Which Max does. Diamond sat out the war in Cuba—if you can call what he did sitting. His Cuban friend gave him a piece of the national lottery, and, believe me, with a very, very small piece of this you could buy like the Baltimore and Ohio. Joe had real connections. Almost everybody inna business needed a route to bring in junk without losses, so Joe organized. The French would get their shit as far as Havana, they would be paid, then Joe had the fishing fleet take it into the Keys, then up to Miami. Everybody was making money, so there was a tendency for Moe and Sam to forget and to talk to the Sicilians so they should forget too. They didn't call it off, you understand, they just forgot it for a little while."

"Mr. Mentor, you are telling me more than I want to know about Joe Diamond. All I want to know is, who approached Gameboy Baker to hire Diamond."

"Listen, I'm witchew. But it takes time. Joe wanted to get back, because now that he had money he had this disease about cops—he wanted to be a big man with the cops. But they should be American cops. Socially, he had to ice Cleveland and Miami and Tucson—a question of personal popularity. So he opened a saloon in Philly, which it was like a club for cops, and all of a sudden he is running all the shit in Philly too. He really thought he had it made. If I was ever in Philly I always went to his place. I would call up first and he would ask me to come in playing the heavy movie gangster to impress the cops—a bunch of patrolmen and sergeants, fahcrissakes—with his big connections. Very funny stuff. But the last time I was there I was like a messenger boy with a message from Gameboy Baker."

Joe Diamond felt sick. He would get in trouble if he vomited going across the lobby of the Santa Rita Hotel in Tucson, but he was afraid it could happen. If he refused to go to Tucson to see Gameboy Baker, Irving Mentor had told him in Philadelphia, then he would be hit. So he went to Tucson even though he now had the kind of a business that needed his personal presence.

Gameboy sent down the word that he was to wait in the lobby. He felt a little better when he sat down. They kept him waiting there from a quarter to eleven in the morning until ten after four in the afternoon. Guys he had known since Woodlands passed three feet away from him all day but they didn't see him; nobody could see him.

At ten after four Jack Lerner told him to come back at nine o'clock. At nine o'clock he was sent right upstairs to Gameboy. Gameboy looked old. All that junk sat on him. He asked Joe if he wanted a sannawitch. They split three pastramis on whole wheat and two bottles of celery tonic. It was lousy pastrami. "If you think the pastrami is bad," Gameboy said, "don't ever try Wild West corned beef."

"It must be the local water," Joe said, trying to be jolly-jaunty.

"Water? Here they cook it in sweat."

"You are looking great, Sam."

"Maybe I am and maybe I'm not, but that isn't what we want to talk about here. I have a contract for you. The biggest contract ever handed out anywheres."

"Me? I'm a restaurant man."

"You are also a thief who was crazy enough to steal from Moey and Sam and Morris and Uncle Louie."

"I want to pay back."

"You are fucking right."

"I can pay back?"

"When you handle this hit you will be paying back. You will be even."

"The thing is—can I do it?"

"Well," Gameboy said, "you know how to answer that."

"How?"

"Don't do it and you're dead."

"What is the contract?"

"Nobody knows yet. But it is big, because they paid big just for me to talk to you."

"But why me, Sam?" Diamond *hated* this. He had a wonderful business, with wonderful built-in friendships with a lot of wonderful guys. Things had never been so good. "Why me when there are maybe two hundred mechanics who can make any hit better than me?"

"That is what Uncle Louie said to them. Four *very* good mechanics were offered to them. But they said no good, because those guys weren't political."

"I'm po*liti*cal?" Diamond asked with horror.

"Uncle Louie said to them: 'What is political? This is business.' They said we had operated in Cuba and that they'd like to have somebody from Cuba. So—and it was very easy, you schmuck—Uncle Louie remembered you. You were eight years in Cuba already, and you are in the FBI files as a political."

"I was never a political in my life! Fah God's sake, Sam."

"You speak a little Cuban. You were *very* good friends with a Cuban minister." Gameboy leered. It was wholly unattractive. "So the man who is paying said you were what the doctor ordered. Because you have a Commie background in the FBI files."

"Commie? Sam, I was out by 1949. Castro didn't

take over until 1959—now—February, this year."

"Joe, what do you want from me? If people like this decide they have to prove you're a Commie, so they'll prove you're a Commie."

"People like who?"

"People like who have been proving that certain people are Commies for six years already."

"This is crazy."

"Anyway you gotta do it."

"Yeah."

"Moey said you could make your own deal, because that's the kind of a little guy he is. Also, you gotta take rifle lessons for as long as you have to, out on Pete Volilica's ranch."

"A rifle?"

The rifle teacher on the Volilica ranch was some
farmer named Turk Fletcher. He could hit anything
from anywhere with a rifle. They put in twenty-six
days, seven hours a day, doing nothing but shooting a
rifle. They shot at a dummy that was strapped into the
back seat of an old-time touring car that Howie Pearl,
who was now the big *macher* in Cleveland, towed
across the field at about a hundred and ten feet away
from where Diamond shot on an eighteen-foot-high
rise of ground. Diamond had to hit the dummy in the
throat. When they had finished he was hitting nine out
of every ten shots. Because he was no dope, he figured
out that they must be going to hit some guy who rode
around in a car with the top down.

Gameboy sent him back to Philadelphia and told
him to wait to hear from somebody named Casper
Williams and that Joe should make his deal with Casper Williams. Joe said good-bye to Gameboy in his
room in Tucson, holding him close with one hand and
squeezing his ass with the other hand. He never saw
Gameboy again. Although Gameboy outlived him,
Gameboy never saw Joe again except on television. So
it goes in the march of the patriots.

When Casper Williams came to his office in the
saloon, Joe Diamond puked right on his own floor
without any warning when Williams told him whom he
was supposed to hit. He had never really been scared
before in his life, he decided. He had to go to bed for a

day and a half. After a while he got used to the idea, because the money they were paying was so good and because he would be working for Captain Heller, who had never made a wrong move in his life.

The cigar smoke in the back of the parked Cadillac in Vincent Street was like suspended meringues, but Nick couldn't open the window, because the engine wasn't running and the windows were automatic. "Open the door, please," he asked. "This smoke is too much for me."

"It could be a signal or something."

"Open the door or I'll shove that cigar down your throat," Nick said savagely. Mentor leaned forward and turned on the ignition, then he opened the windows on both sides. "This is an eighty-five-cent cigar, fahcrissakes," he said. "Wholesale."

"Who was Casper Williams?"

"A Hollywood agent."

"Whaaaat?"

"Yeah, he was dealing for Harry Small, head of the Federal Studios."

"Why would people like that want a President killed?"

"Because that particular President cost them about fifty million dollars in film rentals when Ellamae Irving, who was Federal's biggest star, killed herself because the President told her she couldn't go to a Madison Square Garden rally for him in New York."

"Hardly likely."

"Very likely. He was screwing her, and she took it big. Maybe she had dreams of being the First Lady. That could have made her the biggest grosser in history, even if it was only announced. But chances are she would have killed herself anyway, even if your brother had kept his pants shut."

"Can you set a meeting for me with Casper Williams?"

"He left Hollywood. Somebody said he was working in Rome."

"I'll go to Rome."

"I'll find out."

"Can you set a meeting with Harry Small?"

"What do you read? He's dead for three years already."

Nick got out of the Cadillac and got into a cab across the street in front of the Odeon Grill. He told the driver to take him to the airport. Irving Mentor got out of the back of the car, shut the door, started to open the front door and felt the gun in his back.

Nick called Yvette in New York from the Cleveland airport at 12:55 A.M. The answering service said she still hadn't called in for her messages. He was getting cross-eyed with fury over her perversity. Why was it that only the women one loved behaved like this and never the women one was indifferent to?

The Cleveland flight got Nick to New York at six twenty in the morning. He checked into an airport motel and left a call for half past ten. At eleven thirty he was riding the high-speed elevator in the *National Magazine* building to get some kind of a reasonable explanation from Harry Greenwood as to why the magazine had sent him to a man in Cleveland who, according to the unimpeachable source of Frank Mayo, did not exist as far as the Syndicate was concerned. Nick wanted to have Greenwood's undoubtedly plausible explanation in hand when he made his report to his father about the Mentor meeting.

His name was sent along to Greenwood's office from the editorial reception desk. After about seven minutes he was told Mr. Greenwood would be unable to see him. Was there someone else who could help him?

"Perhaps his secretary doesn't know I had a meeting with Mr. Greenwood here two nights ago. I am Thomas Kegan's son." The receptionist repeated Nick's message to Mr. Greenwood's secretary. There was a short wait, then the receptionist said Mr. Thirkield was to go to the thirty-eighth floor, please.

A young woman was waiting for him at the elevator

bank. "Mr. Thirkield?" He followed her to the uptown side of the building at the eastern end. She led him into an anteroom just as a portly man with heavy eyeglasses and an imperturbable look came through from the far room. "This is Mr. Thirkield," the young woman said.

"What's this about a meeting we had?" the man asked.

"I'm here to see Harry Greenwood."

"I'm Greenwood."

"Like hell you are," Nick said pleasantly, managing to smile.

"Hey, Charlotte," the portly man yelled. The young woman reappeared. "Who am I?" he asked.

"You are Mr. Harry Greenwood."

Greenwood said to Nick, "And you're Tim Kegan's brother?"

Nick nodded with bewilderment.

"Sit down," Greenwood said. "No. You better come inside and tell me what this is all about."

Greenwood's office walls were lined with cork to which production schedules, assignment sheets and oddly shaped pieces of paper were pinned.

"Do you have a writer named Chantal Lamers?" Nick asked.

"On our staff?"

"Yes."

"No."

"*No?*"

"You'd better tell me what happened."

Nick told him how he had met Miss Lamers, who said she worked for the magazine. She had given him her direct-to-desk telephone. The magazine did have direct-to-desk phones? Greenwood nodded. Nick had called Miss Lamers to arrange a meeting. In an office two floors below, off a corridor behind the reception desk, she had introduced him to a man she called Harry Greenwood, who said he was the editor of the *National Magazine*. He gave a careful description of Lamers and the false Greenwood.

"What was the meeting about?"

"I can't say until I clear it with my father. But you have been very helpful. Thank you very much."

Nick told the cab to take him to Chantal's address on East Thirty-first Street.

The doorman was a ratty, if beautifully uniformed, short man who did not look strong enough to protect the tenants from the neighborhood children. He barred the way. He said no one named Chantal Lamers lived in the building. Nick asked him how long he had worked there. The doorman said three and a half years. Nick gave him three one-dollar bills and described Chantal carefully. The doorman shrugged and said they just didn't have any good-looking tenants of any name anywhere in the building. "I don't say this as criticism, buddy," the doorman said, trying to earn the three bucks, "but we have never had a pretty woman live in this building. There could be a jinx on this building."

Nick went to the Walpole Hotel. He felt dazed. Two people who were as convincing in their ways as any two people he had ever met had melted away as if they had never existed. Yet he knew Chantal Lamers existed, because he could still smell her and feel her all too solid flesh, which was incapable of thawing and resolving itself into a dew. Why had she done it? Where was the point of doing what she had done? Whatever her reason, when could it have been planned?—because everything that had happened between them had been accidental. Her car had been wrecked. Her forehead had been cut. The garageman at the crossroads that bore the improbable name of Jane Garnet's Corners, on the Muskogee road, had volunteered the information about the two stoned men who had driven her off the road. *She hadn't called him in New York, he had called her.* He had wandered completely out of her life; then, because he had told her what he thought he needed, she had taken him to the *National Magazine* offices and had produced the magazine's confidential files bearing the cabalistic marks of the magazine's staff. Then, absolutely authentically, she had fallen in love with him.

How, or why, or because of what absurdity should she have pretended to do a thing like that? No one saw anything wrong with simple lust anymore. Subterfuges were silly when two adults wanted to couple for pleasure. Why had any of it happened? It had no shape. It made no sense. What had made any sense since he left Brunei? Keifetz was dead. Nick still could not overtake that terrible fact. Keifetz was dead. One-third of the people in the world who gave a damn about him had been a big breakfast for a shark. Nick knew it was his fault. Keifetz was his friend. If Keifetz had been less of his friend he could be alive. Miles, Tate, Kullers, Sis Ryan and Coney were all dead, as if they had all been playing cards together and he had thrown a live grenade in among them. They had one thing in common and it caused their death: they all knew Nicholas Thirkield. But why was he still alive, eluding such expert killers, who had put away twenty-three people, including Tim? Where was the missing piece? What was its shape? How had it suddenly happened, after almost fifteen years, that he was wandering around in a steam-room, causing the deaths of all the indistinct shapes he happened to bump into? He was on some kind of a bummer through American mythology, a demi-god. Look at the folks: Dawson, the world's richest and most spectacular recluse; Ellamae Irving, a suicidal movie queen; Mayo, a grand vizier of the underworld. It was all so vulgar, with illusion and falsehood used to construct dwellings of steam, buildings on wheels which had rolled him up streets, down corridors. Turk Fletcher had faded into Captain Heller who became Z. K. Dawson who resolved into Chantal Lamers who blended into a dead kitten and an English hit man until all of them fused into Casper Junior who was William Casper or was it Casper Williams. Everyone disappeared almost as soon as he began to talk to them.

Someone, somewhere was trying to teach him futility. This came to him with the clarity of a night ball game—shadowless and static. He had to try to keep in mind that, so far, only one pattern seemed to exist: a pattern of confusion and exhaustion intended to teach him that all striving was fruitless, that when he understood the futility, he would find peace and safety for the people he loved. If that were so, he had to find Yvette and keep her with him. He felt smothered by the terrible fear that these people in the shadows around him were capable of doing to Yvette what they had done to Keifetz and twenty-two others. But if he was on this bummer through a fun house of the American myths, surely Pa's money could save them— Yvette and himself—surely Pa's money was the magic cloak that could cover them and let them survive any darkness?

He left the elevator at the tower floor, opened the door of the apartment and walked into the foyer.

Keifetz was asleep in a large chair that had been placed to face the door. There was a large manila envelope in his lap. Nick stared at him. Nausea hit him. The door slammed behind him. Keifetz awoke suddenly, came to his feet reflexively in one leap, recognized Nick as he focused and said, "Jesus, I thought you'd never get here, baby."

Nick worked it all out by getting hysterical. He sobbed
uncontrollably. Keifetz led him into Tim's bathroom
and put his head under the cold-water shower. Nick
stopped weeping. He dried himself off. "What happened?" he asked Keifetz.

"I was driving to the office with the radio on,"
Keifetz said, "when they announced that Tate and Sis
Ryan had been killed in that automobile accident. I
knew right away what kind of an accident that was. So
I got on the radio phone in the car and called Daisy
and told her to meet me at Fong's—that's kind of a,
you know, kind of a coffee place—and to keep her
mouth shut. I told her to bring every dime there was in
petty cash. This cost you about thirty-five hundred dollars, incidentally."

"That's okay," Nick said. "I'm going to charge it to
my father."

"When she got there I explained that Tate and Sis
had been murdered and that if I just went on about my
business I would be next. Now, I know you don't know
Daisy, but she is a terrific woman. She can do anything
and she has the nerve of ten Apaches. I told her that
you and your father were working on the thing that
had caused the murders of Tate and Sis, and that it was
all in the deposition Tate and Sis had taken at the hospital with us. She was hip. So I told her to go to Tate's
office and say casually that she had come by to pick up
the favor Tate had done for me—she knows Tate's
secretary *very* well—then to go to Sergeant Ali

Kushandra at the cops and to say, nice and easy, that I had sent her over to pick up Fletcher's prints and photographs. We were talking in a room I rented at Fong's—you can get rooms there besides coffee—and I told her to bring everything back to me."

"Daisy knows you're alive?"

"She got me out."

"But she was so stricken with grief on the telephone she could hardly talk."

"She's a terrific woman, Nick. I just told her she had to stay very convincing. Also, she could have thought I'd be killed trying to get this deposition here. She likes me. We're going to be married."

Daisy walked to the Shell offices, then to police headquarters, then to Fong's. She was a small, pretty and dazzlingly intelligent-looking Palawanese woman from the Philippine archipelago whose father had been an American GI who came in with the occupying forces on March 2, 1945. Her father, who owned a Shell station in the Oranges, New Jersey, had paid for her education with the nuns in Brunei. She was nineteen years old. She was the embodiment of Christopher Colombo's inspiration (from previous gossip by Marco Polo) to find a route to the East Indies, where gold was in abundance "to a degree scarcely credible" and "sweet scented trees like sandalwood and camphor, pepper, nutmegs, spikenard, galangal, cubebs, cloves and all other valuable spices abounded."

Keifetz locked the door. He patted her softly on the behind, took the envelope from her and sat down at a table.

"Will they try to kill you, sir?"

"Goddammit, Daisy, don't call me 'sir.' Yes, they will kill me if they can find me. But that's okay, isn't it?"

"Yes, sir. They will not find you."

He stopped opening the envelope. "Come here." She approached. He sat her on his lap as if she were a toy.

"Are you sure you understand that we are going to get married, Daisy?"

"Oh, yes."

"Then you mustn't call me 'sir.' "

"After we are married, if you command me, I will not call you 'sir,' " Daisy said.

"What will you call me?"

"How about 'baby'?"

"Not 'baby.' Too cold. How about 'Your Eminence'?"

"Yes," she sighed. "That fits you best. It is a wonderful private name."

He kissed her enthusiastically, then lifted her off his lap. It was five minutes to seven. The sun was up and very hot. He checked through the pages of the deposition, checked the fingerprints and photographs. "Everything is here," he said. "Sis was a good legal stenographer. This is what we do, Daisy. On the way out, tell Fong to send me up some tea. Then go out to my place with a cardboard box, pack me a change of clothes in it and send it by air mail to General Delivery in Hong Kong. And bring me the pistol. Okay?"

"Sure."

"Fong's cousin has a boat. Which reminds me—did you bring me the money?"

"Sure."

"How much was in petty cash?"

"Thirty-five hundred dollars."

"I have to speak to Nick about switching the petty cash to Swiss francs."

"What about the boat?"

"I don't know. Except I can't leave by plane. They'd have somebody waiting for me when I landed. So I have to go by boat, a private boat, at night. They would expect me to head for the Singapore airport, so that's out."

"Hong Kong is out too, sir. If it isn't Singapore, they'll think of Hong Kong."

"If it's more than one airport, they'll have to check

passenger manifests, so I can't travel with this passport. What name should I use?"

"Gary Cooper!"

He fell about with laughter. She laughed so hard she
had to lean against the wall. When she could speak
again she said, "If you take Fong's cousin's boat to my
island, I can send you to people who will get you to
Manila by plane, then you can fly out from there.
Where are you going, sir?"

"To San Francisco, then I make a call to Palm
Springs and they tell me where to go. Wherever Nick
is."

"I get your clothes." Daisy left. "I will mail them to
General Delivery, Manila, okay?"

"No, they could miss me. Make it registered air
mail, care of General Delivery, San Francisco."

"But if you are all the way to San Francisco in those
clothes, you can buy clothes in San Francisco."

"That's right. Therefore just go down and tell Fong
to send up some tea and come right back."

"But what about the pistol?"

"No. Fong will have to get me a pistol. You and I
have to plan my death here in Brunei today so you can
announce it to the police and the newspaper and radio."

"I will get the tea, sir, while you think."

When she came back with the tea he had it all figured out. They sipped tea. He explained. "You go back
to the office and call Gelbart in from the Number One
rig. He is the safest man and he's a foreman. When
Gelbart gets to the office you hand him a note I am
going to give you in my own writing, which he will dig,
telling him to come here to Fong's. When he gets here
I am going to let him read the deposition, because he
feels almost the same way I feel about Tim Kegan and
the people who killed him. Maybe he's not a nut about
it like me, but killing Kegan was a very important thing
in his life as an American. Okay. Gelbart goes back to
Number One supposedly at about eleven, because you

put him down in the book for a seat on the eleven o'clock chopper going out. Then you call the pier at about twelve thirty and order a seat in the chopper for me to go out to Number One at about two o'clock, just before the rain starts."

"But, sir—"

"No, it's all right. Because the two o'clock chopper is the one Gelbart will actually take. He won't be aboard the eleven o'clock. He goes out to Number One in my seat, wearing my rain rigs. Then at about seven o'clock at night—Number One is about thirty miles out at sea—when the rain is really coming down, he radios to you at the base that I slipped on the deck of the rig and went over the side in shark-infested waters, and because the seas were too heavy and there was no sign of me, they didn't attempt any rescue operation. Okay?"

"Oh, very good, sir!"

"Now, most people know we are crazy about each other, so when you get the news you have to be sad. I am not exactly sure how Filipina women show grief, but I know you will do it correctly."

"We weep."

"Well, as far as I'm concerned you can't overdo it."

"I will make terrible scenes, sir."

"But first tell the police and tell the newspaper and the radio station. Then announce that the office will be closed for two days in mourning. Then you stay right beside my desk and files and post strong security inside and outside the building. Just wait for Nick or Carswell to call, and tell them everything, but don't remember to call them, because you are too grieved."

Keifetz listened to his own obituary on the eight o'clock, nine o'clock and ten o'clock news that night, and, all in all, he wasn't too displeased. If he had known the station would go into such detail, he might have remembered to tell Daisy to slip into his biography that he had gone to Harvard and had once won a

Bollingen Award for poetry. Neither was true, but it would have impressed a lot of people in Brunei.

He got into Fong's cousin's boat at eleven fifteen. It was a compact hydrofoil used to smuggle whiskey to the Mohammedans in the area and transistor electric shavers that fetishists adored using on pubic hair. They ran through the Balabac Strait, then along the south side of Palawan to Puerto Princesa, a distance of about 437 statute miles. They got into Puerto Princesa at a quarter to six the next evening, with Keifetz' teeth hanging out from the banging by the sea. Fong charged him only five hundred dollars each way (the cousin had to get back to Brunei without a tooth in his head), which was a steal. Manila was only four hundred and eighty miles to the northeast, Puerto Princesa had an airfield, and a good old workhorse Beechcraft got him to the Manila airport at eleven the next morning after a marvelous night's sleep. Keifetz could speak Tagalog. Daisy had sent ahead such an exalted description of his position in the world, however, that no one in the meeting party would dare to speak to him. A chief had to be summoned so that Keifetz could find a place to sleep and to make sure he got the plane into Manila.

He slept sublimely on the flight into San Francisco and felt wonderfully refreshed especially when he called Palm Springs and was told that Nick was in New York. But he met a young woman in an airport Pancake Parlor, checked in with her at the airport hotel and got himself exhausted all over again. Then he went on to New York.

Keifetz said, "You don't look so good."

"I was wondering if it is possible that all the others might come back to life."

"What others? Tate and Sis Ryan really caught it."

"Miles Gander is dead."

"Miles? You connected him with this—this business?"

Nick nodded. "He went with me when we found the rifle. It was where Fletcher said it would be, but the police inspector had to get permission from the building manager to look in the room where the rifle was hidden, and there was a tenant who worked in the room—so they all saw the rifle and now they are all dead."

"Why?"

"The rifle has disappeared. No rifle, no witnesses to finding the rifle, just my unsupported story."

"How come you got away?"

"Somebody tried to poison me in Tulsa. I could say I'm pretty sure it was Z. K. Dawson, but the trouble is, it's too open and shut. Nothing else about any of this is open and shut. Then somebody sent a professional killer to throw me out of that window."

"But he didn't."

"I have thought about that a lot. I mean, I'm no puny weakling in the Charles Atlas ad, but this guy was a trained one-hundred-percent mercenary warrior. I mean, he had every advantage—surprise, intent, weapons, strength and experience—and yet, somehow, I vanquished him."

"I see what you mean."

"These people have never been shy about killing. I am the key gofer in all of this—the low man, the god-damn messenger who's here to go-fer things. How come they haven't killed me? I'll tell how come. They don't need to kill me, and they absolutely will not kill me. Why don't they need to kill me?"

"I was just going to ask you that," Keifetz said.

"Better yet, why are they going to such fantastic trouble and expense to confuse me and tire me out?"

"They want you to quit."

"Sure. But not just quit. They want me to quit satisfied that nothing in this world can be done about it, what's the use, that's the way it is, et cetera, et cetera."

"Well, that's the permanent policy the people who own this country have for all the rest of the population, Nicholas, so why not for you? Listen, I hate to say it, but even if someone might call you a co-owner, it looks like, in this, you're just one of the rest of the electorate. After all, on the inside, oligarchies are mutually feuding structures, right? And maybe the guys who are teaching you that famous what's-the-use philosophy are with that same mob, those other fellas who own the country?"

"Keifetz, did you have to go to a Marxist Sunday group when you were a kid?"

"I don't answer tricky questions like that."

"Then what makes you so smart? Come on—what Marxist Sunday group did they make you go to?"

"It's Marxist *study* group. It wasn't a *Sunday* school, fahcrissake. To a socialist worker, what is a Sunday school? It is manipulation by the bosses to interfere with the day of rest."

"I'm glad you went, no kidding. Somebody is trying to teach me futility as a way of life, and you are telling me something that is maybe as old as the first economic figure in American history—you know, one of the basic truths that is always revived as needed."

"What basic truth?" Keifetz asked belligerently.

"That there are a handful of people who own the country and who stay in power by teaching everybody else that all striving is fruitless, that there is no use fighting it—no way—that what's-the-use is the only helpful permanent attitude to have in life."

"Now who was the member of the Marxist Sunday group?" Keifetz asked accusingly.

"The thing is, whoever is teaching me futility this year also killed Tim in 1960. They were able to get close enough to him to kill him; therefore they have to be some of the people who ran him. Let's try on some questions. Why did Z. K. Dawson agree to see me?"

"Your old man asked him." Keifetz' head was as bald as a kneecap, as brown as a GI boot. He had knobby, rosy cheeks over the tan, that comical moustache, and the mock-kindly look of Field Marshal Lord Montgomery of Alamein just after he had consumed a regimental sergeant major and two field ranks for breakfast. He held his mouth pressed together in a permanent expression of belligerence, giving him the look of a prizefighter who was making sure his mouth-piece wouldn't fall out. He was a head taller than Nick, a foot wider and eighteen inches thicker. His voice had overtones of a crocodile with severe indigestion.

"That's not why."

"Why, then?"

"He agreed to see me so that he could pass me along to the next set of phony clues. So they could plant a woman on me named Chantal Lamers, who then set up the third set of phony clues like in a leapfrog game."

"Are you saying the guy in Cleveland was a phony?"

"Frank Mayo says he doesn't even exist."

"Do me a favor and start from the beginning."

"I've been walking around in a maze without a hat. Sometimes I think Tim is alive and well and living in Argentina."

"Just say what happened."

"I got to London, and Carswell was so absolutely impossible that there can no longer be any question about it—he has to go."

"Later, later. Tell me about Philly."

"Okay. Breakfast with Miles. Miles dug up a high-ranking cop. Now, it just happens to work out that fourteen years ago this same cop was in on Tim's murder so deep that he is definitely one of the bad guys."

"Then what?"

"We find the rifle. The cop—who is named Frank Heller—very plausibly takes the rifle to the police lab—he says—except that it never got near the lab. Heller must have tried to blackmail somebody with the rifle, because that same night he was killed."

"Jesus."

"Pa set a meeting with Z. K. Dawson in Tulsa. Dawson gave nothing away, but he went to a lot of trouble to make a case that Tim was good for his business and that the last thing he wanted was to have Tim dead."

"You believe him?"

"I don't see how I can believe anybody. This Casper Junior that Fletcher told us about is all over this thing. He pops up in every nook and cranny of the goddam thing, but I'm no closer to finding out who he was. But he's heavy Texas, and I have to think that he was acting for Dawson, who is very heavy Texas. I did find out that the Philadelphia police were deep into Tim's murder, but Heller is dead. Joe Diamond, the nightclub saloonkeeper, left his muddy footprints everywhere, and I have no doubt that he did everything Fletcher said he did, including shoot Willie Arnold, but he's dead. Willie Arnold, who played Jesus to the Pickering Commission's Pontius Pilate, is dead. It looks like we know everything but we can't prove anything, doesn't it?"

"Sure does."

"Then why did they invent a woman named Chantal

Lamers, who took me to a fake editor of the *National Magazine*, who arranged for me to interview this very dubious Cleveland mobster, who produced a detailed story that the movie industry had had Tim killed?"

"How did *they* get in? Jesus, no wonder there was such a crowd in Hunt Plaza in Philly that day."

"Tim had been laying a movie woman named Ellamae Irving, you know the one, and—"

"Do I know the one? Boyoboy!"

"So the way the story goes from this hoodlum, she killed herself because Tim wouldn't make her First Lady of the Land, and because that cost some movie company fifty million dollars, they had Tim killed."

"It doesn't sound right. I can see how certain guys might miss her, but I don't see them shooting the President of the United States for her. For one thing, they hate to leave Beverly Hills."

"A Lieutenant Doty of the Philadelphia police—a lifetime partner of Heller's—admits that the police opened all the doors for the assassins, but he says they had nothing else to do with the killing. He says the Mob, either on its own or on hire, actually did the work. So I went to what I was *told* were the editors of the *National Magazine* to find me a top mobster."

"But you said you knew Frank Mayo."

"My father knew him, but I didn't know then that my father knew him, or at least I didn't know it until after the magazine had made the hoodlum connection."

"You should have known your old man woulda known Frank Mayo, Nicholas."

"Please, stay with me. We both talked to Turk Fletcher. He was just a Texas farmer. I mean, nobody would say Turk Fletcher was a member of the Mafia or the Syndicate or anything like that."

"Why not? Look at Farmer Rappaport. He was a real dirt farmer from New Jersey. He sold tomatoes to the Campbell Soup Company until he got a job with Lepke in Murder, Inc. My old man was a bushelman in the garment district—that's below Thirty-first Street.

That Farmer Rappaport was a real organization man."

"For Christ's sake! We are fitting a puzzle together! I am saying that it is sensible to reason that if the Mob was in this, they were not acting independently for their own reasons. It is logical that whoever hired Turk Fletcher also may have contacted the Syndicate to hire the other rifleman. If I could find out who hired Joe Diamond, then I'd know who hired Fletcher, and we'd have this all wrapped up."

"So what happened?"

"I found out that is what they wanted me to think, so that when the whole thing collapsed I would have been taught another lesson in futility."

"But how did you find out the broad and the editor were phonies?"

"I went to the magazine this morning, and the real people put me straight. Then I went to Chantal Lamers' building. I found out she never lived there. Then I came here to find you doing your famous impression of The Resurrection and The Light. How do you figure this mess out?"

"I agree with you that they are trying to teach you that anything you do is just going to be futile and hopeless. The owners always do it that way. It has worked for them since the Civil War, so they know it will work with you."

"I haven't even been here a week," Nick said. "I sure haven't been here long enough to figure out any policy."

"There is only one policy."

"If you know it, tell it."

"Don't take any more outside leads like Lamers' or anybody else's. Run everything through your old man. He probably has an organization bigger than the Common Market. And on a thing like Tim's murder he's the only one you can trust."

The telephone rang. It was Pa. He told Nick to get right over to the hospital because Frank Mayo was on his way. Nick didn't mention Keifetz' being alive. He hung up and said, "God knows, I'm happy and grateful that you're alive."

"Okay. So get maudlin."

"So would you if they told you I had been killed by those bastards," Nick flared up.

"Of course. But I'm a Russian Jew. You're a WASP. It doesn't look nice for you." He fingered his moustache, grinned broadly and farted.

"Keifetz, come on. Quit horsing around. The fact is, I am going to need you badly before we get out of this thing, so what I'm saying is, the fewer people who know you are still alive, the better. That includes my father, because he talks all the time, and too many people could find out about it."

"And knock me off."

"That's right. So wait till it's dark before you leave here. Then take the elevator to the cellar and go out through the help's exit. Oh, shit!"

"Whatsamatta?"

"The hotel desk and the manager know you are here, and they file a minute-by-minute log with my father."

"No. I don't know if I thought of that, but they haven't got my real name. I told them I was from the police commissioner's office in Philadelphia. I told them my name was Trudeman Garfunkel."

"Great. That's great! Now I have time to make up a lie. When you get out of here, check into the Waldorf so I can find you. It's just better for you to stay dead a little while longer."

When Nick got to the hospital Pa grandstanded for him by pulling a flat package out from under his pillow and saying, "Here. That's the fifteen grand you gave that fink last night."

"You had him picked up?" Nick wasn't as surprised as he would have been earlier—he had a good sense of Pa now.

"Yeah. You know what he is, this big wheel in the

Syndicate? An actor. But what kind of an actor? An out-of-work actor in blue movies."

"Who hired him?"

"The tape he made for you is with Jim Cerutti now. So is the tape he made with my men who had the talk with him. Cerutti will put it all together."

"The whole peg they tried to hang everything on," Nick said, "was that Tim had been killed by a movie company."

"They must think we're feebleminded!" Pa said. "And they're so *care*less. Just a cursory check would have showed them that a few of my companies own forty-six percent of Federal Studios. Ellamae Irving wasn't worth any fifty million dollars in film rentals. I listened to that Mentor tape. It was fulla false notes. The whole goddam thing was a *romantic* story about a woman who died of a broken heart. Ellamae is supposed to have killed herself because Tim threw her over. But life just didn't work that way with her. And Harry Small had three stars bigger than her—at the box office, that is. Also Harry Small was the kind of a guy who kept so busy that if he was alive right now he might not know Ellamae had killed herself."

"Maybe she didn't kill herself," Nick persisted. "Maybe she's just another one of the twenty-odd people who have died because Tim was killed."

"Don't believe it," Pa said. "First of all, she died a year ahead of Tim. Second, like every other suicide, she had been a suicide inside her head since she was about five years old."

"Okay," Nick said. "Who hired Mentor?"

"The Casper Williams name again. Same description. The interesting thing is the Joe Diamond background they gave Mentor to give to you. It was all designed sideways and backwards, and the funny thing was—"

Rose put her head in the doorway. "Mr. Mayo is here," she said, smiling broadly.

"Send him in, you beautiful thing," Pa said. Frank

Mayo came in and shook hands with Pa and Nick heartily. "Whatever it is you've got," Pa said, "Eve and Rose like it."

"The feeling is entirely mutual," Mr. Mayo said.

"I got a big surprise for you," Pa said. "It'll turn you into a Sicilian again. I got a case of Corvo di Castellodaccio—with four bottles waiting, lightly chilled, right now—to go with—ready?—hey?—crispeddi di riso alla Benedittina, nice and hot, right out of the microwave. I flew them in on my own plane from Catania."

"Holy *Jez*uss, Mr. Kegan!"

"Okay, girls!" Pa yelled.

Eve and Rose rolled the Salton hot cart in. Eve carried two bottles of wine in a cooler. She filled the glasses while Mr. Mayo was tasting the crispeddi and moaning.

"I got four dozen of those deep-frozen for you," Pa said, smiling with great pleasure.

After ten minutes of eating and drinking, Pa said, "Nick is dying to hear the real story on Joe Diamond." To Nick he said, "Frank heard both the Irving Mentor tapes."

Mr. Mayo cleared his throat. "Well, sure, Diamond come from aronn Cleveland originally. He worked for Gameboy Baker in some of Moey's joints, but he never worked in Cuba. He was inna war even. He was infantry in Germany."

"Tim was in Germany," Pa said.

"When he come outta the army he was in Chicago, and him and Max Davidoff got the okay to take over the Grocery and Office Used Box and Paper local after Eddie Brinkman was shot. Davidoff was international president and Diamond was international first vice-president. It was a good thing for them. It threw off maybe two hundred, three hundred thousand a year. That's where he saved up to open a joint in Philly. Davidoff had a son-in-law who was a real hustler in the insurance business, and Davidoff was very solid with

Vonnie Blanik, the international president of the Tubesters, and he made a good deal with Blanik to shove the union insurance through the kid, and there was so much for everybody that Davidoff sold his piece of the Used Box and Paper local to Diamond, and Davidoff moved to Detroit. Whenever this is who killed our President wanted to buy somebody to do it, he went to Blanik, because—which every little kid onna street knows—Blanik hated Tim Kegan more than anybody in the United States, he thought, up until then. Lissen, your brother kept after him, put him in jail, made a monkey of him, called him a crook to his own men, his men that were proud of their crook! Blanik saw how he could hit our President and not get any trouble, so he talked it over with Davidoff."

DECEMBER 5, 1959—DETROIT

Joe Diamond always liked to see Murray Davidoff, a man the Sicilians always called Max for no reason whatsoever, and he always liked to go to Detroit because of the time they had given Elvis Presley his suite at the Book-Cadillac, and by the time they got Presley out of there and he had gone in, very exhausted, while he was having a room-service meal in the living room, four little broads had sneaked into the bedroom without him knowing anything about it. They thought Presley still stayed there. When he threw them out one of them stole his pajama bottoms. The idea of four little broads climbing twenty-one flights of service stairs hoping to get laid by Elvis Presley disgusted him. In fact, when he found one of them still hiding in his room after he had had dinner, he felt like throwing up. But he knew that somewhere in Detroit his pajama bottoms were probably tacked up on the wall of some little broad's room and that they would stay with her for the rest of her life because she thought Elvis had worn them, and that was why he liked Detroit.

So when Murray Davidoff invited him to Detroit he was glad to go. Murray met him at the airport. They drove to Murray's house for a real New England boiled dinner, which, thank God, was boiled flanken, chicken, and tongue with horseradish, and not just corned beef with a lot of boiled vegetables, like plenty of places tried to palm off. Gloria Davidoff was a nice little cook even if she couldn't stand him.

After dinner Cary Davidoff, who was fourteen and

who was going to be a song writer when he grew up,
played sixteen or fifty of his latest tunes and sang them
in the style of Eddie Fisher, or it could have been Eddie Cantor. When Cary finished, with his mother
smirking all over everything, Murray took out the
watch from the grateful members of the Used Box and
Paper local when he had retired and told Diamond that
Vonnie Blanik wanted to meet him.

Diamond had never met Vonnie Blanik, who was,
by any standards, the most famous man in the American labor movement. It gave him the stab of a thrill.
For more than three years he had been consumed with
the idea of organizing a national police union. When
Murray had sold him the Box and Paper local to join
up on Vonnie Blanik's personal staff, Diamond had
tried to get up the nerve to lay the proposition on Murray to have him lay it on Blanik. But who could trust
Murray or Blanik? Diamond knew that if he could be
international president of a national police union, with
an international charter from the Tubesters, he would
like practically come in his pants twice every day. But
he knew all the stories about Blanik. They were greedy
stories. Diamond was not greedy. He would take care
of Blanik and Murray. He didn't care about money in
this instance. The restaurant and the shit traffic in Philadelphia were throwing off plenty. His goal was a national police union.

They drove to the Tubesters' national headquarters.
It was almost half past eleven. They were greeted by
Vonnie himself in his personal office anteroom, but because of a lot of trouble the Justice Department had
made with a wire tap they had put on Vonnie's car
telephone and which he had just found out about, he
and Murray only got to see Vonnie for about two minutes, if that. And it was something Joe Diamond could
just as well have postponed for a week, he thought,
while the meeting was happening.

Vonnie grabbed him by the necktie, which meant he
had to reach away up to get to Diamond's necktie, be-

cause Blanik was no giant—in fact maybe even the opposite. He pulled down hard on the necktie, so Diamond had to bend way over while Vonnie was standing straight up. Vonnie yelled straight into his face, "You do what Murray tells you, you hear, you fink?" He put the heel of his hand on Diamond's chin and pushed. He ran out of the room.

"What kind of a meeting was that?" Joe asked Murray.

"Pay no attention. He is very upset. The White House is persecuting him."

"What did I do? I didn't even vote for Kegan."

"Don't worry. I know Vonnie. You'll see. He will feel terrible and he'll send you a gold cigarette case."

Murray drove them to his son-in-law's office building downtown. On the way Murray explained how Kegan never let up on Vonnie. There were twenty-four hours a day of pressure because Kegan was out to break up the American labor movement. If Vonnie hadn't been made of iron he would have had a complete breakdown long ago. Never, Murray said, had one man—and that included Hitler—persecuted another man the way Kegan was persecuting Vonnie Blanik.

Diamond wasn't listening. He was thinking about what Murray had said about Blanik making it up to him. This could mean an opening. He might get a chance to present his idea, his ideal, with maybe also a chance to break even on it.

Murray led the way down to the cellar of the son-in-law's building. The kid had a whole seven-story building on a Tubesters' mortgage. There were two bent-noses waiting for Murray in the cellar. Murray introduced them. The first was Herm Levin—Hermie the Mole, a legend! The other man was Silk Gabel, who looked like a jewelry salesman Joe knew in Philadelphia. They didn't say much. Everybody sat down. It was like being in the whoopee room of somebody's house. Murray offered a drink. The Mole and Gabel, who were sitting on either side of Diamond on a green plastic sofa, didn't take any. Joe took a Seven-Up. Murray sat behind a dinky wooden desk. He said, "I know you must be wondering why I invited you all the way to Detroit, Joe." He had a very soft voice, because Murray lived on tranquilizers, and was therefore very considerate.

"Listen, it's great to see you again, Murr."

"Vonnie has this friend who he owes a favor to. He hates to be obligated."

Diamond nodded because he couldn't think of anything to say.

"So he asked me to find the best man to help this friend out. So when I heard what it was, I immediately thought of you."

"It's nice to hear it."

"I want you to do a special job for this fellow, the friend of Vonnie's."

"A job?"

"A hit."

"You called me all the way to Detroit for a hit when an absolute legend for hits is sitting right beside me?"

"Joe, the job is so special that it has to be somebody who is not connected in any way, shape or form. You are a man who comes out of the labor movement, who is a respected restaurant owner and a friend of the entire Philadelphia police department, and a man who never made a political statement in his entire life."

"Why political, Murr?"

"The contract is for a certain politician."

"What politician?"

"First I gotta make something clear. This is not Vonnie's contract. It is not my contract. And certainly, God forbid, it has nothing to do with the International Tubesters' Union."

"Whose contract is it?"

"This friend of Vonnie's."

"Who gets hit?" Diamond liked all this talking and he didn't like it. He didn't like it, because Murray was

stretching everything out like he couldn't bring himself
to say who the politician was, which could be bad. But
he was making such a thing out of it that the contract
had to be very important to Blanik. Since the big necktie greeting he didn't like Blanik, but life wasn't a popularity contest, and Blanik could issue a charter for a
national police union. Joe lighted a big cigar, very
calm. Murray waited for him. He puffed on the cigar.
He said, "What politician, Murray?"

"Tim Kegan."

Diamond leaped to his feet. He started for the door
at top speed. Gabel shoved his foot out. Diamond fell
down.

Murray said, "Just take it easy, Joe."

Diamond got up and brushed himself off. He didn't
look at Gabel. He didn't look at anybody. Murray said,
"You didn't give me a chance to tell you, but we have
the total cooperation of the Philadelphia police."

That was Diamond's heartland. "Which police?"

"Captain Heller of the Political Squad."

Diamond sat down on a wooden chair. "Frank Heller?"

"I think so."

Diamond puffed on the cigar elaborately. He was
thinking and he didn't care who knew it. He had a
feeling. If he handled this right he would get his
charter. They were handing him the keys themselves. If
he had gone to Murray with the idea, without them
begging him for something, Blanik would have given
the charter to some stooge. He, Yussel Diamond,
would end up like a ninth vice-president. No more
than that. But even if they didn't know it, they had
just made him international president. He had to make
it very hard for them. He had to make them persuade
him so that he could later on bargain and set a compromise.

He said, "I won't do it, Murray."

Levin and Gabel got up from the sofa and took off
their jackets. They kept their hats on. Both men were

classy dressers. Classy dressers are dainty about everything. They might be willing to shoot him, but they
wouldn't beat him up, because it made a big mess.

Gabel dragged out a galvanized washtub full of
water. He poured in a third of a bag of cement. He
dragged the tub to Diamond's chair and put Joe's legs
in the water—feet, shoes, socks and the bottoms of his
pants. Gabel stirred it all up, then poured more cement
in.

"Stir with your feet," Gabel said.

"What the hell is this?" Diamond asked Murray indignantly. "He ruined my suit and my shoes." After a
while, the way Gabel worked, the cement got very
thick all around Joe's legs.

"Murray!" Diamond said. "What are you doing?"

"Joe, I am personally sorry," Murray said with that
soft voice. "We are going to leave you down here to
think everything over for about twenty-four hours. If
you decide it is yes, then with the shoes and the pants
it won't hurt so much when we knock the cement off."

"What is this *if?*" Diamond asked.

"It's up to you, Joe." The three men left. Diamond
felt scaled with bitterness that Murray could do this to
him. He could have assigned it. They had been good
friends for eleven years and he could have assigned it.
He reconsidered, because he had plenty of time.
Maybe Murray figured he would take the deal right
away. After all, out of all the guys there were, Murray
had picked him for what was essentially a very big job.

In a way it was the rottenest twenty-four hours Diamond had ever spent—from the view of physical dis-
comfort. But he was able to stay happy mentally. He
kept himself euphoric, and sexually excited, with the
thoughts of being the head man among all the police in
the United States. He would be on a first-name basis
with four hundred thousand local police and with
troopers in every state of the union, except never mind
Hawaii and Alaska because he hated long flights.
Wherever he went in God's country he would have

pals, people he really cared about. He thought, Jesus, there will have to be plenty of situations where they get themselves in such jams that only I can get them out. They will have to be grateful. They will have to like me. They will understand me and I will understand them. So in a lot of ways it wasn't the rottenest twenty-four hours he ever spent. Except he wondered if he would ever be able to walk again.

They were right on time. The mechanics sat on the plastic sofa, facing him. Murray went behind the crappy desk again like he was some kind of honest used-car dealer. "What did you decide, Joe?" Murray said, a kindly man.

"I have a conditional answer, Murr."

"What kind of conditional answer, Joe?"

"First: yes, I will do that certain job for you."

Murray slammed his hands together. "Wonderful, Joe!"

"But I will only do it if Vonnie Blanik will do something for me."

"Vonnie has nothing to do with this." And Murray was suddenly not the kindly man.

"I want a charter—I mean a charter made out to me as international president—a charter from the International Tubsters Union that gives only me the right to organize a national police union."

Silence followed. After a while Murray poured a drink—one large bourbon. Someday he was going to take a drink of booze with all those tranquilizers in him, and good-bye Murray, Diamond thought.

"That is what I call an idea," Murray said. "It has so many angles I am dizzy already. Let me make a call. It might take an hour or two, because Vonnie can't use the phones. Okay?"

"Certainly."

"The boys will keep you company."

"Don't bother. Hey, just a minute. When does the cement come off? It doesn't feel so good, believe me."

"Take it off, Herm," Murray said and left the cellar. Diamond found out why there were two men. Gabel put the cement on. Levin took the cement off. They had to have a union. Blanik must have given them a charter. The job took almost two hours. His shoes and pants were a wreck, never mind his socks. Levin had a pack of cards, so they played klob until Murray got back. He was jovial all over.

"You got yourself a deal, Joe," he said. "Vonnie admires you for that idea. The charter will be in your name."

"A dream realized is all I can say," Diamond told them.

"And I was right about the gold cigarette case. It's already on order."

Diamond pretended it wasn't the happiest day of his life. "Come on," he said, "let's take a sannawitch."

When Frank Mayo left the hospital wing Pa told Eve to rush the tape to Cerutti. He lit a cigar, chewing on it as if it were a steak, then climbed down from the high hospital bed like a mauve spider in pajamas. He jammed his feet into a pair of baby-blue quilted muk-luks, shucked on a woolen robe and walked Nick into the large corner living room with its magnificent view of beautiful Queens.

"Siddown, kiddo," he said. Nick chose a stern, up-right chair. Pa sank into the cushions of the sofa. "You're doing a great job," Pa said.

"At what, Pa?"

"As an investigator."

"I would have done better as a designer of hot cross buns," Nick said.

"Don't underestimate yourself. We're getting close here. What we have to do now is to trace back to show who hired Diamond through the Tubesters Union."

"How do we do that?"

"While we sleep, I got guys working on this thing. You're going to the Apostle Islands, on the short Wis-consin side of Lake Superior. That's Cerutti country."

"An Indian tribe?"

"What do you mean?"

"Oh. You meant Professor Jim Cerutti. The man who thinks for computers."

"You think you're kidding, but I can prove that Cerutti thinks better than computers, and he's been an-

alyzing our problem here on a very intensive basis. I
talked to him early this morning. He says he's ready to
make the connection with whoever went to the Tubesters to get them to find a hit man to kill Tim."

"What else has Cerutti been thinking about? I'd like
to have an opinion on Chantal Lamers and why she
faked the *National Magazine* and why she went to such
useless lengths to set that comic meeting in a Cadillac
in Cleveland. Obviously an operation that elaborate
couldn't have seemed useless when it was planned, so
the normal thing would be to question why it was
planned."

"I'll put him on it. You never saw anything like this
guy, no kidding. But I think I ought to warn you. He
has his peculiarities. Anybody who lives alone that
much has to be some kind of an oddball. He just happens to be an egomaniac."

"Who isn't, Pa?"

"No, no—I mean Cerutti thinks he knows better
than anybody else. He actually feels contempt for everybody else. You won't believe this—but he even pa-
tronizes me."

"Pa, why do you think Chantal Lamers set up that
entire useless operation? That is, if she set it up. If she
wasn't just one of the three employees on the deal."

Pa sighed. Maybe it depressed him. What he said
then confirmed this. "I think her orders were to set you
up to be killed."

"How?"

"I don't know. But somewhere along the line during
the time you were with her it figures that she was deliv-
ering you to a convenient place for killers to operate.
Maybe it was set for the magazine building. Maybe she
was the killer and she lost her nerve. It's also logical
that it was supposed to happen in Cleveland but that
they spotted my men who were waiting to pick Mentor
up."

"That's the only theory so far that makes any sense," Nick said.

The feeder airline put Nick down at Ashland on Chequamegon Bay in Wisconsin. Standing on the pier and taking the wet wind off Lake Superior, Nick thought it was colder than Niflheim, the ancient Germanic underground place of eternal damnation. It was so achingly cold that it seemed as though hundreds of long steel pins were being driven deeply into the stiff mask of his face and into all the joints of his body. At 22:05 hours he was taken aboard the *Wendebo,* Cerutti's sixty-eight-foot ice cutter, which was on its outside a copy of a Newfoundland Banks fishing vessel. Below decks the *Wendebo* was beautifully fitted with a companionway ladder that was really a wondrously graceful circular staircase, turning ninety degrees, with a gleaming chrome balustrade leading to a stainless-steel galley. It was warm. He began to thaw. After they were under way he discovered that the chart-table hinge could open to a small electric organ. He began to feel much better about everything. There was a wide-open expanse of the combination dining saloon, main cabin, galley and chart room which created exuberant spaciousness, all of it contained in African mahogany rubbed to a satin finish and splined with holly.

The steward kept putting bacon-and-cheese hors d'oeuvres into a microwave oven. Nick kept eating them and drinking some lovely Pétrus wine until the steward ran out of cheese and the wine bottle was empty. They were running steadily across the international inland sea. Night and the cold were locked out. Nick felt so good he opened the chart table and sat at the organ playing dignified and contrasting pairs of ricercari and capriccios, then moved into the glorious contrapuntals of Franck's *Trois Chorales,* building with thickening dimensions into the choral chaconne of *Jesu der Meine Seele* by J. S. Bach, cantor of Leipzig. It gave him a more stable perspective. It lifted him into

the deity position, reassuring him that he would over-
come. Music was the master illusionist. The music had
created a standoff.

The *Wendebo* took fifty-eight minutes to deliver
them to the Cerutti mooring on Schrader Island. The
captain told him to follow the lighted posts up along
the concrete walk between the snow banks to a low,
immensely square building that had a large main house
behind it. The low house in the foreground was bril-
liantly lighted on the outside, but it had no windows.
The front door was on the latch. He went in.

The room was about the size of a high school gym-
nasium and seemed to be filled with orderly rows of
filing cabinets; hundreds and hundreds of them. A
round-bellied shortish man wearing rimless eyeglasses
arose from behind a large desk at a corner of the room
and walked toward Nick, smiling. "Welcome, Mr.
Thirkield," the man said. "I am Professor Cerutti." He
shook Nick's hand, then locked the only door. He led
Nick forward into the great barracks of facts under a
thirty-foot ceiling. They were enclosed in a cool, sooth-
ing blue shell like the womb of Bessie Smith, but the
piped music, not muted enough, had been written by a
computer and was as far out as Alpha Centauri. Thousands of reference books formed lazy Vs at each corner of the room, shelf upon shelf from floor to ceiling,
all bound in bright yellow as a symbol that Pa's gold
had raised high the roof beams. Nick and Cerutti
walked slowly around the perimeter of the room, and
the view dead ahead was all Nick could see, because
the filing cabinets blocked all else. "This is Corner
One, the writing corner," Cerutti said as they came to
the enormous Florentine desk. Beside the desk were a
powder-blue IBM self-correcting typewriter, a dictating
machine, a microfilm reader and a tabletop Xerox. "I
write all your father's scenarios for all his problematic
and suppositional needs at that desk," the professor
said. They turned to the left and advanced toward Corner Two while Cerutti explained the population of

filing cabinets. "These files hold the fruits of my mission as given me by your father," he said. "They represent about twenty-two years of investigations and interpretations of personal and business motivations in the lives of all industrial and political managers at the crucial decision level with whom your father has done business, is doing business or plans to do business. This room is, of course, the very heart of the Industrial Maintenance Services Corporation and, if I may say it, the secret of your father's prodigious success. There aren't more than eight men in the United States who keep files as nearly complete as these. The files exceed in total security information the combined recorded security effort of Scandinavia plus Benelux and are the equal of the files held by the Republican Party. On your left, ahead, is my communications corner, which we call Corner Two."

Nick saw a twin of the huge Florentine desk at Corner One. Surrounding the chair behind it were three banked telephone switchboard consoles, each held down by a brilliant spotlight. "These give me direct lines to all of your father's installations, to our own offices across the world and to my dear mother's bedside and golf cart. We chat on these lines, of course, but primarily they are for recording tapes for computer retrieval here, tapes of conversations your father or his key agents may have during the course of a twenty-four-hour day. The installation was made by the Army Signal Corps when your brother was President. It represents an annual telephone bill, all in all, of about seven hundred thousand dollars a year, but it earns your father something in the neighborhood of ninety-three million dollars a year. It is a communications hobby nonetheless. A paying hobby, but still a hobby. Your father's real income is from the earnings on the capital that Industrial Maintenance Services Corporation had already earned for him—plus, it goes without saying, the basic fortune that he built with his own fine mind and his two strong hands."

"They won't need to run a benefit for Pa," Nick said.

Behind the ponderous communications desk were two hundred and forty shelves on which rested more than twenty-five hundred yellow-bound volumes. "These are my address books," Cerutti said. "We maintain an up-to-date record of the home, office, extension and hideout telephones of all managers at optimum and secondary decision levels. Your father doesn't like to wait when he places a call. He used to call Charles de Gaulle at his bedside phone late at night until Madame De Gaulle objected. Of course all these numbers are held in the computers, which actually dial the numbers that your father—or the rest of us—asks for by name, but he is still old-fashioned enough to love the idea of his little yellow books."

They reached the far end of the room. "In the far corner on the other side of this room, facing us, which we call Corner Three, you can see my photo desk. In our files here we have stored well over five hundred thousand photographs of people in various kinds of compromised positions, and key specialist photographers everywhere are getting new material for us all the time. On the other hand, in a more exalted sense, we have millions of photographs of computer-retrievable photos of our planet—that is, the planet from the viewpoint of its total physical resources, its points of greatest productivity and richest pollution, and of its least exploited riches. Photography is a very useful discipline."

They came to two facing Edwardian sofas on a Persian carpet in the corridor area between the two working corners. A long, low table separated the two men as they sat down. "Your father maintains his own Earth Resources Technology Satellite in orbit, which photographs the earth's physical data from five hundred and seventy miles out in space. I don't know four other individuals who have taken that trouble to secure their own investments in this way. Our ERTS photographs the entire planet, except for the cones around the poles, every eighteen days. We have our specialists to read the photographs for population shifts, timber, agricultural and water availabilities, and to pinpoint the location of oil deposits and other high-grade mineral ore. An ERTS is a tool, after all. What wine will you have, Mr. Thirkield?"

"Australian wine?" Nick asked with bland malice in the hope of erecting one small dam across this flow of warm smarm. "Houghton's white burgundy? From western Australia? Chilled? About four years old?"

"Anything at all," Cerutti said indifferently. He punched at the console on the tabletop, then leaned back, hardly able to conceal his gratification at having thwarted this young man's ploy so easily, and said, "Although my people were, traditionally, from the Lugano area in the Ticino, then after that from Alexandria, Virginia, historic home of John Dean, I am a tea drinker. Tea is such a reassuring continuity in that it was discovered in 2737 B.C. I drink a blend of twenty-seven teas—fermented, semifermented and unfermented—using black Chinese teas, Panyong and Ichang, as the main base." The lift top at the center of the table opened and the refreshments ascended. Since Nick's own dossier had indicated that he preferred to drink Australian white wine, the correct wine was on the tray.

"This is all too leisurely for me, Professor Cerutti, if you don't mind. I am too pressed to want to hear about tea and satellites."

"Right on," Cerutti said. "You want to know who persuaded the Tubesters to use its—uh—expertise to find them Joe Diamond."

Nick stared at him.

"There are just a few things to clear up before we go on to make that linkage," Cerutti said. "Such as, I think you should know that it wasn't by chance that Miles Gander happened to call on Inspector Heller to accompany you to find that rifle. And, incidentally, perhaps your father hasn't had the chance to tell you that we picked up the rifle at Heller's house the morning after the night he died. I deduced that was where the rifle must be."

Nick felt all systems stop. He felt as if someone had just slammed on his hydraulic brakes. "The next morning," he said slowly. "You had the rifle picked up by a man wearing a police uniform, calling himself Marek, the next morning after Heller died?"

"Yes."

Everything Cerutti had shown him—the dazing files, the dazzling equipment, the paralyzing (to the imagination) reach that Pa had developed toward the end of knowing *anything* he wanted to know—began to purple the edges of Nick's comprehension, began to back him slowly and inexorably toward the edge of some unknown but awful cliff.

"But I told my father more than twenty-four hours after that time that I had deduced where the rifle must be—in the very same place—and Pa arranged for me to ride out to it with the police commissioner of Philadelphia to retrieve that rifle. Why would he let me think that we were on a fresh trail when he had already overtaken the rifle?"

"Ah," Cerutti said, "there is a slight difference. *I*—not your father—had overtaken the rifle. And it is entirely possible that I had not yet reported to your father that we had the rifle."

"But how could you know how to look, where to look? I hadn't told my father that Heller existed until the very night Heller died."

Cerutti smiled with Olympian superiority. "My dear fellow," he said, "Heller was one of the principals in the Philadelphia police department at the time of your brother's assassination. We have held an open file on him since 1960. There was very little about him or his habits that we did not know, and in his case it was remarkably simple, as you demonstrated, to deduce that he would use the rifle to get money and that he would take the rifle to his house."

"Professor—about Miles Gander—"

"Gander faced bankruptcy. Someone whose identity we do not yet know offered him financial assurances that his bankruptcy could be averted if he cooperated on this matter of the rifle. They promised him the moon because they planned to kill him anyway."

"But, Professor Cerutti, how, in the very short time between my London manager's telephone call to Miles Gander for a breakfast appointment with me—to discuss a matter about which Miles was unaware—and our meeting, did these plotters reach Miles to bribe him? Also, since they seem to have planned on killing Heller anyway, how come they didn't take the rifle from him as soon as he got it? We deduced what he did with it, why wouldn't they?"

"You would make a very good little detective," Cerutti said with a patronizing smile.

"Never mind this insolent superior comment," Nick said. "From the icy cores of your gigantic brain please tell me what could have happened."

"From the icy cores of my gigantic brain I will tell you that the answer is: Somewhere along the way you fucked up, and the killers got the information they needed before you ever left Asia."

"How?"

Cerutti stared at him with dislike. "I have no idea where you fucked up, Mr. Thirkield. I, personally, never fuck up. But I expected you to, of course. Indeed. Shall we return to the information I have been told to convey to you?"

"Please do," Nick said. He had to talk this over with Keifetz. He might have had the answer all along. He might have it inside himself right now, but he had to talk it out of himself with Keifetz.

Professor Cerutti picked up his threads and spun them out blandly. "And just as Miles Gander was a straw man, just as Chantal Lamers and Irving Mentor were frauds, there is another even more sinister misrepresentation that stares at us most balefully here."

"If Chantal Lamers was a fraud, who was she?"

"If you would rather talk about a plain and obvious red herring like Lamers, that is all right with me, Mr. Thirkield, but we have come to a fact that is—as I implied—incontrovertibly sinister."

"Which fact?"

"Frank Mayo lied to you and your father with his story about Diamond being recruited by the Tubesters Union. Diamond was never near the union movement. Diamond never met Vonnie Blanik in his life. Nothing Frank Mayo told you and your father ever happened."

Nick felt like a sliding mote within a kaleidoscope aboard a spinning spacecraft above a turning constellation within a limitless universe. "If Mayo was lying," he articulated slowly, "then who did find Joe Diamond for the man who bought the murder?"

"Frank Mayo," Cerutti answered.

Confusion hit Nick like a stomach cramp. Then he stood outside himself: he saw a Nicholas Thirkield sinking into a bog, too hopeless ever to be able to put the whole thing together.

"Nineteen years ago Frank Mayo was the usual run of successful American big crime executive. He probably would have gone on to lead one of their corporate units called a "family," but nineteen years ago, in 1955, there was a dramatic change in Mayo's position, his power and his fortune. Essentially, you could say he owes everything to one person. In 1955 he met and went into business with glamour-beyond-glamour, the ineffable force known merely as "the world's greatest entertainer"—the woman who was once your brother's keystone mistress and procurer, Miss Lola Camonte. Let me tell you about her."

In 1955, at least on the outside, Lola Camonte was still gloriously beautiful, still twelve years away from announcing her last farewell appearance for the first time. The paunch, the wattles, the aqueous ankles, wrists and mouth, the rotting fruits from the cornucopia of her prodigious dissipation were still a decade in the future. In 1955 she was a star at Metro—not yet, however, the great, central Red Giant she was about to become because of her gimmick: a breathtakingly contemporary switch on the Faust legend, in which Faust becomes his own Mephistopheles, his own mirrored, formidable fiend, which then most certainly delivered the goods to Faust as Faust wanted them. In Goethe's version Faust's soul escaped Mephistopheles, but the Faust of Miss Camonte wanted power above all else—and power is known to be very sticky stuff (Professor Cerutti explained).

In 1955 Lola Camonte was perhaps the Number Six star on the Metro list. Six isn't a big number anywhere. Lola's instant identification in the Metro publicity department was "the Mexican sex machine," mostly because of her gleaming blue-black hair and olive-on-pink coloring that she had inherited from her Sicilian parents, who had emigrated to New Orleans. It could also have had to do with her being discovered (for movies) in Acapulco, Mexico, by Harry Small, who was very big on the Metro lot and who had a lock on most of the big-budget musicals. He had discovered Lola on a night when he had a bad cold and had sent out for a hot fifty-dollar hooker to put on his chest (Professor Cerutti chuckled). Lola was so intelligent in those days that though she was only a fifty-dollar hooker in Mexico, it was just to get together enough money to get out of town. At home, in the United States, she was a hundred-dollar hooker. Harry Small liked her style. He put her under personal contract.

In New Orleans, Lola's family had ever leaned upon Mafia benevolence. When the second movie Lola made went into release she flew to New Orleans and asked for an audience with the head of the "family" in her parents' area. She asked him humbly if he would help her to organize a letter-writing campaign telling the studio that the public thought it had a great new star. She explained that the campaign had to be conducted on a national basis, that the letters had to seem to come from all over the United States—obviously from wherever the Mafia was organized (everywhere). Lola averaged two thousand letters a week for eight weeks. Luckily there was a wire-haired terrier in the same movie that had caught the public's fancy, so the picture was doing (mysteriously) big business. The studio connected all the letters about Lola with the unexpected box office. By that time she had the best agent in town.

Lola's intelligence helped her to become a convincing film actress, and she had been born with a skinful of that other stuff that stars squirt off the screen so blindingly. She worked very hard for what she got. She worked hard for it all her life. But beyond energy, intelligence, ambition, talent and beauty she had belief. She believed in the power of the Fratellanza the way a young nun in western Ireland could believe in the power of Rome. It was all and everything. It was the only (American) way to (insured) glory and power.

Aside from her daily prayers to the little brothers, Lola lived by her head. She did this to the square of the degree by which Tim Kegan lived by his head, but precisely to the degree Thomas Kegan lived by his. She was blood over ice. Lola saw the entertainment industry only as a cosmetic that would make her all the more desirable in the seduction of power. Everything it stood for was convenient to her holy goal. Her emergence as the household synonym for sex was just so much rope to pull her up to where she could grab what she had to have, what she told herself she could not live without: power.

Lola wanted that kind of respect from her dead father (who had thrown her down a flight of stairs when she was seventeen because she had come home one night twelve minutes later than he had told her to come home). His soul would grovel in front of her if he could see her as an equal of the Dons. Her mother had had to take shit from him all her life, but if a punk kid who ran coffee for the crap game in the garage across the street came into the store, Pop would practically drop to his knees to kiss that punk's ass. In fact, this was why she believed in the Church. She was a strict Catholic because she wanted to be told over and over again that there was life after death, so that wherever her father was, when he saw her as the equal of any *capo* of the Mafia, he could fall down on his knees and kiss her ass and Mom's ass for fifty thousand years of eternity.

Lola gradually figured out her gimmick when the son of her neighbor at Palm Springs, a square named Kegan, was elected to the U.S. Senate five years before his father said he was going to make it to the White House. First she made good friends with the father. Then she screwed the son. Then he screwed her. Then she screwed him, and so on, and on, and on. It was— like—an idyll. Then she heard both father and son tell her again that he was going to be the next President of the United States. The gimmick began to materialize. She hung around them real close and listened real good. She was able to throw in a few fast angles of her own, so they were more than glad to have her around. After a while, so Tim wouldn't get bored screwing only her, she began to get broads for him. Later on that grew into a major effort. She had a full-time guy on it in Europe because it was worth it. Her cousin lined up broads in New York, and Lola handled Hollywood, Rome and London. She got him the top broads.

Lola wanted a very simple thing for herself. How to get it was just as simple. She wanted to be the national crime industry's lobbyist in Washington. She would be the sole fixer with the federal government, working with the Attorney General's office and the White House. She would be set with every single "family" in the Fratellanza, accepted as the one who could solve their problems with Uncle Sam, from the Congress to offshore deals through the State Department to a lock on the big contracts at the Department of Defense. That was all. To get there would take a little more muscle than she presently had, but she knew she had to be all set at about the same week or, at most, two weeks before Senator Kegan got there as President. When she was ready to make her move she bought the private-line, home telephone number of Salvatore Verdigerri, a/k/a Frank Mayo, a/k/a Frank Brown, at his modest home in Pound Ridge, New York, from where he commuted to the city every day just like any other working stiff, in a Mercedes 600SL.

Mayo was in his workshop in the cellar of his house building a hi-fi set, which was his hobby, with which, by installing it on the roof of an office building, they could bug as many telephones as were necessary to be bugged throughout the structure. Lola spoke to him in a west Sicilian dialect. She said she had important business to talk about and asked permission to fly to New York to see him right away. He knew her in a minute. In fact, he was a fan.

"It wouldn't be good for your business to come to see me, Miss Camonte," he said. "Your reputation and mine, they just wouldn't mix."

"Nobody has to know."

"Look, you my favorite movie stah. I knew the first minute I seen you you wasn't no Mexican. With me, you couldn't do no wrong. You need advice, I wanna help you. Can you get to Havana?"

"Anyplace, Don Francisco."

"Okay. Good. I gotta do some business in Havana. I'll be at the Nacional Thursday night for four, five days. If you want, I'll see you in Havana."

When she called him from her room at the Nacional he told her to come up to room 917-18-19-20-21-22. This was easy for Lola to do because her suite happened to be 923-24-25. She used floral-based perfume because Dons were real straights. When she went into the big parlor, Don Francisco was with a certain man from Naples who had once been from New York for a long time just a little while ago. They were smoking two-dollar cigars, retail cost in Havana. The louvered wooden windows that led to a balcony overlooking the gardens were open. The scents of ginger and frangipani had come into the room. She could see the intensely blue flowers of a tall jacaranda tree in the background behind Don Francisco. Behind and around the tree was a blue, blue sky without a cloud. Overhead in the tall ceiling a four-bladed fan turned lazily, stirring contentment. The sun filled two-thirds of the room in a way that made it seem as if Pissarro had painted them sitting there so motionlessly. The room was tropically warm, but each man remained correctly dressed in a dark suit jacket and wore a dark necktie. Lola was humble and respectful, as they were with her. She addressed them as Don Francisco and Zu Carlo. Zu Carlo was senior. They talked about movies and movie people they all knew for a few minutes. Then her sponsor, Don Francisco, asked her how he could help her. She went directly to the point.

"They are going to make Martin Hanaberry resign," she said. Both men blinked involuntarily. Martin Hanaberry was the big reform mayor of New York in the fifties. He had too strong a grip on the police. Anything that could break the grip would be good for business.

"Who says?" Zu Carlo asked.

"Senator Kegan. He's the junior senator from California."

"That's a long way from City Hall."

"So is Naples."

"The senator or the senator's father?" Don Francisco asked.

"Both."

"Why is Hanaberry out?"

"He's going to have a nervous breakdown. He came out of the war with a very bad condition. He was in a hospital for two years and he picked up a very expensive habit with the treatment. He can hardly support it. When he comes to Palm Springs, I help him."

"How did Kegan find that out?"

"I told him."

"Maybe you shoulda told us," Zu Carlo said sharply.

"New York is big and it can throw off a lot of money," Lola said diffidently. "But when junk comes in like it's gonna come in, and when it takes in the whole country—that's much more money, and it's gonna take much more junk."

"Say what is on your mind."

"If we can bring in, say, ten thousand kilos of the purest and stockpile it, we will have a lock on an industry, not just a business."

"We?"

"An ambassador can go back and forth as much as he wants and nobody bothers him," Lola said. "We could line the whole inside of an ambassador's plane once a week. He could bring in a thousand kilos a week. And nobody would bother him."

"What ambassador?"

"I mentioned to the junior senator from California that it would be a good thing for him and his father to move his father's old friend Martin Hanaberry out of New York and into Mexico now, before he can foul up the next elections. The senator's father has the muscle with the White House to swing it."

"You have good ideas, Miss Camonte," Don Francisco said.

"I like to think I have an investment in my ideas," Lola said.

"First we'll see if you can do it," Zu Carlo told her. "Then we'll talk about your investment."

Lola's long, beautiful hand moved out. Her exquisitely tapered forefinger tapped Zu Carlo on the knee. "Giving you New York—which I have just done—is nothing," she said. "Bringing you an ambassador who will deliver two thousand kilos a week is nothing also. I mean that. Everything is comparative. What I want to talk to you about now is giving you a President of the United States and his entire Cabinet."

"The record of that meeting," Professor Cerutti said to Nick on Schrader Island, "is on a tape Charley Fortunato gave us in Naples the year before he dropped dead. He was the Zu Carlo at the Nacional in Havana. He agreed to give us the tape because your father had been influential in getting him pardoned by the governor before he was deported and because as a patriot he was deeply shocked by your brother's assassination. He also agreed to talk because he had reason to believe that Frank Mayo and Camonte had been giving him a fast count."

"Then they did make a deal with Lola?"

"All the way. Camonte got sixteen and two-thirds percent of their net. In return, to make her what you could say would be an international hostess, when the time came for Lola to move to Washington and establish the new lobby, Zu Carlo and Don Francisco persuaded the national council of the Fratellanza to put out everything to turn Lola into "the world's greatest entertainer"—or certainly the most successful. Tremendous pressure was put on the entire entertainment business and the overcommunications industry. It took them about five years to make Lola the phenomenon she became in world show business—and still is in spite of the paunch and wattles. She suddenly developed as a singer, and her records were pushed day and night, night and day, on every jukebox and by every disc jockey in North America. She was showcased twice a year as the biggest act ever to play Las Vegas. She had a series of her own television shows, the only place she flopped, because even the trained press can't comment on television until after the audience has seen the show, which is bad news in a regimented country, because the viewers just didn't know they were supposed to be watching Lola. But she ran her own movie company. She collected two Oscars. And while she was wowing them from the local Bijou screens to in-person appearances in Tokyo and Paris, she established herself in an enormously effective pleasure complex in Palm Springs which attracted—more and more and more—the highest political figures. She got women for most of the men. She got them whatever they thought they needed. In return they blubbered over her wonderful generosity and fiercely independent spirit, such as when she beat up the mother of a senator in the lobby of the Statler in Washington. Lola's nerves got very taut, and it was up to the press and her powerful friends to make her a law unto herself. As time went on and your brother got closer and closer to the White House, Lola became a very tense, exhausted woman. When Tim got elected, long before his inauguration Lola moved into Washington and her real work began.

"She established herself overnight at the social center of the American government—the lobbyist and fixer for the American crime industry among all top criminal executives of the country. They came to Washington; she entertained them and explained the nature of the services she would offer among all the agencies and branches of the federal government. She was accepted by the greatest of these as a *capo dei capi,* and her father began his fifty-thousand-year term in Purgatory kissing her ass. If Tim had been allowed to serve out his two terms, the lobby would have been es-

tablished forever and would have been just as blandly
self-righteous in its work as the farm or medical lobby.
We might have seen federal price supports for heroin
and evaluations of the lives of John Torrio, Alphonse
Capone and Benjamin Siegel in history books printed
under federal grants.

"It was Lola who handled the Mob's campaign contribution of two million dollars toward Tim's election.
She knew what she was doing. She didn't make the do-
nation directly to Tim. She did it through your father,
whose reaction seems to have been merely that Lola's
friends appreciated as much as he did that Tim was the
man for the job.

"Until the basic deal could be set, the deal by which
Tim would personally acknowledge the contribution of
the two million from Lola's establishment by favoring
them whenever and wherever possible, which is the
only reason for any private campaign contributions—
after all, money's use is to buy not to bless—Lola
waited. This pulled her almost to the breaking point.
She turned to the little doctor on Ninety-seventh Street
for vitamin injections to keep her calm and happy. It
was a miracle cure, but it eventually ruined her looks.

"Tim was elected President. What a wonderful day
for so many different kinds of people, but particularly
for your father. And his friends. In Washington, Lola
began to cultivate, organize and re-establish her place
among the powers. Then—at last—the time came to
affirm the basic deal. The Fratellanza had decided it
would be more dignified to wait until the President
summoned Lola to him to acknowledge the precedent-
smashing contribution they had made to his election.
Eleven months went by and nothing happened for them.
At the end of that time, her own nerves shot, pressed
by her perplexed colleagues, Lola arranged to see Tim
at his father's house in Palm Springs, "the winter
White House"—not knowing that your father records
even the visits of house flies to any of his establish-
ments. She presented her detailed bill for services

rendered, including her services as a fund raiser, emphasizing that the crime industry's offering had been the largest single campaign contribution ever made.

"Lola really thought she had your brother. She was convinced he needed her as though he were some kind of a junkie about sex. She was ready for her great niche in the history of the Mafia. She handed your brother a sheaf of papers that she laughingly identified as the Treaty of Palm Springs. Here is the tape of their conversation." Professor Cerutti touched a button on the console and Tim's distinct, nasal, California voice came into the room:

TIM: No papers, honey. Let's talk about new broads. I'm sick of looking at papers.

LOLA: Read it. It's a big surprise.

TIM: What is it?

LOLA: I call it the Treaty of Palm Springs.

TIM: Okay, but what is it?

LOLA: Did you know I was a Sicilian?

TIM: I knew you weren't a Mexican.

LOLA: Tim, do you remember the Sicilians contributed two million dollars to your campaign?

TIM: Two million dollars? You've lost your mind.

LOLA: We gave it through your father. He handled it. I gave him a check for two million dollars so he would know it was sincere, then he told me to have it made into hundred-dollar bills and put into suitcases. Gucci made the suitcases.

TIM: Is that right? Who are the Sicilians? That's a pretty rich ethnic group.

LOLA: Maybe you better ask your father. [*There is a telephone sound.*]

TIM: Pa? Lola is here. She says some Sicilian organization contributed two million dollars to the campaign and that you took it in hundred-dollar bills. [*There is a long silence on the tape.*] All right. We'll talk about it later. [*There is a sound of a telephone console button being pressed.*] Henry? Get John Don-

nelly out here from Washington. Tell him to bring
me the record of every campaign contribution, legiti-
mate or otherwise. Thanks. [*Sound of telephone
being hung up.*] It's getting clearer anyway. At least
I know who the Sicilians are. Now—what is this
treaty?

LOLA: Look—you sound upset. I mean, I thought you
knew all about the contribution. Let's sleep on it.
There is absolutely no hurry.

TIM: That's good.

LOLA: Tim—don't read it now. Give it back and I'll go
home and we can start all over again.

TIM: I'll be damned. Why—it *is* a treaty!

LOLA: Tim, please. Give it back.

TIM: You will address me as Mr. President, please.
Well! What stately language. . . . Listen to this. I'll
just skim it now, but I will read it through later.
Let's see—the treaty *seeks* the recall of one hundred
and four federal indictments—you'd *like* seventeen
presidential pardons—you respectfully *request* the
elimination of the use of the word "Mafia" by all
federal agencies—you *petition* for greater freedom
for Sicilian importers dealing out of Mexico and
Canada, and you *suggest* that the Treasury Department cease pressuring the Swiss government to allow
them to examine anonymous bank accounts held in
Switzerland.

Lola, are you sure you don't want Joe Bananas
made ambassador to the Court of St. James's?

LOLA: I am very happy that you are taking it this way,
Tim. I was beginning to get a little worried.

TIM: For the last time—I am Mr. President to you,
Lola.

LOLA: Yes, Mr. President.

TIM: You came here for an answer. This is the answer. You may never set foot in Washington again—
unless, of course, you are under investigation. If you
get my drift. Is that clear? And if I hear that you are

entertaining any member of my government from the Vice-President down to the U.S. Marshal in this county, I will see that you are investigated, and I think it will be quite possible that you will be arrested, tried and convicted. This conversation is being recorded, and copies of the tape will be delivered—courtesy of my father—to every one of any consequence in your Sicilian group so that they know where you stand and where they stand. NOW GET THE HELL OUT OF HERE!

[*The tape stopped.*]

"That was why Lola Camonte—and Frank Mayo, for that matter—were happy to cooperate with your brother's assassins by finding Joe Diamond for whoever it was who paid for your brother's murder," Professor Cerutti said.

"But you don't know who that is?"

"Not yet."

"Can Miss Camonte be made to tell who it is?"

Cerutti shrugged. "Maybe. Your father could do it. He is friendly with everyone on the Council. The Council could certainly persuade her to tell who asked her to find Joe Diamond."

"Why hasn't he done that?"

"I would say he hasn't—and I hesitate to conjecture about these things—because he knows they might decide to implicate him and Tim's memory by leaking their version of the two million dollars."

"I don't think so," Nick said. "That was fifteen years ago. Pa and Frank Mayo looked to me to be very good friends. But it could be that Pa is just too close to them to ask them for a favor like that."

"It is not my place to conjecture."

"What happened after the man Donnelly came out from Washington with the information Tim wanted and Tim and Pa had their 'talk' about the two million dollars Pa had accepted in Tim's name?"

Cerutti stared sadly into Nick's eyes. "They met and then your brother never spoke to your father again. He never saw him again. They broke over that issue. It was a terrible blow to your father both personally and financially."

Nick didn't play the organ while the *Wendebo* took
him back to Ashland the next day. He sat in the main
saloon, drank hot tea and felt proud of Tim. He understood all of it, not in its details or even in the inner
meanings of politics, but he knew Tim had been waiting all his life for one black-and-white instance of Pa's
essential unreliability. He suddenly realized that Tim
had lived with what he himself had run away from, and
he began to understand what that signified. They had
both lived in fear of Pa's undependability in any single
moment of time when the existing conditions forced a
choice on Pa of either serving his sons' best interests or
serving Pa.

Nick sat and tried to imagine what had happened
that night in Palm Springs after Tim dismissed
Camonte and called his father in. It must have been a
grisly scene.

Four times, in different places, Nick had read that,
as estimated by historians, psychologists and anthro-
pologists, Tim Kegan had wanted to be President of the
United States more than any other man in the history
of the Republic. To get to the White House he had had
to pay the price of admission to Pa. Somehow his administration had survived Pa's demands during the first
eleven months of Tim's office. Throughout that time
Tim had tried to go forward, carrying the weight of Pa
all alone, taking his cues from Pa on the directions in
which the country was to go, trying to judge when it

would reach a point of no return, living in anguish that the break with Pa would never come.

Then the break came. Lola Camonte gave Tim his freedom. Sometime late that night or early the next morning the finance chairman of the campaign committee arrived at Palm Springs with the records. Tim would have turned everything inside out and would have discovered that two million dollars in hundred-dollar bills had never gone into the campaign fund. A free man, unchained from Pa, Tim would have kicked Pa's door down and would have gone in to tell him that he was barred from the White House and from Washington together with his Sicilian friends, and that if he ever as much as showed his face there again Tim would wind up a Senate committee for an investigation into all of Pa's affairs, including the disappearance of the two million dollars.

It had to have happened that way. In the time he had left, Tim became a different President. Instead of the go-along, frivolous, laissez-faire figure he had offered during his first year of office, he tried to become a strong, pace-setting President of all the people. Nick imagined he could hear Pa shouting that night, "What the hell do you think I made you President for, you little shit—to review the fucking fleet in New York harbor?"

Then Tim would say, cooler than cool, "You had a great ride, Pa. Now you either disappear or I'll drag you at the end of a rope behind the bus."

Nick felt exhilarated. By his own choice, Tim had broken with Pa and had banished him. He felt a wave of love for Tim wash over him. He had always wanted to love Tim. He was ashamed that he had treated Tim the way he had, because Nick knew Pa. He had fled Pa. He should have had understanding of the load Tim had carried within the sound of Pa's voice.

As he was driven into New York, Nick saw all sides of his family clearly for the first time. He was exultant for Tim but he was sorry for Pa. Pa had been Tim's only dominant teacher, and he had conditioned Tim's reflexes the way Pavlov had conditioned his dogs. Pa had bred and trained Tim to be President his way. Pa had inculcated all Tim's attitudes and reactions. Pa had given Tim a religion that money was the only morality or salvation. For Pa (and Pa thought for Tim), if all the criminals and murderers and dope peddlers were on your side to help you make more money, they deserved your support and your country's support. If a bunch of niggers and students and liberals ready to stool-pigeon for the press wanted to try to rock the boat, they had to be clobbered until they could find the carrot held out to get them back on their feet, pulling on the ropes, to keep Pa and his friends moving toward more money.

Pa had thought Tim really understood all that.

Nick called Yvette from Kennedy as soon as he got off the plane. He was self-conscious, spoke stiffly, unable to think of much else except the one big argument they had ever had in three years over a wonderful beef daube that he could still smell. Yvette spoke as if they had never had the argument. She was relaxed and gay.

"Where have you been?" he asked. "I have called you five times from two different cities and maybe five different phones."

"I went to a wedding in Montreal. Best wedding I've ever been to."

"Are you free for dinner?"

"When?"

"Tonight!"

"Yes, I'm free for dinner tonight. What's on your mind?"

"I have to talk to you."

"Have you pinned the killing on Dawson yet?"

"Listen—can't we get whatever it is on your mind dragged out into the open and talk about it?"

"I've been thinking about that all the time."

"Well?"

"I decided—yes—it should be out in the open. We can talk about it tonight."

"That's wonderful. Jesus—I mean, that's great."

"Maybe you better wait until you say it like that. Where shall we meet?"

"I'm at the airport. I have to go to the Walpole to change clothes, but if it's all right with you I'll send a car for you, then you and the car pick me up on the way downtown."

"Fine. What time?"

"Eight twenty your house, eight thirty the Walpole. I'll be in the lobby."

It was snowing. It was freezing and getting colder. The prevailing wind was pushed through the high-walled streets building power, turning each snowflake into a razor blade, driving each one with great force into the faces on the streets of the city.

The table they sat at in the L-shaped top of the dining room at the Canopy—one of the perfect restaurants that Pa owned in New York—put them just out of sight of the rest of the room but directly in line with the main entrance, which was the whole point of the yearning to be seated at one of these six tables that were traditionally reserved for visiting royalty or stately patrons who gave the maître d'hôtel fifty dollars or more. Or for Pa or Nick. Everyone else who entered or departed the place got to see the elite seated to eat against that hallowed wall. Yvette, a seeded international diner, was gratifyingly impressed. She was awed when Nick said offhandedly to the Patron (himself), who hovered over them grinning and rubbing his hands, "You know what we like, Carlo. Do it well, please," and handed the *carte* back to the man without looking at it. Carlo, who was perhaps the third most important man in New York society and in all business conducted on the eastern seaboard, murmured his gratitude and backed away with lowered eyes. The word rolled across the dining room swiftly between and around the packed tables that a British royal was dining at the stem of the L.

"You certainly have a way with tyrants," Yvette said humbly.

"I ought to. My father owns this place."

"*Owns* it?"

"If you like this sort of thing, you should ask your father to buy you a fashionable restaurant. But you have to have a very rich father, and—quite possibly—you have to feel certain that such a headwaiter as Carlo would be cruelly rude to you if you did not."

"As it happens, I do have a very rich father," Yvette said.

"But not the need."

"This is as good a time as any to bring this up and get it over with. My father is Z. K. Dawson."

"Zane Kenneth Dawson?"

"Yes."

"He is your *fath*er?"

"That is why I cannot—will not—marry you."

"I don't understand."

"You and your family think my father had something unspeakable to do with your brother's murder."

"Is that because—are you saying that because of that little reference I made in the letter I mailed from Frankfurt?"

"That was the first time I knew you had any connection with that vile man Thomas Kegan, yes. But you even said yourself that my father was probably the assassin."

"Well, I—you see, Yvette, I—"

"Your father and his people have spread that word from the very first day. From the day your brother died. That wasn't the only word he spread or the only one he blamed, but we know he was the spreader because my father spent a lot of time and money tracking those rumors down."

"This is a very hard thing to talk about, but we've got to do it."

"We are doing it."

"When I wrote that to you it wasn't because of anything my father said to me. My father had never mentioned the name of Z. K. Dawson to me."

"Then how did you——?"

"A man who has turned out to have been the second rifleman at Tim's murder confessed to me on his deathbed just ten days ago tonight. We asked him who hired him. He said he didn't know but that he thought it was probably Z.K. Dawson."

"That's a goddam lie. He's a goddam liar."

"Well, just the same I had to check it out. I went all the way to Tulsa to see your father and——"

"*Tulsa?*"

"The little white house on the Muskogee road. Dentist's chair and everything."

"*Dentist's chair?*"

"He was pretty convincing in an intellectual way about why he hadn't had anything to do with the assassination, but—I'm sorry, Yvette, this is what happened and I've got to say it—he sent me to a motel in Tulsa at the airport, and while I was there—I'm sorry, Yvette—his people tried to kill me."

"Every bit of that actually happened?"

"Every bit."

"Then we both have a bad enemy somewhere. You and me and Daddy. Nick, my daddy hasn't set a foot outside his ranch in the back country of Venezuela in maybe twelve or fourteen years, because he had a bad automobile accident that left him with kind of a crushed face which he is very sensitive about strangers looking at. So much for his living in a little white house outside of Tulsa. Now what is this about the dentist's chair?"

"Z. K. Dawson is famous for holding all his meetings in a dentist's chair."

"Nick, you got a master illusionist working on you.

We've got to be talking 'bout two different people. And as far as daddy ever owning a crappy little motel in a crappy little town like Tulsa, that's silly. He's an Amarillo oil man and a horse-race bettor, and that's all he's ever been or ever wanted to be."

"I saw him. I was with him. Will you let me describe him?"

"I can't wait."

"He's a man of about seventy-five——"

"Ha!"

"——with a great big stomach, a real pink, round face and dead-white hair that curves down over his forehead like a Gay Nineties bartender."

"That tears it. Look, my daddy——that is, Z. K. Dawson of Amarillo, Texas, and Jaime del Arias, Venezuela——is a sixty-two-year-old man with a flat stomach, a dark, dented face and jet black hair that he combs straight back on his head like a Cherokee Indian, of which he happens to be part of, partly."

Nick gulped.

"And if my daddy ever decides to kill you he'll do it in the middle of Main Street at high noon, with a great big loud pistol if not with his bare hands." Yvette fumbled in her purse. She came out with a Polaroid snapshot. Her eyes were filled with tears of indignation. "That is Z. K. Dawson, you turd," she said.

Nick held the picture and stared at it. "I'm knocked out. I'm all out of synch. Not that I'm not glad. I was absolutely wrong. I can't tell you how sorry I am that it all happened that way. But now you can marry me."

There was a delay while the waiter poured wine. Then Nick said, "First, will you accept my profound apologies?"

"Yes. I will. But it hurts to know you're so dumb."

"It all sounds dumb but——"

"I guess I don't really mind if you're dumb. Daddy can support us." He produced a look of such shocked outrage that she giggled.

"Next, are you going to marry me?"

"Yes. I will. If you go to Venezuela and ask Daddy for my hand."

Keifetz had moved into a room at the Waldorf at ten o'clock that night on the supposition that no one would have the time to wire the room for bugging before he and Nick started to talk. Nick had told him to stay out of hotels built after 1962 because there was always the chance that they had had wiring for taps all built in during the construction. Nick got to the hotel at 10:10 P.M. after sending Yvette home in one of Pa's cars.

"How did it go in Wisconsin?" Keifetz asked.

"Interesting. But the real news is that Yvette says she'll marry me."

"Nicholas! Oh boy, that's great."

"So if I take Carswell's job—on account of nobody else wants it—and we move the main office from London to Paris—if that's okay with the tax lawyers—can you handle the operations end alone?"

Keifetz snorted. "What do you think?"

"Okay. Seven percent of the profits, and we apply the other four points of that agreed escalation to start at seven percent."

"What happened to you?"

"No, it's okay. It's fair."

"I'll take it. Any cash?"

"A twenty-percent raise."

"Jesus, now I can take two wives. Daisy won't mind. Her father had four, and she says the second wife is a lot of help around the house."

"You want something to drink?"

"Sure. Why?"

"I have to talk. We have a lot to figure out. It's getting real bad." He picked up the phone and called room service. He ordered a bottle of Scotch, some setups, a platter of cold roast beef and some toast.

"Now think. Did you talk to my father that first day, the day I left Brunei?"

"Yes."

"What did he say?"

"Nothing. He just wanted to know what plane you were on. Why?"

"You are sure that's all you talked about?"

Keifetz thought about it. He said, "I think he asked me why you were going to Philadelphia."

"What did you say?"

"I told him about Fletcher—and I told him about the rifle. And I said you were going on to Palm Springs I think."

"So the only thing he knew before he called you was that I was going to Philadelphia. That means that little sod Carswell called him as soon as he hung up on me."

"What's this all about?"

"Mainly it's about the fact that Pa pretended to me never to have heard the name Fletcher or anything about Fletcher or the rifle when he had discussed everything we knew about Fletcher within an hour after I left Brunei."

"But—what is that supposed to mean?"

"I don't know. I'm going to ask my father. And he wasn't at Palm Springs when I got there. Somebody went to see Miles Gander to bribe him. Somebody knew all about that rifle the instant we found it."

"Your *father*?"

"I don't know. But he was the only one who could have had all those facts. So I'm going to ask him to explain all that to me."

A room-service waiter brought in the food and the liquor and left.

Keifetz poured drinks for both of them. "I lift it to Yvette and you," he said.

"I lift it to your entirely legal harem," Nick said.

They drank. "Enough talk about sex," Keifetz said. "What else about your father?"

"He set up the meeting with Z. K. Dawson for me. Tonight I found out that the man I saw wasn't Dawson, that Dawson hasn't been out of Venezuela for like ten years."

"How could you find out a thing like that tonight and check it out?"

"Because I found out tonight that Z. K. Dawson is Yvette's father, and he comes complete with a photograph."

"But—"

"But what?"

"Well, Jesus. This is a rotten thing to say but—well, what the hell, everybody else has been bending your mind—maybe Yvette gave you a bum steer."

"It didn't happen that way. Besides, she wants me to fly to Venezuela to meet her father. No, it's Pa. And it's not even so much that Pa sent me to the fake Z. K. Dawson, it's that the people who paid to have Tim killed knew I would be at the fake Dawson's, arranged that I be sent to that particular house on that particular road so that they could plant Chantal Lamers and so that everything that led up to Lamers could lead away from her—the magazine, Mentor, the fake stories, everything."

"Then that whole trail led you right back to your father again. Jesus. What are you going to do?"

"You were born in New York. Do you know any cops?"

"My kid brother, Alvin, is a Homicide lieutenant in Bay Ridge."

"Is he straight?"

"Is he straight? My uncle, Doc Lesion, would beat the pole off him if he wasn't straight. He's as straight as a great big Mosler safe at the headquarters of the Boy Scouts of America."

"Good. Now—please get your brother to get a copy of the statement by Martin Keys, the Englishman who tried to throw me out the window. They booked him at the East Sixty-eighth Street station."

"What are you going to be doing?"

"I'm going to Oklahoma to see if I can talk to Chantal Lamers' father in Muskogee. She claimed he was the oldest established pharmacist in town and I have no choice, I have to buy that."

"Don't you think you ought to talk the whole thing over with your father?"

"Yeah, when I have a little more background. After I talk to the Universe Labs in Glendale and buy a copy of their report on that dead cat and the poisoned milk. I'll call you from Palm Springs."

WEDNESDAY, FEBRUARY 6, 1974—
MUSKOGEE AND L.A.

Nick went up and down the main streets of Muskogee very slowly, but there was no Lamers Pharmacy. He looked in the telephone book: no Lamers. He went into three drugstores, and two of them said they were the oldest. Nobody had ever heard the name Lamers. He went through the L's on the tax list at the courthouse. There was nothing in the birth and death records. He was as pleased as he could be. It meant that somebody was convinced that people believed anything they were told. Time and time again, from the beginning of the search, the people up ahead of him in the chase believed that people were all stupid and did what they were told, that they were too lazy to do otherwise. That meant whoever had had Tim killed was somebody who was way out of touch, but, then, anyone who thought he was solving his problems by multiple murders had to be just a little bit out of touch somewhere.

As he drove back toward Tulsa he stopped for a moment on the highway, trying to decide whether he would go into the little white house. He stared at it amazed that he could have thought that Z. K. Dawson, the mystery man of the oil business who had piled up an estimated six hundred million dollars, could have lived in a dinky little house like that. That was why they had invented the dentist's chair gag, he decided. To keep him from thinking about the ordinariness of the house.

He decided he had to go in to be sure, but he shoved the thought out of his mind that he was doing it because of what Keifetz had said—that maybe Yvette was in on the mind-bending from her father's angle. He parked the car in the driveway, went to the front porch and rang the doorbell.

A woman of about thirty-five opened the door. Two small children were holding onto her dress. From where he stood the house looked just as bare inside as it had the last time he had seen it.

"May I speak to Mr. Z. K. Dawson, please?" Nick said.

"Z. K. *Daw*son? The oil king? Here?" The woman was incredulous.

"I wanted to talk to him about buying the dental chair."

"What dental chair? What are you talking about, mister? This is Carson Feenette's place. Z. K. Dawson wouldn't use it to keep his shovels in."

She closed the door. Nick went back to the car and drove back toward Tulsa on the Muskogee road.

He stopped again when he came to the crossroads gas station at Jane Garnet's Corners. For ten dollars the gas pumper told him he had been paid to pretend that there had been two doped guys in the car.

There was no doctor's office next door. There was no state police post across the road.

He spent the night at a motel in Glendale. The next morning he was at the Universe Labs bright and early. They had no record of having received a dead cat and an aspirin bottle of contaminated milk at any time. He was able to reward the girl at the desk with ten dollars for a list of all other principal analytic laboratories. He covered them all by cab. The circuit produced nothing.

He called Keifetz from the Hollywood Biltmore lobby at noon, New York time.

"What happened?" he asked.

"I went with Alvin to the station house. They never picked up or booked any Martin Keys. They haven't had a call from the Walpole Hotel in over a year. Alvin asked me if he should make a little trouble for the manager of the Walpole. I said sure. So we went over and leaned on him. It's a guy named Zendt. Well, you know him. He makes out like he doesn't know what we're talking about."

"Okay, the next thing is, I want you to go to see the police commissioner in Philadelphia, a guy named Frey. I'll call him now. Heller was so meticulous about taping everybody who came into his house that there is just an off chance that he had a concealed camera permanently installed in that room. Frey will have it cased by the time you get there. If there was a camera, what I want you to get from Frey is one clear picture of William Casper. Okay?"

"You got it."

"I'll be with you tomorrow."

Nick called Pa at Palm Springs from Hollywood at twenty minutes after six, but Pa, out of the hospital, would be working at his New York office for the next four days. Nick had dinner at the Mexican Stove on La Cienega and caught an eleven o'clock plane to New York. By the time he got into town it was almost half past nine in the morning. He went directly to the Walpole. The desk said Pa had left for the office at half past seven.

There was a large buff envelope without any stamp addressed to Nick in maroon ink waiting in his letter box. He opened it as he crossed the lobby to the elevator. Reading it, he stopped short in mid-lobby. It had only two lines on it. They were made up of cut-out newspaper type. All the letter said was: IF YOU WANT TO SEE YVETTE MALONE ALIVE STOP INVESTIGATING 1960. WE HAVE HER. STAND BY FOR ORDERS. Nick turned around dully and started for the hotel entrance. He felt as if he had stopped breathing. The force of the fear he felt was suffocating him. He had to stay alive, he told himself dully, to help Yvette. He sat down in the nearest lobby chair, staring at the letter. He had sensed this coming, yet he had done nothing about it. When they thought they had killed Keifetz, there was nothing he could have done. But he could have protected Yvette somehow. He could have done something. He could not find the power to imagine what he would do for the rest of his life if these people harmed Yvette. He got up slowly from the chair and walked, as an old man walks, to the pavement in front of the hotel. He nodded to the doorman to get him a taxi. He gave the driver the address of his father's office.

The taxi swung into Park Avenue and headed downtown. There seemed to be thousands of cars snarling at each other as they ran in their packs, north and south, east and west—predatory, murderous, apocalyptic. Far ahead of them in the thick midtown smog, Nick could see Pa's office building (literally Pa's) as it straddled the broad highway colossally. Nick saw it all at once for what Pa meant it to be: a kindly Maypole for the city, Pa's own phallus towering erectile to one hundred stories tall, one story for each senator Pa ran in the course of his daily work.

It was a spectacular Maypole. From the twelve windows in Pa's private office on the fiftieth floor (above the fifty floors signifying each state in the great American union from which Pa took blood each day in one form or another) a gigantic American flag had been hung straight downward for fifteen stories, faded and thin-looking from exposure to the kinds of weather, over the years, that Pa permitted to happen in New York, but, emphatically striped, starred as a firmament is starred and thereby proclaiming to all who could see that Thomas Xavier Kegan, father of the late, great President of the United States, was toiling personally at his desk at that moment for the greater glory of the American people. The great flag was a gay curtain that obscured the light (such as it was out there in the Kegan-made smog) for one hundred and eighty windows of the building, but it gave Kegan employees great distinction among their peers. Further, since

Thomas Kegan, father of a President, came to his office only about six times a year, and the flag flew only at those times, it could not be said to be a hardship to have to be hidden from the smoky light of the city. Today the flag also hid the combination of falling snow and rain that Pa's satellites could predict but not yet reschedule.

All else Nick had said he had to know from Pa had shrunk away in importance. He had to get Yvette back. That need filled his mind. But to get Yvette back, he realized that Pa would have to answer all the questions Nick and Keifetz had framed. Pa had to make what had happened suddenly make sense. Pa had to explain. When he explained, they would be that much closer to saving Yvette.

Nick felt weak. He hoped he could sit and face his father without his hands shaking. It was one thing to sneer to himself about Pa from the far-off safety of Asia, but now he would be questioning Pa directly to his face. But Pa had to explain, and after he had explained, he had to use his power to bring Yvette back.

As the cab stopped at Pa's office building, Nick made himself think of what Tim had done by facing Pa down after their quarrel and barring him from any access to the government. If Tim could confront Pa, then he must find the courage to confront and question him.

At the fiftieth-floor elevator bank Nick was halted by a security man in uniform who demanded, with the belligerency of a male gorilla whose territory has been entered without permission, to know what he was doing on the fiftieth floor. The man's mean little eyes threatened to beat the bones out of Nick if he didn't come up with an instantly satisfactory answer. He made Nick feel mean. He was already scared by the kidnap note and by going in to beard Pa. He also felt silly, even humiliated, by Pa's grotesque use of the flag as an at-home signal, so he said, "Get out of my way."

As required in the Industrial Maintenance Services Corporation manual of instructions for security precau-

tions on the fiftieth floor, the man hit Nick very hard
directly below his spleen, and when Nick fell to the
floor the man kicked him in the head until he was
unconscious. The man pressed a button in an apparatus
that he took from the outside breast pocket of his uniform. Within twenty seconds two uniformed guards
came running around the corner of the corridor. Using
a metal hook, one of these guards opened the door of
an emergency elevator stationed on the floor. Nick's
body was dragged into the car by the two newly arrived guards. The door closed. The car fell to the basement floor. Nick was put into a panel truck. One guard
drove. The other guard sat on a low bench in the back
beside Nick, who was still unconscious. When the truck
reached its destination the guard handcuffed Nick to
himself. Together the two guards dragged Nick into the
East Sixty-seventh Street police station. Nick was now
more than half conscious. He could stand and move
under his own power. He was booked for forcing entry
and conspiring to do bodily damage. The two guards
left him in a squad room with two detectives.

"Why did you do it?" the fattest detective asked
Nick.

Nick was more fully alert than he had been. "May I
have a moment to think about that?" he asked.

"Take your time, Mac."

"Can I wash up?"

"Sure." The fatter detective pointed to a door.

When Nick sat down across from the two detectives
he said, "If you will take the identification out of my
left rear pocket—it's a credit-card case—and get my
passport out of my right inside breast pocket of the
jacket—that has my picture, okay? My fingerprints are
on file with the FBI."

They told him to take the identification out and
hand it over. "So your name is Nicholas Thirkield and
you look like your picture—what else?"

"My head hurts."

"Why did you do it?" the fatter detective repeated.

"Please look inside the front flap of the card case and at the inside front page of the passport. It tells where to call in case I'm in an emergency."

Each detective took one of the objects and looked.

" 'In case of emergency call Thomas Xavier Kegan, 3 Park Avenue.' " He turned to his partner. "Is that what you got?"

"Yeah."

"Okey-dokey, wise guy," the fatter cop said to Nick, "what's the gag?"

"I had never been to my father's office alone before," Nick said. "I work in Asia. The few times I went to that office I was with my father. You get a different kind of a reception that way. I just didn't understand the security requirements, so his Waffen SS knocked me down and kicked me unconscious because I got off the elevator at the fiftieth floor."

"What is Thomas Kegan's name doing in these, I asked you."

"Thomas Kegan is my father."

The fatter detective called the telephone number written in Nick's passport. Eventually he got through to Thomas Xavier Kegan himself. Nick spoke to his father. His father spoke to the fatter detective, yelling. Nick was released.

"You wanna bring charges against that guard?" the fatter detective asked as they drove Nick back to Pa's building.

"This is a feudal society," Nick said. "I'll bring the charges to my father the duke."

"Say, if you don't mind my askin,' " the thinner detective said, "what was President Kegan really like?"

"He had wit and wisdom," Nick said.

"I *knew* it!"

There was a different security guard at the elevator bank on the fiftieth floor. He was in civilian clothes and he looked as if he was going to cry. He rushed Nick past two successive plainclothes guards along corridors and rooms filled with extraordinarily beautiful furniture to where a giant of about twenty-five years old sat at a small desk.

"This is Mr. Nicholas Thirkield, Mr. Kegan's son," the sponsor said. The brawny youth nodded.

"Do you carry a gun?" Nick asked. "Could they get back this far to you?"

Unsmiling, the young man unbuttoned his jacket and opened it. There was a pistol in each chest holster. Four grenades were suspended from his belt.

"Sorry about that," Pa said when they were alone.

"My head hurts."

"It is a very unpleasant business. But very necessary. There are thousands of Commies and niggers who'd like to get a clear shot at me."

"More every day, I guess," Nick said. He was feeling much, much less compunction about cross-examining Pa.

"I suppose you want that guard fired."

"The one who punched me in the stomach, then kicked me in the head until I was unconscious?"

"Yes."

"No, I don't want him fired. You hired him to do that to people and he does it very, very well."

"I am very happy you can see it that way." Pa beamed. "That is exactly the way to look at it. But how come you're here at all? How come you didn't telephone first. I mean, you *know* the security requirement."

"Pa, listen—I'm going to get married."

"No kidding? Who's the lucky girl?"

"She's been kidnapped."

"Kidnapped? *Kid*—napped?"

Nick handed him the note. Pa read it, his face shattering into dismay. "This is terrible. Let me get to a phone. I'll turn the fucking FBI upside down."

"Not yet, Pa. But what I want to be sure you understand is that we both understand that whoever had Tim killed is also the kidnapper."

"No question about it. Absolutely clear. Oh. I follow

your drift. You mean, we can't get the FBI mixed up in that yet. Okay. Well, I can do better than the FBI. You can have the entire Industrial Maintenance Services Corporation to help you get her back. You can know that I'll do anything in my power to help you any way I can."

"Do you really mean that, Pa?"

"Of course I mean it. Why shouldn't I mean it?"

"Then maybe you'll start helping me by explaining a few things."

"What things?"

"Like how you knew about the rifle before I told you about it. About why you bribed Miles Gander. About why you sent me off on a wild-goose chase to a man you knew was a false Z. K. Dawson, and about the fake murder attempt in that Tulsa motel and the other fake murder attempt at the Walpole. And why you set up that elaborate scheme with Chantal Lamers and the *National Magazine* and Irving Mentor in Cleveland. Just tell me all about those things, Pa. You can help me one goddam heavy great big lot if you'll just tell me all about those things."

Pa's face began to fall apart. Section by section, beginning with his right cheek area, his face seemed to disintegrate, as though he were soluble in the water of the tears that had begun to roll down his seamed, freckled cheeks, which were sinking in imperfect unison, as though he were being punched by small, invisible fists. His eyes rolled in his head. He covered them with his large-knuckled, pale hands. He dropped downward into a leather chair and sat there hunched over, sobbing out obscene heaving sounds.

Nick went to a telephone and called Eddie, Pa's driver-pilot-valet, to come in on the double. Eddie was there in a few seconds, his face stamped with concern. He lifted Pa gently to his feet. He walked him slowly to a doorway almost forty feet away. The door closed after them.

Nick sat down shakily. After a while he got up and

walked to the windows to stare up Park Avenue. The edges of the enormous flag were firmly fixed into steel sleeves that had been built into the window sills for that purpose. It was snowing so hard the sky was dark. The wind drove the hard snow noisily against the window.

Nick was touring among the art objects Pa had spotlighted without price tags around the room when Pa came back into the office. He was erect, but he seemed to be floating. His face had been recomposed, but his eyes seemed to have been stopped down to an impossible f. 64. "Sit down, Nick," he said with great serenity. Nick sat on a straight-backed chair. Pa sat on a sofa facing him.

"I want you to know something," Pa said. "It is a secret so terrible that I could not have conceived until now that I would ever tell it. But you have the right to know."

"I don't want to know, Pa, unless I have to know. And I mean unless it is related directly to the kidnapping of Yvette."

"I think it is."

"Why?"

"Because it will answer your questions about the wild-goose chases."

"Okay, Pa. Tell me."

"A certain person spent four hundred thousand dollars to buy the murder of my son—then I sat with him on a park bench and let him buy me into accepting that."

Fourteen years before, on the twenty-second of February 1960, Pa had been playing high-stakes bridge at the Dial Club in New York when an unknown man suddenly appeared in the doorway and shouted, "Tim Kegan was just shot dead in Philadelphia."

Pa had run out of the club into the street. His driver had stopped him. He told the driver, incoherently, to take him to Philadelphia. The driver took him to the helicopter pad on East Sixty-first Street, telephoning ahead from the car as they went. Pa was in Philadelphia in twenty-nine minutes.

A Dr. Weiler came in to see him in a receiving room at the Philadelphia General Hospital. He was gentle but direct. Tim was dead. They turned Pa over to a police captain named Heller, who managed to get him out of the hospital without meeting the press and drove him to the heliport. By that time Eddie had Pa's own chopper there. Pa gave Captain Heller two hundred dollars, and Heller was too tactful not to take it.

As Pa got into the aircraft he was wondering how he could locate Nick to soften the blow. Ah, what was the use? Tim wasn't there. Tim was dead.

Si was waiting at the apartment in New York. Si gave him a bath and a massage, then he had him take two aspirins with the toddy he made and he wrapped Pa in blankets. Pa slept the night through. When he awoke he wasn't confused anymore. He got up, drank a pot of tea, then called Eldridge Mosely at the White House. He didn't congratulate the new President. He didn't even think about wishing him luck. Eldridge said, "My heart goes out to you, the father. Anything this country can do for the father of its hero is yours to claim."

"Eldridge?"

"Yes, Tom?"

"I want the prick who shot Tim to be nailed. I want him killed. I want that man dead."

"We got him, Tom. We got him yesterday, and he'll pay for what he did."

When Pa hung up he asked Si to bring in all the newspapers. The papers had the whole story. The killer's name was Willie Arnold. He was a Commie. They had nailed him in the finest job of police work the country had ever seen. He was a little punk with a face like a kneecap, sullen and stupid.

In a flash Pa saw how simple it was going to be to kill the son-of-a-bitch. He called the White House again, but the President was not available. He called J. Edgar Hoover, but Mr. Hoover was not in his office. He called Larry Walz, the Governor of Pennsylvania, who was an old-time enemy of Pa's over some aluminum. Walz came to the phone instantly. "Kegan?" he said. "I'm sorry about your son." Then he slammed the phone down. Pa called Pete K. Lascoff, Mayor of Philadelphia. Shaky and a little timid, Lascoff said, "Mr. Kegan?"

"Pete, I want to ask you to get me in to see Willie Arnold." While Pa talked he opened the top drawer of his night table and took out a short-barreled .38 calibre revolver. He looked up at Si. Si didn't change expression, because Si was a man.

"Not in my power, Mr. Kegan," Lascoff said. "The city is overrun with FBI and CIA and Secret Service. There are even two generals mixed up in that crowd somewhere."

"Just get me in with Arnold, Pete, that's all."

"Not my jurisdiction, Mr. Kegan. That's political quicksand out there."

"Then go fuck yourself, Pete," Pa said. Eddie dug out a special number for the police captain who had driven Pa to the heliport. His name was Frank Heller, and Pa called him. Heller got on the phone. He was at police headquarters. He wasn't impressed to be talking to the father of the late President, or sympathetic, or anything but attentive.

"This is Tom Kegan. We met a few hours ago. I want you to get me in to talk to Willie Arnold."

"It can't be done."

"For five thousand bucks."

There was a fair pause. He knew Heller was thinking about it, because he understood Heller. They thought a lot alike. "I can't do it for you, Mr. Kegan," he said slowly, "but if there is anything I can do for you in there—"

"Did he confess?"

"Not yet."

"He didn't confess?"

"No. Sorry. I gotta get back."

"You think he can get off on a thing like this? Is there a chance he can get off?"

"Always a chance."

"Heller, I think you know what I wanted to get in there to talk to him about."

"I think so."

"Follow me on this. Do whatever you can and you'll find out what kind of a friend I can be. You got that?"

"I feel like you do, Mr. Kegan. I am going to do everything I can."

When Joe Diamond killed Willie Arnold, with Captain Heller in entire charge of the detail that was then transferring Arnold to another jail, while Arnold was manacled to Heller's partner, a Lieutenant Ray Doty, Pa knew that he had gotten through to Heller. He had Eddie find out Heller's home address, then he sent Eddie to Heller with a package of twenty-five thousand dollars in cash. Tim was avenged. Pa said to Si, "I don't believe in shit like sins. Tim was murdered, so the man who shot him had to get it from me or through me. Well, Willie Arnold got it, and now I have to find out if he did it on his own or if there were other people I have to pay off in the same way."

Si said he should eat his soup, then he should rest. The funeral had taken a lot out of him.

But Pa couldn't see how a nothing like Willie Arnold could have done it all alone. Just getting as near to Tim as that corner office in the TV Center warehouse in Hunt Plaza took tremendous connections. It was a little plaza. There were only two buildings with rooms and windows. The FBI and the Secret Service would have cased every one of those rooms, and no little punk with a mail-order rifle could just walk into a room and lean out of a window and shoot Tim. Arrangements had to be made. Somebody had to buy his way in to get that close and be so undisturbed.

Pa went to Washington, and Eldridge Mosely moaned out a lot of shit about how there could be another world war if they didn't establish how this kid had done it all by himself, because the CIA was pouring it on how the Russians thought that the Americans thought that they had killed Tim, and they were so overnervous about it that they could be thinking about sending over their own ICBMs first. Eldridge was thinking like a schoolboy.

Pa called the Soviet ambassador and went over to see him. They had done business before on a lot of nickel ore the Russians had wanted to unload, and Pa had helped them out by getting a large piece of wheat together. The ambassador was a helluva guy—no Commie. He convinced Pa that his government didn't feel that way at all. Mosely was grinding a whole different set of axes, Pa decided. Then the White House announced the makeup of the Pickering Commission, and Pa knew the fix was in. So many things were going to get lost and erased from here on in that if he didn't move independently he was never going to find out what he had to know.

So he bought himself the three best investigators in the U.S. government service. He installed them as officers of the Industrial Maintenance Services Corporation, with Jim Cerutti as vice-president of the unit and with an unlimited, open-end budget and plenty of manpower to investigate Tim's assassination. It was the beginning of Pa's own, wholly-owned international security organization, which undertook anything from the routine to the extraordinary in industrial espionage assignments, and which within five years after its establishment was being used by fifty-eight American and foreign corporations, and which, ironically enough, was called upon to carry out one industrial and two labor-union assassinations. It served Pa's basic business tenet: If a service is necessary enough to serve you, the owner, then it is necessary to serve others having similar problems; therefore own everything you use; after you've used it, lease it out, and thereby not only have the services you require at no cost (long-term) but make a profit from the new leased service.

The unit was set up in foam-lined offices in the skyscraper Pa owned over Grand Central Station. Jim Cerutti was established in the Apostle Islands in Lake Superior and directed the search from there, using, at peak point, sixty-one investigators and Pa's formidable access to the records and files of the Pickering Commission, the FBI and the police departments of principal cities. Money was the miracle investigative tool.

Pa had Mosely grant him the special privilege of attending any Pickering Commission hearing, open or closed, and permission to talk to any witness the Commission staff produced. The members of the Commission were all old friends of Pa's and they were glad to see him on two of the fifty-seven times all of them actually got together. Pa went to Philadelphia with Hughie "Horse" Pickering, head of the Federal Synod of American Churches Pro-Christ, chairman of the Commission. They saw Joe Diamond together. Before they went in to see Diamond, Pa arranged for a meeting between Horse and Captain Heller. Heller explained carefully that there was a big TILT light-up on Diamond's forehead. Heller told them that Diamond had paresis and would not last very long, and there was no use going in to talk to him, because he wouldn't talk.

But Diamond did talk. He pleaded. He implored them to get him out of there and into the Commission's own jurisdiction in a cell in the District of Columbia or any other venue except Philadelphia and he would tell them anything they asked. "You gotta understand, Dr. Pickering," he said, almost sobbing, "I can't talk here. I can't. My life is in danger if I talk here. Can't you even figure that out, Dr. Pickering?"

All the time Diamond pleaded with Pickering he never looked at him. He stared at Captain Heller. Dr. Pickering, although a theologian, was quick to understand that paresis produced paranoid responses. He explained that to Pa when they got out of the cell. But Pa didn't think so. To him, Diamond had no symptoms of anything but fright, so he arranged through Harry Matson, the then police commissioner of Philadelphia, to have Captain and Mrs. Heller invited on a Caribbean cruise. Professor Cerutti fixed it for Mrs. Heller to enter a regional baking contest and win a trip for two, and she persuaded her husband that he had to take a rest for ten days after all the terrible strain he had been under. When Heller was gone, Professor Cerutti went into Diamond's cell and they talked everything over. Pa gave Diamond fifty thousand dollars through Cerutti, which must have been a kick in the head for Diamond's estate taxes, because he was dead in just under two months. How it happened, the police said, they would never know, but out of nowhere, in an isolation cell, he developed spinal meningitis, and it killed him. Cerutti said he had been injected with the virus, but there was no autopsy.

Cerutti came away from the talk he had with Diamond with information about a Dallas man named William Casper, including a solid description of the

man. Real work got started. He found out from Diamond that the name of the second rifleman was Arthur
Turkus Fletcher and that he was still at large, having
disappeared on the day of the assassination. Pa was
disappointed that Diamond refused to talk about Captain Heller, but he would not. He was scared witless of
Heller, and, even more unusual, he was in love with
Heller. But he was a lot more scared than he was in
love, Cerutti said. What could a cop do to him that a
judge and jury hadn't already done, Cerutti asked Pa
rhetorically. Kill him, Pa replied. Right, Cerutti said.
So there was nothing, absolutely nothing, about Heller.
But Diamond did say that the Philadelphia police had
set Tim up, so the link with Heller wasn't entirely
moldy, Pa said.

The man they were looking for had his own an-
tenna. He found them before Cerutti could find him.
Cerutti was getting closer, but no cigar. Five weeks af-
ter the Pickering Commission investigation had gotten
under way, on a Saturday afternoon while Pa was at
Rockrimmon trading in forward yen by telephone with
Zurich and playing pinochle with General Nolan, Jim
Cerutti called.

"The man we're looking for contacted me today," he
said.

"Who is he?" Pa yelled into the telephone. He could
feel the adrenalin rush into his bloodstream. His lust to
bring death was so vividly with him that he began to
breathe shallowly.

"He wouldn't say." Cerutti laughed grimly. "He
called from Chicago."

"Then he has men on you?"

"Very good men. I didn't know it. We hope to pick
them up today."

"They won't be there. They were just supposed to
pin you long enough for him to call you."

"Yes."

"What did he say?"

"He wanted to ask me to ask you if you would be willing to talk things over through a friend of his."

"Who's the friend?"

"Alan John Melvin."

"The Assistant Secretary at the Pentagon?"

"Yes."

"What is there to talk over?"

"He wouldn't say."

"How do we confirm with him?"

"Somebody calls Alan John Melvin."

"Let me think about it."

He abandoned the pinochle game and the forward yen trading, left General Nolan and went into the kitchen to find Si. Si was polishing silver.

"The man I'm looking for just got Cerutti on the phone in Venezuela." Si kept polishing. "The man wants me to talk to his man, who is an Assistant Secretary at the Pentagon. What do you think?"

Si stopped polishing. "That is good," he said, looking right at Pa.

"Why?"

"Because the man has been sent to test the temperature. To see if you are serious."

"What is serious?"

"To see if you want to kill his master."

"That's all?"

"That is all. No real talking with the tester. You know how it works. This is big business. This is a very big deal. The man you want has to bet his life that he can talk you down—if you serious."

"I get the picture," Pa said. He went back to the pinochle game. That night when Cerutti called from Bermuda Pa told him he would meet Alan John Melvin at four o'clock at the family apartment at the Walpole in New York. Then Si broke out a platter of roast beef sandwiches and a solid bottle of Pontet-Canet, and General Nolan played them a concert on his ukulele, doing "In a Little Spanish Town," "You're the Cream in My Coffee," "Exactly Where We Are," and other popular favorites. When he had finished, the General said wistfully, "I can't tell you how I miss the little broads Tim used to bring up here."

"You're sixty-eight years old, fahcrissake," Pa said. Pa himself was then sixty.

"Age in sex is a lotta Sunday-supplement crap," the General said. "Sometimes I get so nervous I could bang the cleaning women."

"Why didn't you tell me before?" Pa said indignantly. He picked up the telephone at the big console. "I'll call Eddie in Palm Springs and have him send out some broads from New Haven."

Alan John Melvin was a sweet-faced man with an old-fashioned New York, Greenwich Village, Al Smith accent. The Assistant Secretary was just another civil service employee to Pa. There were no preliminaries and no offers of drinks. Pa didn't even ask him to sit down. He just stared up at the man from his chair beside his drink and said in greeting, "Are you going to tell me who sent you here?"

"No, sir."

"Then take a message and get the hell out of here. Tell him what he knows already—that we're so close behind him that he can hear us breathing. Tell him that when I find him—like next week or the week after that—I'm going to have him killed. Get out of here."

"He wants to talk to you."

Si knew his stuff. Si was right.

"Where? When?"

"At noon tomorrow. On the bench of the traffic island at One Hundred and Twelfth and Broadway."

"How come?"

"You can't kill him there."

"My sniper could."

"He might. However, my principal is counting on the fact that you want to shoot him yourself. For maximum security there will be an extra detail of police in the area."

* * *

He was sitting on the bench on the traffic island, his image distorted by the thick fumes from car exhaust. Pa got out of his limousine on the east side of Broadway. He stared across the monstrous traffic in disbelief. He had known the man who was waiting for him on that bench for thirty years. They had come up together into the ownership of the nation. If the entire country were divided into ten-foot squares of ownership, between them they would have owned three of the squares. What the hell would that man want to kill Tim for?

Pa crossed the half street to the island. As it happened, there was a red light. He had not thought to look for traffic. He was staring in unbalancing hatred at the man who had ordered the death of his son.

The man smiled the way he had always smiled. "Hello, Tom," he said.

Pa fell limply onto the bench beside him.

"I know what you're thinking, Tom," the man said, "because I know how you think. You're thinking how you are going to have your people follow me to wherever I'm going when this is over, and how, when you have me staked out, you're going to kill me there. Well, that's the way you are. That's the way you think. But a man has many levels of resources, doesn't he? While we talk, as we came here to do, I want to address myself to some of the many levels of your mind. Where you really live. To who you really are. That's what I want to do while we're sitting here, Tom."

Women with baby carriages and women with shopping bags walked past them on the way to both sides of Broadway. Old men shuffled slowly in front of them, glaring because they had preempted the old men's bench and a chance to die a little faster in the carbon monoxide. It was very cold, but the sun was up there somewhere behind the smoke. It radiated rather than shone. Pa and the man were oblivious of the hordes of people, the poison that they had helped to put into the air, and the traffic. The man spoke on and Pa gaped at him.

"You and I have more in common than maybe most people in the world, Tom. Better than almost anyone else, we made it our business to find out where the money was, then to go and get it, didn't we? We know that money is neither a production good nor a consumption good. We know there is no satisfactory way to state the value of money. They've used feathers and salt and stones for money. They used human skulls for money once, in Borneo, didn't they? But the true fact is, Tom, over all the millennia nobody—not even you or I—knows what money is or how it works. We know only where and how each man uses it. Isn't that right? We know it has to be portable, durable, divisible and recognizable. But there is an intangible essential that is even more important than all those qualities—and even harder to define. That essential is value."

A woman with a small child holding each of her hands interrupted him to ask how to get to the subway. The man stood up and took off his hat. He showed her the way. He sat down, replacing his hat.

"You might never guess why money was invented, Tom. While we talk here you've got to bear one thing in mind. Money was invented to accommodate human emotion. Human emotion, Tom—not daily needs or trade—human emotion established money among the earliest and most primitive people. Money was invented for only two uses, Tom—and these are anthropological and sociological facts, not any whim of mine— for marriage first, for blood money second. The second use of money by mankind, Tom, was for blood revenge. Blood revenge always demanded a life for a life unless the injured party could be suitably compensated for the loss of services. Simple. Now—the loss of services of your son as President of the United States presents an extraordinary position of advantage for you and goes far beyond the usual measurement in the use of money for blood revenge."

"Are you trying to pay me for the loss of my son's life?" Pa asked incredulously.

"No."

"You haven't talked this much in all the time I've known you. You can save your breath. I'm going to kill you sometime tomorrow."

"I don't think so, Tom. Not after you hear my proposition."

"What proposition?"

"Lemme tell you. Lemme say it the way I thought it all the way through, because that's how it's going to make sense for both of us. Now—the first thing—of course I can't really pay you for your son's life. Sure, the whole blood revenge thing is right there between us, but you have so much money now that for me to try to pay you pro rata would mean I'd have to treble your fortune. I just don't think any one man has any money like that."

Pa had a kind of sense of smell that not many men have, because if more than a few had it, there wouldn't be enough money in the world for all of them or anyone else. The man who was talking to him, who had the gift himself, saw it come over Pa. He had been rambling, waiting for Pa's blinding anger to diminish so that his great natural force could take over again. The time had come.

"Then what are you talking about?" Pa asked.

"I want you to think about one thing, Tom. Just one thing. I want you to think about having three times as much money as you have right now. Then we can call it quits, because the right thing will have been done. Now—I'm going to leave, and your people are going to try to follow me. We'll be in touch."

The red light for north-south traffic on Broadway changed just then. The man got up and walked rapidly across the street to the downtown side and got into a large black limousine. The car rolled before the door closed. Two policemen on roaring motorcycles came out of One Hundred and Twelfth Street, sirens open, to make way for the limousine. A motorcycle escort filled in behind the car as well. The procession picked up enormous speed, turned toward the river at One Hundred and Tenth Street, and disappeared.

Pa goggled after it with admiration.

June was the best time for Pa because it was the time furthest away from Christmas. Christmas always made him feel almost suicidal, because it brought out his feelings of unworthiness when so much emphasis was placed on the time of Christ's birth, the screaming shops, secrecy of the surprises, the last-minute flurries of activity, which muddied the water of his imperfections all over again—everything pointed to that one allegedly perfect figure, all of it suggested the birth of more wives like Nick's mother, who had called him a guttersnipe, proclaiming to all that he was the least of men.

But it was June and he was safer. Christmas was as far away as Nick's mother. She was dead, but he was alive. He had her son in his fist with June and his money to protect him. He would play it loose. He would employ his cardinal rule of living, which was to imagine everyone in the world wearing long, red, lumpy winter underwear. Nobody could dominate him standing out there in lumpy red flannels. Tim was dead. Nothing he could do about that. Amen. God bless you, Tim. He sobbed uncontrollably in the closed room at Rockrimmon. Alan John Melvin must have reached the main gate by now. The car would take him to the country airport and the government plane would fly him back to Washington. It was clear and simple. Proper blood-revenge money had been paid over as the greatest homage ever made to Tim's life and memory. He had done it for Tim.

"The requirement here, Mr. Kegan," Alan John

Melvin had said, "is that you assemble forty-seven blind companies in not less than thirty states that ostensibly have no connection with you and, most important, no connection with any single person or ownership. We think it will be all right if these companies shuttle their tenders through as few as a dozen of the private procurement and lobbying offices in Washington. That could add to the general diffusion. My office will see that these forty-seven firms get the major contracts for the program. Of course the moonshot and the whole space program is a very big and going concern even now, but by sixty-two it is going to be so enormous that you will be required to form probably ninety to a hundred and fifteen more companies as anonymous as the first forty-seven, because several billions—twelve to thirty billions of dollars—are going to be involved here."

During those first years, his busiest years with the space requirement, he certainly didn't want the status quo disturbed (mainly because he didn't want to have to think about it until he had become entirely used to the new arrangement). But as the contracts were transformed into so much money and into the power of so much money he became each year more agitated until, at last, he instructed Professor Cerutti and the unit at Industrial Maintenance Services Corporation to find the second rifleman and to build an apparatus to overtake the evidence that would be a case against the man without in any way seeming to involve Thomas Kegan, because that would have constituted a double cross.

Now that the money had been earned, Tim's and his own honor would be finally avenged.

The trouble was at night. Sometimes late at night he would come wide-awake despite the cold baths and the massages, despite the sleeping pills. He would feel such a guilt of greed, and a father's guilt, and a kinsman's guilt, and the guilt of power, that he would need to scream. He would put on a pair of swimming trunks, go out and lower himself into the heated pool, and try an underwater scream.

He thanked the compassionate Almighty God with large contributions to the Society for the Propagation of the Faith for His mercy in making each year less and less terrible. When three years had gone by, he could live with it. He had his own billion dollars. By the time ten years had gone by and he had three billion dollars of his own, he never thought of it at all. His one hundred and sixty-three companies had done a grand job for the space program, had probably done a better job for being under his direction than discretely owned companies could ever have done, because, in the finest sense, he had done it all for Tim—for President Kegan. The conquest of space had been Tim's own program, originated and installed by Tim, then made possible and practical by his consecrated father.

Pa let his head fall back on the sofa. He closed his eyes. There was a considerable silence. Pa opened his eyes.

Nick said, "I see."

"In a sense I betrayed him. In another sense I did not."

Nick said, "So you have known all these years who murdered Tim."

"Yes."

"When I found that rifle it must have upset you greatly."

"I didn't know what to do."

"So you called the man and asked for orders."

"Yes."

"He told you to send me to that house on the Muskogee road."

Pa closed his eyes. "Yes."

"Then all those other things to throw me off the track."

"Yes."

Nick leaned forward. His voice rose and trembled. "Well, I didn't make any whoring deal with the son-of-a-bitch—*who is he?* He has Yvette. He's holding Yvette. Who is he, Pa?"

"Z. K. Dawson."

"*Daw*son."

"The real Dawson. But no use your going after him. He made that deal with me, but he isn't the one who had Tim killed."

"Who was it, then?"

"His daughter."

"What?" It was a cry of pain.

"Dawson only made the deal to buy safety for his daughter."

"Pa, open your eyes."

Pa's eyes opened.

"Z. K. Dawson's daughter was only about sixteen when Tim was killed."

"Oh, no. She was older than that. She had to be. She was sleeping with Tim. She was laying men at Lola Camonte's. She planned Tim's killing with cold blood. We have the whole story. Cerutti dug up the whole story."

Z. K. Dawson's daughter met Tim Kegan in Washington when he was a young "bachelor senator" just three weeks after his nomination to the candidacy as President, three weeks before his official campaign for election began. It was so exciting for such a country girl. She had hardly ever left her daddy's ranch—which surrounded Bryson, Texas—until she was fourteen. Daddy ran eight or ten thousand head of cattle as a tax gimmick. He wasn't a rancher. He was an oil man: fields, pipelines, gas, refineries, tankers, gas stations, trucks and money. He had big oil and helium plants in Amarillo. He was heavy with grain elevators, zinc smelters, meat-packing and flour-milling in the Amarillo area. The ranch straddled the New Mexico border for hundreds of square miles on either side and swole out all over Deaf Smith County. It was just about the healthiest place in the world to raise a little girl.

Her culture was rounded off in three finishing schools in three altogether different European countries so she could have the power of talking foreign languages plus American and West Texan. Her daddy was as proud as proud can be (Pa said): "She sure as hell is entitled to a warm corner. She can speak Italian, French and German just like she was a wop, a frog or a kraut."

When she was sixteen she was sent to school in Italy for two years, under the tutelage and protection of the Duchessa di Giorgio, who ran a school for five young

girls each year in different parts of the Italian penin-
sula, depending on the seasons. It was after the long
series of operations, and she was a lovely child, with
hair the color of an almond skin and eyes like laurel
leaves. She was tall, with a wistfully faraway expression, yet with enormous animal vitality. Italy was her
dream. Italy was the distilled adventure of all history.
Italy was the romantic time of the world.

After two springs with the duchessa at Villa Somali,
twenty-three kilometers from Venice on the Treviso
road, then two summers at another Villa Somali (next
door to the central residence of the late, thrilling Ga-
briele D'Annunzio Rapagnetta, Prince of Monte Nev-
oso, at Lago di Garda), two autumns at yet another
Villa Somali at Siena to learn the supreme enunciation
of the Italian language, and two winters in Rome at the
Palazzo di Giorgio, she was no longer a virgin. The
duchessa was firm, almost harsh, with her girls about
virginity. She not only did not believe in it for young
civilized women but she had two almost-elderly clients
among the Black nobility who paid her well to deliver
them.

One of these was a marchese, Luigi Debole, a diplomat who had served his country steadfastly in the Ar-
gentine, France and Yugoslavia, who had certain difficulties in sexual expression. Signorina Dawson's youth
meant a great deal to him, so much so that, on her
ninetcenth birthday, when he was sixty-two, they married in Rome in a civil ceremony that was accompanied
by a marriage contract drawn by Daddy's lawyers. In
the contract it was stated that Signore Debole had an
aversion to using his title, although it was acknowledged that his wife could use it after his death if that
suited her.

After the wedding, Daddy, through the President
and the Secretary of State, arranged to have the Deboles posted to Washington, where her beauty trans-
fixed the diplomatic corps and the press.

What started her on being the first roundly educated member the family had ever had was the bad car accident she had with Daddy (Pa explained), which had nearly ruined her face. In less than a year she had recovered nicely from all the plastic operations, but Daddy couldn't bear to look at her, because they wouldn't have gotten into the accident at all if Daddy hadn't been such a heavy drinking man in those days. She wouldn't have been a fraction as lovely as those three Japanese surgeons made her if it hadn't been for the accident. If she had looked the way she had been born to look, it seemed an easy thing to say that Tim would not have glanced twice in her direction, and very well might have had another shot at the Presidency after taking a four-year rest at the end of his second term.

But there had been the terrible accident. She had been sent away to school in Siena, Lausanne and Baden-Baden. She had married an Italian diplomat named Luigi Debole, who was always described in Washington society pages as "an older man." The Deboles were assigned to the Italian Embassy in Washington because Daddy had explained to the President that it was something close to his heart.

Tim was never sure where it was they met in Washington. It would be fair to say that they met at about thirty cocktail parties, dinners, balls, late suppers, hunts, charity auctions and lunches that they both attended on a professional basis. Unknown to her, and for reasons of appeasing his own conscience, Daddy had hired the best, most accepted high-pressure public-relations firm in the country to undertake the job of establishing in print—as if it weren't true unless it had been set and seen in print over and over again—that she was the most beautiful woman to grace official Washington since Evalina Hunt, daughter of the British ambassador in the time of the thirty-one day Harrison administration in 1841. Since he was a modern man, it is possible that it was these repeated published claims measuring the extraordinary beauty of Signora Debole that first moved Tim to "pay attention" to her, rather than when, where or how often they had met. However, it was generally decided by both of them after the fun and games had gotten under way that they had been introduced by Lola Camonte at her "magnificent Georgetown house." During this time Lola was hard at work as an erection engineer on Signore Debole. As an Italo-American, she was determined to be decorated by the Italian government for the undoubted effect it would have upon many key members of her own (invisible) organization.

Before the campaign started, Tim and Signora Debole had about eight days of callid copulating in a flat that the wily senator had rented for the purpose. Then he had to become inseparable from his entourage of press and politicians, and he found himself under total scrutiny. He had become almost physically addicted to her (and she to him). Pa noticed how distracted he was when he should have been giving all his attention to the campaign. He and Tim had a showdown about it, screaming at each other (in whispers) in Tim's compartment on the plane, Pa attacking him obscenely for what he clearly saw to be a dangerous weakness, but Tim said he was just unable to accommodate Pa without any relief for himself. So a compromise was reached. Rockrimmon was named as the place of withdrawal to which the candidate would go whenever possible during the campaign and where, by common agreement with the press, he would be allowed to recharge his vigor without any encroachment by them. They watched every entrance and exit to the place, but they couldn't get closer to the candidate than two miles. He never overdid it. Three days away from them was the most he was ever able to achieve, but each time he visited Rockrimmon Signora Debole would have been flown in by a small Jovair helicopter at least twenty-four hours before the candidate's arrival. The signora and her husband solemnly told each other that she needed to visit her father in Texas each time she had to be away with Tim.

An irreparable thing happened. Tim was able to transfer his physical addiction to six or so other ladies while, almost simultaneously and certainly against her will, Signora Debolc fell hopelessly in love with him. It was not only irreparable. It was incompatible with serenity.

The time between his election and his inauguration, Tim reasoned, would be the logical time to let the signora cool off. He had had a lot of fun with her, even though in a confined way upon a small space, but now there was work to do (as opposed to what he had been doing in the Senate) and other beds to activate. From the beginning of his time with her he had said all the usual words, because she seemed to have become a passionate Italianate by adoption, utterly denying herself the laconics of an uncomplicated Texas girl in love. But the accident with Daddy in that terrible swaying, roaring car had turned her into an extraordinarily complicated woman. The awful fright of the long drive on the high mountain road with a drunken man at the wheel began it, and it never ended. If she dozed without the right drugs to put her completely to sleep with a wiped mind, that all came back to her. The pain throughout her body between the periods of oblivion brought by the morphine and the Demerol impressed itself upon the country-girl placidity she had been born with and changed all its smoothness into the contours of a serpentine nebula. Then the mysterious Japanese surgeons had appeared riding in on the carpet of Daddy's money. A face, a new chest and legs, had been chosen for her from the arcane records of the faces and figures of wonderful fairies who lived amid the flowers of a child's dream, and she had been transformed. Everyone soon came to see what the surgeons showed

them as being her. But she knew the molded flesh between the back of her eyes and the tip of her nose was
not her. She was wearing a mask. She knew the perfect
bosoms, more flawlessy sculpted than anything by Ber-
nini, and the incomparable legs were a shell she had
been packed into, a suit of armor that concealed the
real plainness of a piano-legged, flat-chested, turnip-
chinned country girl with teeth like a mouse's and eyes
so close together that they turned her full face into a
profile. All the press carried on about her beauty, but
she knew. Her husband rhapsodized about her beauty,
but she knew. When Tim happened to her, she was lib-
erated from the mean little prison of her surgery. In
Tim's arms, listening to him make love, she not only
forgot all about what she had looked like once, but she
didn't care. She didn't have to care. The most important man in the world wanted her and needed her so
deeply and frantically that he could not understand
how he survived when they were apart.

She asked him fifty times with many variations, "If I
weren't already married, would you marry me?" And
Tim would say, "We'd be married right now if it
weren't for that." She would dream about being married to Tim, then she would extend it, as any sheltered
country girl from West Texas, raised purposely without
a view of television or American magazines would do
it. She fantasized becoming the First Lady of the Land.
She would have to convert to do it, but she would at-
tend his exotic church services with him every Sunday.
She was a darned good cook, and she'd make them
give her a private kitchen in the White House so Tim
could find out what real bardele coi Morai and
sucama-growl dumplings tasted like. She saw Tim for
three days a month at Rockrimmon, and she thought
of nothing else but Tim for the rest of the time. She
told her husband she had discovered wonderful health
treatments at a new, inexpensive fat farm in Connecticut, and he patted her on the behind and waved good-

bye, having decided realistically that her little tussle with the almost-certain next President, as reported to him by his ambassador—with many protestations of how a young wife must be allowed to use her wings now and then—would essentially be good for Italo-American relations.

Then Tim got bored with sex games because there were so many other electrifying discoveries connected with the Presidency, and in his mind and body became as totally finished with Signora Debole as if they had never met. It was a brutal changeover. She was in multiple orgasm, dreaming edifying dreams of breaking wine bottles over the prows of new aircraft carriers— then she was alone on an iceberg drifting northward into the Arctic Sea. But she understood. She most certainly didn't blame Tim. She knew it would be at least three weeks after the inauguration before she could see him again. She waited. She began to telephone the White House ten and twelve times a day, until Secret Service men appeared to say that someone had somehow gotten the use of her telephone and had been calling the White House to oppress the President. She threw everything in the room she could lift at them. She screamed. She tried to set fire to the drapes. Her maid, Pucinella, had to give her a bath and two Seconals to calm her down. When she felt strong enough she went to see her only real friend in Washington, Lola Camonte. She sat in the wicker armchair while Lola took a bath and she said, "I can't sleep. I can't eat. But I knew he was carrying the country on his back while he was learning a new job, so I was able to stand it." They spoke in Italian, because Lola wanted to get all the practice she could, because after she got the decoration from the Italian government which this broad and her husband could get her, she was going to visit Italy and meet a lot of very important, aristocratic people. Let Frank Mayo and Ginzo Porchesa try a thing like that—and out on their ass in the Quirinale.

"I didn't go near him at any of the receptions. He didn't dare look at me when we were both in the same room at the White House, because he knew he would have had to drag me off to the Secret Service john, the way he used to. But I can't keep this up. What am I going to do?"

"You look terrible."

"I do?"

"You look absolutely terrible. Hasn't your husband said anything to you?"

"About what?"

"About looking terrible."

"He wouldn't say it like that. But—yes—I think he did. He said perhaps I was overdieting."

"The first thing is to get you physically back on your feet," Lola said.

"How? I can't think about things like that. All I can think about is Tim, Tim, Tim."

"I'll handle it. Say, have you heard anything around the embassy about the Order of Merit that Luigi said he was arranging for me?"

"How long can he go on this way? It must be tearing him apart. I just can't get out of my mind the anguished picture of a man achieving his dream—the American Presidency—only to have it turn to ashes because he cannot be with the woman he loves."

"Luigi already talked it over with the ambassador. They want to set me as a Commander of the Order, and I then wear the badge on a green, red and white bow. Come on! What is the use of crying? Give him a chance to get his administration started. Let him figure out how he is going to shake the newspapermen."

Signora Debole was able to sustain herself admirably for exactly five more weeks. Then, when she saw Tim taking the wife of the Tanzanian chargé d'affaires into the Secret Service john, her mind snapped. She made a terrible scene at the Mother's Day reception for the diplomatic corps which was instantly concealed from the public, but was the scandal of the season among the people in those circles that mattered most to the President's father.

Pa went into a towering rage that night in the presidential apartments.

"How did you ever get yourself involved with that crazy Guinea broad?" Pa shouted.

"She isn't a Guinea broad, Pa," Tim said in his unruffled way, puffing on a long, thin cigar. "She's a West Texas broad whose father, Z. K. Dawson, is one of your more cherished enemies."

"She's the wife of a ranking Italian diplomat. That means she has to be invited wherever other key diplomats are invited. She's out of her mind. You didn't see the worst of it, because the detail made you disappear, thank God."

"It was pretty rough on Bijou Kanaawarili," Tim said. "I mean, it's bad enough being black and having to live in Washington."

"The Deboles have to be shipped back home. No two ways about it," Pa said.

"That wouldn't be a bad idea," Tim said, "if any of us survived after we did it. If she ever thought she was being sent back to Italy—where she never came from—because of me, I swear I think she'd shoot me at the next reception."

"That's a possibility," Pa said. "I mean she might take it so big that she'd round off to the Italian press, and they'll print anything."

"What do we do?"

"We'll have to get Lola her decoration. But they'll have to give it to her in Rome. Lola will have to insist that the Debole woman goes to Rome with her to give her moral support, and they'll have to go by boat. The day they go, Luigi Debole will have to be promoted to some cockamamie job in the Italian foreign ministry and fly home. Then he'll meet the boat and break the news to his wife, and we'll have her safe in Italy."

"Not bad, Pa. When?"

"I'll see Lola tonight. I'll see the ambassador tomorrow and set the decoration. Then we'll allow two weeks for Lola to get Mrs. Debole to agree to sail with her on the *Conde di Locarno,* which goes on the twenty-fifth. Say three weeks at the outside."

"Okay. I'll visit the fleet in Hawaii, then some work at Palm Springs, then an inspection of the guerrilla training in Panama. That'll fill it."

There were two complications. The first was that Lola took the signora to New York to introduce her to the wonderful little doctor on Ninety-seventh Street who had the power to make people so happy by the simple injection of vitamins. Lola figured correctly that if the signora was very, very happy and relaxed to the point of being zonked out of even remembering who Tim Kegan was, she might be all the more willing to voyage with Lola to Italy. The signora took to the vitamin shots in the most maximum kind of way. When they left New York, Lola had arranged for the doctor to make up an enormous travel kit, then to send like a year's supply in a crate to go out with Lola in the pouch. The signora took doubles and triples. She really zonked Tim right out of her mind.

The second complication was that in her third month in Italy, almost eight months since she had been with Tim, Signora Debole became pregnant. Lola's erection lessons and his share of the enriching vitamin shots from the little happy-doctor on Ninety-seventh Street had made it possible for Signor (actually a marchese) Debole to have sex with Signora Debole. However, through some quirk of need in her neurosis, which through the strain of the rejection by Tim and by passing through the sieve of the massive vitamin injections (which turned out to contain quite a bit of methadrine as part of their recipe) had evolved into psychosis, Signora Debole became convinced that the child she was going to have was Tim's.

Luigi Debole knew his wife had wandered away from sanity. He had her attended by two of the best professors of medicine and psychiatry, respectively, then she was taken quietly by ambulance and plane to the very best psychiatric clinic in the Canton of Zurich, where she was slowly taken off the miraculous vitamins and where an obstetrician consulted with the medical and psychiatric doctors who were treating her.

She got stronger. Her mind became much clearer and more sure of itself. The great obstacle to her full recovery was her conviction that she had burdened the great American President with the shackles of tragedy that would forever keep him from breaking free into the sprint to glorious achievement. She had utterly forgotten Bijou Kanaawarili's finding love in the Secret Service loo. She could think only of what she had cost Tim and the world, because that kind of feeling was the sort of massive punishment she deserved to match the dimensions of the sin she had committed. Now she was bearing Tim's son. He had the right to know that he had fathered a son. That knowledge could force him to light a torch that would light up the world so that his boy could live beyond the present darkness. She wrote to tell him. She addressed the letter to Lola Camonte at Palm Springs, then enclosed a sealed envelope within that envelope for Tim.

It arrived two days after Lola had taken the Treaty of Palm Springs to Tim at Pa's house. Lola had always believed that she had been touched by the Hand of God, which had given her access to wonder and to privilege remotely beyond any opportunities shown to any other people, but she had not believed in any of the essences of justice as that concept might have been taught in the civics classes or in the Sunday schools. But, as if from the Hand of God again, here was her right to justice held in her hand. Everything came to her in its final shape. She saw her armies assembled on the plain, as it were. She thought she was inventing the domino theory, by which if she could move this crazy lady now in Switzerland in the right direction, that lady was rich enough and crazy enough to give it to Kegan right where he deserved to get it. She flew east with her makeup man, who was also her bodyguard, in last year's Gulfstream II, because it could go farther faster, to check everything out with Frank Mayo, because this wasn't something she wanted to make a mistake about twice. The essence of Don Francisco's considered judgment was, "Listen, that prick took two million dollars from us and did nothing for it. If you got it figured out as close as this, I say it can't do us any harm and can only do us a lotta good."

So Lola went into her files and got some samples of Rockrimmon stationery. She had a studio printer copy a few sheets. She fooled around with a couple of drafts, then she typed out the letter to the signora in Switzerland, and copying his signature from notes in her files, she signed it "T." The letter said:

Signora:
A long time ago we had some pleasure together—good, wholesome, light-hearted fun. Apart from the fairly sick scene you made at the reception I haven't set eyes on you in about seven months. Now from your booby hatch in Switzerland you write me that diseased letter to tell me that I am to be the father of a child you are expecting. For once and for all, I am sorry you are ill, I hope you recover in good time. If you continue with these wild allegations I will feel that they must be reported to your physicians. I am sorry for you, but I will not be victimized by a silly, deluded woman.

Sincerely,
T

On the second day of its life the Debole infant was

strangled to death by its mother in the Rütliberg Clinic. No charges were pressed, due to the weight of psychiatric evidence. Luigi Debole entered a petition for the annulment of his marriage by the Church. Z. K. Dawson had his daughter flown to the family ranch, which was six hundred and ten miles in the interior of Venezuela. Because he was a very busy man he left her mostly in the care of the devoted man who had been assigned to her as a companion and counsel ever since childhood, William John Casper.

For as long as she could remember, Billy John Casper had been there to help. He had no kin of his own. He had been Daddy's right hand for thirty years. He was sort of given to her when she was a little girl because Daddy wanted her to have a good, strong man to lean on whenever she needed one. They had long talks. They did a lot of riding. She had a chance to cook again, and since there was nothing for almost six hundred miles that she could complicate, she just kept getting better and better until, when the time came that Daddy had to be in Libya and Lola invited her to Palm Springs, she just couldn't bear it to have everything so quiet anymore, so she went. Daddy had left a little Dassault Fan Jet behind in case she wanted to go shopping in Puerto Rico or cut over to see the bulls at Cali, so she had Billy John lay a couple of pilots on, and they worked their way over to Panama, then up to Acapulco, then straight on in to Palm Springs and Lola.

It wasn't the same old Lola. She was glum. She was upset. The house was just empty of people, and that just wasn't normal. They had a quiet dinner together with Lola hardly speaking at all, then finally, when they were sitting out in the patio staring at the pool, she said to Lola abruptly, "Say, what's the matter with you?"

"I'm all upset."

"Well, *tell* me about it."

"That's why I'm so upset, honey. I feel I gotta tell you about it, but I can't do it."

"I am just going to make you tell me. I never saw you like this. You've got yourself all worked up."

"I'm just torn in half. I mean, you know how hard the truth can be. I have this great feeling for Tim because he is the President, but much more than that you are my dearest friend, and right is right."

"What about Tim?"

"He has been calling me about you for about two months. Ever since—about the time you sent him that letter from Switzerland through me."

"What does he say when he calls you?"

"It got so bad I began to make tapes of the calls. I just couldn't believe it and I just couldn't stand it."

"Stand what?"

"Before I could believe it was him saying it I had to go over to his father's when they were out here and stand up in front of him and hear him say it."

"Say *what,* Lola?"

"Well, he uses you for the cheapest kind of laughs."

"How?"

"He says things like you've been trying to blackmail him into marrying you. He said you were the joke of Washington and that somebody had started a pool to bet how many times you could call him in a single day."

"No!"

"I'm sorry, baby. But I had to tell you."

"How could I blackmail him into marrying me? I was married to an Italian who could never agree to a divorce. Tim pleaded with me to marry him. He asked me a dozen times last fall. He said he couldn't live without me, Lola—he wanted to throw the Presidency away because he said he couldn't go through with it without me to give him strength. It was like going to a play! I see it now. It was just like watching a performance in a play."

"Do you want to hear the tapes of his calls?"

"Yes!"

"No. I'm sorry I asked. You mustn't hear them. Getting yourself sick over him isn't worth it."

"I have to hear them, Lola. I have to *know* what he is saying about me."

"I can't stay here. I can't sit through them again."

"Just show me how to turn the machine on. Just show me."

Lola rolled the playback out. She slipped a set of headphones over her friend's head on either side of the wild eyes so filled with fear, then she pressed the PLAY button and withdrew into the house. What Lola had done was as easy as editing tape anywhere, from the White House to Watergate. She had recorded telephone conversations of Tim talking about four hundred women in the past six years. It had once been a breakfast ritual with which he had started the day. The worst things he had had to say about the stupidest, dullest and most aggressive women had been edited by Lola into one relentless tape.

The tape rolled and spoke. Signora Debole wept. After a while she stopped weeping. Her eyes stopped looking wild and fearful. Her eyes became dry and hard. She thought of everything Daddy had done for her and how this man had shamed him. Any man who could do a thing like that to her daddy just didn't deserve to live.

She slipped off the headphones and walked slowly back into Lola's house.

The next morning she called Billy John in Venezuela and asked him to meet her at the apartment in Dallas. Daddy was still in Libya. She left Lola's and got out to the Palm Springs airport before Lola woke up. She flew straight to Dallas. Billy John got in two hours later flying his own Riley Dove, which had a twelve-hundred-and-ninety-mile range but which he insisted on flying anyway, even if he did have to stop to refuel between Caracas and Dallas.

She had taken a pretty good-sized traveling kit of the special vitamins away from Lola's, but this time nobody but she and the little happy doctor were going to know that she was back taking treatments again. They made her feel simply sensational. She knew what she had to do as clearly as if it were just a walk to the schoolhouse. When Billy John got in she told him everything. She told him what she had meant to the President and what the President had done to her because she had chosen to remain at her husband's side in Italy. Billy John was horrified that any man would dare to do and say such things to Z. K. Dawson's only daughter.

"He deserves to die, Billy John," she said evenly.

"I have been saying that for a very long time," Billy John said, "and so has your daddy and every other loyal Texan. And I don't mean just Texas. There are plenty in Oklahoma too."

"Well, we are going to have him killed," she said.

Billy John had taken orders from the Dawson family for over thirty years. Z. K. Dawson did not encourage independent thinking and neither did his daughter. Billy John had never thought himself to be very bright, but he knew enough to know that these two were just about the most brilliant people who ever lived. The kind of money they had proved it. This little ole girl might be Number Two Thousand in the line of people who said Tim Kegan ought to be shot, but it was characteristic of the Dawson leadership that she was going to be the first one to do something about it.

"What can I do to help?" he asked.

"Remember when Neiman's had that Italian Week and we all came down here and one Sunday we were out to Judge Sissons' spread and they had that big-money rifle competition?"

"Sure do."

"Remember the shooter who won just about everything? Shooter name of Turk Fletcher?"

"Sure do."

"You go on and find him and see if he'd like to make a day's pay shooting for us."

After Billy John left she stayed in the apartment shooting vitamins and thinking real hard. She had to get some inside help. She knew from all the newspapers that he was going to Philadelphia and the Liberty Bell on Washington's Birthday. She decided that, no matter what else, the advance man was going to have to lean a whole lot on the Philadelphia city police, because they were the ones who would know how to take him the best way from the airport and into the city and out again. She had to get to know a key Philadelphia cop, that's all. She'd have to put the problem to him with a large piece of cash money. She had to know from an inside man like that where the best place would be along the route for Turk Fletcher to wait to pick him off. Lola knew everybody. She called Lola.

"Sweetheart, can you introduce me to a real important policeman in Philadelphia?" she asked. "Not me personally but a friend of mine name of Billy John Casper?"

"I could ask around."

"Sure would appreciate it."

"What do you need it for?"

She was stacked to the eyelids with the special vitamins, so she didn't mind saying, "Nobody can expect me to take what *he* has been saying about me. He's going to be in Philadelphia on the twenty-second of February and I'm going to do something about it."

"Give me a couple of hours. Where are you, honey, so I can call you right back?"

It took Lola closer to four hours, because Frank Mayo was out of the office. "You're okay, honey," Lola said when she called back. "Tell your man to see a fella name of Joe Diamond who runs the Casino Latino in Philly. Police are his business. He expects a call.

Whoever calls, tell him to say Frank Brown."

Billy John saw Joe Diamond in Philadelphia. Diamond sent him to see Captain Heller. When all the business arrangements were worked out, Billy John brought Turk Fletcher up from Dallas and together they all murdered the President in exchange for Z. K. Dawson's daughter's money.

When Pa finished talking in the enormous twelve-window office, they sat silent. Nick stared at the floor. He understood why Yvette had refused to marry him, but he couldn't understand how a girl who could look straight out into anything the way she could look and who could laugh the way she laughed could ever have had a whole, different shadow soul nailed onto her, a soul made of lead and pain that she dragged behind her wherever she went.

He forced himself to stand. He walked slowly, swaying, to the wall bar and poured whiskey into a glass. The bottle clanked rhythmically against the crystal like a drummer making a set of rim shots. He tried to bring the glass to his mouth, but his hand was shaking too badly. He spilled it over the front of his shirt. At last he got part of the enormous shot down, then he walked across the room to Pa's john and was sick. When he came out, colorless and haunted, he said, "Where is she now, Pa?"

"She's dead."

"Dead?" He held onto the back of a sofa, with his eyes tight shut. He would never see Yvette again. He would never see her again, and everything went into collision inside his mind, stopping him from thinking anything except that she was dead.

"I'm very sorry, Nick."

Nick slumped down upon the sofa and gripped his face in his hands.

"Who killed her, Pa?"

"She killed herself. She put a bullet through her head."

"When?"

"Sometime last night. She's lying in the city morgue right now."

"Pa?" Nick lifted his head out of his hands and stared at his father. "How do you know she's in the morgue? How do you know she shot herself?" Nick could see his father so hazily, in such distortion, that he knew he must be weeping.

"My people are connected. They flooded the police departments with the picture we got at the hotel and the picture we picked up from Commissioner Frey. I put out a five-thousand-dollar reward for information. A morgue attendant collected it this morning when the police brought the body in."

"I want to see her."

"Of course. We'll call ahead. They'll be expecting you."

"Pa—that isn't enough! How did you know she was dead?"

"We read the note she left for you at the Walpole."

"The kidnap note?"

"Yes."

"*She* left it?"

"Yes, she left it. Zendt read it and called me. I decided she was going to disappear the worst way. That she was going to kill herself."

"I—*Jesus!*"

"I'm sorry, Nick."

"What a mess. What a terrible mess." He turned toward the door. "I have to see her."

"The name is Mrs. Luigi Debole," Pa said. "Nick!"

Nick turned to face his father. "I never had even the wildest notion that she meant this much to you, that feeling like this could build up in such a short time. But no matter what, kiddo, we've got to keep realizing that a certain kind of justice did triumph here, because Z. K. Dawson was struck in his heart this morning the way I was struck when I got the news that Tim had been cut down."

"Fuck you and Z. K. Dawson, Pa," Nick said. "You're both the disease of this world."

Nick stood in front of Pa's building below the gigantic flag, looking up Park Avenue with his arm in the air until a cab stopped in front of him. He told the driver to take him to the city morgue.

Pa's people had called ahead. He was taken directly to the body without any delay. The attendant rolled the drawer open. He saw the bare feet with the tagged toe come out first, then he made himself move his eyes up along the sheet, and after an agony of effort, made himself look at the head.

He was staring down into Chantal Lamers' dead face. He stared. He blinked. As he blinked, everything seemed to fall into place. He understood where the mistake had been made, and he knew to the last drop of blood what the mistake was going to cost. He felt as if he now held a map in his hands, a map that was going to lead him directly to Tim's murderer, Chantal's murderer, and the murderer of twenty-two other people who had just happened to get in the way. More than that, more than anything else, he knew where to find Yvette.

When he left the morgue he dropped a fifty-dollar bill on the driver's lap, realizing that it was the first extravagant thing he had ever done in his life.

"What the hell is that?" the driver said.

"That's for taking me to good news," Nick said. "Now take me to a phone booth."

He called Keifetz. "Did you get the photograph in Philadelphia?"

"Right here."

"Is your brother the cop still in good shape?"

"He's a real jock," Keifetz said. "He keeps in shape to watch pro football on television."

"Where is he?"

"Right here in front of the set."

"Can he take the weekend off?"

"I'll ask him." Keifetz was back on the phone immediately. "Sure. He can take the weekend. What's up?"

"Meet me at the Park Avenue entrance in fifteen minutes," Nick said. "Bring the picture, and tell your brother to bring his badge and gun."

Keifetz' brother Alvin didn't talk very much, and he had spent a lot of time in his life practicing looking menacing. Never had a man mastered his art as well as Alvin. Nick stared at the photograph that Captain Heller's concealed camera had taken of William Casper, a/k/a Casper Junior, a/k/a Billy John Casper, a/k/a Hilliard Casper II. It was a face he could have described in his sleep: round and fat, with faithful-dog eyes and white hair—a broad part showing a lot of pink skin—hair curving down over his forehead as though his was the hand that had shaken the hand of John L. Sullivan. Nick could imagine the face at any time of its life, because although it had been corrupted by age, it had not been matured by it. It was still the face of a boy—eager, untested, immature, untouched by empathy or feeling.

His earlier elation had turned into euphoria. Yvette had been condemned, ruined, doomed, killed and resurrected, saved, cleansed and restored to him all on the same morning. As Pa had predicted, justice, an unexpected justice, might even triumph, but first he wanted to retrieve Yvette whole and unharmed before he turned away to collect eyes for eyes and teeth for teeth. They drove to La Guardia. While Keifetz and his brother Alvin chartered a two-engine jet, Nick went to a telephone and called Keith Lee at the Riverside Hospital in California.

The two-engine jet flew them to Ashland, Wisconsin.
The Fairchild-Hiller FH-1100, a utility five-seater helicopter, had been flown up from Chicago and was waiting to take them out to Schrader Island pad. They were
set down beside Professor Cerutti's big house in twelve
minutes' time. There was a short scuffle. A guard with
a machine rifle told them they were trespassing. Nick
identified himself, but it didn't seem to mean anything
to the guard, so Alvin knocked him down and dis-
armed him so he wouldn't lose his head.

With Alvin carrying the rifle, the three men walked
around the large, pink box, a copy of a late Georgian
house, and kept walking to the long, low laboratory
building where much of Pa's power was stored. Professor Cerutti was annoyed to see them. They went into
the enormous file room. Professor Cerutti was at his
writing center in view of the door. When he saw them
he exploded. "Look here, Thirkield," he said coldly, "I
don't know what the hell you think you are doing here,
but you are not here at my invitation, and you are most
distinctly not welcome."

"We've come for Yvette Malone," Nick said.

"Did your father send you for her?"

"No," Nick said.

"You mean you yourself deduced that Miss Malone
was here?"

"Elementary, my dear Watson," Nick said, unsmiling, "considering all the blunders you made." If
Cerutti's sense of superiority was his self-image, the

mirror held up to his tiny world, Nick had decided this would be the quickest way, perhaps the only way, to break him down. The statement inflamed Cerutti. He gasped at the size of the insult. His face became mottled. *"Blun*ders?" he said with outraged incredulity. "What are you talking about—blunders?"

"Tell us where Miss Malone is, then you and I can talk about that."

"She's in the main house. Who are these men?"

"New York Police Department," Nick said.

Alvin flashed his badge. Keifetz tried to look as mean as Alvin.

"Call the main house," Alvin said to Cerutti. "Tell them we're on our way. Tell them to watch their manners." Cerutti telephoned the main house and gave instructions. Alvin and Keifetz left.

Professor Cerutti, trembling with rage, led Nick to the facing sofas at the far end of the building. They sat down opposite each other. "What blunders?" Cerutti said.

"You mean you'd like to hear the worst blunder first, I guess. It has to do with Z. K. Dawson's daughter, Professor. In your most recent scenario for my father you killed the wrong woman."

"Do you mean Lamers?" Cerutti said with disdain. "I knew Lamers wasn't Dawson's daughter. But I also knew you knew nothing about Dawson, had never met him, and were absolutely ready to accept any plausible woman as his daughter—so what are you talking about?"

"I am going to marry Yvette Malone."

"Really? How nice for you."

"Yvette Malone is Z. K. Dawson's only daughter."

Cerutti's face puckered. It began to fold in upon itself—a dutiful company man's mock-up of his employer's face when in crisis, Nick thought. For a moment it seemed possible that he was going to cry, but he recovered as he stared at Nick with bulging eyes like wet grapes and said, "His daughter?"

"This morning my father told me the story you had written for him. The rousing scenario about Mrs.—I mean Signora—Luigi Debole, and all the while he told it he was thinking about Chantal Lamers and I was thinking about Yvette. We were talking and threatening and weeping about two different women, Professor. He didn't know Yvette, really didn't know she was alive, much less that she was Z. K. Dawson's daughter. He meant Lamers, so he thought I meant Lamers. He thought I had fallen in love with Lamers. I mean it was just about the lousiest piece of staff work and research anybody ever handed his boss. I mean it is such a lousy piece of staff work that it is going to hang you or electrocute you or whatever it is they are going to do to you, because you are cooked, Professor Cerutti. When I went to that morgue in New York and looked down at Chantal Lamers, baby, I knew you were cooked."

"Cooked? Hanged? Me? You are mistaken, Mr. Thirkield. I did nothing. I killed no one. All I did was to make up scenarios. I gave your father some perfectly harmless stories. It is a method we developed many, many years ago. In business, as in all other life situations, people tend to accept the plausible if it is wondrously documented; they definitely tend to believe what they want to believe. We stumbled on this system when your father wanted to take over a certain large corporation, but his way was blocked by the company president and two members of their board. Your father said to me—this is almost thirty-five years ago, Mr. Nicholas Thirkield—if he could only get something on those men, he could use it as a lever to pry them out of their places, and I told him I would think about it. I did. I decided that in our modern society truths did not matter. The illusion of truth, the appearance of truth, indeed, let us say the application of the techniques of fiction playing like searchlights upon a fancied façade of truth, would entirely suffice. We pioneered these methods in modern society, we did it—until today, as we see, our politicians and political structure could not exist without them. Life and truth have been turned into diverting, gripping, convincing scenarios, Nicholas Thirkield. All they require is a command of an extensive research facility and a fixed target upon which to project the new truth."

"The New Truth," Nick murmured.

"Communications has come a long, long way from Dr. Goebbels, the father of our science."

Nick slid the photograph out of its envelope and extended it to Cerutti. "Who is this?"

Cerutti looked at the picture of the round old man with the sweeping white forelock and the wide pink hair part. "In my scenario that was Casper Junior or William Casper. And other variants."

"Who was it really?" Nick said harshly.

Cerutti grinned at him. It was a proverbial ear-to-ear grin. "Actually, it was Major General James Nolan," he said.

Nick's jaw dropped. Cerutti giggled. "Counting everything," Nick said, "he must be a fairly filthy son-of-a-bitch."

"Why do you say that?"

"Because my father would never let me meet him."

"Yes. The General has been a background character for thirty years. But so have I. I made a tremendous amount of money, but I never found myself anyplace where I could spend it."

"It's probably just as well."

"Why?" asked Cerutti quickly, feeling cheated of a main chance to prove his devotion to duty.

"That way you had less of a chance to fuck up. But why did every succeeding scenario conflict with and contradict the one before it?"

"The use of these techniques both personally, as in your case, or upon masses of people—as, for instance, when the techniques are used by politicians—requires that the subject remain confused, that he become exhausted by the unrelenting confusion and, ultimately, hopeless that anything he could ever do, any effort he might ever make would produce any solution whatever inside his maze. We were, after all—the politicians and I—able to stay ahead of you."

Nick took a deep breath. He exhaled very slowly. "Professor," he said, staring into Cerutti's eyes with loathing, "the police who arrived with me don't know why they are here, except that they know they are to take Mrs. Malone out. They don't know who you are or what you've done under instructions from my father. I'll just assume for the time being that you would rather not be hanged or that you would rather be hanged than to go into a building with twelve thousand other prisoners, sleep in a cell with five other men in a three-level bed, the other men sharing you."

Cerutti became pale. A small tic developed at the corner of his mouth. He had been feeling the pressure, but now he was beginning to understand what pressure was.

"I am prepared to offer you this deal on my own," Nick said. "If you don't accept it, these police will take you in. After that no deals can possibly be made, as you can understand, considering the nature of the charges that will be brought against you."

"Mr. Nicholas Thirkield, I want you to understand something. These records you see all around you are so terribly incriminating to your father, to me and to hundreds of people whom they involve, that this entire building is wired with an explosive charge so tremendous that nothing on this island could live once it is detonated."

"Very sensible precaution, I'm sure," Nick said.

"You don't think I am intimidated by a New York cop flashing his badge?"

"I think you would regret being executed for kidnapping. Let's put it that way."

"In short, you are defying me. You are saying to me, 'Go ahead, Cerutti, blow us all up.'"

"I am counting on you fucking up, Cerutti."

"What do you mean?" the professor snapped.

"I mean you are very fond of what you like, and you like Cerutti being alive, therefore no crazy idea of my father's orders to blow this place up would have any effect on you if you had to be blown up with it."

"What is the deal you are offering me?"

"Tell me everything you know about my brother's assassination, Professor, and everything that followed it—*everything*. Then I can let you disappear in any way you choose."

"I'll accept that. Very kind of you, I'm sure."

"Not at all. Please don't thank me. They'll catch you anyway."

"I don't think so," Cerutti said. "I have been thinking about this for some years."

"Professor, what was real and what was a scenario?"

Cerutti dialed at the console. The table opened and a tray with a pot of tea and one cup and saucer ascended. Cerutti poured the tea and said, "Captain Heller, Joe Diamond, Turk Fletcher and Willie Arnold were as real as real can be. That guard who beat you up on the fiftieth floor of your father's building was very real. He was telling you specifically and incontrovertibly that you were to stop."

"The rest was fantasy?" Nick asked.

"Almost."

"Except the twenty-four murders."

"I had nothing to do with those. Furthermore, most of those deaths were only coincidental—people wanted to believe they were connected with the assassination."

"What did Z. K. Dawson have to do with any of it?"

"Nothing. Dawson was just a mistake of your father's. He was off Dawson because of an aluminum deal Dawson won about twenty-six years ago, so he thought he'd give Dawson a hard time—create a public scapegoat and pay off an old score. But your father's mistakes got worse. He decided he wanted to protect Fletcher. He wouldn't let us find Fletcher. Are you going to tell me that a man who doesn't even bother to change his own name, who has limited means of earn-

ing a living, who has to be in touch with his centenar-
ian mother and who had an Amarillo accent like a
knife sharpener in Indonesia could have gotten away
from our people?"

"But, why would Pa—"

"Oh, your father knew where he was. He told General Nolan to give Fletcher a letter of reference, and
your father followed Fletcher straight through to Bangladesh and Brunei, but I think he wanted Fletcher
alive to keep himself sharp. There was no way for him
to get old and flaccid while Fletcher was still alive, and
then there was the biggest reason of all, which your father didn't know himself. He could not stand the guilt
of what he had done. He wanted to get caught and he
wanted to be punished. Deep, deep down in his mind
and in his soul he had put the whole combination together. He knew Fletcher was working for you. Maybe
he even told Nolan to tell Fletcher that there would be
a safe job for him with you. Then he waited for something to happen that would make Fletcher talk, make
Fletcher draw you in, because your father knew absolutely that if you could get pulled into this you would
surely turn to him, and with him steering the whole investigation through you, he could force its course and
could bring about his own apprehension."

"Pa was using me to make sure he was punished for
what he did to Tim?"

"Yes. But he didn't know that. And considering all
that he had done over fourteen years' time to cover his
tracks, he didn't have to lay down an order on the first
day that you were to be protected—no matter what—
that no harm was to come to you. He didn't have to
demand that I bring Lola Camonte into the scenarios.
That was getting close to the bone, that was right down
at the real issue."

"Camonte and Frank Mayo were real, then. Just the
way the witnesses said they were?"

"Camonte and Mayo are real people, God knows,"
Cerutti said. "But except for one section, they were

just characters in the scenarios and therefore unreal. The real part was the tape your father had made about the meeting between Camonte and the President, when the President heard for the first time that your father had stolen the two-million-dollar campaign contribution that had been made through Camonte by the crime industry. All of the rest about Camonte I fabricated, because our science functions in the balance between the real and the fanciful, and that is what makes our scenarios the marvelously effective things they are—the task-force strength of all modern American political action."

Nick inhaled very deeply again. "Professor"—he sighed helplessly—"did Pa have Tim killed?"

"Yes."

There was a silence. Nick covered his face with his hands. Then he released them and sat back, staring at Cerutti.

"Your brother knew that your father and his friends had been taking him down the wrong road in the Presidency. For eleven months he had gone along because he could see no way to break with the men who had elected him. Then your father gave him his chance over the issue of the stolen campaign contribution, and the President barred your father and the rest of the oligarchs he could identify from access to the White House and key government offices. He became, so to speak, his own President. When he did that he sealed his death warrant."

"His death warrant?" Nick cried out. "Who signed it? Who ordered it? Who are these—the rest of the oligarchs Tim barred?"

"The executive committee of the men and women who own this country met and voted. Your brother had to be punished, and a man they could trust had to be moved into the White House in his place. They controlled the CIA, the Secret Service and the FBI, and it was understood that one of these would organize the strike, but your father said it was his right to get that part of the work done. It was he who had lost your brother in the first instance. It was his job to make it all good and to re-establish himself among his peers. That motion was carried."

The two spokesmen for the executive committee arrived at Rockrimmon in a sweet little Jovair that was affected by its pilot. It was a red, white and blue four-seater, tandem-rotor helicopter, with egg-shaped tail fins mounted on outriggers below the rear rotor head. It was supercharged with a 235 horsepower 6A-350 Franklin engine, and it had a range of 200 miles at 105 miles per hour. Its owner-pilot was Francis Manning Winikus, "the grand old man of the CIA," cultivated, healthy and pink behind his neat white moustache and his twinkling eyeglasses. "The Incomparable Spymaster," Georges Marton, the espionage chronicler, had called him. His passenger was Dr. Hugh "Horse" Pickering, leader of the Federal Synod of American Churches Pro-Christ, who was heavy-boned, hearty and cunning. The two men were dressed for the country, except that Dr. Pickering wore a black-and-white-checked sports jacket and black slacks and loafers, as befitted his calling, and Winikus wore a blood-red-flecked and -lined tweed jacket with blood-red slacks and kerchief, as befitted his.

Pa and General Nolan were waiting for them at the pad. For the day only, the General wore his full kit: brass glowing, fruit salad bulging, overseas cap at a merry tilt. It had not been the uniform he had worn in World War II. He had gained sixty-one pounds since the old, flat days, but Pa liked him to be dressed out for ceremonial occasions, and the uniform had been measured, cut and tailored by Welshman in London only five weeks before. Pa wore knickers and a pullover under a heavy overcoat.

They rode to the house in two golf carts under sable throws, Pa riding in the lead cart with Francis Winikus, the General handling the rear guard in the cart with Dr. Pickering. Si had a bowl of hot punch waiting for them. Winikus asked for a Dr. Pepper drink. Dr. Pickering wanted Ovaltine laced with Southern Comfort. General Nolan waded into the hot punch. Pa drank beer.

There was a roaring fire going in the high-manteled, wide fireplace. Standing around it, sipping their drinks, they settled what had gone wrong with the Army-Navy game the previous Saturday. In a little while luncheon was called.

At Dr. Pickering's curate's request, Pa had laid on a sound, high-protein meal (because Dr. Pickering did not feel it right for his presbytery to buy and serve proteins openly): jambon persillé, slabs of cold roast beef, cold haricot beans in oil and garlic, and a magnum of 1949 Bonnes Mares. Francis kept them entertained with stories of how he had gotten ITT into France the day before World War II was over, what an advantage it had turned out to be, and how it had all become quite a large pot. Dr. Pickering ate 2.3 pounds of beef, 1.2 pounds of ham, but bypassed the beans. After lunch they went into Pa's study, with its four five-foot-wide balconies cantilevered high up on the forty-two-foot-high walls to get at the upper books. They sat around the open fire this time, the two visitors on sofas on either side of Pa, Pa in a low, comfortable, calfskin chair. General Nolan was at a desk, making notes to keep up the pretense that the conversations were not being recorded.

Si brought in a glass *cona* of black South African coffee on a battery-operated heating stand. The General passed among them with a bottle of Pelisson cognac that had been in the cask for thirty years. When Si left, Francis said in his wonderful voice that could speak so many languages, "We are interested to hear your final reactions, Tom."

Pa stayed impassive. Everything had been handled courteously and skillfully, as though to convey the impression that he really had a choice in the matter—which he did not. The owners of America in plenary session had voted death for Tim unanimously. Pa's loyalty to himself and to them—call it bushido, call it omertà, call it love of country—now required that Pa re-establish himself for having made the move that had disaffected Tim, rendering the President useless to them. Pa felt no mawkishness about what he would have to do. Tim knew better than most people about what would happen to him once he dared to pull this man-of-the-people stunt. Now it was either Tim or Pa. As far as Pa was concerned, Tim had already stretched him out on the ice as though he were an old Eskimo whose time was up—over a couple of suitcases filled with some lousy campaign money that they used to buy whores and burglars with. He had barred Pa from Washington. He had locked the door on Pa's mutual owners of the country, and that was ritual murder. Pa could tell himself with total confidence that if Tim had ever had to have him killed, the way Pa now had to have Tim killed, Tim would have done it with a big, toothy grin. All right. If he didn't get rid of Tim himself, personally, to hold the esteem of the men like Francis Manning Winikus and Hugh Pickering, he would go down. He would be brought down swiftly, efficiently, painlessly and impersonally. If he didn't insist, as he had, on doing this job himself, it would be the end. So Pa answered Francis imperturbably. "I thought we'd make the move on the twenty-second of February," he said. "That's Washington's Birthday, and the President will be making the traditional visit to the Liberty Bell in Philadelphia. We'll be able to lay out a pretty good plan."

"Is there *any*thing we can do to ease the way for you, Tom?" Francis asked courteously. "Do you need weapons, disguises, master keys, infrared cameras, surveillance equipment—*any*thing?"

"Do you have plants inside the White House detail of the Secret Service?" Pa asked.

"Yes. Eleven men."

"When the time comes, we'd like to eliminate building checks on the site."

"Of course."

"We'll need some safe weapons. Just what we'll need we'll have figured down to a T by the eighth or ninth."

"Have you set your contacts with the police?"

"We're doing that now."

"Have you chosen the marksmen you'll want?"

"We're organizing that right now too, Francis."

"I have a sound list of men, if you think that can help you."

"No," Pa said flatly, "I think we'll be all right there. We'll have the marksmen and the police and a fall guy for the press and TV. We'll look to you for weapons and some help from the Secret Service boys, and I think we'll be all right."

"We know you'll understand, Tom, that the Committee decided it would be necessary," Dr. Pickering rumbled, "to back you up with an independent team."

"Perfectly all right, Horse," Pa said. "I certainly understand and approve. I just would like it understood, however, that when my team breaks through and does the whole job in the perfect manner in which it is going to be done, it is agreed that this back-up team, this team that is in effect a witnessing element, will be eliminated by Francis' people."

"Oh, absolutely," Dr. Pickering said.

"That is understood," Francis Winikus assured Pa. He turned a red carnation from his buttonhole in his two hands and stared into the fire speaking almost wistfully. "These are sad days for all of us," he said, "but the saddest for you. I am very, very fond of Tim, as well you know. But, sentimentality to the contrary, I know of no other American whom I would rather have in charge of what must be done."

"So say we all of us," Dr. Pickering intoned.

When Francis Winikus and Dr. Pickering took off in the Jovair, Pa and General Nolan drove back to the house silently in a golf cart, then settled down to play pinochle. After a while the General asked, "How do we find this corrupt, well-placed cop, Tom?"

"Frank Mayo will find him."

The General brightened. "Oh—sure. And how will we find the marksmen?"

"We'll import one and use a local for the other."

"A local?"

"The cop will find him."

"Where do we import the other one from?"

"What was your mother's maiden name?"

"Casper."

"Okay. You are now William Casper. You go back to Dallas, where you like it, where you came from, and you call Eddie Tropek at the National Rifle Association, the state office, and ask him to dig you out just the names of the three best marksmen in the state. Then you talk to them one by one until you get a feel of the one who'll move anything for money. Then we import him to Philadelphia."

"When do I talk to this corrupt policeman?"

"I'll talk to Mayo right now," Pa said.

General Nolan had been born a Texan, and that had meant just about everything to him. He felt he was a Texan to the marrow of his bones, from the soles of his feet to the top of his head. It meant a very great deal to him to get this assignment from Tom to go back to the land of the sons of the pioneers and to become William Casper/Casper Junior. He could talk again as

he had talked as a boy without any fear that he would
not be understood. He loved the sound of Texas
speech. It was like a concert of massed banjos. At last,
after a lifetime of uniforms and eastern clothes, he
would be able to dress as his father had dressed. He
bought real thick, old b'ar-grease hair tonic. He trained
his hair down over his forehead the way his daddy had
worn his. He liked the style of it so much that he
vowed never to change it back. He got himself a big,
old-fashioned gold watch and chain in a New Haven
pawn shop. It had a huge elk's tooth suspended from
it. He carried a package of quill toothpicks and one
pure gold toothpick for after Sunday dinner. He listed
and did all the things his father had done, such as polishing anything he picked up or farting unexpectedly
and unself-consciously. It had been near to forty years
since he'd even stepped inside the Texas line. He had
forgotten how much he liked people like ole Turk
Fletcher, who was as plain as a sweaty old hatband.

Everything went well. There was no need to use the
back-up team. They were eliminated on the afternoon
of the assassination in an airplane explosion over
Champaign, Illinois.

There was a certain amount of mopping up to do for
the intensive four-month period after the assassination
until the Pickering Commission could complete its report and disband. Francis Manning Winikus' specialists
handled the elimination of those people who had either
observed something inconsistent in Hunt Plaza or who
had followed their own hunches in various directions,
such as journalists, blackmailers or amateur detectives.

Then everything settled down. The public bought
the Pickering Commission's recommendations without
question, and, happily, the men and women who
owned the country could return to their work for a better world, for a better America.

Fourteen years went by, each one of them a busy
and profitable year for Pa. General Nolan gained

twenty-six additional pounds. He had to give up coitus and accept fellatio as a way of life, because there was just no other way for him to do otherwise. "I don't see how can you find it even to pee," Pa said.

SUNDAY, JANUARY 27, 1974—PALM SPRINGS

The call from Carswell had come at 1:05 P.M. It was eleven o'clock at night in London and ten in the morning, on Monday, in Brunei, so Pa figured he could pick up about a full day's start on Nick, considering the time differences and the traveling Nick still had to do. All Carswell knew was that Nick was going to Philadelphia and wanted a meeting with Miles Gander. It could be oil business, but Pa didn't think so. Nick had two of the best geologists in the world aboard the *Teekay* if he had any geological questions. There was no reason to fly halfway around the world to see Gander because he was a geologist.

When Pa called Keifetz to get the question answered he got a shock equal to a circus sledgehammer crashing into the side of his head. Fletcher had talked to Nick and had spilled everything he knew. Fletcher had hidden the rifle, and Nick knew where to find it. For no reason—and this was what frightened Pa most—when he should have felt metallic and wary and dangerous, he felt suddenly euphoric. He felt extraordinarily released from he did not know what. He sat motionless after he hung up on Keifetz, thinking not about the complex of protective moves he would need to construct but that a strong, warming light seemed to have been switched on within him, illuminating every inner part of him in all the places he could not see and, even now, seventy-four years later, could not understand. *Nick is smart. Nick doesn't like you. You could get into bad trouble over this.* But he knew the bad trouble he could find was that he loved Nick too. He had loved Tim, but he had cheated himself by loving Tim for what he could bring in, as a cat's paw. He loved Nick for being a fine man, his own man, a brave and a responsible man—and he didn't want to have to face any chance of harm for him. But it had been so long since Pa had known what trouble was that the habituated part of his mind spoke to him soothingly and promised pleasure. *This is a game. You must enjoy it. Nick has never lived by his wits. Play with him as long as it amuses you, then send him back to Asia, baffled and empty-handed.*

He paid Cerutti just to outthink people like Nick, and Cerutti had handled far tougher assignments than this one with the greatest of ease. Nolan could certainly use one last adventure before he ate himself to death or some little girl ate him to death. They would line up against Nick and play an exciting game and Pa would have the deep, elemental satisfaction of getting his own back from that smarmy little kid who thought he was a guttersnipe.

All at once Pa was able to switch the reasons for what he was going to do over to and upon Nick's mother, that tone-deaf, pathetic snob who had scrounged all that money and all that pride out of him all because of one little dose of clap. The mother and the son had thought they were so superior to the father. Nick still thought he was superior. Therefore let it be considered that the chips are down, Pa thought. We'll see which one is the better man. They would play this out, and when it was done he would let Nick know somehow—with a contemptuous grin or the gift of a tourist-class ticket back to his day-laboring job in Asia—that Nick hadn't been up to winning the most important thing he'd ever sought.

Pa turned to the telephone console and flipped a red switch. In a moment a green light went on. "Cerutti?"

Pa asked into the microphone.

"Yes, sir."

Pa watched the small screen as it lined up Cerutti's voice print and the intermittent confirming light flashed around the edges of the screen.

"I'll be there in about three hours, probably less."

"Yes, sir. Do you want to give me a little thinking time on it, sir?"

"The 1960 business has come up again. You remember Turk Fletcher?"

"Yes, sir."

"He just died in Brunei. He talked to my son Nick before he died. I'll see you in about two and a half hours."

Pa flipped off. He told Eddie to find him Miles Gander in Philadelphia and to have the Gulfstream ready to leave for Wisconsin as soon as possible. Eddie had Gander on the telephone in less than five minutes.

"Miles," Pa said, "I have to be in Philly tonight, and I hear you're in a bind. I'd like to help you out. Meet me at the Barclay for dinner tonight at eight thirty." Pa flipped off. He called Eddie Dillon again. "Listen, Eddie," Pa said, "when I come back we'll put down at Palm Springs and come in by chopper. I want to come in with maximum flash. I want you to have a real brassy, bright young girl waiting for me at Palm Springs. I'll tell her what to do when I see her."

At Pa's apartment at the Barclay that night Miles Gander looked as if the threat of bankruptcy was keeping him from sleeping. He couldn't eat much either. After Pa had a good dinner he lighted a big, chocolate Monte Cristo, which the CIA got him from Cuba in monthly shipments, and said, "How much are you stuck for, Miles?"

"Four hundred and eight thousand," Miles said.

"You got any leases you could sign over as collateral if I pick up the tab?"

"Why should you pick up the tab, Mr. Kegan?"

"Because I'm your friend, Miles. You got any leases?"

"Yes," Miles said sadly. "Leases in Honduras and Morocco. That's where I should have started drilling instead of letting them talk me into starting where I did start."

"A man who is his own geologist has a fool for a geologist. Can you get the leases over here by tomorrow morning?"

"I have a breakfast meeting with your son Nick at nine thirty. All right if I come here before that?"

"Make it eight fifteen," Pa said. "Just one thing. Are these leases worth four hundred and eight thousand?"

"My professional estimate, an objective estimate, as if I were making it for somebody else, is that the leases are more likely worth three hundred million dollars."

"If we hit with them," Pa said. "All right. Don't fret. No matter what comes out of the ground we'll be eighty-twenty partners on my capital expenditure. If we bring in a field, Miles, your twenty percent will make you a rich man."

"Not being a bankrupt is the only thing I have on my mind, Mr. Kegan."

"Miles—when you see Nick tomorrow morning he's going to ask you to find him a police official to be a witness for something he has to get done. I don't want Nick to think I'm interfering in his affairs, but I want him protected, I want him to get a good high-up police official if police help is what he thinks he wants." Pa took a slip of paper out of his vest pocket and tossed it across the table. "Just call that number. It's Police Inspector Frank Heller. You know how it is. Sons don't like their fathers helping them out if they can avoid it, so I'll appreciate it if you keep quiet about our meeting and about my asking you to call Heller."

Gander was back at Pa's apartment at the Barclay

promptly at eight fifteen the next morning. He endorsed the Honduran and Moroccan leases over to a name of a company that Pa dictated and he received in return a check for four hundred and eight thousand dollars from the Corinna Soar Foundation for Isotope Research which was signed by someone called Denis Ashby-Yassir. He left Pa at five minutes to nine to return to the Petroleum Club to await Nick's arrival.

General Nolan arrived from Rockrimmon at nine forty-five, which was forty-five minutes late, because he had taken the opportunity to drive across country in his Ferrari, and it had seized up in Trenton and had overheated in the Philadelphia traffic. He had had to journey the last twelve miles by taxi. Pa and General Nolan spent the next hour and a half on a "conference call" with Professor Cerutti, which Pa was able to set up instantly and with total electronic safety with his portable Signal Corps switchboard.

Professor Cerutti explained the Z. K. Dawson-Muskogee road scenario to General Nolan, then dictated his lines into Pa's recording equipment so that the General could study them at his leisure. Then he laid out the scenario for the woman who would flag Nick down on the Muskogee road, outlining what would follow it. When he finished he asked General Nolan to check in at the Hadley Hotel, Philadelphia, registering as William Casper. "I'll have the woman there at noon. You'll be running her, and she knows that. She is a good, professional actress with a criminal record. The full scenario, her first pay envelope, and her background are waiting for you at the Hadley now."

When the conference call was done, Pa said to the General, "I have a clear understanding with Cerutti, kiddo, and I want just as clear an understanding with you. No rough stuff with Nick. We'll just handle Nick with our heads and not with assault weapons—get it?"

"Whatever you say, Tom. You know that."

"But—and this is a big but—if this rifle is where Fletcher said it is, wherever that might be, then whoever sees it found—except Nick—is an entirely different proposition. Heller and Gander will go with Nick to look for it. So that means we gotta shut up Heller and Gander. You follow, Jim?"

"Tom, you are one of the people who own and run our country. I am a simple soldier. I am what you have armies for—to kill your enemies." General Nolan was a thoroughgoing professional soldier who had made a brilliant career, and necessary killing had never seemed in any way prohibited to him. He was not some street person or some narcotics-drenched criminal who could run amok, doing murder. Necessary killing meant killing ordered by authority. He was a soldier.

"Okay," Pa said. "That's an order. Whoever is there—except Nick—when they find that rifle—they all have to go."

"Check," General Nolan said.

"Cerutti will put men on Gander, so you can handle him when you're ready. Incidentally, he's carrying a check of mine on the Soar Foundation. Pick it up, please."

"Check," General Nolan acknowledged.

The General raced to the Hadley Hotel in a taxi, registered, picked up the waiting envelope, then settled down in his suite of rooms with a pot of tea and read the woman's dossier through.

Her name was Jane Talbot. She would work with him under the name of Chantal Lamers. She had been assistant to the director of "What's My Line," then, through his influence, a television actress in daytime soap opera, then in evening drama. She had appeared live in a play called *The Cloisonné Nose* for sixteen performances on Broadway and for four performances as an inmate at Tehachapi Prison, California, where she had been sentenced to five to seven and a half years for fraud. It was her only conviction out of nineteen arrests on fraud charges. Miss Talbot, a/k/a Chantal Lamers, was a methadrine addict. She was at her best under "pretense conditions."

General Nolan considered her to be a strikingly handsome woman. Her bright, intelligent eyes were remarkably clear. She had elegance and she had character, he saw instantly. She also had a gorgeous set of knockers. She stood before him in the doorway, her head mounted on a collar of beaver, under a beaver hat. He felt instant admiration for her. She was a gallant figure.

"Miss Chantal Lamers?" he asked as instructed, so that the stimulation of "pretense conditions" could take hold immediately. She smiled at him with such brilliant appreciation of this new name she had never heard before that he was dazzled. It became impossible for him to imagine her standing before him in a prison uniform. He took her coat. He asked her to sit down. He offered her tea, which she refused. He told her his name was Billy John Casper.

They went through her assignment with care. She asked relevant questions. She seemed delighted with what she would have to do. He began to imagine that he could smell the soft, perfumed skin along the inside of her thighs. He stared at her loose mouth. He seemed to be wishing for things about her breasts. Age and sex are not related, he had often told Tom Kegan. Only if one reaches can one grasp. He was monstrously shaped now. He wished she could have seen him as a young captain of infantry when he had marched with General MacArthur to drive the Bonus Army out of the Anacostia Flats in 1932, when he had been flat and fit, years ago, before she had been born. He had been younger than she was now, once, and the sperm had poured out of him like wine from a skin.

With great courtliness he handed over her sealed envelope with her money for doing the work. They did not discuss money. In any event she did not seem interested in the money, only in the excitement of the pretense to come. She smiled across at him and said in a new, pronounced Oklahoma accent, "I just get this feelin' that you are a very, very sweet man." With a stately movement that General Nolan did not feel compromised her dignity for a moment, she lifted the light veil away from her face, swept it to the top of her hat, and knelt on the floor in front of him as he sat on the chair. With a deft gesture she unzipped his fly, put her hand inside his trousers and exposed him. "Now I am just goin' to taste you to find out."

It was a little present from Pa.

General Nolan looked old because he had eaten so much over such a long time. It was as though the weight of all that good food had sagged and ballooned him grotesquely. He was an old, fat, quaint figure who balanced a billycock bowler on his head. He wore striped four-button suits, with white piping showing at the edges of the waistcoat, over a pink or a lavender shirt. He was short enough and round enough to appear to be sitting in his suits. When he moved with the slow and careful gait of a brittle man of seventy-five, he seemed to glide as if he were on an old-fashioned wheeled chair made of wicker and pushed by a black man along the edges of a seaside a half century before.

So did he move carefully and elegantly when he killed John Kullers late in the day in Kullers' office, Room 603 of the Engelson Building. He knocked politely and enquired if he might enter. He closed the door carefully before he sat down in the chair in front of Mr. Kullers' desk and shot Kullers through the head with a weapon that Francis Manning Winikus' agency had lent them, fitted with a silencer.

He had to travel out to the Main Line to kill Mr. Coney. He did not dare take the Ferrari, because that slow-moving traffic would most definitely have heated it up and he could have been hours getting back to the hotel.

He removed the Corinna Soar Foundation check

from Miles Gander's wallet after he had struck him at the back of the head with a government-issue sap, before he left him in the closed car with the engine running.

When he killed Chantal Lamers she was kneeling directly in front of him, so he was able to place the bullet into her temple painlessly at extremely close range.

It was his present to Pa.

When Nick left the small white house on the Muskogee road for the first time, after his interview with Z. K. Dawson, General Nolan padded out to the back porch and told the two government men to take out the dentist's chair on the half-track truck that was waiting behind the garage. Then the General opened the garage doors and got into the Ferrari, looking forward to a wonderful open-road drive to the Tulsa airport on the good, well-paved shunpikes that avoided the main road. The Ferrari worked like a dear little watch all the way. He called Pa from the airport and told him how well everything had gone.

"You are absolutely sure that the man who is taking the cream and that cat into Nick's room is reliable?"

"Of course he's reliable, Tom. He's one of Cerutti's people. And—oh, hey—some business came up at the meeting with your boy."

"What?"

"When he gets to Tulsa he's going to hire a man named Ed Blenheim. Is that any use to you?"

"Blenheim! Shit, I forgot all about Blenheim. He'd be a great man for running those Miles Gander leases. We need him, Jim. Get on the phone right now, tell him you are old Z. K. Dawson himself, and offer him a job. When he asks how much it pays, you tell him it'll be a damned sight more than he's getting now, and say Eddie Dillon will contact him tomorrow morning at eight o'clock at his house."

"Where do I go now, Tom?"

"You go back to the Hadley in Philadelphia. Cerutti

will have an envelope waiting for you there. A man named Ira Skutch will contact you. He's a memory wizard and a good actor. There'll be an envelope there for him."

General Nolan drove the Ferrari aboard the old Boeing KC-97G Stratofreighter, which had been phased out in 1956 and which Pa had been able to pick up for a song from the Georgia State Air Guard in '67. It was handy to move cars, wire-tap equipment, favorite pieces of furniture and cases of wine around the country. Pa had a soft spot in his head for Nolan. "You know what, kiddo," he had said to the General once, "combined we represent the military-industrial complex that is making this country rich."

"I'm not so military anymore, and I never was complex," the General said, hugely flattered.

Pa knew how much Nolan enjoyed roaring around in that Ferrari when he could get it out on the open road, so, operationally, the plane was almost entirely the General's. When Pa knew he wouldn't need Nolan around for a couple of days, the General would pile the Ferrari into the old Stratocruiser and they'd fly out to the Utah salt flats or up to the Alcan Highway, and the General would really open that car up and have a helluva time.

From Tulsa the Boeing flew General Nolan and his car to the Philadelphia airport, but on the way into town the damned car heated up like a Zippo lighter in the stop-and-go traffic, and he had to take a taxi into town (again) for the meeting with Ira Skutch. He got to the hotel with thirty-nine minutes to spare and immediately settled down to read the scenario from Professor Cerutti that was for Skutch's use. He was astonished, if not saddened, because Heller had been such a greedy brute of a man, to learn, in a note from Cerutti, that Captain Heller had passed on. He had instinctively felt that Chantal Lamers would be a keen operative, but even he had not been ready to accept that she would have caught on that quickly. She was certainly a very exciting woman, he thought, feeling the faintest stirrings of an erection.

Skutch was a man in his late sixties. He was tall, skinny, and had bright red skin. In the friendliest sort of way he asked General Nolan if they had not met in Joliet prison in 1943.

"I was in London in 1943," the General said, wondering all the while how Cerutti could have said this man was such a memory wizard.

"You sure are a ringer for this guy, I mean," Skutch said.

"I was also thirty-one years younger in 1943," the General reminded him.

"Ah! That's it. That's how I almost made a mistake," Skutch said. "Because I never forget a face."

The man not only had an inferior memory, General Nolan thought, but he might be a moron.

They went through the scenario together.

"Will there be just the one stand or will there be a follow-up?" Skutch asked.

"From the notes we have just gone over," the General said, "I take it your orders are to stand by for two weeks at a rooming house in Amalauk, New Jersey. If Mr. Thirkield wants to see you again, we'll contact you."

After Skutch left, with memories of his most recent admiration for Chantal Lamers in his mind, General Nolan telephoned a young eighty-dollar hooker whose number he had had the foresight to get from Pa's logistics man, Eddie Dillon. Nolan thought eighty dollars was an odd sort of inflationary number for a hooker, but this was Philadelphia. It wasn't really that it was high; he'd paid more and he'd paid less—but it was such an odd number. When she arrived he was pleased to find that she was a pretty little thing, quite pleasant, but that she had a pathetically unformed style at fellatio.

While she was blowing him ineffectively the General

pondered the deep truth in the method that Professor Cerutti used with his scenarios. With sure skill he made certain to parallel American mythology, history, customs and usage. Just so, on a vastly larger scale, the White House, the Pickering Commission and the political oligarchy had screened and made mystifying all the facts about Tim's assassination, obfuscating, ignoring, overlooking and denying reality while they fed out to the boyish, panting press a stream of half truths and nontruths until, in a not-very-long time, the American people had become so confused, so culturally exhausted, that they had abandoned all hope of ever making the sets of facts about any area whatsoever of the assassination match the facts of any other area. They had flaccidly accepted the corpse of Willie Arnold as the sacrificial goat. What Cerutti had done had been to concentrate the essence of all that fraudulence and fantasy into his short, continually contrasting and masterful scenarios. Nick, as their present target, represented in microcosm what the American people had been fourteen years before. General Nolan had never met Nicholas Thirkield, but even though he was one-half Tom Kegan or more, he would not be able to withstand the force of Professor Cerutti's projected illusions.

The General reached out and signaled the young woman by patting the top of her bobbing head affectionately. He told her that would be enough, that he had to get along.

"Of course, we had no problem finding the people to play Harry Greenwood, the magazine editor, or Irving Mentor, the false Syndicate man," Professor Cerutti explained to Nick in the enormous files room at Schrader Island. "But they were the last of the professional actors we used. Everything else was purest fiction, to be sure, but it was allowed to play out in your own imagination, using established premises as the stuff such dreams are made on—such as the known enmity between your brother and the head of the Tube-sters Union. We were prepared to go on weaving scenarios until we had exhausted you. Fictionized facts. Fantasized facts. Those are the steady cultural nourishment of the American people, forcefed down their throats through the power hoses of the most powerful and pervasive overcommunications design ever dreamed of by man to enslave other men. Still, the subtlety of lying can be fun, as we all know. It wasn't the exposure of the Watergate tragedy that told Americans of the glorious Freedom of Their Press institutions—also called the Triumph of the Little Man Over the Forces of Repression—because, after all, the Glorious Free Press and the readers of that press had known about the Watergate since June of 1972, well before the presidential elections, in time for the Glorious Free Press to expose the Forces of Repression and prevent them from ever reaching the White House again. The skill there was that we could experience the thrill of the fantasy of a free press through which the Watergate was *re*-exposed, after our free press had gotten permission to do so. And that is where our collective genius really lies—in the extraordinary American ability to perceive only when we are told to perceive and to believe only when we are told to believe. Not before. All the facts of your brother's murder have been there to be examined for fourteen years, Mr. Thirkield. It is only now that you have been told to disbelieve them."

"Told by whom, Professor Cerutti?"

"By your father, who has lost whatever power he had to contain his guilt any longer."

Yvette and Nick, Keifetz and Alvin got back to New York at five minutes to three and went directly to the apartment at the Walpole. Nick called Mr. Zendt and asked him to arrange his marriage to Yvette aboard the S.S. *France,* which was to sail the following evening.

"If that's the way it's going to be," Yvette said, "what am I doing here? I have to get home to pack."

"Don't go home yet," Nick said. "Please wait right here until I get back. I don't see how I can be more than an hour." The doorbell rang. Keifetz opened the door on Keith Lee. The four men left the duplex. Yvette went to bed.

It was snowing heavily as the big limousine moved down Park Avenue into a cold, cutting wind. Far down the avenue they could see the colors of the superflag bleeding through the hazing screen of the falling snow as the cup of smog pressed down, distilling out much of the light.

"My God," Keith said, "I heard about your father's house flag, but I hadn't ever seen it before."

Nick couldn't answer. He was thinking about Tim. Tim had believed everything Pa had taught him, so he could not ever have won over Pa. They were the long, long yesterday. Nick shivered in the ice cave of Now. He shivered from the mindlessness and helplessness of Now, but he shivered out of fear of what tomorrow would be like—how tomorrow would contrast with Pa's image.

Pa greeted Nick jovially as Nick went into Pa's office alone. Alvin and Keifetz had subdued the floor security men. The people who worked in Pa's executive suite had been locked in one room and the telephones had been ripped out of the walls.

Pa and Nick settled into deep leather chairs.

"Have a little wine?" Pa asked.

"No, thanks."

"On your way back to Asia?"

"Very soon."

"I think you're doing the right thing, Nick. If you leave with as much fanfare as we can lay on, whoever has your girl will know that you've decided to wrap the whole thing up—then I'll be able to negotiate for her return, and I'll bundle her up and send her on to you."

"Thanks, Pa. But that's okay. I got her back. A few hours ago."

"You got her *back?*" Pa was uncomprehending. He knew he had not heard Nick correctly.

"I spent almost two hours in a very frank talk with Professor Cerutti. He cooperated, Pa."

"What the hell do you mean?"

"He told me everything, Pa."

"But—if he told you everything, why did you come here? I've done everything I could do to save you, and now you do this. Now I am going to have to have you put away, Nick. I am going to have to have you certified and put away."

"Pa—please. Just tell me why you had Tim killed. I can't get that part straight. I have to hear it from you. Please—in the little time we have left—I want to talk about that, Pa."

Pa took off his glasses and began to polish them with a handkerchief. He was trying to assemble reality. He hadn't been ready, and he couldn't understand why he hadn't been ready. But this boy had become deadly dangerous. He had to be put away for everyone's protection, most of all his own.

Pa hunched forward in his chair and slipped his

glasses on again. "I had to do it, Nick. Tim was dying. He would have been a hopeless invalid—just as paralyzed and helpless as Woodrow Wilson. I—I could not have stood that, Nick. He was the meaning of youth and the force of youth to the whole world. Could anyone have been able to see that golden hero turned into a twisted thing? I committed an act of mercy. I made immortality fall on him while he was at the greatest glory of his powers. I had him killed so that the American ideal he stood for might live on forever."

"That is a total lie, Pa. Why did you have him killed?"

Pa stared at Nick, his face draining of color. Murder burned in his eyes. His voice trembled. White sputum bubbled at the left corner of his mouth. His lips worked silently, then he found his voice. "Why did I have him killed?" he almost screamed. "I'll tell you why I had him killed. I spent eleven million dollars to build him up from a cunt-simple college boy to the President of the United States! I drilled him every day and every night on what he was to become. For twenty years I told him what was going to happen and how and why we were going to do it and everything that was going to happen after we did it. He knew better than anyone alive that I hadn't made him the President of the United States so that we could review the fucking fleet together! It was a cold-assed business proposition just like everything else in this life. Let the rope-pullers have 'Hail to the Chief' and those wonderful evenings in the East Room with Alice Cooper and Pablo Casals. I put Tim in the White House because that's where you can generate the most cash. What the hell do you think American politics is all about, kiddo? What the hell do we send the niggers out to fight the wars for? What is all this Latin-American brotherhood shit, our new pals the Chinks and the fucking Russians? Watch the price of oil go up the way we've been pushing it up, and soon it will be worthwhile to have those Arabs blown apart by our brave free-world fighters, and that small town they call Canada taken over and annexed if they don't go along. Tim had known all his adult life that he was going to be sitting in the White House as my sales-promotion manager, and he knew he had to deliver on a quota basis."

"If he knew all that, Pa, then what went wrong? What happened?"

"What happened? It went to his head. Lunch with De Gaulle. Dinner with Khrushchev. A thousand built-in broads. The Marine with the box. Five-star generals shining his shoes. Front pages with his name everywhere he looked. It all turned him into a flag-kisser, for Christ's sake. He was all right for almost one year, then the whole razzle-dazzle turned his head. He peed all over his quotas. He decided to teach the niggers to read. He began to think we were all living in a democracy. He double-crossed me while he double-crossed himself. And I had every right to put out a life I had created in the first place. That's logical, isn't it?"

"Sure is, Pa."

"I let him trade in the Presidency for a sainthood. I gave him open-end immortality in exchange for spitting in my eye. That was more than fair, wasn't it?"

"Sure was, Pa."

"And yet—in spite of the fact that everyone out there in this country believes in and lives in the very same dog-eat-dog way, in spite of the fact that every one of them would use any angle they could find to make a fast buck, if you were to tell them that I had Tim killed, they'd want to tear me limb from limb. What the hell. That's the system we wanted, and we're goddam lucky to have it. That's the American way. But they have to catch you first. That's the whole secret. Cover your tracks and don't get caught, and that's why—as sorry as I am about it, as much as I regret it, Nick—you are going to have to be locked away for a long time, and I'm going to have to see that you get a prefrontal lobotomy to help you wait for the years to go past."

"Good-bye, Pa," Nick said as he watched Keith Lee, the Keifetz brothers and two city patrolmen come into the room far behind Pa's chair. Pa heard the rustle they made. He turned. Without a second of hesitation he darted out of the chair to the far side of the room and stood beside the farthest window.

"Stay where you are," he said loudly. Nick stood up, twenty feet on Pa's right. The block of men stopped dead, thirty feet on Pa's left. Pa turned quickly and opened the window wide.

"All right, boys," he said. "You asked for it. You are finished. I am going out on that ledge, fifty stories above the street in the most prominent location in Manhattan. In ten minutes I'll draw a crowd of maybe three thousand, maybe seven thousand people. In half an hour the television crews will have set up in the building just across the street. They'll interview me with parabolic mikes and I will expose this conspiracy by my son, Nicholas Thirkield, who, with bribed police and a crooked doctor, plans to take over my fortune on trumped-up charges so fantastic that they cannot be believed by any honest, freedom-loving, right-thinking Americans." He climbed up on the windowsill with athletic agility. "We will see then whether the enduring American system will allow you to conspire to break the heart of the father of its greatest President."

He slipped out on the ledge. He began to sidle away from the window. The men rushed to the window to grab his legs. As they rushed at him he pulled back involuntarily, even though he was already too far away from them to be reached. Had he not pulled back he might have won it all—just as he had said. But as he pulled back reflexively, his foot slipped on the ice-coated ledge. He fell, dragging the other foot off the snow on the ledge.

As he fell he grabbed at the folds of the gigantic flag, his house signal, as it hung downward for fifteen stories. He held onto the flag desperately four feet below the window ledge, just too far below for the hands above him to reach down to grasp his clothing and pull him up to safety. He looked up at Nick's face with terror.

"Son! Help me! Help me!" he screamed, his eyes popping with the fear of death. There was the sudden sound of ripping. The years Pa had exposed the great flag in every kind of weather had rotted it.

The flag began to tear just above Pa's gripping hands. There was a terrible ripping sound as the flag burst apart. Staring upward and screaming into Nick's eyes, Pa fell down and down and down until he hit the pavement fifty floors below.